DOVE.

MW00614146

The Complete
John Silence Stories

ALGERNON BLACKWOOD

Edited and with an introduction by

S. T. JOSHI

DOVER PUBLICATIONS, INC.
Mineola, New York

To M. L. W. The Original of John Silence
and
My Companion in Many Adventures

DOVER HORROR CLASSICS

GENERAL EDITOR: S. T. JOSHI

Bibliographical Note

The Complete John Silence Stories, first published by Dover Publications, Inc., in 1997, is an unabridged republication of stories that first appeared in *John Silence, Physician Extraordinary* (London: Eveleigh Nash, 1908) and *Day and Night Stories* (London: Cassell, 1917).

Library of Congress Cataloging-in-Publication Data

Blackwood, Algernon, 1869–1951.
    The complete John Silence stories / by Algernon Blackwood ; edited and with an introduction by S. T. Joshi.
        p. cm.
    Contents: Case I: A psychical invasion — Case II: Ancient sorceries — Case III: The nemesis of fire — Case IV: Secret worship — Case V: The camp of the dog — Case VI: A victim of higher space.
    ISBN-13: 978-0-486-29942-6
    ISBN-10: 0-486-29942-2
    I. Detective and mystery stories, English. 2. Physicians — Fiction. I. Joshi, S. T., 1958– . II. Title.
PR6003.L3C6   1997
823'.912 — dc21   97-29663
                                                                                         CIP

Manufactured in the United States by LSC Communications
4500056509
www.doverpublications.com

Contents

Introduction

John Silence—Physician Extraordinary (1908) is a landmark work—as much in the realm of weird fiction as in the career of its author, Algernon Blackwood (1869–1951). It was one of Blackwood's first successes—both artistic and commercial—and made much of the rest of his literary work possible. And that body of work may well establish him as the greatest weird writer in all literature.

It is unlikely that Algernon Henry Blackwood ever thought of becoming a literary man, for until he was close to forty he pursued almost every other career except that of writer. Born in Kent, England, and the son of a distinguished father—Sir Stevenson Arthur Blackwood, who ultimately became Secretary of the Post Office—Blackwood spent his youth absorbing the rigid Evangelical teachings of his parents, although secretly rebelling by surreptitiously reading the *Bhagavad Gita* and theosophy. Throughout his life Blackwood remained a religious mystic, but one who vigorously opposed the dogmas of conventional religion.

Much of Blackwood's adolescence and early manhood was spent in travel—and the whole of his literary work reveals the expansion of mental horizons he gained from his visits to four continents. After spending time at a series of private schools in England, he was sent for a year-long stay (1885–86) at the School of the Moravian Brotherhood in Königsfeld, Germany. He spent the summer of 1887 in Switzerland, after which his father sent him to Canada for business. In 1888 Blackwood enrolled in Edinburgh University in Scotland but withdrew the next year.

Returning to Canada in 1890, Blackwood attempted to start a dairy farm, but it failed and he lost much of his investment. After an idyllic summer in the Canadian backwoods in 1892 (later the setting for some of his most powerful tales of supernatural horror, including "The Wendigo"), Blackwood came to New York, where he became a reporter for the *Evening Sun*. The brutal contrast between the pristine forests of Canada and the phantasmagoric civilization of New York was, I believe, a crucial turning point for Blackwood. Consider his description of the metropolis in his piquant autobiography, *Episodes Before Thirty* (1923):

The awful city, with its torrential, headlong life, held for me something of the monstrous. Everything about it was exaggerated. Its racing speed, its roofs amid the clouds with the canyon gulfs below, its gaudy avenues dripping gold that ran almost arm in arm with streets little better than sewers of human decay and misery, its frantic noise, both of voices and mechanism, its lavishly organized charity and boastful splendour, and its deep corruption in the grip of heartless and degraded Tammany—it was all this that painted the horror into my imagination as of something monstrous, non-human, almost unearthly.

It is scarcely to be wondered that Blackwood developed a kind of mystic pantheism that saw all good to be housed in the untenanted wilderness and all evil in the teeming labyrinths of modern urban life.

Blackwood returned to England in 1899, remaining involved in a variety of business ventures but still giving apparently little thought to writing. He had, indeed, written various articles on his early travels as well as a few stories (the first was "A Mysterious House" [1889]); but now he not only continued his travels—to France, to his old school in Germany, and to the Danube (the setting for his later masterpiece, "The Willows")—but also turned increasingly to literature. His essays and stories began appearing with some regularity in the magazines of the day; but it was only a chance meeting with a friend, Angus Hamilton, that led to Blackwood's submission of his first volume, *The Empty House and Other Ghost Stories,* to the publisher Eveleigh Nash. The book was published in 1906, and—although the significant collection *The Listener and Other Stories,* containing "The Willows," "The Old Man of Visions," "The Woman's Ghost Story," and other fine tales, appeared in 1907—it was only *John Silence* that made Blackwood a best-seller.

To trace the history of the "psychic detective" in literature would be a fascinating exercise. Here we can perhaps pinpoint two significant forerunners: Dr. Martin Hesselius, the German doctor who appears (though oftentimes fleetingly and tangentially) in the tales that make up Joseph Sheridan LeFanu's landmark volume, *In a Glass Darkly* (1872), most notably "Green Tea" and "Carmilla"; and, of course, Professor Van Helsing, the antagonist of Count Dracula in Bram Stoker's *Dracula* (1897). It is, indeed, significant that both Hesselius and Van Helsing make pretensions to medical knowledge; for Blackwood never uses the term "psychic detective" about John Silence, referring to him only as a "psychic doctor."

Of course, the influence of Sherlock Holmes (recall that by 1908 three collections of tales and three short novels by Sir Arthur Conan

Doyle about the cerebral detective had appeared) is also evident in the figure of John Silence. In "A Psychical Invasion" he sits in his consulting room and listens to a woman telling the story of a haunted house; later he engages in pseudo-Holmesian ratiocinative detection, perceiving at a glance that a character has been taking drugs. In "The Nemesis of Fire" there is, as throughout the Holmesian saga, a tantalizing reference to an unwritten John Silence case.

It might seem as if this element of scientific rationality would be fatal to the atmosphere of cosmic wonder that Blackwood is clearly attempting to create in these tales; and, indeed, this tension persists throughout the volume and also figures in the differing roles John Silence plays from one story to the next. The most orthodox instance is "A Psychical Invasion," where Silence is summoned to a house apparently haunted by some of its former tenants; he promptly "solves" the case. In "Ancient Sorceries" Silence acts merely as an interlocutor, listening to the account of a man's strange experiences in a small town in France and adding only a few concluding comments in a somewhat pedantic know-it-all detective fashion. "The Nemesis of Fire" introduces John Silence's assistant, a man named Hubbard, who acts as a Dr. Watson-like narrator while Silence energetically probes and solves another haunting. Hubbard returns as the narrator of "The Camp of the Dog." In "Secret Worship" Silence acts as a literal *deus ex machina*, rescuing the hapless narrator at the last minute from spiritual and perhaps physical death. "A Victim of Higher Space"—a story not published in the 1908 volume, although written at about the same time (it was first collected in *Day and Night Stories*, 1917)—finds Silence back in his consulting room, although with a new assistant, Barker.

It might be startling at first to hear John Silence say, in "The Nemesis of Fire," that "I have yet to come across a problem that is not natural, and has not a natural explanation"; but what he means is that the seemingly supernatural can really be encompassed within the realm of a kind of higher rationality that takes both spiritual and physical phenomena into account. In a sense Blackwood is perhaps trying to have his cake and eat it, too—trying to retain the mystery of an awesome universe while at the same time remaining within the domain of human reason—and if the attempt is not always successful, then it has still resulted in the creation of some of the most powerful vignettes in weird fiction.

H. P. Lovecraft, who thought some of the tales immeasurably powerful, nevertheless criticized Blackwood for "credulousness regarding 'occultism' which causes him to employ now and then a professional mediumistic jargon of woefully weakening effect." It is true that when a "knowledge of occultism" is attributed to him, John Silence expostulates in mock horror, "Oh, please—that dreadful word!" But this may be a case of protesting too much. Silence clearly claims to be a clairvoyant, and in "The Nemesis of Fire" he and other characters hold a kind of séance as a way of bringing forth the supernatural entity.

Blackwood himself did indeed reveal a certain "credulousness" in the occult. His early studies in Buddhism and Hinduism endowed him with a fixed belief in reincarnation. In his brief school days at Edinburgh he participated in a number of séances. Then in 1900 he joined the Hermetic Order of the Golden Dawn. His dissatisfaction with this occultist organization led him into a splinter group, the Holy Order of the Golden Dawn, headed by A. E. Waite, and he remained a member until 1914. Indeed, the Blackwood scholar Mike Ashley believes that the character of John Silence himself is based upon a member of this group, although his identity is as yet uncertain. Blackwood himself acknowledges in his enigmatic dedication to "M. L. W." that John Silence is indeed derived from some real person.

There are other autobiographical connections in the John Silence tales. The most obvious instance is "Secret Worship," whose opening pages transparently and movingly convey Blackwood's respect for the simple piety of the Moravian Brothers and irritation at their stern discipline. An early article, "About the Moravians" (*Methodist Magazine*, February 1891), anticipates many features of the story:

> To the visitor anxious to see a Moravian settlement to its best advantage, no place offers greater attractions than Königsfeld. Remote from the world, it is a perfect model for its earnest, active life and at the same time its perfect peacefulness. Here the round of life goes on undisturbed from year to year. . . . A long day of hard study is commenced at six o'clock with a reading out of the Bible, the same portion being read in all Moravian settlements all the world over at the same time. . . . Nothing was more conspicuous in this school . . . than the beautiful spirit of gentleness and merciful justice, tempered by true brotherly sympathy, with which the boys of as many temperaments as nationalities were taught to live.

The extensive references to Egypt in "The Nemesis of Fire" are intriguing: although Blackwood did not visit Egypt in person until 1911, his fascination is already evident; and many of his later works (notably "Sand" in *Pan's Garden* and "A Descent into Egypt" in *Incredible Adventures*) are the direct results of his absorption of the mysteries of this ancient land. "The Camp of the Dog," although set in Scandinavia, clearly echoes Blackwood's camping trips in Canada.

The overriding dangers of a serial character are, of course, monotony

and repetitiousness. Blackwood manages to avoid these pitfalls by ingenious variations in narration. As already mentioned, Blackwood's assistant, Hubbard, narrates two stories in the first person ("The Nemesis
of Fire" and "The Camp of the Dog"), playing a far more active role in
the actual events of the tales than Dr. Watson ordinarily would. Three
other stories—"A Psychical Invasion," "Secret Worship," and "A Victim
of Higher Space"—are told in a fairly orthodox first person; indeed, the
fact that "A Psychical Invasion"—presumably the first of the John
Silence stories—does not feature Hubbard suggests that John Silence
was not initially conceived as having an assistant and that Hubbard was
added later precisely for the purpose of imparting diversity to the nar-
ratives. From this perspective the most effective story is "Ancient
Sorceries," featuring an interesting mixture of pseudo-first-person narration (the monologues of Arthur Vezin) and third-person narration.

But none of these narrative devices would be effective if the tales
themselves did not have the power and substance of theme to bear
them. In the best of the John Silence stories, Blackwood has discovered
a secret that many other weird writers have come upon but that few others have tapped as cannily: the aptness of the novelette form for con-
veying supernatural horror. This form allows for all the dramatic intensity that Poe sought in his quest for "unity of effect" while at the same
time developing the textural richness of a novel in its expansive scope.
Blackwood's tales are the more remarkable because not much "happens" in them; instead, it is the slow accumulation of telling details that
fosters an insidious atmosphere of almost unendurable tension and fore-
boding. Blackwood was a master of narrative pacing, and all his best
tales build to an apocalyptic climax that fully justifies their length.

John Silence—Physician Extraordinary was an immediate success,
partially because of an aggressive advertising campaign on the part of
Blackwood's publishers. As Mike Ashley notes in his definitive *Algernon Blackwood: A Bio-Bibliography* (1987): "A distinctive poster de-
picting a bearded John Silence gazing out of an open balcony window
at the night sky bore the slogan 'JOHN SILENCE—the Most
Mysterious Character of Modern Fiction.' The advertisement held the
distinction of being the largest illustrated book poster to appear on
hoardings in England at that time."

The result for Blackwood was especially felicitous. It allowed him to
spend the next six years in a mountain village in Switzerland and write
some of his most remarkable weird work: the story collections *The Lost
Valley* (1910), *Pan's Garden* (1912), and *Incredible Adventures* (1914),
the latter being perhaps the greatest weird collection of all time; the de-

lightful children's stories *Jimbo: A Fantasy* (1909) and *The Education of Uncle Paul* (1909); and the novels *The Human Chord* (1910), *The Centaur* (1911), and *A Prisoner in Fairyland* (1913).

The rest of Blackwood's career, indeed, was a vain attempt to duplicate the potency of these imperishable works. Although such novels as *Julius LeVallon* (1916), *The Wave* (1916), *The Garden of Survival* (1918), and *The Bright Messenger* (1921) have their moments of power and there are some worthy tales in such later collections as *Day and Night Stories* (1917), *The Wolves of God* (1921), *Tongues of Fire* (1924), and *Shocks* (1935), it seems as if Blackwood's creative energies were dissipating. In the late 1920s he returned to children's writing, producing a number of delightful stories and novels, including *Dudley and Gilderoy* (1929) and *The Fruit Stoners* (1934).

But Blackwood showed vigor to the end. In the mid-1930s he began a new career reading stories on BBC radio, and he even became a pioneering presence in the new medium of television, where his long, gaunt, skeletal face was the perfect embodiment of weirdness. Throughout World War II—even though his residence in London was destroyed in the Battle of Britain and he was almost killed—Blackwood continued his radio talks; this valiant work led ultimately to his becoming a Commander of the British Empire.

Algernon Blackwood has left a legacy of weird writing unsurpassed in both quality and quantity. The fact that his reputation now survives, if at all, on the basis of a few anthology chestnuts like "The Willows" and "The Wendigo" surely casts doubt on the facile belief that literary merit always prevails. In his long life he watched his best work slowly go out of print; one hopes that this Dover collection will help to elevate him once again to the place he deserves in the literature of the weird.

S. T. JOSHI

CASE I

A PSYCHICAL INVASION

I

"And what is it makes you think I could be of use in this particular case?" asked Dr. John Silence, looking across somewhat sceptically at the Swedish lady in the chair facing him.

"Your sympathetic heart and your knowledge of occultism——"

"Oh, please—that dreadful word!" he interrupted, holding up a finger with a gesture of impatience.

"Well, then," she laughed, "your wonderful clairvoyant gift and your trained psychic knowledge of the processes by which a personality may be disintegrated and destroyed—these strange studies you've been experimenting with all these years——"

"If it's only a case of multiple personality I must really cry off," interrupted the doctor again hastily, a bored expression in his eyes.

"It's not that; now, please, be serious, for I want your help," she said; "and if I choose my words poorly you must be patient with my ignorance. The case I know will interest you, and no one else could deal with it so well. In fact, no ordinary professional man could deal with it at all, for I know of no treatment nor medicine that can restore a lost sense of humour!"

"You begin to interest me with your 'case,'" he replied, and made himself comfortable to listen.

Mrs. Sivendson drew a sigh of contentment as she watched him go to the tube and heard him tell the servant he was not to be disturbed.

"I believe you have read my thoughts already," she said; "your intuitive knowledge of what goes on in other people's minds is positively uncanny."

Her friend shook his head and smiled as he drew his chair up to a convenient position and prepared to listen attentively to what she had to say. He closed his eyes, as he always did when he wished to absorb the real meaning of a recital that might be inadequately expressed, for by this method he found it easier to set himself in tune with the living thoughts that lay behind the broken words.

By his friends John Silence was regarded as an eccentric, because he was rich by accident, and by choice—a doctor. That a man of independent means should devote his time to doctoring, chiefly doctoring

1

folk who could not pay, passed their comprehension entirely. The native nobility of a soul whose first desire was to help those who could not help themselves, puzzled them. After that, it irritated them, and, greatly to his own satisfaction, they left him to his own devices.

Dr. Silence was a free-lance, though, among doctors, having neither consulting-room, bookkeeper, nor professional manner. He took no fees, being at heart a genuine philanthropist, yet at the same time did no harm to his fellow-practitioners, because he only accepted unremunerative cases, and cases that interested him for some very special reason. He argued that the rich could pay, and the very poor could avail themselves of organised charity, but that a very large class of ill-paid, self-respecting workers, often followers of the arts, could not afford the price of a week's comforts merely to be told to travel. And it was these he desired to help: cases often requiring special and patient study—things no doctor can give for a guinea, and that no one would dream of expecting him to give.

But there was another side to his personality and practice, and one with which we are now more directly concerned; for the cases that especially appealed to him were of no ordinary kind, but rather of that intangible, elusive, and difficult nature best described as psychical afflictions; and, though he would have been the last person himself to approve of the title, it was beyond question that he was known more or less generally as the "Psychic Doctor."

In order to grapple with cases of this peculiar kind, he had submitted himself to a long and severe training, at once physical, mental, and spiritual. What precisely this training had been, or where undergone, no one seemed to know,—for he never spoke of it, as, indeed, he betrayed no single other characteristic of the charlatan,—but the fact that it had involved a total disappearance from the world for five years, and that after he returned and began his singular practice no one ever dreamed of applying to him the so easily acquired epithet of quack, spoke much for the seriousness of his strange quest and also for the genuineness of his attainments.

For the modern psychical researcher he felt the calm tolerance of the "man who knows." There was a trace of pity in his voice—contempt he never showed—when he spoke of their methods.

"This classification of results is uninspired work at best," he said once to me, when I had been his confidential assistant for some years. "It leads nowhere, and after a hundred years will lead nowhere. It is playing with the wrong end of a rather dangerous toy. Far better, it would be, to examine the causes, and then the results would so easily slip into place and explain themselves. For the sources are accessible, and open to all who have the courage to lead the life that alone makes practical investigation safe and possible."

And towards the question of clairvoyance, too, his attitude was significantly sane, for he knew how extremely rare the genuine power was, and that what is commonly called clairvoyance is nothing more than a keen power of visualising.

"It connotes a slightly increased sensibility, nothing more," he would say. "The true clairvoyant deplores his power, recognising that it adds a new horror to life, and is in the nature of an affliction. And you will find this always to be the real test."

Thus it was that John Silence, this singularly developed doctor, was able to select his cases with a clear knowledge of the difference between mere hysterical delusion and the kind of psychical affliction that claimed his special powers. It was never necessary for him to resort to the cheap mysteries of divination; for, as I have heard him observe, after the solution of some peculiarly intricate problem—

"Systems of divination, from geomancy down to reading by tea-leaves, are merely so many methods of obscuring the outer vision, in order that the inner vision may become open. Once the method is mastered, no system is necessary at all."

And the words were significant of the methods of this remarkable man, the keynote of whose power lay, perhaps, more than anything else, in the knowledge, first, that thought can act at a distance, and, secondly, that thought is dynamic and can accomplish material results.

"Learn how to *think*," he would have expressed it, "and you have learned to tap power at its source."

To look at—he was now past forty—he was sparely built, with speaking brown eyes in which shone the light of knowledge and self-confidence, while at the same time they made one think of that wondrous gentleness seen most often in the eyes of animals. A close beard concealed the mouth without disguising the grim determination of lips and jaw, and the face somehow conveyed an impression of transparency, almost of light, so delicately were the features refined away. On the fine forehead was that indefinable touch of peace that comes from identifying the mind with what is permanent in the soul, and letting the impermanent slip by without power to wound or distress; while, from his manner,—so gentle, quiet, sympathetic,—few could have guessed the strength of purpose that burned within like a great flame.

"I think I should describe it as a psychical case," continued the Swedish lady, obviously trying to explain herself very intelligently, "and just the kind you like. I mean a case where the cause is hidden deep down in some spiritual distress, and——"

"But the symptoms first, please, my dear Svenska," he interrupted, with a strangely compelling seriousness of manner, "and your deductions afterwards."

She turned round sharply on the edge of her chair and looked him in the face, lowering her voice to prevent her emotion betraying itself too obviously.

"In my opinion there's only one symptom," she half whispered, as though telling something disagreeable—"fear—simply fear."

"Physical fear?"

"I think not; though how can I say? I think it's a horror in the psychical region. It's no ordinary delusion; the man is quite sane; but he lives in mortal terror of something——"

"I don't know what you mean by his 'psychical region,'" said the doctor, with a smile; "though I suppose you wish me to understand that his spiritual, and not his mental, processes are affected. Anyhow, try and tell me briefly and pointedly what you know about the man, his symptoms, his need for help, my peculiar help, that is, and all that seems vital in the case. I promise to listen devotedly."

"I am trying," she continued earnestly, "but must do so in my own words and trust to your intelligence to disentangle as I go along. He is a young author, and lives in a tiny house off Putney Heath somewhere. He writes humorous stories—quite a genre of his own: Pender—you must have heard the name—Felix Pender? Oh, the man had a great gift, and married on the strength of it; his future seemed assured. I say 'had,' for quite suddenly his talent utterly failed him. Worse, it became transformed into its opposite. He can no longer write a line in the old way that was bringing him success——"

Dr. Silence opened his eyes for a second and looked at her.

"He still writes, then? The force has not gone?" he asked briefly, and then closed his eyes again to listen.

"He works like a fury," she went on, "but produces nothing"—she hesitated a moment—"nothing that he can use or sell. His earnings have practically ceased, and he makes a precarious living by book-reviewing and odd jobs—very odd, some of them. Yet, I am certain his talent has not really deserted him finally, but is merely——"

Again Mrs. Sivendson hesitated for the appropriate word.

"In abeyance," he suggested, without opening his eyes.

"Obliterated," she went on, after a moment to weigh the word, "merely obliterated by something else——"

"By some *one* else?"

"I wish I knew. All I can say is that he is haunted, and temporarily his sense of humour is shrouded—gone—replaced by something dreadful that writes other things. Unless something competent is done, he will simply starve to death. Yet he is afraid to go to a doctor for fear of being pronounced insane; and, anyhow, a man can hardly ask a doctor to take a guinea to restore a vanished sense of humour, can he?"

"Has he tried any one at all——?"

"Not doctors yet. He tried some clergymen and religious people; but they *know* so little and have so little intelligent sympathy. And most of them are so busy balancing on their own little pedestals——"

John Silence stopped her tirade with a gesture.

"And how is it that you know so much about him?" he asked gently.

"I know Mrs. Pender well—I knew her before she married him——"

"And is she a cause, perhaps?"

"Not in the least. She is devoted; a woman very well educated, though without being really intelligent, and with so little sense of humour herself that she always laughs at the wrong places. But she has nothing to do with the cause of his distress; and, indeed, has chiefly guessed it from observing him, rather than from what little he has told her. And he, you know, is a really lovable fellow, hard-working, patient—altogether worth saving."

Dr. Silence opened his eyes and went over to ring for tea. He did not know very much more about the case of the humorist than when he first sat down to listen; but he realised that no amount of words from his Swedish friend would help to reveal the real facts. A personal interview with the author himself could alone do that.

"All humorists are worth saving," he said with a smile, as she poured out tea. "We can't afford to lose a single one in these strenuous days. I will go and see your friend at the first opportunity."

She thanked him elaborately, effusively, with many words, and he, with much difficulty, kept the conversation thenceforward strictly to the teapot.

And, as a result of this conversation, and a little more he had gathered by means best known to himself and his secretary, he was whizzing in his motor-car one afternoon a few days later up the Putney Hill to have his first interview with Felix Pender, the humorous writer who was the victim of some mysterious malady in his "psychical region" that had obliterated his sense of the comic and threatened to wreck his life and destroy his talent. And his desire to help was probably of equal strength with his desire to know and to investigate.

The motor stopped with a deep purring sound, as though a great black panther lay concealed within its hood, and the doctor—the "psychic doctor," as he was sometimes called—stepped out through the gathering fog, and walked across the tiny garden that held a blackened fir tree and a stunted laurel shrubbery. The house was very small, and it was some time before any one answered the bell. Then, suddenly, a light appeared in the hall, and he saw a pretty little woman standing on the top step begging him to come in. She was dressed in grey, and the gaslight fell on a mass of deliberately brushed light hair. Stuffed, dusty birds, and a shabby array of African spears, hung on the wall behind her. A hat-rack, with a bronze plate full of very large cards, led his eye swiftly to a dark staircase beyond. Mrs. Pender had round eyes like a child's, and she greeted him with an effusiveness that barely concealed her emotion, yet strove to appear naturally cordial. Evidently she had been looking out for his arrival, and had outrun the servant girl. She was a little breathless.

"I hope you've not been kept waiting—I think it's *most* good of you to come——" she began, and then stopped sharp when she saw his face in the gaslight. There was something in Dr. Silence's look that did not encourage mere talk. He was in earnest now, if ever man was.

"Good evening, Mrs. Pender," he said, with a quiet smile that won confidence, yet deprecated unnecessary words, "the fog delayed me a little. I am glad to see you."

They went into a dingy sitting-room at the back of the house, neatly furnished but depressing. Books stood in a row upon the mantelpiece. The fire had evidently just been lit. It smoked in great puffs into the room.

"Mrs. Sivendson said she thought you might be able to come," ventured the little woman again, looking up engagingly into his face and betraying anxiety and eagerness in every gesture. "But I hardly dared to believe it. I think it is really too good of you. My husband's case is so peculiar that—well, you know, I am quite sure any *ordinary* doctor would say at once the asylum——"

"Isn't he in, then?" asked Dr. Silence gently.

"In the asylum?" she gasped. "Oh dear, no—not yet!"

"In the house, I meant," he laughed.

She gave a great sigh.

"He'll be back any minute now," she replied, obviously relieved to see him laugh; "but the fact is, we didn't expect you so early—I mean, my husband hardly thought you would come at all."

"I am always delighted to come—when I am really wanted, and can be of help," he said quickly; "and, perhaps, it's all for the best that your husband is out, for now that we are alone you can tell me something about his difficulties. So far, you know, I have heard very little."

Her voice trembled as she thanked him, and when he came and took a chair close beside her she actually had difficulty in finding words with which to begin.

"In the first place," she began timidly, and then continuing with a nervous incoherent rush of words, "he will be simply delighted that you've really come, because he said you were the only person he would consent to see at all—the only doctor, I mean. But, of course, he doesn't know how frightened I am, or how much I have noticed. He pretends with me that it's just a nervous breakdown, and I'm sure he doesn't realise all the odd things I've noticed him doing. But the main thing, I suppose——"

"Yes, the main thing, Mrs. Pender," he said, encouragingly, noticing her hesitation.

"—— is that he thinks we are not alone in the house. That's the chief thing."

"Tell me more facts—just facts."

"It began last summer when I came back from Ireland; he had been here alone for six weeks, and I thought him looking tired and queer—ragged and scattered about the face, if you know what I mean, and his manner worn out. He said he had been writing hard, but his inspiration had somehow failed him, and he was dissatisfied with his work. His sense of humour was leaving him, or changing into something else, he said. There was something in the house, he declared, that"—she emphasised the words—"prevented his feeling funny."

"Something in the house that prevented his feeling funny," repeated the doctor. "Ah, now we're getting to the heart of it!"

"Yes," she resumed vaguely, "that's what he kept saying."

"And what was it he *did* that you thought strange?" he asked sympathetically. "Be brief, or he may be here before you finish."

"Very small things, but significant it seemed to me. He changed his workroom from the library, as we call it, to the sitting-room. He said all his characters became wrong and terrible in the library; they altered, so that he felt like writing tragedies—vile, debased tragedies, the tragedies of broken souls. But now he says the same of the sitting-room, and he's gone back to the library."

"Ah!"

"You see, there's so little I can tell you," she went on, with increasing speed and countless gestures. "I mean it's only very small things he does and says that are queer. What frightens me is that he assumes there is some one else in the house all the time—some one I never see. He does not actually say so, but on the stairs I've seen him standing aside to let some one pass; I've seen him open a door to let some one in or out; and often in our bedrooms he puts chairs about as though for some one else to sit in. Oh—oh yes, and once or twice," she cried—"once or twice——"

She paused, and looked about her with a startled air.

"Yes?"

"Once or twice," she resumed hurriedly, as though she heard a sound that alarmed her, "I've heard him running — coming in and out of the rooms breathless as if something were after him——"

The door opened while she was still speaking, cutting her words off in the middle, and a man came into the room. He was dark and clean-shaven, sallow rather, with the eyes of imagination, and dark hair growing scantily about the temples. He was dressed in a shabby tweed suit, and wore an untidy flannel collar at the neck. The dominant expression of his face was startled — hunted; an expression that might any moment leap into the dreadful stare of terror and announce a total loss of self-control.

The moment he saw his visitor a smile spread over his worn features, and he advanced to shake hands.

"I hoped you would come; Mrs. Sivendson said you might be able to find time," he said simply. His voice was thin and needy. "I am very glad to see you, Dr. Silence. It is 'Doctor,' is it not?"

"Well, I am entitled to the description," laughed the other, "but I rarely get it. You know, I do not practise as a regular thing; that is, I only take cases that specially interest me, or——"

He did not finish the sentence, for the men exchanged a glance of sympathy that rendered it unnecessary.

"I have heard of your great kindness."

"It's my hobby," said the other quickly, "and my privilege."

"I trust you will still think so when you have heard what I have to tell you," continued the author, a little wearily. He led the way across the hall into the little smoking-room where they could talk freely and undisturbed.

In the smoking-room, the door shut and privacy about them, Pender's attitude changed somewhat, and his manner became very grave. The doctor sat opposite, where he could watch his face. Already, he saw, it looked more haggard. Evidently it cost him much to refer to his trouble at all.

"What I have is, in my belief, a profound spiritual affliction," he began quite bluntly, looking straight into the other's eyes.

"I saw that at once," Dr. Silence said.

"Yes, you saw that, of course; my atmosphere must convey that much to any one with psychic perceptions. Besides which, I feel sure from all I've heard, that you are really a soul-doctor, are you not, more than a healer merely of the body?"

"You think of me too highly," returned the other; "though I prefer cases, as you know, in which the spirit is disturbed first, the body afterwards."

"I understand, yes. Well, I have experienced a curious disturbance in — not in my physical region primarily. I mean my nerves are all right, and my body is all right. I have no delusions exactly, but my spirit is tortured by a calamitous fear which first came upon me in a strange manner."

John Silence leaned forward a moment and took the speaker's hand and held it in his own for a few brief seconds, closing his eyes as he did so. He was not feeling his pulse, or doing any of the things that doctors ordinarily do; he was merely absorbing into himself the main note of the man's mental condition, so as to get completely his own point of view, and thus be able to treat his case with true sympathy. A very close observer might perhaps have noticed that a slight tremor ran through his frame after he had held the hand for a few seconds.

"Tell me quite frankly, Mr. Pender," he said soothingly, releasing the hand, and with deep attention in his manner, "tell me all the steps that led to the beginning of this invasion. I mean tell me what the particular drug was, and why you took it, and how it affected you——"

"Then you know it began with a drug!" cried the author, with undisguised astonishment.

"I only know from what I observe in you, and in its effect upon myself. You are in a surprising psychical condition. Certain portions of your atmosphere are vibrating at a far greater rate than others. This is the effect of a drug, but of no ordinary drug. Allow me to finish, please. If the higher rate of vibration spreads all over, you will become, of course, permanently cognisant of a much larger world than the one you know normally. If, on the other hand, the rapid portion sinks back to the usual rate, you will lose these occasional increased perceptions you now have."

"You amaze me!" exclaimed the author; "for your words exactly describe what I have been feeling——"

"I mention this only in passing, and to give you confidence before you approach the account of your real affliction," continued the doctor. "All perception, as you know, is the result of vibrations; and clairvoyance simply means becoming sensitive to an increased scale of vibrations. The awakening of the inner senses we hear so much about means no more than that. Your partial clairvoyance is easily explained. The only thing that puzzles me is how you managed to procure the drug, for it is not easy to get in pure form, and no adulterated tincture could have given you the terrific impetus I see you have acquired. But, please proceed now and tell me your story in your own way."

"This *Cannabis indica*," the author went on, "came into my possession last autumn while my wife was away. I need not explain how I got it, for that has no importance; but it was the genuine fluid extract, and I could not resist the temptation to make an experiment. One of its effects, as you know, is to induce torrential laughter——"

"Yes: sometimes."

"——I am a writer of humorous tales, and I wished to increase my own sense of laughter—to see the ludicrous from an abnormal point of view. I wished to study it a bit, if possible, and——"

"Tell me!"

"I took an experimental dose. I starved for six hours to hasten the effect, locked myself into this room, and gave orders not to be disturbed. Then I swallowed the stuff and waited."

"And the effect?"

"I waited one hour, two, three, four, five hours. Nothing happened. No laughter came, but only a great weariness instead. Nothing in the room or in my thoughts came within a hundred miles of a humorous aspect."

"Always a most uncertain drug," interrupted the doctor. "We make very small use of it on that account."

"At two o'clock in the morning I felt so hungry and tired that I decided to give up the experiment and wait no longer. I drank some milk and went upstairs to bed. I felt flat and disappointed. I fell asleep at once and must have slept for about an hour, when I awoke suddenly with a great noise in my ears. It was the noise of my own laughter! I was simply shaking with merriment. At first I was bewildered and thought I had been laughing in dreams, but a moment later I remembered the drug, and was delighted to think that after all I had got an effect. It had been working all along, only I had miscalculated the time. The only unpleasant thing *then* was an odd feeling that I had not waked naturally, but had been wakened by some one else—deliberately. This came to me as a certainty in the middle of my noisy laughter and distressed me."

"Any impression who it could have been?" asked the doctor, now listening with close attention to every word, very much on the alert.

Pender hesitated and tried to smile. He brushed his hair from his forehead with a nervous gesture.

"You must tell me all your impressions, even your fancies; they are quite as important as your certainties."

"I had a vague idea that it was some one connected with my forgotten dream, some one who had been at me in my sleep, some one of great strength and great ability—of great force—quite an unusual personality—and, I was certain, too—a woman."

"A good woman?" asked John Silence quietly.

Pender started a little at the question and his sallow face flushed; it seemed to surprise him. But he shook his head quickly with an indefinable look of horror.

"Evil," he answered briefly, "appallingly evil, and yet mingled with the sheer wickedness of it was also a certain perverseness—the perversity of the unbalanced mind."

He hesitated a moment and looked up sharply at his interlocutor. A shade of suspicion showed itself in his eyes.

"No," laughed the doctor, "you need not fear that I'm merely humouring you, or think you mad. Far from it. Your story interests me exceedingly and you furnish me unconsciously with a number of clues as you tell it. You see, I possess some knowledge of my own as to these psychic byways."

"I was shaking with such violent laughter," continued the narrator, reassured in a moment, "though with no clear idea what was amusing me, that I had the greatest difficulty in getting up for the matches, and was afraid I should frighten the servants overhead with my explosions. When the gas was lit I found the room empty, of course, and the door locked as usual. Then I half dressed and went out on to the landing, my hilarity better under control, and proceeded to go downstairs. I wished to record my sensations. I stuffed a handkerchief into my mouth so as not to scream aloud and communicate my hysterics to the entire household."

"And the presence of this—this——?"

"It was hanging about me all the time," said Pender, "but for the moment it seemed to have withdrawn. Probably, too, my laughter killed all other emotions."

"And how long did you take getting downstairs?"

"I was just coming to that. I see you know all my 'symptoms' in advance, as it were; for, of course, I thought I should never get to the bottom. Each step seemed to take five minutes, and crossing the narrow hall at the foot of the stairs—well, I could have sworn it was half an hour's journey had not my watch certified that it was a few seconds. Yet I walked fast and tried to push on. It was no good. I walked apparently without advancing, and at that rate it would have taken me a week to get down Putney Hill."

"An experimental dose radically alters the scale of time and space sometimes——"

"But, when at last I got into my study and lit the gas, the change came horridly, and sudden as a flash of lightning. It was like a douche of icy water, and in the middle of this storm of laughter——"

"Yes; what?" asked the doctor, leaning forward and peering into his eyes.

"——I was overwhelmed with terror," said Pender, lowering his reedy voice at the mere recollection of it.

He paused a moment and mopped his forehead. The scared, hunted look in his eyes now dominated the whole face. Yet, all the time, the corners of his mouth hinted of possible laughter as though the recollection of that merriment still amused him. The combination of fear and laughter in his face was very curious, and lent great conviction to his story; it also lent a bizarre expression of horror to his gestures.

"Terror, was it?" repeated the doctor soothingly.

"Yes, terror; for, though the Thing that woke me seemed to have gone, the memory of it still frightened me, and I collapsed into a chair. Then I locked the door and tried to reason with myself, but the drug made my movements so prolonged that it took me five minutes to reach the door, and another five to get back to the chair again. The laughter, too, kept bubbling up inside me—great wholesome laughter that shook me like gusts of wind—so that even my terror almost made me laugh. Oh, but I may tell you, Dr. Silence, it was altogether vile, that mixture of fear and laughter, altogether vile!

"Then, all at once, the things in the room again presented their funny side to me and set me off laughing more furiously than ever. The bookcase was ludicrous, the arm-chair a perfect clown, the way the clock looked at me on the mantelpiece too comic for words; the arrangement of papers and inkstand on the desk tickled me till I roared and shook and held my sides and the tears streamed down my cheeks. And that footstool! Oh, that absurd footstool!"

He lay back in his chair, laughing to himself and holding up his hands at the thought of it, and at the sight of him Dr. Silence laughed, too.

"Go on, please," he said, "I quite understand. I know something myself of the hashish laughter."

The author pulled himself together and resumed, his face growing quickly grave again.

"So, you see, side by side with this extravagant, apparently causeless merriment, there was also an extravagant, apparently causeless terror. The drug produced the laughter, I knew; but what brought in the terror I could not imagine. Everywhere behind the fun lay the fear. It was terror masked by cap and bells; and I became the playground for two opposing emotions, armed and fighting to the death. Gradually, then, the impression grew in me that this fear was caused by the invasion—so you called it just now—of the 'person' who had wakened me: she was utterly evil; inimical to my soul, or at least to all in me that wished for good. There I stood, sweating and trembling, laughing at everything in the room, yet all the while with this white terror mastering my heart. And this creature was putting——putting her——"

He hesitated again, using his handkerchief freely.

"Putting what?"

"——putting ideas into my mind," he went on glancing nervously about the room. "Actually tapping my thought-stream so as to switch off the usual current and inject her own. How mad that sounds! I know it, but it's true. It's the only way I can express it. Moreover, while the operation terrified me, the skill with which it was accomplished filled me afresh with laughter at the clumsiness of men by comparison. Our ignorant, bungling methods of teaching the minds of others, of inculcating ideas, and so on, overwhelmed me with laughter when I understood this superior and diabolical method. Yet my laughter seemed hollow and ghastly, and ideas of evil and tragedy trod close upon the heels of the comic. Oh, doctor, I tell you again, it was unnerving!"

John Silence sat with his head thrust forward to catch every word of the story which the other continued to pour out in nervous, jerky sentences and lowered voice.

"You *saw* nothing—no one—all this time?" he asked.

"Not with my eyes. There was no visual hallucination. But in my mind there began to grow the vivid picture of a woman—large, dark-skinned, with white teeth and masculine features, and one eye—the left—so drooping as to appear almost closed. Oh, such a face——!"

"A face you would recognise again?"

Pender laughed dreadfully.

"I wish I could forget it," he whispered, "I only wish I could forget it!" Then he sat forward in his chair suddenly, and grasped the doctor's hand with an emotional gesture.

"I *must* tell you how grateful I am for your patience and sympathy," he cried, with a tremor in his voice, "and—that you do not think me mad. I have told no one else a quarter of all this, and the mere freedom of speech—the relief of sharing my affliction with another—has helped me already more than I can possibly say."

Dr. Silence pressed his hand and looked steadily into the frightened eyes. His voice was very gentle when he replied.

"Your case, you know, is very singular, but of absorbing interest to me," he said, "for it threatens, not your physical existence but the temple of your psychical existence—the inner life. Your mind would not be permanently affected here and now, in this world; but in the existence after the body is left behind, you might wake up with your spirit

so twisted, so distorted, so befouled, that you would be *spiritually insane*—a far more radical condition than merely being insane here."

There came a strange hush over the room, and between the two men
sitting there facing one another.

"Do you really mean—Good Lord!" stammered the author as soon
as he could find his tongue.

"What I mean in detail will keep till a little later, and I need only say
now that I should not have spoken in this way unless I were quite positive of being able to help you. Oh, there's no doubt as to that, believe
me. In the first place, I am very familiar with the workings of this extraordinary drug, this drug which has had the chance effect of opening
you up to the forces of another region; and, in the second, I have a firm
belief in the reality of supersensuous occurrences as well as considerable knowledge of psychic processes acquired by long and painful experiment. The rest is, or should be, merely sympathetic treatment and
practical application. The hashish has partially opened another world
to you by increasing your rate of psychical vibration, and thus render-
ing you abnormally sensitive. Ancient forces attached to this house
have attacked you. For the moment I am only puzzled as to their
precise nature; for were they of an ordinary character, I should myself
be psychic enough to feel them. Yet I am conscious of feeling nothing
as yet. But now, please continue, Mr. Pender, and tell me the rest of
your wonderful story; and when you have finished, I will talk about the
means of cure."

Pender shifted his chair a little closer to the friendly doctor and then
went on in the same nervous voice with his narrative.

"After making some notes of my impressions I finally got upstairs
again to bed. It was four o'clock in the morning. I laughed all the way
up—at the grotesque banisters, the droll physiognomy of the staircase
window, the burlesque grouping of the furniture, and the memory of
that outrageous footstool in the room below; but nothing more happened to alarm or disturb me, and I woke late in the morning after a
dreamless sleep, none the worse for my experiment except for a slight
headache and a coldness of the extremities due to lowered circulation."

"Fear gone, too?" asked the doctor.

"I seemed to have forgotten it, or at least ascribed it to mere nervousness. Its reality had gone, anyhow for the time, and all that day I
wrote and wrote and wrote. My sense of laughter seemed wonderfully
quickened and my characters acted without effort out of the heart of
true humour. I was exceedingly pleased with this result of my experiment. But when the stenographer had taken her departure and I came
to read over the pages she had typed out, I recalled her sudden glances

of surprise and the odd way she had looked up at me while I was dic-
tating. I was amazed at what I read and could hardly believe I had uttered it."

"And why?"

"It was so distorted. The words, indeed, were mine so far as I could
remember, but the meanings seemed strange. It frightened me. The
sense was so altered. At the very places where my characters were intended to tickle the ribs, only curious emotions of sinister amusement
resulted. Dreadful innuendoes had managed to creep into the phrases.
There was laughter of a kind, but it was bizarre, horrible, distressing;
and my attempt at analysis only increased my dismay. The story, as it
read then, made me shudder, for by virtue of these slight changes it had
come somehow to hold the soul of horror, of horror disguised as merriment. The framework of humour was there, if you understand me,
but the characters had turned sinister, and their laughter was evil."

"Can you show me this writing?"

The author shook his head.

"I destroyed it," he whispered. "But, in the end, though of course
much perturbed about it, I persuaded myself that it was due to some
after-effect of the drug, a sort of reaction that gave a twist to my mind
and made me read macabre interpretations into words and situations
that did not properly hold them."

"And, meanwhile, did the presence of this person leave you?"

"No; that stayed more or less. When my mind was actively employed
I forgot it, but when idle, dreaming, or doing nothing in particular,
there she was beside me, influencing my mind horribly——"

"In what way, precisely?" interrupted the doctor.

"Evil, scheming thoughts came to me, visions of crime, hateful pictures of wickedness, and the kind of bad imagination that so far has
been foreign, indeed impossible, to my normal nature——"

"The pressure of the Dark Powers upon the personality," murmured
the doctor, making a quick note.

"Eh? I didn't quite catch——"

"Pray, go on. I am merely making notes; you shall know their purport
fully later."

"Even when my wife returned I was still aware of this Presence in the
house; it associated itself with my inner personality in most intimate
fashion; and outwardly I always felt oddly constrained to be polite and
respectful towards it—to open doors, provide chairs and hold myself
carefully deferential when it was about. It became very compelling at
last, and, if I failed in any little particular, I seemed to know that it pursued me about the house, from one room to another, haunting my very

soul in its inmost abode. It certainly came before my wife so far as my attentions were concerned.

"But, let me first finish the story of my experimental dose, for I took it again the third night, and underwent a very similar experience, delayed like the first in coming, and then carrying me off my feet when it did come with a rush of this false demon-laughter. This time, however, there was a reversal of the changed scale of space and time; it shortened instead of lengthened, so that I dressed and got downstairs in about twenty seconds, and the couple of hours I stayed and worked in the study passed literally like a period of ten minutes."

"That is often true of an overdose," interjected the doctor, "and you may go a mile in a few minutes, or a few yards in a quarter of an hour. It is quite incomprehensible to those who have never experienced it, and is a curious proof that time and space are merely forms of thought."

"This time," Pender went on, talking more and more rapidly in his excitement, "another extraordinary effeot came to me, and I experienced a curious changing of the senses, so that I perceived external things through one large main sense-channel instead of through the five divisions known as sight, smell, touch, and so forth. You will, I know, understand me when I tell you that I *heard* sights and *saw* sounds. No language can make this comprehensible, of course, and I can only say, for instance, that the striking of the clock I saw as a visible picture in the air before me. I saw the sounds of the tinkling bell. And in precisely the same way I heard the colours in the room, especially the colours of those books in the shelf behind you. Those red bindings I heard in deep sounds, and the yellow covers of the French bindings next to them made a shrill, piercing note not unlike the chattering of starlings. That brown bookcase muttered, and those green curtains opposite kept up a constant sort of rippling sound like the lower notes of a wood-horn. But I only was conscious of these sounds when I looked steadily at the different objects, and thought about them. The room, you understand, was not full of a chorus of notes; but when I concentrated my mind upon a colour, I heard, as well as saw, it."

"That is a known, though rarely obtained, effect of *Cannabis indica*," observed the doctor. "And it provoked laughter again, did it?"

"Only the muttering of the cupboard-bookcase made me laugh. It was so like a great animal trying to get itself noticed, and made me think of a performing bear—which is full of a kind of pathetic humour, you know. But this mingling of the senses produced no confusion in my brain. On the contrary, I was unusually clear-headed and experienced an intensification of consciousness, and felt marvellously alive and keen-minded.

"Moreover, when I took up a pencil in obedience to an impulse to sketch—a talent not normally mine—I found that I could draw nothing but heads, nothing, in fact, but one head—always the same—the head of a dark-skinned woman, with huge and terrible features and a very drooping left eye; and so well drawn, too, that I was amazed, as you may imagine——"

"And the expression of the face——?"

Pender hesitated a moment for words, casting about with his hands in the air and hunching his shoulders. A perceptible shudder ran over him.

"What I can only describe as—*blackness*," he replied in a low tone; "the face of a dark and evil soul."

"You destroyed that, too?" queried the doctor sharply.

"No; I have kept the drawings," he said, with a laugh, and rose to get them from a drawer in the writing-desk behind him.

"Here is all that remains of the pictures, you see," he added, pushing a number of loose sheets under the doctor's eyes; "nothing but a few scrawly lines. That's all I found the next morning. I had really drawn no heads at all—nothing but those lines and blots and wriggles. The pictures were entirely subjective, and existed only in my mind which constructed them out of a few wild strokes of the pen. Like the altered scale of space and time it was a complete delusion. These all passed, of course, with the passing of the drug's effects. But the other thing did not pass. I mean, the presence of that Dark Soul remained with me. It is here still. It is real. I don't know how I can escape from it."

"It is attached to the house, not to you personally. You must leave the house."

"Yes. Only I cannot afford to leave the house, for my work is my sole means of support, and—well, you see, since this change I cannot even write. They are horrible, these mirthless tales I now write, with their mockery of laughter, their diabolical suggestion. Horrible? I shall go mad if this continues."

He screwed his face up and looked about the room as though he expected to see some haunting shape.

"This influence in this house induced by my experiment, has killed in a flash, in a sudden stroke, the sources of my humour, and though I still go on writing funny tales—I have a certain name you know—my inspiration has dried up, and much of what I write I have to burn—yes, doctor, to burn, before any one sees it."

"As utterly alien to your own mind and personality?"

"Utterly! As though some one else had written it——"

"Ah!"

"And shocking!" He passed his hand over his eyes a moment and let the breath escape softly through his teeth. "Yet most damnably clever in the consummate way the vile suggestions are insinuated under cover of a kind of high drollery. My stenographer left me of course—and I've been afraid to take another——"

John Silence got up and began to walk about the room leisurely without speaking; he appeared to be examining the pictures on the wall and reading the names of the books lying about. Presently he paused on the hearthrug, with his back to the fire, and turned to look his patient quietly in the eyes. Pender's face was grey and drawn; the hunted expression dominated it; the long recital had told upon him.

"Thank you, Mr. Pender," he said, a curious glow showing about his fine, quiet face; "thank you for the sincerity and frankness of your account. But I think now there is nothing further I need ask you." He indulged in a long scrutiny of the author's haggard features drawing purposely the man's eyes to his own and then meeting them with a look of power and confidence calculated to inspire even the feeblest soul with courage. "And, to begin with," he added, smiling pleasantly, "let me assure you without delay that you need have no alarm, for you are no more insane or deluded than I myself am——"

Pender heaved a deep sigh and tried to return the smile.

"——and this is simply a case, so far as I can judge at present, of a very singular psychical invasion, and a very sinister one, too, if you perhaps understand what I mean——"

"It's an odd expression; you used it before, you know," said the author wearily, yet eagerly listening to every word of the diagnosis, and deeply touched by the intelligent sympathy which did not at once indicate the lunatic asylum.

"Possibly," returned the other, "and an odd affliction, too, you'll allow, yet one not unknown to the nations of antiquity, nor to those moderns, perhaps, who recognise the freedom of action under certain pathogenic conditions between this world and another."

"And you think," asked Pender hastily, "that it is all primarily due to the *Cannabis?* There is nothing radically amiss with myself—nothing incurable, or——?"

"Due entirely to the overdose," Dr. Silence replied emphatically, "to the drug's direct action upon your psychical being. It rendered you ultra-sensitive and made you respond to an increased rate of vibration. And, let me tell you, Mr. Pender, that your experiment might have had results far more dire. It has brought you into touch with a somewhat singular class of Invisible, but of one, I think, chiefly human in character. You might, however, just as easily have been drawn out of human range altogether, and the results of such a contingency would have been exceedingly terrible. Indeed, you would not now be here to tell the tale. I need not alarm you on that score, but mention it as a warning you will not misunderstand or underrate after what you have been through.

"You look puzzled. You do not quite gather what I am driving at; and it is not to be expected that you should, for you, I suppose, are the nominal Christian with the nominal Christian's lofty standard of ethics, and his utter ignorance of spiritual possibilities. Beyond a somewhat childish understanding of 'spiritual wickedness in high places,' you probably have no conception of what is possible once you break-down the slender gulf that is mercifully fixed between you and that Outer World. But my studies and training have taken me far outside these orthodox trips, and I have made experiments that I could scarcely speak to you about in language that would be intelligible to you."

He paused a moment to note the breathless interest of Pender's face and manner. Every word he uttered was calculated; he knew exactly the value and effect of the emotions he desired to waken in the heart of the afflicted being before him.

"And from certain knowledge I have gained through various experiences," he continued calmly, "I can diagnose your case as I said before to be one of psychical invasion."

"And the nature of this—er—invasion?" stammered the bewildered writer of humorous tales.

"There is no reason why I should not say at once that I do not yet quite know," replied Dr. Silence. "I may first have to make one or two experiments——"

"On me?" gasped Pender, catching his breath.

"Not exactly," the doctor said, with a grave smile, "but with your assistance, perhaps. I shall want to test the conditions of the house—to ascertain, if possible, the character of the forces, of this strange personality that has been haunting you——"

"At present you have no idea exactly who—what—why——" asked the other in a wild flurry of interest, dread and amazement.

"I have a very good idea, but no proof rather," returned the doctor. "The effects of the drug in altering the scale of time and space, and merging the senses have nothing primarily to do with the invasion. They come to any one who is fool enough to take an experimental dose. It is the other features of your case that are unusual. You see, you are now in touch with certain violent emotions, desires, purposes, still active in this house, that were produced in the past by some powerful and evil personality that lived here. How long ago, or why they still persist so forcibly, I cannot positively say. But I should judge that they are merely forces acting automatically with the momentum of their terrific original impetus."

"Not directed by a living being, a conscious will, you mean?"

"Possibly not—but none the less dangerous on that account, and more difficult to deal with. I cannot explain to you in a few minutes the nature of such things, for you have not made the studies that would enable you to follow me; but I have reason to believe that on the dissolution at death of a human being, its forces may still persist and continue to act in a blind, unconscious fashion. As a rule they speedily dissipate themselves, but in the case of a very powerful personality they may last a long time. And, in some cases—of which I incline to think this is one—these forces may coalesce with certain non-human entities who thus continue their life indefinitely and increase their strength to an unbelievable degree. If the original personality was evil, the beings attracted to the left-over forces will also be evil. In this case, I think there has been an unusual and dreadful aggrandisement of the thoughts and purposes left behind long ago by a woman of consummate wickedness and great personal power of character and intellect. Now, do you begin to see what I am driving at a little?"

Pender stared fixedly at his companion, plain horror showing in his eyes. But he found nothing to say, and the doctor continued—

"In your case, predisposed by the action of the drug, you have experienced the rush of these forces in undiluted strength. They wholly obliterate in you the sense of humour, fancy, imagination,—all that makes for cheerfulness and hope. They seek, though perhaps automatically only, to oust your own thoughts and establish themselves in their place. You are the victim of a psychical invasion. At the same time, you have become clairvoyant in the true sense. You are also a clairvoyant victim."

Pender mopped his face and sighed. He left his chair and went over to the fireplace to warm himself.

"You must think me a quack to talk like this, or a madman," laughed Dr. Silence. "But never mind that. I have come to help you, and I can help you if you will do what I tell you. It is very simple: you must leave this house at once. Oh, never mind the difficulties; we will deal with those together. I can place another house at your disposal, or I would take the lease here off your hands, and later have it pulled down. Your case interests me greatly, and I mean to see you through, so that you have no anxiety, and can drop back into your old groove of work tomorrow! The drug has provided you, and therefore me, with a short-cut to a very interesting experience. I am grateful to you."

The author poked the fire vigorously, emotion rising in him like a tide. He glanced towards the door nervously.

"There is no need to alarm your wife or to tell her the details of our conversation," pursued the other quietly. "Let her know that you will soon be in possession again of your sense of humour and your health, and explain that I am lending you another house for six months. Meanwhile I may have the right to use this house for a night or two for my experiment. Is that understood between us?"

"I can only thank you from the bottom of my heart," stammered Pender, unable to find words to express his gratitude.

Then he hesitated for a moment, searching the doctor's face anxiously. "And your experiment with the house?" he said at length.

"Of the simplest character, my dear Mr. Pender. Although I am myself an artificially trained psychic, and consequently aware of the presence of discarnate entities as a rule, I have so far felt nothing here at all. This makes me sure that the forces acting here are of an unusual description. What I propose to do is to make an experiment with a view of drawing out this evil, coaxing it from its lair, so to speak, in order that it may *exhaust itself through me* and become dissipated for ever. I have already been inoculated," he added; "I consider myself to be immune."

"Heavens above!" gasped the author, collapsing on to a chair.

"Hell beneath! might be a more appropriate exclamation," the doctor laughed. "But, seriously, Mr. Pender, this is what I propose to do— with your permission."

"Of course, of course," cried the other, "you have my permission and my best wishes for success. I can see no possible objection, but——"

"But what?"

"I pray to Heaven you will not undertake this experiment alone, will you?"

"Oh, dear, no; not alone."

"You will take a companion with good nerves, and reliable in case of disaster, won't you?"

"I shall bring two companions," the doctor said.

"Ah, that's better. I feel easier. I am sure you must have among your acquaintances men who——"

"I shall not think of bringing men, Mr. Pender."

The other looked up sharply.

"No, or women either; or children."

"I don't understand. Who will you bring, then?"

"Animals," explained the doctor, unable to prevent a smile at his companion's expression of surprise—"two animals, a cat and a dog."

Pender stared as if his eyes would drop out upon the floor, and then led the way without another word into the adjoining room where his wife was awaiting them for tea.

II

A few days later the humorist and his wife, with minds greatly relieved, moved into a small furnished house placed at their free disposal in another part of London; and John Silence, intent upon his approaching experiment, made ready to spend a night in the empty house on the top of Putney Hill. Only two rooms were prepared for occupation: the study on the ground floor and the bedroom immediately above it; all other doors were to be locked, and no servant was to be left in the house. The motor had orders to call for him at nine o'clock the following morning.

And, meanwhile, his secretary had instructions to look up the past history and associations of the place, and learn everything he could concerning the character of former occupants, recent or remote.

The animals, by whose sensitiveness he intended to test any unusual conditions in the atmosphere of the building, Dr. Silence selected with care and judgment. He believed (and had already made curious experiments to prove it) that animals were more often, and more truly, clairvoyant than human beings. Many of them, he felt convinced, possessed powers of perception far superior to that mere keenness of the senses common to all dwellers in the wilds where the senses grow specially alert; they had what he termed "animal clairvoyance," and from his experiments with horses, dogs, cats, and even birds, he had drawn certain deductions, which, however, need not be referred to in detail here.

Cats, in particular, he believed, were almost continuously conscious of a larger field of vision, too detailed even for a photographic camera, and quite beyond the reach of normal human organs. He had, further, observed that while dogs were usually terrified in the presence of such phenomena, cats on the other hand were soothed and satisfied. They welcomed manifestations as something belonging peculiarly to their own region.

He selected his animals, therefore, with wisdom so that they might afford a differing test, each in its own way, and that one should not merely communicate its own excitement to the other. He took a dog and a cat.

The cat he chose, now full grown, had lived with him since kittenhood, a kittenhood of perplexing sweetness and audacious mischief. Wayward it was and fanciful, ever playing its own mysterious games in the corners of the room, jumping at invisible nothings, leaping sideways into the air and falling with tiny moccasined feet on to another part of the carpet, yet with an air of dignified earnestness which showed that the performance was necessary to its own well-being, and not done merely to impress a stupid human audience. In the middle of elaborate washing it would look up, startled, as though to stare at the approach of some Invisible, cocking its little head sideways and putting out a velvet pad to inspect cautiously. Then it would get absent-minded, and stare with equal intentness in another direction (just to confuse the onlookers), and suddenly go on furiously washing its body again, but in quite a new place. Except for a white patch on its breast it was coal black. And its name was—Smoke.

"Smoke" described its temperament as well as its appearance. Its movements, its individuality, its posing as a little furry mass of concealed mysteries, its elfin-like elusiveness, all combined to justify its name; and a subtle painter might have pictured it as a wisp of floating smoke, the fire below betraying itself at two points only—the glowing eyes.

All its forces ran to intelligence—secret intelligence, the wordless incalculable intuition of the Cat. It was, indeed, *the* cat for the business in hand.

The selection of the dog was not so simple, for the doctor owned many; but after much deliberation he chose a collie, called Flame from his yellow coat. True, it was a trifle old, and stiff in the joints, and even beginning to grow deaf, but, on the other hand, it was a very particular friend of Smoke's, and had fathered it from kittenhood upwards so that a subtle understanding existed between them. It was this that turned the balance in its favour, this and its courage. Moreover, though good-tempered, it was a terrible fighter, and its anger when provoked by a righteous cause was a fury of fire, and irresistible.

It had come to him quite young, straight from the shepherd, with the air of the hills yet in its nostrils, and was then little more than skin and bones and teeth. For a collie it was sturdily built, its nose blunter than most, its yellow hair stiff rather than silky, and it had full eyes, unlike the slit eyes of its breed. Only its master could touch it, for it ignored strangers, and despised their pattings—when any dared to pat it. There was something patriarchal about the old beast. He was in earnest, and went through life with tremendous energy and big things in view, as though he had the reputation of his whole race to uphold. And to watch him fighting against odds was to understand why he was terrible.

In his relations with Smoke he was always absurdly gentle; also he was fatherly; and at the same time betrayed a certain diffidence or shyness. He recognised that Smoke called for strong yet respectful management. The cat's circuitous methods puzzled him, and his elaborate pretences perhaps shocked the dog's liking for direct, undisguised action. Yet, while he failed to comprehend these tortuous feline mysteries, he was never contemptuous or condescending; and he presided over the safety of his furry black friend somewhat as a father, loving, but intuitive, might superintend the vagaries of a wayward and talented child. And, in return, Smoke rewarded him with exhibitions of fascinating and audacious mischief.

And these brief descriptions of their characters are necessary for the proper understanding of what subsequently took place.

With Smoke sleeping in the folds of his fur coat, and the collie lying watchful on the seat opposite, John Silence went down in his motor after dinner on the night of November 15th.

And the fog was so dense that they were obliged to travel at quarter speed the entire way.

It was after ten o'clock when he dismissed the motor and entered the dingy little house with the latchkey provided by Pender. He found the hall gas turned low, and a fire in the study. Books and food had also been placed ready by the servant according to instructions. Coils of fog rushed in after him through the open door and filled the hall and passage with its cold discomfort.

The first thing Dr. Silence did was to lock up Smoke in the study with a saucer of milk before the fire, and then make a search of the house with Flame. The dog ran cheerfully behind him all the way while he tried the doors of the other rooms to make sure they were locked. He nosed about into corners and made little excursions on his own account. His manner was expectant. He knew there must be something unusual about the proceeding, because it was contrary to the habits of his whole life not to be asleep at this hour on the mat in front of the fire. He kept looking up into his master's face, as door after door was tried, with an expression of intelligent sympathy, but at the same time a certain air of disapproval. Yet everything his master did was good in his eyes, and he betrayed as little impatience as possible with all this unnecessary journeying to and fro. If the doctor was pleased to play this sort of game at such an hour of the night, it was surely not for him to object. So he played it, too; and was very busy and earnest about it into the bargain.

After an uneventful search they came down again to the study, and here Dr. Silence discovered Smoke washing his face calmly in front of the fire. The saucer of milk was licked dry and clean; the preliminary examination that cats always make in new surroundings had evidently been satisfactorily concluded. He drew an arm-chair up to the fire, stirred the coals into a blaze, arranged the table and lamp to his satisfaction for reading, and then prepared surreptitiously to watch the animals. He wished to observe them carefully without their being aware of it.

Now, in spite of their respective ages, it was the regular custom of these two to play together every night before sleep. Smoke always made the advances, beginning with grave impudence to pat the dog's tail, and Flame played cumbrously, with condescension. It was his duty, rather than pleasure; he was glad when it was over, and sometimes he was very determined and refused to play at all.

And this night was one of the occasions on which he was firm.

The doctor, looking cautiously over the top of his book, watched the cat begin the performance. It started by gazing with an innocent expression at the dog where he lay with nose on paws and eyes wide open in the middle of the floor. Then it got up and made as though it meant to walk to the door, going deliberately and very softly. Flame's eyes followed it until it was beyond the range of sight, and then the cat turned sharply and began patting his tail tentatively with one paw. The tail moved slightly in reply, and Smoke changed paws and tapped it again. The dog, however, did not rise to play as was his wont, and the cat fell to patting it briskly with both paws. Flame still lay motionless.

This puzzled and bored the cat, and it went round and stared hard into its friend's face to see what was the matter. Perhaps some inarticulate message flashed from the dog's eyes into its own little brain, making it understand that the programme for the night had better not begin with play. Perhaps it only realised that its friend was immovable. But, whatever the reason, its usual persistence thenceforward deserted it, and it made no further attempts at persuasion. Smoke yielded at once to the dog's mood; it sat down where it was and began to wash.

But the washing, the doctor noted, was by no means its real purpose; it only used it to mask something else; it stopped at the most busy and furious moments and began to stare about the room. Its thoughts wandered absurdly. It peered intently at the curtains; at the shadowy corners; at empty space above; leaving its body in curiously awkward positions for whole minutes together. Then it turned sharply and stared with a sudden signal of intelligence at the dog, and Flame at once rose somewhat stiffly to his feet and began to wander aimlessly and restlessly to and fro about the floor. Smoke followed him, padding quietly at his heels. Between them they made what seemed to be a deliberate search of the room.

And, here, as he watched them, noting carefully every detail of the performance over the top of his book, yet making no effort to interfere, it seemed to the doctor that the first beginnings of a faint distress betrayed themselves in the collie, and in the cat the stirrings of a vague excitement.

He observed them closely. The fog was thick in the air, and the tobacco smoke from his pipe added to its density; the furniture at the far end stood mistily, and where the shadows congregated in hanging clouds under the ceiling, it was difficult to see clearly at all; the lamplight only reached to a level of five feet from the floor, above which came layers of comparative darkness, so that the room appeared twice as lofty as it actually was. By means of the lamp and the fire, however, the carpet was everywhere clearly visible.

The animals made their silent tour of the floor, sometimes the dog leading, sometimes the cat; occasionally they looked at one another as though exchanging signals; and once or twice, in spite of the limited space, he lost sight of one or other among the fog and the shadows. Their curiosity, it appeared to him, was something more than the excitement lurking in the unknown territory of a strange room; yet, so far, it was impossible to test this, and he purposely kept his mind quietly receptive lest the smallest mental excitement on his part should communicate itself to the animals and thus destroy the value of their independent behaviour.

They made a very thorough journey, leaving no piece of furniture unexamined, or unsmelt. Flame led the way, walking slowly with lowered head, and Smoke followed demurely at his heels, making a transparent pretence of not being interested, yet missing nothing. And, at length, they returned, the old collie first, and came to rest on the mat before the fire. Flame rested his muzzle on his master's knee, smiling beatifically while he patted the yellow head and spoke his name; and Smoke, coming a little later, pretending he came by chance, looked from the empty saucer to his face, lapped up the milk when it was given him to the last drop, and then sprang upon his knees and curled round for the sleep it had fully earned and intended to enjoy.

Silence descended upon the room. Only the breathing of the dog upon the mat came through the deep stillness, like the pulse of time marking the minutes; and the steady drip, drip of the fog outside upon the window-ledges dismally testified to the inclemency of the night beyond. And the soft crashings of the coals as the fire settled down into the grate became less and less audible as the fire sank and the flames resigned their fierceness.

It was now well after eleven o'clock, and Dr. Silence devoted himself again to his book. He read the words on the printed page and took in their meaning superficially, yet without starting into life the correlations of thought and suggestions that should accompany interesting reading. Underneath, all the while, his mental energies were absorbed in watching, listening, waiting for what might come. He was not over-sanguine himself, yet he did not wish to be taken by surprise. Moreover, the animals, his sensitive barometers, had incontinently gone to sleep.

After reading a dozen pages, however, he realised that his mind was really occupied in reviewing the features of Pender's extraordinary story, and that it was no longer necessary to steady his imagination by studying the dull paragraphs detailed in the pages before him. He laid down his book accordingly, and allowed his thoughts to dwell upon the features of the Case. Speculations as to the meaning, however, he rigorously suppressed, knowing that such thoughts would act upon his imagination like wind upon the glowing embers of a fire.

As the night wore on the silence grew deeper and deeper, and only at rare intervals he heard the sound of wheels on the main road a hundred yards away, where the horses went at a walking pace owing to the density of the fog. The echo of pedestrian footsteps no longer reached him, the clamour of occasional voices no longer came down the side street. The night, muffled by fog, shrouded by veils of ultimate mystery, hung about the haunted villa like a doom. Nothing in the house stirred. Stillness, in a thick blanket, lay over the upper storeys. Only the mist in the room grew more dense, he thought, and the damp cold more penetrating. Certainly, from time to time, he shivered.

The collie, now deep in slumber, moved occasionally,—grunted, sighed, or twitched his legs in dreams. Smoke lay on his knees, a pool of warm, black fur, only the closest observation detecting the movement of his sleek sides. It was difficult to distinguish exactly where his head and body joined in that circle of glistening hair; only a black satin nose and a tiny tip of pink tongue betrayed the secret.

Dr. Silence watched him, and felt comfortable. The collie's breathing was soothing. The fire was well built, and would burn for another two hours without attention. He was not conscious of the least nervousness. He particularly wished to remain in his ordinary and normal state of mind, and to force nothing. If sleep came naturally, he would let it come—and even welcome it. The coldness of the room, when the fire died down later, would be sure to wake him again; and it would then be time enough to carry these sleeping barometers up to bed. From various psychic premonitions he knew quite well that the night would not pass without adventure; but he did not wish to force its arrival; and he wished to remain normal, and let the animals remain normal, so that, when it came, it would be unattended by excitement or by any straining of the attention. Many experiments had made him wise. And, for the rest, he had no fear.

Accordingly, after a time, he did fall asleep as he had expected, and the last thing he remembered, before oblivion slipped up over his eyes like soft wool, was the picture of Flame stretching all four legs at once, and sighing noisily as he sought a more comfortable position for his paws and muzzle upon the mat.

It was a good deal later when he became aware that a weight lay upon his chest, and that something was pencilling over his face and mouth. A soft touch on the cheek woke him. Something was patting him.

He sat up with a jerk, and found himself staring straight into a pair of brilliant eyes, half green, half black. Smoke's face lay level with his own; and the cat had climbed up with its front paws upon his chest.

The lamp had burned low and the fire was nearly out, yet Dr. Silence saw in a moment that the cat was in an excited state. It kneaded with its front paws into his chest, shifting from one to the other. He felt them prodding against him. It lifted a leg very carefully and patted his cheek gingerly. Its fur, he saw, was standing ridgewise upon its back; the ears were flattened back somewhat; the tail was switching sharply. The cat, of course, had wakened him with a purpose, and the instant he realised this, he set it upon the arm of the chair and sprang up with a quick turn to face the empty room behind him. By some curious instinct, his arms of their own accord assumed an attitude of defence in front of him, as though to ward off something that threatened his safety. Yet nothing was visible. Only shapes of fog hung about rather heavily in the air, moving slightly to and fro.

His mind was now fully alert, and the last vestiges of sleep gone. He turned the lamp higher and peered about him. Two things he became aware of at once: one, that Smoke, while excited, was *pleasurably* excited; the other, that the collie was no longer visible upon the mat at his feet. He had crept away to the corner of the wall farthest from the window, and lay watching the room with wide-open eyes, in which lurked plainly something of alarm.

Something in the dog's behaviour instantly struck Dr. Silence as unusual, and, calling him by name, he moved across to pat him. Flame got up, wagged his tail, and came over slowly to the rug, uttering a low sound that was half growl, half whine. He was evidently perturbed about something, and his master was proceeding to administer comfort when his attention was suddenly drawn to the antics of his other four-footed companion, the cat.

And what he saw filled him with something like amazement.

Smoke had jumped down from the back of the arm-chair and now occupied the middle of the carpet, where, with tail erect and legs stiff as ramrods, it was steadily pacing backwards and forwards in a narrow space, uttering, as it did so, those curious little guttural sounds of pleasure that only an animal of the feline species knows how to make expressive of supreme happiness. Its stiffened legs and arched back made it appear larger than usual, and the black visage wore a smile of beatific joy. Its eyes blazed magnificently; it was in an ecstasy.

At the end of every few paces it turned sharply and stalked back again along the same line, padding softly, and purring like a roll of little muffled drums. It behaved precisely as though it were rubbing against the ankles of some one who remained invisible. A thrill ran down the doctor's spine as he stood and stared. His experiment was growing interesting at last.

He called the collie's attention to his friend's performance to see whether he too was aware of anything standing there upon the carpet, and the dog's behaviour was significant and corroborative. He came as far as his master's knees and then stopped dead, refusing to investigate closely. In vain Dr. Silence urged him; he wagged his tail, whined a little, and stood in a half-crouching attitude, staring alternately at the cat and at his master's face. He was, apparently, both puzzled and alarmed, and the whine went deeper and deeper down into his throat till it changed into an ugly snarl of awakening anger.

Then the doctor called to him in a tone of command he had never known to be disregarded; but still the dog, though springing up in response, declined to move nearer. He made tentative motions, pranced a little like a dog about to take to water, pretended to bark, and ran to and fro on the carpet. So far there was no actual fear in his manner, but he was uneasy and anxious, and nothing would induce him to go within touching distance of the walking cat. Once he made a complete circuit, but always carefully out of reach; and in the end he returned to his master's legs and rubbed vigorously against him. Flame did not like the performance at all: that much was quite clear.

For several minutes John Silence watched the performance of the cat with profound attention and without interfering. Then he called to the animal by name.

"Smoke, you mysterious beastie, what in the world are you about?" he said, in a coaxing tone.

The cat looked up at him for a moment, smiling in its ecstasy, blinking its eyes, but too happy to pause. He spoke to it again. He called to it several times, and each time it turned upon him its blazing eyes, drunk with inner delight, opening and shutting its lips, its body large and rigid with excitement. Yet it never for one instant paused in its short journeys to and fro.

He noted exactly what it did: it walked, he saw, the same number of paces each time, some six or seven steps, and then it turned sharply and retraced them. By the pattern of the great roses in the carpet he measured it. It kept to the same direction and the same line. It behaved precisely as though it were rubbing against something solid. Undoubtedly, there was something standing there on that strip of carpet, something invisible to the doctor, something that alarmed the dog, yet caused the cat unspeakable pleasure.

"Smokie!" he called again, "Smokie, you black mystery, what is it excites you so?"

Again the cat looked up at him for a brief second, and then continued its sentry-walk, blissfully happy, intensely preoccupied. And, for an instant, as he watched it, the doctor was aware that a faint uneasiness stirred in the depths of his own being, focusing itself for the moment upon this curious behaviour of the uncanny creature before him.

There rose in him quite a new realisation of the mystery connected with the whole feline tribe, but especially with that common member of it, the domestic cat—their hidden lives, their strange aloofness, their incalculable subtlety. How utterly remote from anything that human beings understood lay the sources of their elusive activities. As he watched the indescribable bearing of the little creature mincing along the strip of carpet under his eyes, coquetting with the powers of darkness, welcoming, maybe, some fearsome visitor, there stirred in his heart a feeling strangely akin to awe. Its indifference to human kind, its serene superiority to the obvious, struck him forcibly with fresh meaning; so remote, so inaccessible seemed the secret purposes of its real life, so alien to the blundering honesty of other animals. Its absolute poise of bearing brought into his mind the opium-eater's words that "no dignity is perfect which does not at some point ally itself with the mysterious"; and he became suddenly aware that the presence of the dog in this foggy, haunted room on the top of Putney Hill was uncommonly welcome to him. He was glad to feel that Flame's dependable personality was with him. The savage growling at his heels was a pleasant sound. He was glad to hear it. That marching cat made him uneasy.

Finding that Smoke paid no further attention to his words, the doctor decided upon action. Would it rub against his leg, too? He would take it by surprise and see.

He stepped quickly forward and placed himself upon the exact strip of carpet where it walked.

But no cat is ever taken by surprise! The moment he occupied the space of the Intruder, setting his feet on the woven roses midway in the line of travel, Smoke suddenly stopped purring and sat down. If lifted up its face with the most innocent stare imaginable of its green eyes. He could have sworn it laughed. It was a perfect child again. In a single second it had resumed its simple, domestic manner; and it gazed at him in such a way that he almost felt Smoke was the normal being, and *his* was the eccentric behaviour that was being watched. It was consummate, the manner in which it brought about this change so easily and so quickly.

"Superb little actor!" he laughed in spite of himself, and stooped to stroke the shining black back. But, in a flash, as he touched its fur, the cat turned and spat at him viciously, striking at his hand with one paw. Then, with a hurried scutter of feet, it shot like a shadow across the floor and a moment later was calmly sitting over by the window-curtains washing its face as though nothing interested it in the whole world but the cleanness of its cheeks and whiskers.

John Silence straightened himself up and drew a long breath. He realised that the performance was temporarily at an end. The collie, meanwhile, who had watched the whole proceeding with marked disapproval, had now lain down again upon the mat by the fire, no longer growling. It seemed to the doctor just as though something that had entered the room while he slept, alarming the dog, yet bringing happiness to the cat, had now gone out again, leaving all as it was before. Whatever it was that excited its blissful attentions had retreated for the moment.

He realised this intuitively. Smoke evidently realised it, too, for presently he deigned to march back to the fireplace and jump upon his master's knees. Dr. Silence, patient and determined, settled down once more to his book. The animals soon slept; the fire blazed cheerfully; and the cold fog from outside poured into the room through every available chink and crannie.

For a long time silence and peace reigned in the room and Dr. Silence availed himself of the quietness to make careful notes of what had happened. He entered for future use in other cases an exhaustive analysis of what he had observed, especially with regard to the effect upon the two animals. It is impossible here, nor would it be intelligible to the reader unversed in the knowledge of the region known to a scientifically trained psychic like Dr. Silence, to detail these observations. But to him it was clear, up to a certain point—for the rest he must still wait and watch. So far, at least, he realised that while he slept in the chair—that is, while his will was dormant—the room had suffered intrusion from what he recognised as an intensely active Force, and might later be forced to acknowledge as something more than merely a blind force, namely, a distinct personality.

So far it had affected himself scarcely at all, but had acted directly upon the simpler organisms of the animals. It stimulated keenly the centres of the cat's psychic being, inducing a state of instant happiness (intensifying its consciousness probably in the same way a drug or stimulant intensifies that of a human being); whereas it alarmed the less sensitive dog, causing it to feel a vague apprehension and distress.

His own sudden action and exhibition of energy had served to disperse it temporarily, yet he felt convinced—the indications were not lacking even while he sat there making notes—that it still remained near to him, conditionally if not spatially, and was, as it were, gathering force for a second attack.

And, further, he intuitively understood that the relations between the two animals had undergone a subtle change: that the cat had become immeasurably superior, confident, sure of itself in its own peculiar region, whereas Flame had been weakened by an attack he could not comprehend and knew not how to reply to. Though not yet afraid, he was defiant—ready to act against a fear that he felt to be approaching. He was no longer fatherly and protective towards the cat. Smoke held the key to the situation; and both he and the cat knew it.

Thus, as the minutes passed, John Silence sat and waited, keenly on the alert, wondering how soon the attack would be renewed, and at what point it would be diverted from the animals and directed upon himself.

The book lay on the floor beside him, his notes were complete. With one hand on the cat's fur, and the dog's front paws resting against his feet, the three of them dozed comfortably before the hot fire while the night wore on and the silence deepened towards midnight.

It was well after one o'clock in the morning when Dr. Silence turned the lamp out and lighted the candle preparatory to going up to bed. Then Smoke suddenly woke with a loud sharp purr and sat up. It neither stretched, washed nor turned: it listened. And the doctor, watching it, realised that a certain indefinable change had come about that very moment in the room. A swift readjustment of the forces within the four walls had taken place—a new disposition of their personal equations. The balance was destroyed, the former harmony gone. Smoke, most sensitive of barometers, had been the first to feel it, but the dog was not slow to follow suit, for on looking down he noted that Flame was no longer asleep. He was lying with eyes wide open, and that same instant he sat up on his great haunches and began to growl.

Dr. Silence was in the act of taking the matches to re-light the lamp when an audible movement in the room behind him made him pause. Smoke leaped down from his knee and moved forward a few paces across the carpet. Then it stopped and stared fixedly; and the doctor stood up on the rug to watch.

As he rose the sound was repeated, and he discovered that it was not in the room as he first thought, but outside, and that it came from more directions than one. There was a rushing, sweeping noise against the window-panes, and simultaneously a sound of something brushing against the door—out in the hall. Smoke advanced sedately across the carpet, twitching his tail, and sat down within a foot of the door. The influence that had destroyed the harmonious conditions of the room had apparently moved in advance of its cause. Clearly, something was about to happen.

For the first time that night John Silence hesitated; the thought of that dark narrow hall-way, choked with fog, and destitute of human comfort, was unpleasant. He became aware of a faint creeping of his flesh. He knew, of course, that the actual opening of the door was not necessary to the invasion of the room that was about to take place, since neither doors nor windows, nor any other solid barriers could interpose an obstacle to what was seeking entrance. Yet the opening of the door would be significant and symbolic, and he distinctly shrank from it.

But for a moment only. Smoke, turning with a show of impatience, recalled him to his purpose, and he moved past the sitting, watching creature, and deliberately opened the door to its full width.

What subsequently happened, happened in the feeble and flickering light of the solitary candle on the mantlepiece.

Through the opened door he saw the hall, dimly lit and thick with fog. Nothing, of course, was visible—nothing but the hat-stand, the African spears in dark lines upon the wall and the high-backed wooden chair standing grotesquely underneath on the oilcloth floor. For one instant the fog seemed to move and thicken oddly; but he set that down to the score of the imagination. The door had opened upon nothing.

Yet Smoke apparently thought otherwise, and the deep growling of the collie from the mat at the back of the room seemed to confirm his judgment.

For, proud and self-possessed, the cat had again risen to his feet, and having advanced to the door, was now ushering some one slowly into the room. Nothing could have been more evident. He paced from side to side, bowing his little head with great *empressement* and holding his stiffened tail aloft like a flag-staff. He turned this way and that, mincing to and fro, and showing signs of supreme satisfaction. He was in his element. He welcomed the intrusion, and apparently reckoned that his companions, the doctor and the dog, would welcome it likewise.

The Intruder had returned for a second attack.

Dr. Silence moved slowly backwards and took up his position on the hearthrug, keying himself up to a condition of concentrated attention.

He noted that Flame stood beside him, facing the room, with body motionless, and head moving swiftly from side to side with a curious swaying movement. His eyes were wide open, his back rigid, his neck and jaws thrust forward, his legs tense and ready to leap. Savage, ready for attack or defence, yet dreadfully puzzled and perhaps already a little cowed, he stood and stared, the hair on his spine and sides positively bristling outwards as though a wind played through it. In the dim firelight he looked like a great yellow-haired wolf, silent, eyes shooting dark fire, exceedingly formidable. It was Flame, the terrible.

Smoke, meanwhile, advanced from the door towards the middle of the room, adopting the very slow pace of an invisible companion. A few feet away it stopped and began to smile and blink its eyes. There was something deliberately coaxing in its attitude as it stood there undecided on the carpet, clearly wishing to effect some sort of introduction between the Intruder and its canine friend and ally. It assumed its most winning manners, purring, smiling, looking persuasively from one to the other, and making quick tentative steps first in one direction and then in the other. There had always existed such perfect understanding between them in everything. Surely Flame would appreciate Smoke's intention now, and acquiesce.

But the old collie made no advances. He bared his teeth, lifting his lips till the gums showed, and stood stockstill with fixed eyes and heaving sides. The doctor moved a little farther back, watching intently the smallest movement, and it was just then he divined suddenly from the cat's behaviour and attitude that it was not only a single companion it had ushered into the room, but *several.* It kept crossing over from one to the other, looking up at each in turn. It sought to win over the dog to friendliness with them all. The original Intruder had come back with reinforcements. And at the same time he further realised that the Intruder was something more than a blindly acting force, impersonal though destructive. It was a Personality, and moreover a great personality. And it was accompanied for the purposes of assistance by a host of other personalities, minor in degree, but similar in kind.

He braced himself in the corner against the mantelpiece and waited, his whole being roused to defence, for he was now fully aware that the attack had spread to include himself as well as the animals, and he must be on the alert. He strained his eyes through the foggy atmosphere, trying in vain to see what the cat and dog saw; but the candlelight threw an uncertain and flickering light across the room and his eyes discerned nothing. On the floor Smoke moved softly in front of him like a black shadow, his eyes gleaming as he turned his head, still trying with many insinuating gestures and much purring to bring about the introductions he desired.

But it was all in vain. Flame stood riveted to one spot, motionless as a figure carved in stone.

Some minutes passed, during which only the cat moved, and then there came a sharp change. Flame began to back towards the wall. He moved his head from side to side as he went, sometimes turning to snap at something almost behind him. *They* were advancing upon him, trying to surround him. His distress became very marked from now onwards, and it seemed to the doctor that his anger merged into genuine terror and became overwhelmed by it. The savage growl sounded perilously like a whine, and more than once he tried to dive past his master's legs, as though hunting for a way of escape. He was trying to avoid something that everywhere blocked the way.

This terror of the indomitable fighter impressed the doctor enormously; yet also painfully; stirring his impatience; for he had never before seen the dog show signs of giving in, and it distressed him to witness it. He knew, however, that he was not giving in easily, and understood that it was really impossible for him to gauge the animal's sensations properly at all. What Flame felt, and saw, must be terrible indeed to turn him all at once into a coward. He faced something that made him afraid of more than his life merely. The doctor spoke a few quick words of encouragement to him, and stroked the bristling hair. But without much success. The collie seemed already beyond the reach of comfort such as that, and the collapse of the old dog followed indeed very speedily after this.

And Smoke, meanwhile, remained behind, watching the advance, but not joining in it; sitting, pleased and expectant, considering that all was going well and as it wished. It was kneading on the carpet with its front paws—slowly, laboriously, as though its feet were dipped in treacle. The sound its claws made as they caught in the threads was distinctly audible. It was still smiling, blinking, purring.

Suddenly the collie uttered a poignant short bark and leaped heavily to one side. His bared teeth traced a line of whiteness through the gloom. The next instant he dashed past his master's legs, almost upsetting his balance, and shot out into the room, where he went blundering wildly against walls and furniture. But that bark was significant; the doctor had heard it before and knew what it meant: for it was the cry of the fighter against odds and it meant that the old beast had found his courage again. Possibly it was only the courage of despair, but at any rate the fighting would be terrific. And Dr. Silence understood, too, that he dared not interfere. Flame must fight his own enemies in his own way.

But the cat, too, had heard that dreadful bark; and it, too, had understood. This was more than it had bargained for. Across the dim shadows of that haunted room there must have passed some secret signal of distress between the animals. Smoke stood up and looked swiftly about him. He uttered a piteous meow and trotted smartly away into the greater darkness by the windows. What his object was only those endowed with the spirit-like intelligence of cats might know. But, at any rate, he had at last ranged himself on the side of his friend. And the little beast meant business.

At the same moment the collie managed to gain the door. The doctor saw him rush through into the hall like a flash of yellow light. He shot across the oilcloth, and tore up the stairs, but in another second he appeared again, flying down the steps and landing at the bottom in a tumbling heap, whining, cringing, terrified. The doctor saw him slink back into the room again and crawl round by the wall towards the cat. Was, then, even the staircase occupied? Did *They* stand also in the hall? Was the whole house crowded from floor to ceiling?

The thought came to add to the keen distress he felt at the sight of the collie's discomfiture. And, indeed, his own personal distress had increased in a marked degree during the past minutes, and continued to increase steadily to the climax. He recognised that the drain on his own vitality grew steadily, and that the attack was now directed against himself even more than against the defeated dog, and the too much deceived cat.

It all seemed so rapid and uncalculated after that—the events that took place in this little modern room at the top of Putney Hill between midnight and sunrise—that Dr. Silence was hardly able to follow and remember it all. It came about with such uncanny swiftness and terror; the light was so uncertain; the movements of the black cat so difficult to follow on the dark carpet, and the doctor himself so weary and taken by surprise—that he found it almost impossible to observe accurately, or to recall afterwards precisely what it was he had seen or in what order the incidents had taken place. He never could understand what defect of vision on his part made it seem as though the cat had duplicated itself at first, and then increased indefinitely, so that there were at least a dozen of them darting silently about the floor, leaping softly on to chairs and tables, passing like shadows from the open door to the end of the room, all black as sin, with brilliant green eyes flashing fire in all directions. It was like the reflections from a score of mirrors placed round the walls at different angles. Nor could he make out at the time why the size of the room seemed to have altered, grown much larger, and why it extended away behind him where ordinarily the wall should have been. The snarling of the enraged and terrified collie sounded sometimes so far away; the ceiling seemed to have raised itself so much higher than before, and much of the furniture had changed in appearance and shifted marvellously.

It was all so confused and confusing, as though the little room he knew had become merged and transformed into the dimensions of quite another chamber, that came to him, with its host of cats and its strange distances, in a sort of vision.

But these changes came about a little later, and at a time when his attention was so concentrated upon the proceedings of Smoke and the collie, that he only observed them, as it were, subconsciously. And the excitement, the flickering candlelight, the distress he felt for the collie, and the distorting atmosphere of fog were the poorest possible allies to careful observation.

At first he was only aware that the dog was repeating his short dangerous bark from time to time, snapping viciously at the empty air, a foot or so from the ground. Once, indeed, he sprang upwards and forwards, working furiously with teeth and paws, and with a noise like wolves fighting, but only to dash back the next minute against the wall behind him. Then, after lying still for a bit, he rose to a crouching position as though to spring again, snarling horribly and making short half-circles with lowered head. And Smoke all the while meowed piteously by the window as though trying to draw the attack upon himself.

Then it was that the rush of the whole dreadful business seemed to turn aside from the dog and direct itself upon his own person. The collie had made another spring and fallen back with a crash into the corner, where he made noise enough in his savage rage to waken the dead before he fell to whining and then finally lay still. And directly afterwards the doctor's own distress became intolerably acute. He had made a half movement forward to come to the rescue when a veil that was denser than mere fog seemed to drop down over the scene, draping room, walls, animals and fire in a mist of darkness and folding also about his own mind. Other forms moved silently across the field of vision, forms that he recognised from previous experiments, and wel-

comed not. Unholy thoughts began to crowd into his brain, sinister suggestions of evil presented themselves seductively. Ice seemed to settle
about his heart, and his mind trembled. He began to lose memory—
memory of his identity, of where he was, of what he ought to do.
The very foundations of his strength were shaken. His will seemed
paralysed.

And it was then that the room filled with this horde of cats, all dark as
the night, all silent, all with lamping eyes of green fire. The dimensions
of the place altered and shifted. He was in a much larger space. The
whining of the dog sounded far away, and all about him the cats flew
busily to and fro, silently playing their tearing, rushing game of evil,
weaving the pattern of their dark purpose upon the floor. He strove hard
to collect himself and remember the words of power he had made use
of before in similar dread positions where his dangerous practice had
sometimes led; but he could recall nothing consecutively; a mist lay
over his mind and memory; he felt dazed and his forces scattered. The
deeps within were too troubled for healing power to come out of them.

It was glamour, of course, he realised afterwards, the strong glamour
thrown upon his imagination by some powerful personality behind the
veil; but at the time he was not sufficiently aware of this and, as with all
true glamour, was unable to grasp where the true ended and the false
began. He was caught momentarily in the same vortex that had sought
to lure the cat to destruction through its delight, and threatened utterly
to overwhelm the dog through its terror.

There came a sound in the chimney behind him like wind booming
and tearing its way down. The windows rattled. The candle flickered
and went out. The glacial atmosphere closed round him with the cold
of death, and a great rushing sound swept by overhead as though the
ceiling had lifted to a great height. He heard the door shut. Far away it
sounded. He felt lost, shelterless in the depths of his soul. Yet still he
held out and resisted while the climax of the fight came nearer and
nearer. . . . He had stepped into the stream of forces awakened by
Pender and he knew that he must withstand them to the end or come
to a conclusion that it was not good for a man to come to. Something
from the region of utter cold was upon him.

And then quite suddenly, through the confused mists about him,
there slowly rose up the Personality that had been all the time directing
the battle. Some force entered his being that shook him as the tempest
shakes a leaf, and close against his eyes—clean level with his face—he
found himself staring into the wreck of a vast dark Countenance, a
countenance that was terrible even in its ruin.

For ruined it was, and terrible it was, and the mark of spiritual evil was branded everywhere upon its broken features. Eyes, face and hair rose level with his own, and for a space of time he never could properly measure, or determine, these two, a man and a woman, looked straight into each other's visages and down into each other's hearts.

And John Silence, the soul with the good, unselfish motive, held his own against the dark discarnate woman whose motive was pure evil, and whose soul was on the side of the Dark Powers.

It was the climax that touched the depth of power within him and began to restore him slowly to his own. He was conscious, of course, of effort, and yet it seemed no superhuman one, for he had recognised the character of his opponent's power, and he called upon the good within him to meet and overcome it. The inner forces stirred and trembled in response to his call. They did not at first come readily as was their habit, for under the spell of glamour they had already been diabolically lulled into inactivity, but come they eventually did, rising out of the inner spiritual nature he had learned with so much time and pain to awaken to life. And power and confidence came with them. He began to breathe deeply and regularly, and at the same time to absorb into himself the forces opposed to him, and to *turn them to his own account*. By ceasing to resist, and allowing the deadly stream to pour into him unopposed, he used the very power supplied by his adversary and thus enormously increased his own.

For this spiritual alchemy he had learned. He understood that force ultimately is everywhere one and the same; it is the motive behind that makes it good or evil; and his motive was entirely unselfish. He knew—provided he was not first robbed of self-control—how vicariously to absorb these evil radiations into himself and change them magically into his own good purposes. And, since his motive was pure and his soul fearless, they could not work him harm.

Thus he stood in the main stream of evil unwittingly attracted by Pender, deflecting its course upon himself; and after passing through the purifying filter of his own unselfishness these energies could only add to his store of experience, of knowledge, and therefore of power. And, as his self-control returned to him, he gradually accomplished this purpose, even though trembling while he did so.

Yet the struggle was severe, and in spite of the freezing chill of the air, the perspiration poured down his face. Then, by slow degrees, the dark and dreadful countenance faded, the glamour passed from his soul, the normal proportions returned to walls and ceiling, the forms melted back into the fog, and the whirl of rushing shadow-cats disappeared whence they came.

And with the return of the consciousness of his own identity John Silence was restored to the full control of his own will-power. In a deep, modulated voice he began to utter certain rhythmical sounds that slowly rolled through the air like a rising sea, filling the room with powerful vibratory activities that whelmed all irregularities of lesser vibrations in its own swelling tone. He made certain sigils, gestures and movements at the same time. For several minutes he continued to utter these words, until at length the growing volume dominated the whole room and mastered the manifestation of all that opposed it. For just as he understood the spiritual alchemy that can transmute evil forces by raising them into higher channels, so he knew from long study the occult use of sound, and its direct effect upon the plastic region wherein the powers of spiritual evil work their fell purposes. Harmony was restored first of all to his own soul, and thence to the room and all its occupants.

And, after himself, the first to recognise it was the old dog lying in his corner. Flame began suddenly uttering sounds of pleasure, that "something" between a growl and a grunt that dogs make upon being restored to their master's confidence. Dr. Silence heard the thumping of the collie's tail against the floor. And the grunt and the thumping touched the depth of affection in the man's heart, and gave him some inkling of what agonies the dumb creature had suffered.

Next, from the shadows by the window, a somewhat shrill purring announced the restoration of the cat to its normal state. Smoke was advancing across the carpet. He seemed very pleased with himself, and smiled with an expression of supreme innocence. He was no shadow-cat, but real and full of his usual and perfect self-possession. He marched along, picking his way delicately, but with a stately dignity that suggested his ancestry with the majesty of Egypt. His eyes no longer glared; they shone steadily before him, they radiated, not excitement, but knowledge. Clearly he was anxious to make amends for the mischief to which he had unwittingly lent himself owing to his subtle and electric constitution.

Still uttering his sharp high purrings he marched up to his master and rubbed vigorously against his legs. Then he stood on his hind feet and pawed his knees and stared beseechingly up into his face. He turned his head towards the corner where the collie still lay, thumping his tail feebly and pathetically.

John Silence understood. He bent down and stroked the creature's living fur, noting the line of bright blue sparks that followed the motion of his hand down its back. And then they advanced together towards the corner where the dog was.

Smoke went first and put his nose gently against his friend's muzzle, purring while he rubbed, and uttering little soft sounds of affection in his throat. The doctor lit the candle and brought it over. He saw the collie lying on its side against the wall; it was utterly exhausted, and foam still hung about its jaws. Its tail and eyes responded to the sound of its name, but it was evidently very weak and overcome. Smoke continued to rub against its cheek and nose and eyes, sometimes even standing on its body and kneading into the thick yellow hair. Flame replied from time to time by little licks of the tongue, most of them curiously misdirected.

But Dr. Silence felt intuitively that something disastrous had happened, and his heart was wrung. He stroked the dear body, feeling it over for bruises or broken bones, but finding none. He fed it with what remained of the sandwiches and milk, but the creature clumsily upset the saucer and lost the sandwiches between its paws, so that the doctor had to feed it with his own hand. And all the while Smoke meowed piteously.

Then John Silence began to understand. He went across to the farther side of the room and called aloud to it.

"Flame, old man! come!"

At any other time the dog would have been upon him in an instant, barking and leaping to the shoulder. And even now he got up, though heavily and awkwardly, to his feet. He started to run, wagging his tail more briskly. He collided first with a chair, and then ran straight into a table. Smoke trotted close at his side, trying his very best to guide him. But it was useless. Dr. Silence had to lift him up into his own arms and carry him like a baby. For he was blind.

III

It was a week later when John Silence called to see the author in his new house, and found him well on the way to recovery and already busy again with his writing. The haunted look had left his eyes, and he seemed cheerful and confident.

"Humour restored?" laughed the doctor, as soon as they were comfortably settled in the room overlooking the Park.

"I've had no trouble since I left that dreadful place," returned Pender gratefully; "and thanks to you——"

The doctor stopped him with a gesture.

"Never mind that," he said, "we'll discuss your new plans afterwards, and my scheme for relieving you of the house and helping you settle elsewhere. Of course it must be pulled down, for it's not fit for any sensitive person to live in, and any other tenant might be afflicted in the same way you were. Although, personally, I think the evil has exhausted itself by now."

He told the astonished author something of his experiences in it with the animals.

"I don't pretend to understand," Pender said, when the account was finished, "but I and my wife are intensely relieved to be free of it all. Only I must say I should like to know something of the former history of the house. When we took it six months ago I heard no word against it."

Dr. Silence drew a typewritten paper from his pocket.

"I can satisfy your curiosity to some extent," he said, running his eye over the sheets, and then replacing them in his coat; "for by my secretary's investigations I have been able to check certain information obtained in the hypnotic trance by a 'sensitive' who helps me in such cases. The former occupant who haunted you appears to have been a woman of singularly atrocious life and character who finally suffered death by hanging, after a series of crimes that appalled the whole of England and only came to light by the merest chance. She came to her end in the year 1798, for it was not this particular house she lived in, but a much larger one that then stood upon the site it now occupies, and was then, of course, not in London, but in the country. She was a person of intellect, possessed of a powerful, trained will, and of consummate audacity, and I am convinced availed herself of the resources of the lower magic to attain her ends. This goes far to explain the virulence of the attack upon yourself, and why she is still able to carry on after death the evil practices that formed her main purpose during life."

"You think that after death a soul can still consciously direct——" gasped the author.

"I think, as I told you before, that the forces of a powerful personality may still persist after death in the line of their original momentum," replied the doctor; "and that strong thoughts and purposes can still react upon suitably prepared brains long after their originators have passed away.

"If you knew anything of magic," he pursued, "you would know that thought is dynamic, and that it may call into existence forms and pictures that may well exist for hundreds of years. For, not far removed from the region of our human life is another region where float the waste and drift of all the centuries, the limbo of the shells of the dead; a densely populated region crammed with horror and abomination of all descriptions, and sometimes galvanised into active life again by the will of a trained manipulator, a mind versed in the practices of lower magic. That this woman understood its vile commerce, I am persuaded, and the forces she set going during her life have simply been accumulating ever since, and would have continued to do so had they not been drawn down upon yourself, and afterwards discharged and satisfied through me.

"Anything might have brought down the attack, for, besides drugs, there are certain violent emotions, certain moods of the soul, certain spiritual fevers, if I may so call them, which directly open the inner being to a cognisance of this astral region I have mentioned. In your case it happened to be a peculiarly potent drug that did it.

"But now, tell me," he added, after a pause, handing to the perplexed author a pencil drawing he had made of the dark countenance that had appeared to him during the night on Putney Hill—"tell me if you recognise this face?"

Pender looked at the drawing closely, greatly astonished. He shuddered a little as he looked.

"Undoubtedly," he said, "it is the face I kept trying to draw—dark, with the great mouth and jaw, and the drooping eye. That is the woman."

Dr. Silence then produced from his pocket-book an old-fashioned woodcut of the same person which his secretary had unearthed from the records of the Newgate Calendar. The woodcut and the pencil drawing were two different aspects of the same dreadful visage. The men compared them for some moments in silence.

"It makes me thank God for the limitations of our senses," said Pender quietly, with a sigh; "continuous clairvoyance must be a sore affliction."

"It is indeed," returned John Silence significantly, "and if all the people nowadays who claim to be clairvoyant were really so, the statistics of suicide and lunacy would be considerably higher than they are. It is little wonder," he added, "that your sense of humour was clouded, with the mind-forces of that dead monster trying to use your brain for their dissemination. You have had an interesting adventure, Mr. Felix Pender, and, let me add, a fortunate escape."

The author was about to renew his thanks when there came a sound of scratching at the door, and the doctor sprang up quickly.

"It's time for me to go. I left my dog on the step, but I suppose——"

Before he had time to open the door, it had yielded to the pressure behind it and flew wide open to admit a great yellow-haired collie. The dog, wagging his tail and contorting his whole body with delight, tore across the floor and tried to leap up upon his owner's breast. And there was laughter and happiness in the old eyes; for they were clear again as the day.

ANCIENT SORCERIES

I

There are, it would appear, certain wholly unremarkable persons, with none of the characteristics that invite adventure, who yet once or twice in the course of their smooth lives undergo an experience so strange that the world catches its breath—and looks the other way! And it was cases of this kind, perhaps, more than any other, that fell into the widespread net of John Silence, the psychic doctor, and, appealing to his deep humanity, to his patience, and to his great qualities of spiritual sympathy, led often to the revelation of problems of the strangest complexity, and of the profoundest possible human interest.

Matters that seemed almost too curious and fantastic for belief he loved to trace to their hidden sources. To unravel a tangle in the very soul of things—and to release a suffering human soul in the process—was with him a veritable passion. And the knots he untied were, indeed, after passing strange.

The world, of course, asks for some plausible basis to which it can attach credence—something it can, at least, pretend to explain. The adventurous type it can understand: such people carry about with them an adequate explanation of their exciting lives, and their characters obviously drive them into the circumstances which produce the adventures. It expects nothing else from them, and is satisfied. But dull, ordinary folk have no right to out-of-the-way experiences, and the world having been led to expect otherwise, is disappointed with them, not to say shocked. Its complacent judgment has been rudely disturbed.

"Such a thing happened to *that* man!" it cries—"a commonplace person like that! It is too absurd! There must be something wrong!"

Yet there could be no question that something did actually happen to little Arthur Vezin, something of the curious nature he described to Dr. Silence. Outwardly or inwardly, it happened beyond a doubt, and in spite of the jeers of his few friends who heard the tale, and observed wisely that "such a thing might perhaps have come to Iszard, that crackbrained Iszard, or to that odd fish Minski, but it could never have happened to commonplace little Vezin, who was fore-ordained to live and die according to scale."

But, whatever his method of death was, Vezin certainly did not "live according to scale" so far as this particular event in his otherwise un-eventful life was concerned; and to hear him recount it, and watch his pale delicate features change, and hear his voice grow softer and more hushed as he proceeded, was to know the conviction that his halting words perhaps failed sometimes to convey. He lived the thing over again each time he told it. His whole personality became muffled in the recital. It subdued him more than ever, so that the tale became a lengthy apology for an experience that he deprecated. He appeared to excuse himself and ask your pardon for having dared to take part in so fantastic an episode. For little Vezin was a timid, gentle, sensitive soul, rarely able to assert himself, tender to man and beast, and almost con-stitutionally unable to say No, or to claim many things that should rightly have been his. His whole scheme of life seemed utterly remote from anything more exciting than missing a train or losing an umbrella on an omnibus. And when this curious event came upon him he was already more years beyond forty than his friends suspected or he cared to admit.

John Silence, who heard him speak of his experience more than once, said that he sometimes left out certain details and put in others; yet they were all obviously true. The whole scene was unforgettably cinematographed on to his mind. None of the details were imagined or invented. And when he told the story with them all complete, the ef-fect was undeniable. His appealing brown eyes shone, and much of the charming personality, usually so carefully repressed, came forward and revealed itself. His modesty was always there, of course, but in the telling he forgot the present and allowed himself to appear almost vividly as he lived again in the past of his adventure.

He was on the way home when it happened, crossing northern France from some mountain trip or other where he buried himself soli-tary-wise every summer. He had nothing but an unregistered bag in the rack, and the train was jammed to suffocation, most of the passengers being unredeemed holiday English. He disliked them, not because they were his fellow-countrymen, but because they were noisy and ob-trusive, obliterating with their big limbs and tweed clothing all the quieter tints of the day that brought him satisfaction and enabled him to melt into insignificance and forget that he was anybody. These English clashed about him like a brass band, making him feel vaguely that he ought to be more self-assertive and obstreperous, and that he did not claim insistently enough all kinds of things that he didn't want and that were really valueless, such as corner seats, windows up or down, and so forth.

So that he felt uncomfortable in the train, and wished the journey were over and he was back again living with his unmarried sister in Surbiton.

And when the train stopped for ten panting minutes at the little station in northern France, and he got out to stretch his legs on the platform, and saw to his dismay a further batch of the British Isles debouching from another train, it suddenly seemed impossible to him to continue the journey. Even *his* flabby soul revolted, and the idea of staying a night in the little town and going on next day by a slower, emptier train, flashed into his mind. The guard was already shouting *"en voiture"* and the corridor of his compartment was already packed when the thought came to him. And, for once, he acted with decision and rushed to snatch his bag.

Finding the corridor and steps impassable, he tapped at the window (for he had a corner seat) and begged the Frenchman who sat opposite to hand his luggage out to him, explaining in his wretched French that he intended to break the journey there. And this elderly Frenchman, he declared, gave him a look, half of warning, half of reproach, that to his dying day he could never forget; handed the bag through the window of the moving train; and at the same time poured into his ears a long sentence, spoken rapidly and low, of which he was able to comprehend only the last few words: *"à cause du sommeil et à cause des chats."*

In reply to Dr. Silence, whose singular psychic acuteness at once seized upon this Frenchman as a vital point in the adventure, Vezin admitted that the man had impressed him favourably from the beginning, though without being able to explain why. They had sat facing one another during the four hours of the journey, and though no conversation had passed between them—Vezin was timid about his stuttering French—he confessed that his eyes were being continually drawn to his face, almost, he felt, to rudeness, and that each, by a dozen nameless little politenesses and attentions, had evinced the desire to be kind. The men liked each other and their personalities did not clash, or would not have clashed had they chanced to come to terms of acquaintance. The Frenchman, indeed, seemed to have exercised a silent protective influence over the insignificant little Englishman, and without words or gestures betrayed that he wished him well and would gladly have been of service to him.

"And this sentence that he hurled at you after the bag?" asked John Silence, smiling that peculiarly sympathetic smile that always melted the prejudices of his patient, "were you unable to follow it exactly?"

"It was so quick and low and vehement," explained Vezin, in his small voice, "that I missed practically the whole of it. I only caught the few words at the very end, because he spoke them so clearly, and his face was bent down out of the carriage window so near to mine."

"'À cause du sommeil et à cause des chats'?" repeated Dr. Silence, as though half speaking to himself.

"That's it exactly," said Vezin; "which, I take it, means something like 'because of sleep and because of the cats,' doesn't it?"

"Certainly, that's how I should translate it," the doctor observed shortly, evidently not wishing to interrupt more than necessary.

"And the rest of the sentence—all the first part I couldn't understand, I mean—was a warning not to do something—not to stop in the town, or at some particular place in the town, perhaps. That was the impression it made on me."

Then, of course, the train rushed off, and left Vezin standing on the platform alone and rather forlorn.

The little town climbed in straggling fashion up a sharp hill rising out of the plain at the back of the station, and was crowned by the twin towers of the ruined cathedral peeping over the summit. From the station itself it looked uninteresting and modern, but the fact was that the mediæval position lay out of sight just beyond the crest. And once he reached the top and entered the old streets, he stepped clean out of modern life into a bygone century. The noise and bustle of the crowded train seemed days away. The spirit of this silent hill-town, remote from tourists and motor-cars, dreaming its own quiet life under the autumn sun, rose up and cast its spell upon him. Long before he recognised this spell he acted under it. He walked softly, almost on tiptoe, down the winding narrow streets where the gables all but met over his head, and he entered the doorway of the solitary inn with a deprecating and modest demeanour that was in itself an apology for intruding upon the place and disturbing its dream.

At first, however, Vezin said, he noticed very little of all this. The attempt at analysis came much later. What struck him then was only the delightful contrast of the silence and peace after the dust and noisy rattle of the train. He felt soothed and stroked like a cat.

"Like a cat, you said?" interrupted John Silence, quickly catching him up.

"Yes. At the very start I felt that." He laughed apologetically. "I felt as though the warmth and the stillness and the comfort made me purr. It seemed to be the general mood of the whole place—then."

The inn, a rambling ancient house, the atmosphere of the old coaching days still about it, apparently did not welcome him too warmly. He felt he was only tolerated, he said. But it was cheap and comfortable, and the delicious cup of afternoon tea he ordered at once made him feel really very pleased with himself for leaving the train in this bold, original way. For to him it had seemed bold and original. He felt something of a dog. His room, too, soothed him with its dark panelling and low irregular ceiling, and the long sloping passage that led to it seemed the natural pathway to a real Chamber of Sleep—a little dim cubby hole out of the world where noise could not enter. It looked upon the courtyard at the back. It was all very charming, and made him think of himself as dressed in very soft velvet somehow, and the floors seemed padded, the walls provided with cushions. The sounds of the streets could not penetrate there. It was an atmosphere of absolute rest that surrounded him.

On engaging the two-franc room he had interviewed the only person who seemed to be about that sleepy afternoon, an elderly waiter with Dundreary whiskers and a drowsy courtesy, who had ambled lazily towards him across the stone yard; but on coming downstairs again for a little promenade in the town before dinner he encountered the proprietress herself. She was a large woman whose hands, feet, and features seemed to swim towards him out of a sea of person. They emerged, so to speak. But she had great dark, vivacious eyes that counteracted the bulk of her body, and betrayed the fact that in reality she was both vigorous and alert. When he first caught sight of her she was knitting in a low chair against the sunlight of the wall, and something at once made him see her as a great tabby cat, dozing, yet awake, heavily sleepy, and yet at the same time prepared for instantaneous action. A great mouser on the watch occurred to him.

She took him in with a single comprehensive glance that was polite without being cordial. Her neck, he noticed, was extraordinarily supple in spite of its proportions, for it turned so easily to follow him, and the head it carried bowed so very flexibly.

"But when she looked at me, you know," said Vezin, with that little apologetic smile in his brown eyes, and that faintly deprecating gesture of the shoulders that was characteristic of him, "the odd notion came to me that really she had intended to make quite a different movement, and that with a single bound she could have leaped at me across the width of that stone yard and pounced upon me like some huge cat upon a mouse."

He laughed a little soft laugh, and Dr. Silence made a note in his book without interrupting, while Vezin proceeded in a tone as though he feared he had already told too much and more than we could believe.

"Very soft, yet very active she was, for all her size and mass, and I felt she knew what I was doing even after I had passed and was behind her back. She spoke to me, and her voice was smooth and running. She asked if I had my luggage, and was comfortable in my room, and then added that dinner was at seven o'clock, and that they were very early people in this little country town. Clearly, she intended to convey that late hours were not encouraged."

Evidently, she contrived by voice and manner to give him the impression that here he would be "managed," that everything would be arranged and planned for him, and that he had nothing to do but fall into the groove and obey. No decided action or sharp personal effort would be looked for from him. It was the very reverse of the train. He walked quietly out into the street feeling soothed and peaceful. He realised that he was in a *milieu* that suited him and stroked him the right way. It was so much easier to be obedient. He began to purr again, and to feel that all the town purred with him.

About the streets of that little town he meandered gently, falling deeper and deeper into the spirit of repose that characterised it. With no special aim he wandered up and down, and to and fro. The September sunshine fell slantingly over the roofs. Down winding alleyways, fringed with tumbling gables and open casements, he caught fairylike glimpses of the great plain below, and of the meadows and yellow copses lying like a dream-map in the haze. The spell of the past held very potently here, he felt.

The streets were full of picturesquely garbed men and women, all busy enough, going their respective ways; but no one took any notice of him or turned to stare at his obviously English appearance. He was even able to forget that with his tourist appearance he was a false note in a charming picture, and he melted more and more into the scene, feeling delightfully insignificant and unimportant and unself-conscious. It was like becoming part of a softly coloured dream which he did not even realise to be a dream.

On the eastern side the hill fell away more sharply, and the plain below ran off rather suddenly into a sea of gathering shadows in which the little patches of woodland looked like islands and the stubble fields like deep water. Here he strolled along the old ramparts of ancient fortifications that once had been formidable, but now were only vision-like with their charming mingling of broken grey walls and wayward vine and ivy. From the broad coping on which he sat for a moment, level with the rounded tops of clipped plane trees, he saw the esplanade far below lying in shadow. Here and there a yellow sunbeam crept in and lay upon the fallen yellow leaves, and from the height he looked down and saw that the townsfolk were walking to and fro in the cool of the evening. He could just hear the sound of their slow footfalls, and the murmur of their voices floated up to him through the gaps between the trees. The figures looked like shadows as he caught glimpses of their quiet movements far below.

He sat there for some time pondering, bathed in the waves of murmurs and half-lost echoes that rose to his ears, muffled by the leaves of the plane trees. The whole town, and the little hill out of which it grew as naturally as an ancient wood, seemed to him like a being lying there half asleep on the plain and crooning to itself as it dozed.

And, presently, as he sat lazily melting into its dream, a sound of horns and strings and wood instruments rose to his ears, and the town band began to play at the far end of the crowded terrace below to the accompaniment of a very soft, deep-throated drum. Vezin was very sensitive to music, knew about it intelligently, and had even ventured, unknown to his friends, upon the composition of quiet melodies with low-running chords which he played to himself with the soft pedal when no one was about. And this music floating up through the trees from an invisible and doubtless very picturesque band of the townspeople wholly charmed him. He recognised nothing that they played, and it sounded as though they were simply improvising without a conductor. No definitely marked time ran through the pieces, which ended and began oddly after the fashion of wind through an Æolian harp. It was part of the place and scene, just as the dying sunlight and faintly breathing wind were part of the scene and hour, and the mellow notes of old-fashioned plaintive horns, pierced here and there by the sharper strings, all half smothered by the continuous booming of the deep drum, touched his soul with a curiously potent spell that was almost too engrossing to be quite pleasant.

There was a certain queer sense of bewitchment in it all. The music seemed to him oddly unartificial. It made him think of trees swept by the wind, of night breezes singing among wires and chimney-stacks, or in the rigging of invisible ships; or—and the simile leaped up in his thoughts with a sudden sharpness of suggestion—a chorus of animals, of wild creatures, somewhere in desolate places of the world, crying and singing as animals will, to the moon. He could fancy he heard the wailing, half-human cries of cats upon the tiles at night, rising and falling with weird intervals of sound, and this music, muffled by distance and the trees, made him think of a queer company of these creatures on some roof far away in the sky, uttering their solemn music to one another and the moon in chorus.

It was, he felt at the time, a singular image to occur to him, yet it expressed his sensation pictorially better than anything else. The instruments played such impossibly odd intervals, and the crescendos and diminuendos were so very suggestive of cat-land on the tiles at night, rising swiftly, dropping without warning to deep notes again, and all in such strange confusion of discords and accords. But, at the same time a plaintive sweetness resulted on the whole, and the discords of these half-broken instruments were so singular that they did not distress his musical soul like fiddles out of tune.

He listened a long time, wholly surrendering himself as his character was, and then strolled homewards in the dusk as the air grew chilly.

"There was nothing to alarm?" put in Dr. Silence briefly.

"Absolutely nothing," said Vezin; "but you know it was all so fantastical and charming that my imagination was profoundly impressed. Perhaps, too," he continued, gently explanatory, "it was this stirring of my imagination that caused other impressions; for, as I walked back, the spell of the place began to steal over me in a dozen ways, though all intelligible ways. But there were other things I could not account for in the least, even then."

"Incidents, you mean?"

"Hardly incidents, I think. A lot of vivid sensations crowded themselves upon my mind and I could trace them to no causes. It was just after sunset and the tumbled old buildings traced magical outlines against an opalescent sky of gold and red. The dusk was running down the twisted streets. All round the hill the plain pressed in like a dim sea, its level rising with the darkness. The spell of this kind of scene, you know, can be very moving, and it was so that night. Yet I felt that what came to me had nothing directly to do with the mystery and wonder of the scene."

"Not merely the subtle transformations of the spirit that come with beauty," put in the doctor, noticing his hesitation.

"Exactly," Vezin went on, duly encouraged and no longer so fearful of our smiles at his expense. "The impressions came from somewhere else. For instance, down the busy main street where men and women were bustling home from work, shopping at stalls and barrows, idly gossiping in groups, and all the rest of it, I saw that I aroused no interest and that no one turned to stare at me as a foreigner and stranger. I was utterly ignored, and my presence among them excited no special interest or attention.

"And then, quite suddenly, it dawned upon me with conviction that all the time this indifference and inattention were merely feigned. Everybody as a matter of fact was watching me closely. Every movement I made was known and observed. Ignoring me was all a pretence—an elaborate pretence."

He paused a moment and looked at us to see if we were smiling, and then continued, reassured—

"It is useless to ask me how I noticed this, because I simply cannot explain it. But the discovery gave me something of a shock. Before I got back to the inn, however, another curious thing rose up strongly in my mind and forced my recognition of it as true. And this, too, I may as well say at once, was equally inexplicable to me. I mean I can only give you the fact, as fact it was to me."

The little man left his chair and stood on the mat before the fire. His diffidence lessened from now onwards, as he lost himself again in the magic of the old adventure. His eyes shone a little already as he talked.

"Well," he went on, his soft voice rising somewhat with his excitement, "I was in a shop when it came to me first—though the idea must have been at work for a long time subconsciously to appear in so complete a form all at once. I was buying socks, I think," he laughed, "and struggling with my dreadful French, when it struck me that the woman in the shop did not care two pins whether I bought anything or not. She was indifferent whether she made a sale or did not make a sale. She was only pretending to sell.

"This sounds a very small and fanciful incident to build upon what follows. But really it was not small. I mean it was the spark that lit the line of powder and ran along to the big blaze in my mind.

"For the whole town, I suddenly realised, was something other than I so far saw it. The real activities and interests of the people were elsewhere and otherwise than appeared. Their true lives lay somewhere out of sight behind the scenes. Their busy-ness was but the outward semblance that masked their actual purposes. They bought and sold, and ate and drank, and walked about the streets, yet all the while the main stream of their existence lay somewhere beyond my ken, underground, in secret places. In the shops and at the stalls they did not care whether I purchased their articles or not; at the inn, they were indifferent to my staying or going; their life lay remote from my own, springing from hidden, mysterious sources, coursing out of sight, unknown. It was all a great elaborate pretence, assumed possibly for my benefit, or possibly for purposes of their own. But the main current of their energies ran elsewhere. I almost felt as an unwelcome foreign substance might be expected to feel when it has found its way into the human system and the whole body organises itself to eject it or to absorb it. The town was doing this very thing to me.

"This bizarre notion presented itself forcibly to my mind as I walked home to the inn, and I began busily to wonder wherein the true life of this town could lie and what were the actual interests and activities of its hidden life.

"And, now that my eyes were partly opened, I noticed other things

too that puzzled me, first of which, I think, was the extraordinary silence of the whole place. Positively, the town was muffled. Although
the streets were paved with cobbles the people moved about silently,
softly, with padded feet, like cats. Nothing made noise. All was hushed,
subdued, muted. The very voices were quiet, low-pitched like purring.
Nothing clamorous, vehement or emphatic seemed able to live in the
drowsy atmosphere of soft dreaming that soothed this little hill-town
into its sleep. It was like the woman at the inn—an outward repose
screening intense inner activity and purpose.

"Yet there was no sign of lethargy or sluggishness anywhere about it.
The people were active and alert. Only a magical and uncanny softness
lay over them all like a spell."

Vezin passed his hand across his eyes for a moment as though the
memory had become very vivid. His voice had run off into a whisper so
that we heard the last part with difficulty. He was telling a true thing
obviously, yet something that he both liked and hated telling.

"I went back to the inn," he continued presently in a louder voice,
"and dined. I felt a new strange world about me. My old world of reality receded. Here, whether I liked it or no, was something new and incomprehensible. I regretted having left the train so impulsively. An
adventure was upon me, and I loathed adventures as foreign to my nature. Moreover, this was the beginning apparently of an adventure
somewhere deep within me, in a region I could not check or measure,
and a feeling of alarm mingled itself with my wonder—alarm for the
stability of what I had for forty years recognised as my 'personality.'

"I went upstairs to bed, my mind teeming with thoughts that were
unusual to me, and of rather a haunting description. By way of relief I
kept thinking of that nice, prosaic noisy train and all those wholesome,
blustering passengers. I almost wished I were with them again. But my
dreams took me elsewhere. I dreamed of cats, and soft-moving creatures, and the silence of life in a dim muffled world beyond the senses."

II

Vezin stayed on from day to day, indefinitely, much longer than he had
intended. He felt in a kind of dazed, somnolent condition. He did
nothing in particular, but the place fascinated him and he could not
decide to leave. Decisions were always very difficult for him and he
sometimes wondered how he had ever brought himself to the point of
leaving the train. It seemed as though some one else must have
arranged it for him, and once or twice his thoughts ran to the swarthy
Frenchman who had sat opposite. If only he could have understood

that long sentence ending so strangely with "*à cause du sommeil et à cause des chats.*" He wondered what it all meant.

Meanwhile the hushed softness of the town held him prisoner and he sought in his muddling, gentle way to find out where the mystery lay, and what it was all about. But his limited French and his constitutional hatred of active investigation made it hard for him to buttonhole anybody and ask questions. He was content to observe, and watch, and remain negative.

The weather held on calm and hazy, and this just suited him. He wandered about the town till he knew every street and alley. The people suffered him to come and go without let or hindrance, though it became clearer to him every day that he was never free himself from observation. The town watched him as a cat watches a mouse. And he got no nearer to finding out what they were all so busy with or where the main stream of their activities lay. This remained hidden. The people were as soft and mysterious as cats.

But that he was continually under observation became more evident from day to day.

For instance, when he strolled to the end of the town and entered a little green public garden beneath the ramparts and seated himself upon one of the empty benches in the sun, he was quite alone — at first. Not another seat was occupied; the little park was empty, the paths deserted. Yet, within ten minutes of his coming, there must have been fully twenty persons scattered about him, some strolling aimlessly along the gravel walks, staring at the flowers, and others seated on the wooden benches enjoying the sun like himself. None of them appeared to take any notice of him; yet he understood quite well they had all come there to watch. They kept him under close observation. In the street they had seemed busy enough, hurrying upon various errands; yet these were suddenly all forgotten and they had nothing to do but loll and laze in the sun, their duties unremembered. Five minutes after he left, the garden was again deserted, the seats vacant. But in the crowded street it was the same thing again; he was never alone. He was ever in their thoughts.

By degrees, too, he began to see how it was he was so cleverly watched, yet without the appearance of it. The people did nothing *directly*. They behaved *obliquely*. He laughed in his mind as the thought thus clothed itself in words, but the phrase exactly described it. They looked at him from angles which naturally should have led their sight in another direction altogether. Their movements were oblique, too, so far as these concerned himself. The straight, direct thing was not their way evidently. They did nothing obviously. If he entered a shop to buy, the woman walked instantly away and busied herself with something at the farther end of the counter, though answering at once when he spoke, showing that she knew he was there and that this was only her way of attending to him. It was the fashion of the cat she followed. Even in the dining-room of the inn, the be-whiskered and courteous waiter, lithe and silent in all his movements, never seemed able to come straight to his table for an order or a dish. He came by zigzags, indirectly, vaguely, so that he appeared to be going to another table altogether, and only turned suddenly at the last moment, and was there beside him.

Vezin smiled curiously to himself as he described how he began to realize these things. Other tourists there were none in the hostel, but he recalled the figures of one or two old men, inhabitants, who took their *déjeuner* and dinner there, and remembered how fantastically they entered the room in similar fashion. First, they paused in the doorway, peering about the room, and then, after a temporary inspection, they came in, as it were, sideways, keeping close to the walls so that he wondered which table they were making for, and at the last minute making almost a little quick run to their particular seats. And again he thought of the ways and methods of cats.

Other small incidents, too, impressed him as all part of this queer, soft town with its muffled, indirect life, for the way some of the people appeared and disappeared with extraordinary swiftness puzzled him exceedingly. It may have been all perfectly natural, he knew, yet he could not make it out how the alleys swallowed them up and shot them forth in a second of time when there were no visible doorways or openings near enough to explain the phenomenon. Once he followed two elderly women who, he felt, had been particularly examining him from across the street—quite near the inn this was—and saw them turn the corner a few feet only in front of him. Yet when he sharply followed on their heels he saw nothing but an utterly deserted alley stretching in front of him with no sign of a living thing. And the only opening through which they could have escaped was a porch some fifty yards away, which not the swiftest human runner could have reached in time.

And in just such sudden fashion people appeared, when he never expected them. Once when he heard a great noise of fighting going on behind a low wall, and hurried up to see what was going on, what should he see but a group of girls and women engaged in vociferous conversation which instantly hushed itself to the normal whispering note of the town when his head appeared over the wall. And even then none of them turned to look at him directly, but slunk off with the most unaccountable rapidity into doors and sheds across the yard. And their voices, he thought, had sounded so like, so strangely like, the angry snarling of fighting animals, almost of cats.

The whole spirit of the town, however, continued to evade him as something elusive, protean, screened from the outer world, and at the same time intensely, genuinely vital; and, since he now formed part of its life, this concealment puzzled and irritated him; more—it began rather to frighten him.

Out of the mists that slowly gathered about his ordinary surface thoughts, there rose again the idea that the inhabitants were waiting for him to declare himself, to take an attitude, to do this, or to do that; and that when he had done so they in their turn would at length make some direct response, accepting or rejecting him. Yet the vital matter concerning which his decision was awaited came no nearer to him.

Once or twice he purposely followed little processions or groups of the citizens in order to find out, if possible, on what purpose they were bent; but they always discovered him in time and dwindled away, each individual going his or her own way. It was always the same: he never could learn what their main interest was. The cathedral was ever empty, the old church of St. Martin, at the other end of the town, deserted. They shopped because they had to, and not because they wished to. The booths stood neglected, the stalls unvisited, the little *cafés* desolate. Yet the streets were always full, the townsfolk ever on the bustle.

"Can it be," he thought to himself, yet with a deprecating laugh that he should have dared to think anything so odd, "can it be that these people are people of the twilight, that they live only at night their real life, and come out honestly only with the dusk? That during the day they make a sham though brave pretence, and after the sun is down their true life begins? Have they the souls of night-things, and is the whole blessed town in the hands of the cats?"

The fancy somehow electrified him with little shocks of shrinking and dismay. Yet, though he affected to laugh, he knew that he was beginning to feel more than uneasy, and that strange forces were tugging with a thousand invisible cords at the very centre of his being. Something utterly remote from his ordinary life, something that had not waked for years, began faintly to stir in his soul, sending feelers abroad into his brain and heart, shaping queer thoughts and penetrating even into certain of his minor actions. Something exceedingly vital to himself, to his soul, hung in the balance.

And, always when he returned to the inn about the hour of sunset, he saw the figures of the townsfolk stealing through the dusk from their shop doors, moving sentry-wise to and fro at the corners of the streets, yet always vanishing silently like shadows at his near approach. And as the inn invariably closed its doors at ten o'clock he had never yet found the opportunity he rather half-heartedly sought to see for himself what account the town could give of itself at night.

"——*à cause du sommeil et à cause des chats*"—the words now rang in his ears more and more often, though still as yet without any definite meaning.

Moreover, something made him sleep like the dead.

III

It was, I think, on the fifth day—though in this detail his story sometimes varied—that he made a definite discovery which increased his alarm and brought him up to a rather sharp climax. Before that he had already noticed that a change was going forward and certain subtle transformations being brought about in his character which modified several of his minor habits. And he had affected to ignore them. Here, however, was something he could no longer ignore; and it startled him.

At the best of times he was never very positive, always negative rather, compliant and acquiescent; yet, when necessity arose he was capable of reasonably vigorous action and could take a strongish decision. The discovery he now made that brought him up with such a sharp turn was that this power had positively dwindled to nothing. He found it impossible to make up his mind. For, on this fifth day, he realised that he had stayed long enough in the town and that for reasons he could only vaguely define to himself it was wiser *and safer* that he should leave.

And he found that he could not leave!

This is difficult to describe in words, and it was more by gesture and the expression of his face that he conveyed to Dr. Silence the state of impotence he had reached. All this spying and watching, he said, had as it were spun a net about his feet so that he was trapped and powerless to escape; he felt like a fly that had blundered into the intricacies of a great web; he was caught, imprisoned, and could not get away. It was a distressing sensation. A numbness had crept over his will till it had become almost incapable of decision. The mere thought of vigorous action—action towards escape—began to terrify him. All the currents of his life had turned inwards upon himself, striving to bring to the surface something that lay buried almost beyond reach, determined to force his recognition of something he had long forgotten—forgotten years upon years, centuries almost ago. It seemed as though a window deep within his being would presently open and reveal an entirely new world, yet somehow a world that was not unfamiliar. Beyond that, again, he fancied a great curtain hung; and when that too rolled up he would see still farther into this region and at last understand something of the secret life of these extraordinary people.

"Is this why they wait and watch?" he asked himself with rather a shaking heart, "for the time when I shall join them—or refuse to join them? Does the decision rest with me after all, and not with them?"

And it was at this point that the sinister character of the adventure first really declared itself, and he became genuinely alarmed. The stability of his rather fluid little personality was at stake, he felt, and something in his heart turned coward.

Why otherwise should he have suddenly taken to walking stealthily, silently, making as little sound as possible, for ever looking behind him? Why else should he have moved almost on tiptoe about the passages of the practically deserted inn, and when he was abroad have found himself deliberately taking advantage of what cover presented itself? And why, if he was not afraid, should the wisdom of staying indoors after sundown have suddenly occurred to him as eminently desirable? Why, indeed?

And, when John Silence gently pressed him for an explanation of these things, he admitted apologetically that he had none to give.

"It was simply that I feared something might happen to me unless I kept a sharp look-out. I felt afraid. It was instinctive," was all he could say. "I got the impression that the whole town was after me—wanted me for something; and that if it got me I should lose myself, or at least the Self I knew, in some unfamiliar state of consciousness. But I am not a psychologist, you know," he added meekly, "and I cannot define it better than that."

It was while lounging in the courtyard half an hour before the evening meal that Vezin made this discovery, and he at once went upstairs to his quiet room at the end of the winding passage to think it over alone. In the yard it was empty enough, true, but there was always the possibility that the big woman whom he dreaded would come out of some door, with her pretence of knitting, to sit and watch him. This had happened several times, and he could not endure the sight of her. He still remembered his original fancy, bizarre though it was, that she would spring upon him the moment his back was turned and land with one single crushing leap upon his neck. Of course it was nonsense, but then it haunted him, and once an idea begins to do that it ceases to be nonsense. It has clothed itself in reality.

He went upstairs accordingly. It was dusk, and the oil lamps had not yet been lit in the passages. He stumbled over the uneven surface of the ancient flooring, passing the dim outlines of doors along the corridor—doors that he had never once seen opened—rooms that seemed never occupied. He moved, as his habit now was, stealthily and on tiptoe.

Half-way down the last passage to his own chamber there was a sharp turn, and it was just here, while groping round the walls with out-stretched hands, that his fingers touched something that was not wall—something that moved. It was soft and warm in texture, indescribably fragrant, and about the height of his shoulder; and he immediately thought of a furry, sweet-smelling kitten. The next minute he knew it was something quite different.

Instead of investigating, however,—his nerves must have been too overwrought for that, he said,—he shrank back as closely as possible against the wall on the other side. The thing, whatever it was, slipped past him with a sound of rustling and, retreating with light footsteps down the passage behind him, was gone. A breath of warm, scented air was wafted to his nostrils.

Vezin caught his breath for an instant and paused, stockstill, half leaning against the wall—and then almost ran down the remaining distance and entered his room with a rush, locking the door hurriedly behind him. Yet it was not fear that made him run: it was excitement, pleasurable excitement. His nerves were tingling, and a delicious glow made itself felt all over his body. In a flash it came to him that this was just what he had felt twenty-five years ago as a boy when he was in love for the first time. Warm currents of life ran all over him and mounted to his brain in a whirl of soft delight. His mood was suddenly become tender, melting, loving.

The room was quite dark, and he collapsed upon the sofa by the win-dow, wondering what had happened to him and what it all meant. But the only thing he understood clearly in that instant was that something in him had swiftly, magically changed: he no longer wished to leave, or to argue with himself about leaving. The encounter in the passage-way had changed all that. The strange perfume of it still hung about him, bemusing his heart and mind. For he knew that it was a girl who had passed him, a girl's face that his fingers had brushed in the darkness, and he felt in some extraordinary way as though he had been actually kissed by her, kissed full upon the lips.

Trembling, he sat upon the sofa by the window and struggled to col-lect his thoughts. He was utterly unable to understand how the mere passing of a girl in the darkness of a narrow passage-way could com-municate so electric a thrill to his whole being that he still shook with the sweetness of it. Yet, there it was! And he found it as useless to deny as to attempt analysis. Some ancient fire had entered his veins, and now ran coursing through his blood; and that he was forty-five instead of twenty did not matter one little jot. Out of all the inner turmoil and confusion emerged the one salient fact that the mere atmosphere, the merest casual touch, of this girl, unseen, unknown in the darkness, had been sufficient to stir dormant fires in the centre of his heart, and rouse his whole being from a state of feeble sluggishness to one of tearing and tumultuous excitement.

After a time, however, the number of Vezin's years began to assert their cumulative power; he grew calmer, and when a knock came at length upon his door and he heard the waiter's voice suggesting that dinner was nearly over, he pulled himself together and slowly made his way downstairs into the dining-room.

Every one looked up as he entered, for he was very late, but he took his customary seat in the far corner and began to eat. The trepidation was still in his nerves, but the fact that he had passed through the court-yard and hall without catching sight of a petticoat served to calm him a little. He ate so fast that he had almost caught up with the current stage of the table d'hôte, when a slight commotion in the room drew his attention.

His chair was so placed that the door and the greater portion of the long *salle à manger* were behind him, yet it was not necessary to turn round to know that the same person he had passed in the dark passage had now come into the room. He felt the presence long before he heard or saw any one. Then he became aware that the old men, the only other guests, were rising one by one in their places, and exchang-ing greetings with some one who passed among them from table to table. And when at length he turned with his heart beating furiously to ascertain for himself, he saw the form of a young girl, lithe and slim, moving down the centre of the room and making straight for his own table in the corner. She moved wonderfully, with sinuous grace, like a young panther, and her approach filled him with such delicious be-wilderment that he was utterly unable to tell at first what her face was like, or discover what it was about the whole presentment of the crea-ture that filled him anew with trepidation and delight.

"Ah, Ma'mselle est de retour!" he heard the old waiter murmur at his side, and he was just able to take in that she was the daughter of the proprietress, when she was upon him, and he heard her voice. She was addressing him. Something of red lips he saw and laughing white teeth, and stray wisps of fine dark hair about the temples; but all the rest was a dream in which his own emotion rose like a thick cloud before his eyes and prevented his seeing accurately, or knowing exactly what he did. He was aware that she greeted him with a charming little bow; that her beautiful large eyes looked searchingly into his own; that the perfume he had noticed in the dark passage again assailed his nostrils, and that she was bending a little towards him and leaning with one hand on the table at this side. She was quite close to him—that was the chief thing he knew—explaining that she had been asking after the comfort of her mother's guests, and now was introducing herself to the latest arrival—himself.

"M'sieur has already been here a few days," he heard the waiter say; and then her own voice, sweet as singing, replied—

"Ah, but M'sieur is not going to leave us just yet, I hope. My mother is too old to look after the comfort of our guests properly, but now I am here I will remedy all that." She laughed deliciously. "M'sieur shall be well looked after."

Vezin, struggling with his emotion and desire to be polite, half rose to acknowledge the pretty speech, and to stammer some sort of reply, but as he did so his hand by chance touched her own that was resting upon the table, and a shock that was for all the world like a shock of electricity, passed from her skin into his body. His soul wavered and shook deep within him. He caught her eyes fixed upon his own with a look of most curious intentness, and the next moment he knew that he had sat down wordless again on his chair, that the girl was already half-way across the room, and that he was trying to eat his salad with a dessert-spoon and a knife.

Longing for her return, and yet dreading it, he gulped down the remainder of his dinner, and then went at once to his bedroom to be alone with his thoughts. This time the passages were lighted, and he suffered no exciting contretemps; yet the winding corridor was dim with shadows, and the last portion, from the bend of the walls onwards, seemed longer than he had ever known it. It ran downhill like the pathway on a mountain side, and as he tiptoed softly down it he felt that by rights it ought to have led him clean out of the house into the heart of a great forest. The world was singing with him. Strange fancies filled his brain, and once in the room, with the door securely locked, he did not light the candles, but sat by the open window thinking long, long thoughts that came unbidden in troops to his mind.

IV

This part of the story he told to Dr. Silence, without special coaxing, it is true, yet with much stammering embarrassment. He could not in the least understand, he said, how the girl had managed to affect him so profoundly, and even before he had set eyes upon her. For her mere proximity in the darkness had been sufficient to set him on fire. He knew nothing of enchantments, and for years had been a stranger to anything approaching tender relations with any member of the opposite sex, for he was encased in shyness, and realised his overwhelming defects only too well. Yet this bewitching young creature came to him deliberately. Her manner was unmistakable, and she sought him out on every possible occasion. Chaste and sweet she was undoubtedly, yet frankly inviting; and she won him utterly with the first glance of her shining eyes, even if she had not already done so in the dark merely by the magic of her invisible presence.

"You felt she was altogether wholesome and good!" queried the doctor. "You had no reaction of any sort—for instance, of alarm?"

Vezin looked up sharply with one of his inimitable little apologetic smiles. It was some time before he replied. The mere memory of the adventure had suffused his shy face with blushes, and his brown eyes sought the floor again before he answered.

"I don't think I can quite say that," he explained presently. "I acknowledged certain qualms, sitting up in my room afterwards. A conviction grew upon me that there was something about her—how shall I express it?—well, something unholy. It is not impurity in any sense, physical or mental, that I mean, but something quite indefinable that gave me a vague sensation of the creeps. She drew me, and at the same time repelled me, more than—than——"

He hesitated, blushing furiously, and unable to finish the sentence.

"Nothing like it has ever come to me before or since," he concluded, with lame confusion. "I suppose it was, as you suggested just now, something of an enchantment. At any rate, it was strong enough to make me feel that I would stay in that awful little haunted town for years if only I could see her every day, hear her voice, watch her wonderful movements, and sometimes, perhaps, touch her hand."

"Can you explain to me what you felt was the source of her power?" John Silence asked, looking purposely anywhere but at the narrator.

"I am surprised that *you* should ask me such a question," answered Vezin, with the nearest approach to dignity he could manage. "I think no man can describe to another convincingly wherein lies the magic of the woman who ensnares him. I certainly cannot. I can only say this slip of a girl bewitched me, and the mere knowledge that she was living and sleeping in the same house filled me with an extraordinary sense of delight.

"But there's one thing I can tell you," he went on earnestly, his eyes aglow, "namely, that she seemed to sum up and synthesise in herself all the strange hidden forces that operated so mysteriously in the town and its inhabitants. She had the silken movements of the panther, going smoothly, silently to and fro, and the same indirect, oblique methods as the townsfolk, screening, like them, secret purposes of her own—purposes that I was sure had *me* for their objective. She kept me, to my terror and delight, ceaselessly under observation, yet so carelessly, so consummately, that another man less sensitive, if I may say so"—he made a deprecating gesture—"or less prepared by what had gone before, would never have noticed it at all. She was always still, always reposeful, yet she seemed to be everywhere at once, so that I never could escape from her. I was continually meeting the stare and laughter of her great eyes, in the corners of the rooms, in the passages, calmly looking at me through the windows, or in the busiest parts of the public streets."

Their intimacy, it seems, grew very rapidly after this first encounter which had so violently disturbed the little man's equilibrium. He was naturally very prim, and prim folk live mostly in so small a world that anything violently unusual may shake them clean out of it, and they therefore instinctively distrust originality. But Vezin began to forget his primness after awhile. The girl was always modestly behaved, and as her mother's representative she naturally had to do with the guests in the hotel. It was not out of the way that a spirit of camaraderie should spring up. Besides, she was young, she was charmingly pretty, she was French, and—she obviously liked him.

At the same time, there was something indescribable—a certain indefinable atmosphere of other places, other times—that made him try hard to remain on his guard, and sometimes made him catch his breath with a sudden start. It was all rather like a delirious dream, half delight, half dread, he confided in a whisper to Dr. Silence; and more than once he hardly knew quite what he was doing or saying, as though he were driven forward by impulses he scarcely recognised as his own.

And though the thought of leaving presented itself again and again to his mind, it was each time with less insistence, so that he stayed on from day to day, becoming more and more a part of the sleepy life of this dreamy mediæval town, losing more and more of his recognisable personality. Soon, he felt, the Curtain within would roll up with an awful rush, and he would find himself suddenly admitted into the secret purposes of the hidden life that lay behind it all. Only, by that time, he would have become transformed into an entirely different being.

And, meanwhile, he noticed various little signs of the intention to make his stay attractive to him: flowers in his bedroom, a more comfortable arm-chair in the corner, and even special little extra dishes on his private table in the dining-room. Conversations, too, with "Mademoiselle Ilsé" became more and more frequent and pleasant, and although they seldom travelled beyond the weather, or the details of the town, the girl, he noticed, was never in a hurry to bring them to an end, and often contrived to interject little odd sentences that he never properly understood, yet felt to be significant.

And it was these stray remarks, full of a meaning that evaded him, that pointed to some hidden purpose of her own and made him feel uneasy. They all had to do, he felt sure, with reasons for his staying on in the town indefinitely.

"And has M'sieur not even yet come to a decision?" she said softly in his ear, sitting beside him in the sunny yard before *déjeuner*, the acquaintance having progressed with significant rapidity. "Because, if it's so difficult, we must all try together to help him!"

The question startled him, following upon his own thoughts. It was spoken with a pretty laugh, and a stray bit of hair across one eye, as she turned and peered at him half roguishly. Possibly he did not quite understand the French of it, for her near presence always confused his small knowledge of the language distressingly. Yet the words, and her manner, and something else that lay behind it all in her mind, frightened him. It gave such point to his feeling that the town was waiting for him to make his mind up on some important matter.

At the same time, her voice, and the fact that she was there so close beside him in her soft dark dress, thrilled him inexpressibly.

"It is true I find it difficult to leave," he stammered, losing his way deliciously in the depths of her eyes, "and especially now that Mademoiselle Ilsé has come."

He was surprised at the success of his sentence, and quite delighted with the little gallantry of it. But at the same time he could have bitten his tongue off for having said it.

"Then after all you like our little town, or you would not be pleased to stay on," she said, ignoring the compliment.

"I am enchanted with it, and enchanted with you," he cried, feeling that his tongue was somehow slipping beyond the control of his brain. And he was on the verge of saying all manner of other things of the wildest description, when the girl sprang lightly up from her chair beside him, and made to go.

"It is *soupe à l'onion* to-day!" she cried, laughing back at him through the sunlight, "and I must go and see about it. Otherwise, you know, M'sieur will not enjoy his dinner, and then, perhaps, he will leave us!"

He watched her cross the courtyard, moving with all the grace and lightness of the feline race, and her simple black dress clothed her, he thought, exactly like the fur of the same supple species. She turned once to laugh at him from the porch with the glass door, and then stopped a moment to speak to her mother, who sat knitting as usual in her corner seat just inside the hall-way.

But how was it, then, that the moment his eye fell upon this ungainly woman, the pair of them appeared suddenly as other than they were? Whence came that transforming dignity and sense of power that enveloped them both as by magic? What was it about that massive woman that made her appear instantly regal, and set her on a throne in some dark and dreadful scenery, wielding a sceptre over the red glare of some tempestuous orgy? And why did this slender stripling of a girl, graceful as a willow, lithe as a young leopard, assume suddenly an air of sinister majesty, and move with flame and smoke about her head, and the darkness of night beneath her feet?

Vezin caught his breath and sat there transfixed. Then, almost simultaneously with its appearance, the queer notion vanished again, and the sunlight of day caught them both, and he heard her laughing to her mother about the *soupe à l'onion*, and saw her glancing back at him over her dear little shoulder with a smile that made him think of a dew-kissed rose bending lightly before summer airs.

And, indeed, the onion soup was particularly excellent that day, because he saw another cover laid at his small table, and, with fluttering heart, heard the waiter murmur by way of explanation that "Ma'mselle Ilsé would honour M'sieur to-day at *déjeuner*, as her custom sometimes is with her mother's guests."

So actually she sat by him all through that delirious meal, talking quietly to him in easy French, seeing that he was well looked after, mixing the salad-dressing, and even helping him with her own hand. And, later in the afternoon, while he was smoking in the courtyard, longing for a sight of her as soon as her duties were done, she came again to his side, and when he rose to meet her, she stood facing him a moment, full of a perplexing sweet shyness before she spoke—

"My mother thinks you ought to know more of the beauties of our little town, and I think so too! Would M'sieur like me to be his guide, perhaps? I can show him everything, for our family has lived here for many generations."

She had him by the hand, indeed, before he could find a single word to express his pleasure, and led him, all unresisting, out into the street, yet in such a way that it seemed perfectly natural she should do so, and without the faintest suggestion of boldness or immodesty. Her face glowed with the pleasure and interest of it, and with her short dress and tumbled hair she looked every bit the charming child of seventeen that she was, innocent and playful, proud of her native town, and alive beyond her years to the sense of its ancient beauty.

So they went over the town together, and she showed him what she considered its chief interest: the tumble-down old house where her forebears had lived; the sombre, aristocratic-looking mansion where her mother's family dwelt for centuries, and the ancient market-place where several hundred years before the witches had been burnt by the score. She kept up a lively running stream of talk about it all, of which he understood not a fiftieth part as he trudged along by her side, cursing his forty-five years and feeling all the yearnings of his early manhood revive and jeer at him. And, as she talked, England and Surbiton seemed very far away indeed, almost in another age of the world's history. Her voice touched something immeasurably old in him, something that slept deep. It lulled the surface parts of his consciousness to sleep, allowing what was far more ancient to awaken. Like the town, with its elaborate pretence of modern active life, the upper layers of his being became dulled, soothed, muffled, and what lay underneath began to stir in its sleep. That big Curtain swayed a little to and fro. Presently it might lift altogether. . . .

He began to understand a little better at last. The mood of the town was reproducing itself in him. In proportion as his ordinary external self became muffled, that inner secret life, that was far more real and vital, asserted itself. And this girl was surely the high-priestess of it all, the chief instrument of its accomplishment. New thoughts, with new interpretations, flooded his mind as she walked beside him through the winding streets, while the picturesque old gabled town, softly coloured in the sunset, had never appeared to him so wholly wonderful and seductive.

And only one curious incident came to disturb and puzzle him, slight in itself, but utterly inexplicable, bringing white terror into the child's face and a scream to her laughing lips. He had merely pointed to a column of blue smoke that rose from the burning autumn leaves and made a picture against the red roofs, and had then run to the wall and called her to his side to watch the flames shooting here and there through the heap of rubbish. Yet, at the sight of it, as though taken by surprise, her face had altered dreadfully, and she had turned and run like the wind, calling out wild sentences to him as she ran, of which he had not understood a single word, except that the fire apparently frightened her, and she wanted to get quickly away from it, and to get him away too.

Yet five minutes later she was as calm and happy again as though nothing had happened to alarm or waken troubled thoughts in her, and they had both forgotten the incident.

They were leaning over the ruined ramparts together listening to the weird music of the band as he had heard it the first day of his arrival. It moved him again profoundly as it had done before, and somehow he managed to find his tongue and his best French. The girl leaned across the stones close beside him. No one was about. Driven by some remorseless engine within he began to stammer something—he hardly knew what—of his strange admiration for her. Almost at the first word she sprang lightly off the wall and came up smiling in front of him, just touching his knees as he sat there. She was hatless as usual, and the sun caught her hair and one side of her cheek and throat.

"Oh, I'm *so* glad!" she cried, clapping her little hands softly in his face, "so very glad, because that means that if you like me you must also like what I do, and what I belong to."

Already he regretted bitterly having lost control of himself. Something in the phrasing of her sentence chilled him. He knew the fear of embarking upon an unknown and dangerous sea.

"You will take part in our real life, I mean," she added softly, with an indescribable coaxing of manner, as though she noticed his shrinking. "You will come back to us."

Already this slip of a child seemed to dominate him; he felt her power coming over him more and more; something emanated from her that stole over his senses and made him aware that her personality, for all its simple grace, held forces that were stately, imposing, august. He saw her again moving through smoke and flame amid broken and tempestuous scenery, alarmingly strong, her terrible mother by her side. Dimly this shone through her smile and appearance of charming innocence.

"You will, I know," she repeated, holding him with her eyes.

They were quite alone up there on the ramparts, and the sensation that she was overmastering him stirred a wild sensuousness in his blood. The mingled abandon and reserve in her attracted him furiously, and all of him that was man rose up and resisted the creeping influence, at the same time acclaiming it with the full delight of his forgotten youth. An irresistible desire came to him to question her, to summon what still remained to him of his own little personality in an effort to retain the right to his normal self.

The girl had grown quiet again, and was now leaning on the broad wall close beside him, gazing out across the darkening plain, her elbows on the coping, motionless as a figure carved in stone. He took his courage in both hands.

"Tell me, Ilsé," he said, unconsciously imitating her own purring softness of voice, yet aware that he was utterly in earnest, "what is the meaning of this town, and what is this real life you speak of? And why is it that the people watch me from morning to night? Tell me what it all means? And, tell me," he added more quickly with passion in his voice, "what you really are—yourself?"

She turned her head and looked at him through half-closed eyelids, her growing inner excitement betraying itself by the faint colour that ran like a shadow across her face.

"It seems to me,"—he faltered oddly under her gaze—"that I have some right to know——"

Suddenly she opened her eyes to the full. "You love me, then?" she asked softly.

"I swear," he cried impetuously, moved as by the force of a rising tide, "I never felt before—I have never known any other girl who——"

"Then you *have* the right to know," she calmly interrupted his confused confession, "for love shares all secrets."

She paused, and a thrill like fire ran swiftly through him. Her words lifted him off the earth, and he felt a radiant happiness, followed almost the same instant in horrible contrast by the thought of death. He became aware that she had turned her eyes upon his own and was speaking again.

"The real life I speak of," she whispered, "is the old, old life within, the life of long ago, the life to which you, too, once belonged, and to which you still belong."

A faint wave of memory troubled the deeps of his soul as her low voice sank into him. What she was saying he knew instinctively to be true, even though he could not as yet understand its full purport. His present life seemed slipping from him as he listened, merging his personality in one that was far older and greater. It was this loss of his present self that brought to him the thought of death.

"You came here," she went on, "with the purpose of seeking it, and the people felt your presence and are waiting to know what you decide, whether you will leave them without having found it, or whether——"

Her eyes remained fixed upon his own, but her face began to change, growing larger and darker with an expression of age.

"It is their thoughts constantly playing about your soul that makes you feel they watch you. They do not watch you with their eyes. The purposes of their inner life are calling to you, seeking to claim you. You were all part of the same life long, long ago, and now they want you back again among them."

Vezin's timid heart sank with dread as he listened; but the girl's eyes held him with a net of joy so that he had no wish to escape. She fascinated him, as it were, clean out of his normal self.

"Alone, however, the people could never have caught and held you," she resumed. "The motive force was not strong enough; it has faded through all these years. But I"—she paused a moment and looked at him with complete confidence in her splendid eyes—"I possess the spell to conquer you and hold you: the spell of old love. I can win you back again and make you live the old life with me, for the force of the ancient tie between us, if I choose to use it, is irresistible. And I do choose to use it. I still want you. And you, dear soul of my dim past"— she pressed closer to him so that her breath passed across his eyes, and her voice positively sang—"I mean to have you, for you love me and are utterly at my mercy."

Vezin heard, and yet did not hear; understood, yet did not understand. He had passed into a condition of exaltation. The world was beneath his feet, made of music and flowers, and he was flying somewhere far above it through the sunshine of pure delight. He was breathless and giddy with the wonder of her words. They intoxicated him. And, still, the terror of it all, the dreadful thought of death, pressed ever behind her sentences. For flames shot through her voice out of black smoke and licked at his soul.

And they communicated with one another, it seemed to him, by a process of swift telepathy, for his French could never have compassed all he said to her. Yet she understood perfectly, and what she said to him was like the recital of verses long since known. And the mingled pain and sweetness of it as he listened were almost more than his little soul could hold.

"Yet I came here wholly by chance——" he heard himself saying.

"No," she cried with passion, "you came here because I called to you. I have called to you for years, and you came with the whole force of the past behind you. You had to come, for I own you, and I claim you."

She rose again and moved closer, looking at him with a certain insolence in the face—the insolence of power.

The sun had set behind the towers of the old cathedral and the darkness rose up from the plain and enveloped them. The music of the band had ceased. The leaves of the plane trees hung motionless, but the chill of the autumn evening rose about them and made Vezin shiver. There was no sound but the sound of their voices and the occasional soft rustle of the girl's dress. He could hear the blood rushing in his ears. He scarcely realised where he was or what he was doing. Some terrible magic of the imagination drew him deeply down into the tombs of his own being, telling him in no unfaltering voice that her words shadowed forth the truth. And this simple little French maid, speaking beside him with so strange authority, he saw curiously alter into quite another being. As he stared into her eyes, the picture in his mind grew and lived, dressing itself vividly to his inner vision with a degree of reality he was compelled to acknowledge. As once before, he saw her tall and stately, moving through wild and broken scenery of forests and mountain caverns, the glare of flames behind her head and clouds of shifting smoke about her feet. Dark leaves encircled her hair, flying loosely in the wind, and her limbs shone through the merest rags of clothing. Others were about her, too, and ardent eyes on all sides cast delirious glances upon her, but her own eyes were always for One only, one whom she held by the hand. For she was leading the dance in some tempestuous orgy to the music of chanting voices, and the dance she led circled about a great and awful Figure on a throne, brooding over the scene through lurid vapours, while innumerable other wild faces and forms crowded furiously about her in the dance. But the one she held by the hand he knew to be himself, and the monstrous shape upon the throne he knew to be her mother.

The vision rose within him, rushing to him down the long years of buried time, crying aloud to him with the voice of memory reawakened. . . . And then the scene faded away and he saw the clear circle of the girl's eyes gazing steadfastly into his own, and she became once more the pretty little daughter of the innkeeper, and he found his voice again.

"And you," he whispered tremblingly—"you child of visions and enchantment, how is it that you so bewitch me that I loved you even before I saw?"

She drew herself up beside him with an air of rare dignity.

"The call of the Past," she said; "and besides," she added proudly, "in the real life I am a princess——"

"A princess!" he cried.

"——and my mother is a queen!"

At this, little Vezin utterly lost his head. Delight tore at his heart and swept him into sheer ecstasy. To hear that sweet singing voice, and to see those adorable little lips utter such things, upset his balance beyond all hope of control. He took her in his arms and covered her unresisting face with kisses.

But even while he did so, and while the hot passion swept him, he felt that she was soft and loathsome, and that her answering kisses stained his very soul. . . . And when, presently, she had freed herself and vanished into the darkness, he stood there, leaning against the wall in a state of collapse, creeping with horror from the touch of her yielding

body, and inwardly raging at the weakness that he already dimly realised must prove his undoing.

And from the shadows of the old buildings into which she disappeared there rose in the stillness of the night a singular, long-drawn cry,
which at first he took for laughter, but which later he was sure he recognised as the almost human wailing of a cat.

V

For a long time Vezin leant there against the wall, alone with his surg-
ing thoughts and emotions. He understood at length that he had done
the one thing necessary to call down upon him the whole force of this
ancient Past. For in those passionate kisses he had acknowledged the tie
of olden days, and had revived it. And the memory of that soft impal-
pable caress in the darkness of the inn corridor came back to him with
a shudder. The girl had first mastered him, and then led him to the one
act that was necessary for her purpose. He had been waylaid, after the
lapse of centuries—caught, and conquered.

Dimly he realised this, and sought to make plans for his escape. But,
for the moment at any rate, he was powerless to manage his thoughts
or will, for the sweet, fantastic madness of the whole adventure
mounted to his brain like a spell, and he gloried in the feeling that he
was utterly enchanted and moving in a world so much larger and
wilder than the one he had ever been accustomed to.

The moon, pale and enormous, was just rising over the sea-like
plain, when at last he rose to go. Her slanting rays drew all the houses
into new perspective, so that their roofs, already glistening with dew,
seemed to stretch much higher into the sky than usual, and their gables
and quaint old towers lay far away in its purple reaches.

The cathedral appeared unreal in a silver mist. He moved softly,
keeping to the shadows; but the streets were all deserted and very silent;
the doors were closed, the shutters fastened. Not a soul was astir. The
hush of night lay over everything; it was like a town of the dead, a
churchyard with gigantic and grotesque tombstones.

Wondering where all the busy life of the day had so utterly disappeared to, he made his way to a back door that entered the inn by
means of the stables, thinking thus to reach his room unobserved. He
reached the courtyard safely and crossed it by keeping close to the
shadow of the wall. He sidled down it, mincing along on tiptoe, just as
the old men did when they entered the *salle à manger*. He was horri-
fied to find himself doing this instinctively. A strange impulse came to
him, catching him somehow in the centre of his body—an impulse to

drop upon all fours and run swiftly and silently. He glanced upwards and the idea came to him to leap up upon his window-sill overhead instead of going round by the stairs. This occurred to him as the easiest, and most natural way. It was like the beginning of some horrible transformation of himself into something else. He was fearfully strung up.

The moon was higher now, and the shadows very dark along the side of the street where he moved. He kept among the deepest of them, and reached the porch with the glass doors.

But here there was light; the inmates, unfortunately, were still about. Hoping to slip across the hall unobserved and reach the stairs, he opened the door carefully and stole in. Then he saw that the hall was not empty. A large dark thing lay against the wall on his left. At first he thought it must be household articles. Then it moved, and he thought it was an immense cat, distorted in some way by the play of light and shadow. Then it rose straight up before him and he saw that it was the proprietress.

What she had been doing in this position he could only venture a dreadful guess, but the moment she stood up and faced him he was aware of some terrible dignity clothing her about that instantly recalled the girl's strange saying that she was a queen. Huge and sinister she stood there under the little oil lamp; alone with him in the empty hall. Awe stirred in his heart, and the roots of some ancient fear. He felt that he must bow to her and make some kind of obeisance. The impulse was fierce and irresistible, as of long habit. He glanced quickly about him. There was no one there. Then he deliberately inclined his head toward her. He bowed.

"Enfin! M'sieur s'est donc décidé. C'est bien alors. J'en suis contente."

Her words came to him sonorously as through a great open space.

Then the great figure came suddenly across the flagged hall at him and seized his trembling hands. Some overpowering force moved with her and caught him.

"On pourrait faire un p'tit tour ensemble, n'est-ce pas? Nous y allons cette nuit et il faut s'exercer un peu d'avance pour cela. Ilsé, Ilsé, viens donc ici. Viens vite!"

And she whirled him round in the opening steps of some dance that seemed oddly and horribly familiar. They made no sound on the stones, this strangely assorted couple. It was all soft and stealthy. And presently, when the air seemed to thicken like smoke, and a red glare as of flame shot through it, he was aware that some one else had joined them and that his hand the mother had released was now tightly held by the daughter. Ilsé had come in answer to the call, and he saw her with leaves of vervain twined in her dark hair, clothed in tattered vestiges of some curious garment, beautiful as the night, and horribly, odiously, loathsomely seductive.

"To the Sabbath! to the Sabbath!" they cried. "On to the Witches' Sabbath!"

Up and down that narrow hall they danced, the women on each side of him, to the wildest measure he had ever imagined, yet which he dimly, dreadfully remembered, till the lamp on the wall flickered and went out, and they were left in total darkness. And the devil woke in his heart with a thousand vile suggestions and made him afraid.

Suddenly they released his hands and he heard the voice of the mother cry that it was time, and they must go. Which way they went he did not pause to see. He only realised that he was free, and he blundered through the darkness till he found the stairs and then tore up them to his room as though all hell was at his heels.

He flung himself on the sofa, with his face in his hands, and groaned. Swiftly reviewing a dozen ways of immediate escape, all equally impossible, he finally decided that the only thing to do for the moment was to sit quiet and wait. He must see what was going to happen. At least in the privacy of his own bedroom he would be fairly safe. The door was locked. He crossed over and softly opened the window which gave upon the courtyard and also permitted a partial view of the hall through the glass doors.

As he did so the hum and murmur of a great activity reached his ears from the streets beyond—the sound of footsteps and voices muffled by distance. He leaned out cautiously and listened. The moonlight was clear and strong now, but his own window was in shadow, the silver disc being still behind the house. It came to him irresistibly that the inhabitants of the town, who a little while before had all been invisible behind closed doors, were now issuing forth, busy upon some secret and unholy errand. He listened intently.

At first everything about him was silent, but soon he became aware of movements going on in the house itself. Rustlings and cheepings came to him across that still, moonlit yard. A concourse of living beings sent the hum of their activity into the night. Things were on the move everywhere. A biting, pungent odour rose through the air, coming he knew not whence. Presently his eyes became glued to the windows of the opposite wall where the moonshine fell in a soft blaze. The roof overhead, and behind him, was reflected clearly in the panes of glass, and he saw the outlines of dark bodies moving with long footsteps over the tiles and along the coping. They passed swiftly and silently, shaped like immense cats, in an endless procession across the pictured glass, and then appeared to leap down to a lower level where he lost sight of them. He just caught the soft thudding of their leaps. Sometimes their shadows fell upon the white wall opposite, and then he could not make out whether they were the shadows of human beings or of cats. They seemed to change swiftly from one to the other. The transformation looked horribly real, for they leaped like human beings, yet changed swiftly in the air immediately afterwards, and dropped like animals.

The yard, too, beneath him, was now alive with the creeping movements of dark forms all stealthily drawing towards the porch with the glass doors. They kept so closely to the wall that he could not determine their actual shape, but when he saw that they passed on to the great congregation that was gathering in the hall, he understood that these were the creatures whose leaping shadows he had first seen reflected in the windowpanes opposite. They were coming from all parts of the town, reaching the appointed meeting-place across the roofs and tiles, and springing from level to level till they came to the yard.

Then a new sound caught his ear, and he saw that the windows all about him were being softly opened, and that to each window came a face. A moment later figures began dropping hurriedly down into the yard. And these figures, as they lowered themselves down from the windows, were human, he saw; but once safely in the yard they fell upon all fours and changed in the swiftest possible second into—cats—huge, silent cats. They ran in streams to join the main body in the hall beyond.

So, after all, the rooms in the house had not been empty and unoccupied.

Moreover, what he saw no longer filled him with amazement. For he remembered it all. It was familiar. It had all happened before just so, hundreds of times, and he himself had taken part in it and known the wild madness of it all. The outline of the old building changed, the yard grew larger, and he seemed to be staring down upon it from a much greater height through smoky vapours. And, as he looked, half remembering, the old pains of long ago, fierce and sweet, furiously assailed him, and the blood stirred horribly as he heard the Call of the Dance again in his heart and tasted the ancient magic of Ilsé whirling by his side.

Suddenly he started back. A great lithe cat had leaped softly up from the shadows below on to the sill close to his face, and was staring fixedly at him with the eyes of a human. "Come," it seemed to say, "come with us to the Dance! Change as of old! Transform yourself swiftly and come!" Only too well he understood the creature's soundless call.

It was gone again in a flash with scarcely a sound of its padded feet on the stones, and then others dropped by the score down the side of the house, past his very eyes, all changing as they fell and darting away rapidly, softly, towards the gathering point. And again he felt the dreadful desire to do likewise; to murmur the old incantation, and then drop upon hands and knees and run swiftly for the great flying leap into the air. Oh, how the passion of it rose within him like a flood, twisting his very entrails, sending his heart's desire flaming forth into the night for the old, old Dance of the Sorcerers at the Witches' Sabbath! The whirl of the stars was about him; once more he met the magic of the moon. The power of the wind, rushing from precipice and forest, leaping from cliff to cliff across the valleys, tore him away. . . . He heard the cries of the dancers and their wild laughter, and with this savage girl in his embrace he danced furiously about the dim Throne where sat the Figure with the sceptre of majesty. . . .

Then, suddenly, all became hushed and still, and the fever died down a little in his heart. The calm moonlight flooded a courtyard empty and deserted. They had started. The procession was off into the sky. And he was left behind—alone.

Vezin tiptoed softly across the room and unlocked the door. The murmur from the streets, growing momentarily as he advanced, met his ears. He made his way with the utmost caution down the corridor. At the head of the stairs he paused and listened. Below him, the hall where they had gathered was dark and still, but through opened doors and windows on the far side of the building came the sound of a great throng moving farther and farther into the distance.

He made his way down the creaking wooden stairs, dreading yet longing to meet some straggler who should point the way, but finding no one; across the dark hall, so lately thronged with living, moving things, and out through the opened front doors into the street. He could not believe that he was really left behind, really forgotten, that he had been purposely permitted to escape. It perplexed him.

Nervously he peered about him, and up and down the street; then, seeing nothing, advanced slowly down the pavement.

The whole town, as he went, showed itself empty and deserted, as though a great wind had blown everything alive out of it. The doors and windows of the houses stood open to the night; nothing stirred; moonlight and silence lay over all. The night lay about him like a cloak. The air, soft and cool, caressed his cheek like the touch of a great furry paw. He gained confidence and began to walk quickly, though still keeping to the shadowed side. Nowhere could he discover the faintest sign of the great unholy exodus he knew had just taken place. The moon sailed high over all in a sky cloudless and serene.

Hardly realising where he was going, he crossed the open market-place and so came to the ramparts, whence he knew a pathway descended to the high road and along which he could make good his escape to one of the other little towns that lay to the northward, and so to the railway.

But first he paused and gazed out over the scene at his feet where the great plain lay like a silver map of some dream country. The still beauty of it entered his heart, increasing his sense of bewilderment and unreality. No air stirred, the leaves of the plane trees stood motionless, the near details were defined with the sharpness of day against dark shadows, and in the distance the fields and woods melted away into haze and shimmering mistiness.

But the breath caught in his throat and he stood stockstill as though transfixed when his gaze passed from the horizon and fell upon the near prospect in the depth of the valley at his feet. The whole lower slopes of the hill, that lay hid from the brightness of the moon, were aglow, and through the glare he saw countless moving forms, shifting thick and fast between the openings of the trees; while overhead, like leaves driven by the wind, he discerned flying shapes that hovered darkly one moment against the sky and then settled down with cries and weird singing through the branches into the region that was aflame.

Spellbound, he stood and stared for a time that he could not measure. And then, moved by one of the terrible impulses that seemed to control the whole adventure, he climbed swiftly upon the top of the broad coping, and balanced a moment where the valley gaped at his feet. But in that very instant, as he stood hovering, a sudden movement among the shadows of the houses caught his eye, and he turned to see the outline of a large animal dart swiftly across the open space behind him, and land with a flying leap upon the top of the wall a little lower down. It ran like the wind to his feet and then rose up beside him upon the ramparts. A shiver seemed to run through the moonlight, and his sight trembled for a second. His heart pulsed fearfully. Ilsé stood beside him, peering into his face.

Some dark substance, he saw, stained the girl's face and skin, shining in the moonlight as she stretched her hands towards him; she was dressed in wretched tattered garments that yet became her mightily; rue and vervain twined about her temples; her eyes glittered with unholy light. He only just controlled the wild impulse to take her in his arms and leap with her from their giddy perch into the valley below.

"See!" she cried, pointing with an arm on which the rags fluttered in the rising wind towards the forest aglow in the distance. "See where they await us! The woods are alive! Already the Great Ones are there, and the dance will soon begin! The salve is here! Anoint yourself and come!"

Though a moment before the sky was clear and cloudless, yet even while she spoke the face of the moon grew dark and the wind began to toss in the crests of the plane trees at his feet. Stray gusts brought the sounds of hoarse singing and crying from the lower slopes of the hill, and the pungent odour he had already noticed about the courtyard of the inn rose about him in the air.

"Transform, transform!" she cried again, her voice rising like a song. "Rub well your skin before you fly. Come! Come with me to the Sabbath, to the madness of its furious delight, to the sweet abandonment of its evil worship! See! the Great Ones are there, and the terrible Sacraments prepared. The Throne is occupied. Anoint and come! Anoint and come!"

She grew to the height of a tree beside him, leaping upon the wall with flaming eyes and hair strewn upon the night. He too began to change swiftly. Her hands touched the skin of his face and neck, streaking him with the burning salve that sent the old magic into his blood with the power before which fades all that is good.

A wild roar came up to his ears from the heart of the wood, and the girl, when she heard it, leaped upon the wall in the frenzy of her wicked joy.

"Satan is there!" she screamed, rushing upon him and striving to draw him with her to the edge of the wall. "Satan has come. The Sacraments call us! Come, with your dear apostate soul, and we will worship and dance till the moon dies and the world is forgotten!"

Just saving himself from the dreadful plunge, Vezin struggled to release himself from her grasp, while the passion tore at his reins and all but mastered him. He shrieked aloud, not knowing what he said, and then he shrieked again. It was the old impulses, the old awful habits instinctively finding voice; for though it seemed to him that he merely shrieked nonsense, the words he uttered really had meaning in them, and were intelligible. It was the ancient call. And it was heard below. It was answered.

The wind whistled at the skirts of his coat as the air round him darkened with many flying forms crowding upwards out of the valley. The crying of hoarse voices smote upon his ears, coming closer. Strokes of wind buffeted him, tearing him this way and that along the crumbling top of the stone wall; and Ilsé clung to him with her long shining arms, smooth and bare, holding him fast about the neck. But not Ilsé alone, for a dozen of them surrounded him, dropping out of the air. The pun-

gent odour of the anointed bodies stifled him, exciting him to the old
madness of the Sabbath, the dance of the witches and sorcerers doing
honour to the personified Evil of the world.

"Anoint and away! Anoint and away!" they cried in wild chorus about
him. "To the Dance that never dies! To the sweet and fearful fantasy of
evil!"

Another moment and he would have yielded and gone, for his will
turned soft and the flood of passionate memory all but overwhelmed
him, when—so can a small thing after the whole course of an adventure—he caught his foot upon a loose stone in the edge of the wall, and
then fell with a sudden crash on to the ground below. But he fell towards the houses, in the open space of dust and cobblestones, and fortunately not into the gaping depth of the valley on the farther side.

And they, too, came in a tumbling heap about him, like flies upon a
piece of food, but as they fell he was released for a moment from the
power of their touch, and in that brief instant of freedom there flashed
into his mind the sudden intuition that saved him. Before he could re-
gain his feet he saw them scrabbling awkwardly back upon the wall, as
though bat-like they could only fly by dropping from a height, and had
no hold upon him in the open. Then, seeing them perched there in a
row like cats upon a roof, all dark and singularly shapeless, their eyes
like lamps, the sudden memory came back to him of Ilsé's terror at the
sight of fire.

Quick as a flash he found his matches and lit the dead leaves that lay
under the wall.

Dry and withered, they caught fire at once, and the wind carried the
flame in a long line down the length of the wall, licking upwards as it
ran; and with shrieks and wailings, the crowded row of forms upon the
top melted away into the air on the other side, and were gone with a
great rush and whirring of their bodies down into the heart of the
haunted valley, leaving Vezin breathless and shaken in the middle of
the deserted ground.

"Ilsé!" he called feebly; "Ilsé!" for his heart ached to think that she
was really gone to the great Dance without him, and that he had lost
the opportunity of its fearful joy. Yet at the same time his relief was so
great, and he was so dazed and troubled in mind with the whole thing,
that he hardly knew what he was saying, and only cried aloud in the
fierce storm of his emotion. . . .

The fire under the wall ran its course, and the moonlight came
out again, soft and clear, from its temporary eclipse. With one last
shuddering look at the ruined ramparts, and a feeling of horrid wonder
for the haunted valley beyond, where the shapes still crowded and flew,

he turned his face towards the town and slowly made his way in the direction of the hotel.

And as he went, a great wailing of cries, and a sound of howling, followed him from the gleaming forest below, growing fainter and fainter with the bursts of wind as he disappeared between the houses.

VI

"It may seem rather abrupt to you, this sudden tame ending," said Arthur Vezin, glancing with flushed face and timid eyes at Dr. Silence sitting there with his notebook, "but the fact is—er—from that moment my memory seems to have failed rather. I have no distinct recollection of how I got home or what precisely I did.

"It appears I never went back to the inn at all. I only dimly recollect racing down a long white road in the moonlight, past woods and villages, still and deserted, and then the dawn came up, and I saw the towers of a biggish town and so came to a station.

"But, long before that, I remember pausing somewhere on the road and looking back to where the hill-town of my adventure stood up in the moonlight, and thinking how exactly like a great monstrous cat it lay there upon the plain, its huge front paws lying down the two main streets, and the twin and broken towers of the cathedral marking its torn ears against the sky. That picture stays in my mind with the utmost vividness to this day.

"Another thing remains in my mind from that escape—namely, the sudden sharp reminder that I had not paid my bill, and the decision I made, standing there on the dusty highroad, that the small baggage I had left behind would more than settle for my indebtedness.

"For the rest, I can only tell you that I got coffee and bread at a café on the outskirts of this town I had come to, and soon after found my way to the station and caught a train later in the day. That same evening I reached London."

"And how long altogether," asked John Silence quietly, "do you think you stayed in the town of the adventure?"

Vezin looked up sheepishly.

"I was coming to that," he resumed, with apologetic wrigglings of his body. "In London I found that I was a whole week out in my reckoning of time. I had stayed over a week in the town, and it ought to have been September 15th,—instead of which it was only September 10th!"

"So that, in reality, you had only stayed a night or two in the inn?" queried the doctor.

Vezin hesitated before replying. He shuffled upon the mat.

"I must have gained time somewhere," he said at length—"somewhere or somehow. I certainly had a week to my credit. I can't explain it. I can only give you the fact."

"And this happened to you last year, since when you have never been back to the place?"

"Last autumn, yes," murmured Vezin; "and I have never dared to go back. I think I never want to."

"And, tell me," asked Dr. Silence at length, when he saw that the little man had evidently come to the end of his words and had nothing more to say, "had you ever read up the subject of the old witchcraft practices during the Middle Ages, or been at all interested in the subject?"

"Never!" declared Vezin emphatically. "I had never given a thought to such matters so far as I know——"

"Or to the question of reincarnation, perhaps?"

"Never—before my adventure; but I have since," he replied significantly.

There was, however, something still on the man's mind that he wished to relieve himself of by confession, yet could only with difficulty bring himself to mention; and it was only after the sympathetic tactfulness of the doctor had provided numerous openings that he at length availed himself of one of them, and stammered that he would like to show him the marks he still had on his neck where, he said, the girl had touched him with her anointed hands.

He took off his collar after infinite fumbling hesitation, and lowered his shirt a little for the doctor to see. And there, on the surface of the skin, lay a faint reddish line across the shoulder and extending a little way down the back towards the spine. It certainly indicated exactly the position an arm might have taken in the act of embracing. And on the other side of the neck, slightly higher up, was a similar mark, though not quite so clearly defined.

"That was where she held me that night on the ramparts," he whispered, a strange light coming and going in his eyes.

It was some weeks later when I again found occasion to consult John Silence concerning another extraordinary case that had come under my notice, and we fell to discussing Vezin's story. Since hearing it, the doctor had made investigations on his own account, and one of his secretaries had discovered that Vezin's ancestors had actually lived for generations in the very town where the adventure came to him. Two of them, both women, had been tried and convicted as witches, and had been burned alive at the stake. Moreover, it had not been difficult to prove that the very inn where Vezin stayed was built about 1700 upon the spot where the funeral pyres stood and the executions took place. The town was a sort of headquarters for all the sorcerers and witches of the entire region, and after conviction they were burnt there literally by scores.

"It seems strange," continued the doctor, "that Vezin should have remained ignorant of all this; but, on the other hand, it was not the kind of history that successive generations would have been anxious to keep alive, or to repeat to their children. Therefore I am inclined to think he still knows nothing about it.

"The whole adventure seems to have been a very vivid revival of the memories of an earlier life, caused by coming directly into contact with the living forces still intense enough to hang about the place, and, by a most singular chance, too, with the very souls who had taken part with him in the events of that particular life. For the mother and daughter who impressed him so strangely must have been leading actors, with himself, in the scenes and practices of witchcraft which at that period dominated the imaginations of the whole country.

"One has only to read the histories of the times to know that these witches claimed the power of transforming themselves into various animals, both for the purposes of disguise and also to convey themselves swiftly to the scenes of their imaginary orgies. Lycanthropy, or the power to change themselves into wolves, was everywhere believed in, and the ability to transform themselves into cats by rubbing their bodies with a special salve or ointment provided by Satan himself, found equal credence. The witchcraft trials abound in evidences of such universal beliefs."

Dr. Silence quoted chapter and verse from many writers on the subject, and showed how every detail of Vezin's adventure had a basis in the practices of those dark days.

"But that the entire affair took place subjectively in the man's own consciousness, I have no doubt," he went on, in reply to my questions; "for my secretary who has been to the town to investigate, discovered his signature in the visitors' book, and proved by it that he had arrived on September 8th, and left suddenly without paying his bill. He left two days later, and they still were in possession of his dirty brown bag and some tourist clothes. I paid a few francs in settlement of his debt, and have sent his luggage on to him. The daughter was absent from home, but the proprietress, a large woman very much as he described her, told my secretary that he had seemed a very strange, absent-minded kind of gentleman, and after his disappearance she had feared for a long time that he had met with a violent end in the neighbouring forest where he used to roam about alone.

"I should like to have obtained a personal interview with the daughter so as to ascertain how much was subjective and how much actually took place with her as Vezin told it. For her dread of fire and the sight of burning must, of course, have been the intuitive memory of her former painful death at the stake, and have thus explained why he fancied more than once that he saw her through smoke and flame."

"And that mark on his skin, for instance?" I inquired.

"Merely the marks produced by hysterical brooding," he replied, "like the stigmata of the *religieuses,* and the bruises which appear on the bodies of hypnotised subjects who have been told to expect them. This is very common and easily explained. Only it seems curious that these marks should have remained so long in Vezin's case. Usually they disappear quickly."

"Obviously he is still thinking about it all, brooding, and living it all over again," I ventured.

"Probably. And this makes me fear that the end of his trouble is not yet. We shall hear of him again. It is a case, alas! I can do little to alleviate."

Dr. Silence spoke gravely and with sadness in his voice.

"And what do you make of the Frenchman in the train?" I asked further—"the man who warned him against the place, *à cause du sommeil et à cause des chats?* Surely a very singular incident?"

"A very singular incident indeed," he made answer slowly, "and one I can only explain on the basis of a highly improbable coincidence——"

"Namely?"

"That the man was one who had himself stayed in the town and undergone there a similar experience. I should like to find this man and ask him. But the crystal is useless here, for I have no slightest clue to go upon, and I can only conclude that some singular psychic affinity, some force still active in his being out of the same past life, drew him thus to the personality of Vezin, and enabled him to fear what might happen to him, and thus to warn him as he did.

"Yes," he presently continued, half talking to himself, "I suspect in this case that Vezin was swept into the vortex of forces arising out of the intense activities of a past life, and that he lived over again a scene in which he had often played a leading part centuries before. For strong actions set up forces that are so slow to exhaust themselves, they may be said in a sense never to die. In this case they were not vital enough to render the illusion complete, so that the little man found himself caught in a very distressing confusion of the present and the past; yet he was sufficiently sensitive to recognise that it was true, and to fight against the degradation of returning, even in memory, to a former and lower state of development.

"Ah yes!" he continued, crossing the floor to gaze at the darkening sky, and seemingly quite oblivious of my presence, "subliminal up-rushes of memory like this can be exceedingly painful, and sometimes exceedingly dangerous. I only trust that this gentle soul may soon escape from this obsession of a passionate and tempestuous past. But I doubt it, I doubt it."

His voice was hushed with sadness as he spoke, and when he turned back into the room again there was an expression of profound yearning upon his face, the yearning of a soul whose desire to help is sometimes greater than his power.

THE NEMESIS OF FIRE

I

By some means which I never could fathom, John Silence always contrived to keep the compartment to himself, and as the train had a clear run of two hours before the first stop, there was ample time to go over the preliminary facts of the case. He had telephoned to me that very morning, and even through the disguise of the miles of wire the thrill of incalculable adventure had sounded in his voice.

"As if it were an ordinary country visit," he called, in reply to my question; "and don't forgot to bring your gun."

"With blank cartridges, I suppose?" for I knew his rigid principles with regard to the taking of life, and guessed that the guns were merely for some obvious purpose of disguise.

Then he thanked me for coming, mentioned the train, snapped down the receiver, and left me, vibrating with the excitement of anticipation, to do my packing. For the honour of accompanying Dr. John Silence on one of his big cases was what many would have considered an empty honour—and risky. Certainly the adventure held all manner of possibilities, and I arrived at Waterloo with the feelings of a man who is about to embark on some dangerous and peculiar mission in which the dangers he expects to run will not be the ordinary dangers to life and limb, but of some secret character difficult to name and still more difficult to cope with.

"The Manor House has a high sound," he told me, as we sat with our feet up and talked, "but I believe it is little more than an overgrown farmhouse in the desolate heather country beyond D——, and its owner, Colonel Wragge, a retired soldier with a taste for books, lives there practically alone, I understand, with an elderly invalid sister. So you need not look forward to a lively visit, unless the case provides some excitement of its own."

"Which is likely?"

By way of reply he handed me a letter marked "Private." It was dated a week ago, and signed "Yours faithfully, Horace Wragge."

"He heard of me, you see, through Captain Anderson," the doctor explained modestly, as though his fame were not almost world-wide; "you remember that Indian obsession case——"

I read the letter. Why it should have been marked private was difficult to understand. It was very brief, direct, and to the point. It referred by way of introduction to Captain Anderson, and then stated quite simply that the writer needed help of a peculiar kind and asked for a personal interview—a morning interview, since it was impossible for him to be absent from the house at night. The letter was dignified even to the point of abruptness, and it is difficult to explain how it managed to convey to me the impression of a strong man, shaken and perplexed. Perhaps the restraint of the wording, and the mystery of the affair had something to do with it; and the reference to the Anderson case, the horror of which lay still vivid in my memory, may have touched the sense of something rather ominous and alarming. But, whatever the cause, there was no doubt that an impression of serious peril rose somehow out of that white paper with the few lines of firm writing, and the spirit of a deep uneasiness ran between the words and reached the mind without any visible form of expression.

"And when you saw him——?" I asked, returning the letter as the train rushed clattering noisily through Clapham Junction.

"I have not seen him," was the reply. "The man's mind was charged to the brim when he wrote that; full of vivid mental pictures. Notice the restraint of it. For the main character of his case psychometry could be depended upon, and the scrap of paper his hand has touched is sufficient to give to another mind—a sensitive and sympathetic mind—clear mental pictures of what is going on. I think I have a very sound general idea of his problem."

"So there may be excitement, after all?"

John Silence waited a moment before he replied.

"Something very serious is amiss there," he said gravely, at length. "Some one—not himself, I gather,—has been meddling with a rather dangerous kind of gunpowder. So—yes, there may be excitement, as you put it."

"And my duties?" I asked, with a decidedly growing interest. "Remember, I am your 'assistant.'"

"Behave like an intelligent confidential secretary. Observe everything, without seeming to. Say nothing—nothing that means anything. Be present at all interviews. I may ask a good deal of you, for if my impressions are correct this is——"

He broke off suddenly.

"But I won't tell you my impressions yet," he resumed after a moment's thought. "Just watch and listen as the case proceeds. Form your own impressions and cultivate your intuitions. We come as ordinary visitors, of course," he added, a twinkle showing for an instant in his eye; "hence, the guns."

Though disappointed not to hear more, I recognised the wisdom of his words and knew how valueless my impressions would be once the powerful suggestion of having heard his own lay behind them. I likewise reflected that intuition joined to a sense of humour was of more use to a man than double the quantity of mere "brains," as such.

Before putting the letter away, however, he handed it back, telling me to place it against my forehead for a few moments and then describe any pictures that came spontaneously into my mind.

"Don't deliberately look for anything. Just imagine you see the inside of the eyelid, and wait for pictures that rise against its dark screen."

I followed his instructions, making my mind as nearly blank as possible. But no visions came. I saw nothing but the lines of light that pass to and fro like the changes of a kaleidoscope across the blackness. A momentary sensation of warmth came and went curiously.

"You see—what?" he asked presently.

"Nothing," I was obliged to admit disappointedly; "nothing but the usual flashes of light one always sees. Only, perhaps, they are more vivid than usual."

He said nothing by way of comment or reply.

"And they group themselves now and then," I continued, with painful candour, for I longed to see the pictures he had spoken of, "group themselves into globes and round balls of fire, and the lines that flash about sometimes look like triangles and crosses—almost like geometrical figures. Nothing more."

I opened my eyes again, and gave him back the letter.

"It makes my head hot," I said, feeling somehow unworthy for not seeing anything of interest. But the look in his eyes arrested my attention at once.

"That sensation of heat is important," he said significantly.

"It was certainly real, and rather uncomfortable," I replied, hoping he would expand and explain. "There was a distinct feeling of warmth—internal warmth somewhere—oppressive in a sense."

"That is interesting," he remarked, putting the letter back in his pocket, and settling himself in the corner with newspapers and books. He vouchsafed nothing more, and I knew the uselessness of trying to make him talk. Following his example I settled likewise with magazines into my corner. But when I closed my eyes again to look for the flashing lights and the sensation of heat, I found nothing but the usual phantasmagoria of the day's events—faces, scenes, memories,—and in due course I fell asleep and then saw nothing at all of any kind.

When we left the train, after six hours' travelling, at a little wayside station standing without trees in a world of sand and heather, the late October shadows had already dropped their sombre veil upon the landscape, and the sun dipped almost out of sight behind the moorland hills. In a high dogcart, behind a fast horse, we were soon rattling across the undulating stretches of an open and bleak country, the keen air stinging our cheeks and the scents of pine and bracken strong about us. Bare hills were faintly visible against the horizon, and the coachman pointed to a bank of distant shadows on our left where he told us the sea lay. Occasional stone farmhouses, standing back from the road among straggling fir trees, and large black barns that seemed to shift past us with a movement of their own in the gloom, were the only signs of humanity and civilisation that we saw, until at the end of a bracing five miles the lights of the lodge gates flared before us and we plunged into a thick grove of pine trees that concealed the Manor House up to the moment of actual arrival.

Colonel Wragge himself met us in the hall. He was the typical army officer who had seen service, real service, and found himself in the process. He was tall and well built, broad in the shoulders, but lean as a greyhound, with grave eyes, rather stern, and a moustache turning grey. I judged him to be about sixty years of age, but his movements showed a suppleness of strength and agility that contradicted the years. The face was full of character and resolution, the face of a man to be depended upon, and the straight grey eyes, it seemed to me, wore a veil of perplexed anxiety that he made no attempt to disguise. The whole appearance of the man at once clothed the adventure with gravity and importance. A matter that gave such a man cause for serious alarm, I felt, must be something real and of genuine moment.

His speech and manner, as he welcomed us, were like his letter, simple and sincere. He had a nature as direct and undeviating as a bullet. Thus, he showed plainly his surprise that Dr. Silence had not come alone.

"My confidential secretary, Mr. Hubbard," the doctor said, introducing me, and the steady gaze and powerful shake of the hand I then received were well calculated, I remember thinking, to drive home the impression that here was a man who was not to be trifled with, and whose perplexity must spring from some very real and tangible cause. And, quite obviously, he was relieved that we had come. His welcome was unmistakably genuine.

He led us at once into a room, half library, half smoking-room, that opened out of the low-ceilinged hall. The Manor House gave the impression of a rambling and glorified farmhouse, solid, ancient, comfortable, and wholly unpretentious. And so it was. Only the heat of the place struck me as unnatural. This room with the blazing fire may have seemed uncomfortably warm after the long drive through the night air; yet it seemed to me that the hall itself, and the whole atmosphere of the house, breathed a warmth that hardly belonged to well-filled grates or the pipes of hot air and water. It was not the heat of the greenhouse; it was an oppressive heat that somehow got into the head and mind. It stirred a curious sense of uneasiness in me, and I caught myself thinking of the sensation of warmth that had emanated from the letter in the train.

I heard him thanking Dr. Silence for having come; there was no preamble, and the exchange of civilities was of the briefest description. Evidently here was a man who, like my companion, loved action rather than talk. His manner was straightforward and direct. I saw him in a flash: puzzled, worried, harassed into a state of alarm by something he could not comprehend; forced to deal with things he would have preferred to despise, yet facing it all with dogged seriousness and making no attempt to conceal that he felt secretly ashamed of his incompetence.

"So I cannot offer you much entertainment beyond that of my own company, and the queer business that has been going on here, and is still going on," he said, with a slight inclination of the head towards me by way of including me in his confidence.

"I think, Colonel Wragge," replied John Silence impressively, "that we shall none of us find the time hangs heavy. I gather we shall have our hands full."

The two men looked at one another for the space of some seconds, and there was an indefinable quality in their silence which for the first time made me admit a swift question into my mind; and I wondered a little at my rashness in coming with so little reflection into a big case of this incalculable doctor. But no answer suggested itself, and to withdraw was, of course, inconceivable. The gates had closed behind me now, and the spirit of the adventure was already besieging my mind with its advance guard of a thousand little hopes and fears.

Explaining that he would wait till after dinner to discuss anything serious, as no reference was ever made before his sister, he led the way upstairs and showed us personally to our rooms; and it was just as I was finishing dressing that a knock came at my door and Dr. Silence entered.

He was always what is called a serious man, so that even in moments of comedy you felt he never lost sight of the profound gravity of life, but as he came across the room to me I caught the expression of his face and understood in a flash that he was now in his most grave and earnest mood. He looked almost troubled. I stopped fumbling with my black tie and stared.

"It *is* serious," he said, speaking in a low voice, "more so even than I imagined. Colonel Wragge's control over his thoughts concealed a great deal in my psychometrising of the letter. I looked in to warn you to keep yourself well in hand—generally speaking."

"Haunted house?" I asked, conscious of a distinct shiver down my back.

But he smiled gravely at the question.

"Haunted House of Life more likely," he replied, and a look came into his eyes which I had only seen there when a human soul was in the toils and he was thick in the fight of rescue. He was stirred in the deeps.

"Colonel Wragge—or the sister?" I asked hurriedly, for the gong was sounding.

"Neither directly," he said from the door. "Something far older, something very, very remote indeed. This thing has to do with the ages, unless I am mistaken greatly, the ages on which the mists of memory have long lain undisturbed."

He came across the floor very quickly with a finger on his lips, looking at me with a peculiar searchingness of gaze.

"Are you aware yet of anything—odd here?" he asked in a whisper. "Anything you cannot quite define, for instance. Tell me, Hubbard, for I want to know all your impressions. They may help me."

I shook my head, avoiding his gaze, for there was something in the eyes that scared me a little. But he was so in earnest that I set my mind keenly searching.

"Nothing yet," I replied truthfully, wishing I could confess to a real emotion; "nothing but the strange heat of the place."

He gave a little jump forward in my direction.

"The heat again, that's it!" he exclaimed, as though glad of my corroboration. "And how would you describe it, perhaps?" he asked quickly, with a hand on the door knob.

"It doesn't seem like ordinary physical heat," I said, casting about in my thoughts for a definition.

"More a mental heat," he interrupted, "a glowing of thought and desire, a sort of feverish warmth of the spirit. Isn't that it?"

I admitted that he had exactly described my sensations.

"Good!" he said, as he opened the door, and with an indescribable gesture that combined a warning to be ready with a sign of praise for my correct intuition, he was gone.

I hurried after him, and found the two men waiting for me in front of the fire.

"I ought to warn you," our host was saying as I came in, "that my sister, whom you will meet at dinner, is not aware of the real object of your visit. She is under the impression that we are interested in the same line of study—folklore—and that your researches have led to my seeking acquaintance. She comes to dinner in her chair, you know. It will be a great pleasure to her to meet you both. We have few visitors."

So that on entering the dining-room we were prepared to find Miss Wragge already at her place, seated in a sort of bath-chair. She was a vivacious and charming old lady, with smiling expression and bright eyes, and she chatted all through dinner with unfailing spontaneity. She had that face, unlined and fresh, that some people carry through life from the cradle to the grave; her smooth plump cheeks were all pink and white, and her hair, still dark, was divided into two glossy and sleek halves on either side of a careful parting. She wore gold-rimmed glasses, and at her throat was a large scarab of green jasper that made a very handsome brooch.

Her brother and Dr. Silence talked little, so that most of the conversation was carried on between herself and me, and she told me a great deal about the history of the old house, most of which I fear I listened to with but half an ear.

"And when Cromwell stayed here," she babbled on, "he occupied the very rooms upstairs that used to be mine. But my brother thinks it safer for me to sleep on the ground floor now in case of fire."

And this sentence has stayed in my memory only because of the sudden way her brother interrupted her and instantly led the conversation on to another topic. The passing reference to fire seemed to have disturbed him, and thenceforward he directed the talk himself.

It was difficult to believe that this lively and animated old lady, sitting beside me and taking so eager an interest in the affairs of life, was practically, we understood, without the use of her lower limbs, and that her whole existence for years had been passed between the sofa, the bed, and the bath-chair in which she chatted so naturally at the dinner-table. She made no allusion to her affliction until the dessert was reached, and then, touching a bell, she made us a witty little speech about leaving us "like time, on noiseless feet," and was wheeled out of the room by the butler and carried off to her apartments at the other end of the house.

And the rest of us were not long in following suit, for Dr. Silence and myself were quite as eager to learn the nature of our errand as our host was to impart it to us. He led us down a long flagged passage to a room at the very end of the house, a room provided with double doors, and windows, I saw, heavily shuttered. Books lined the walls on every side, and a large desk in the bow window was piled up with volumes, some open, some shut, some showing scraps of paper stuck between the leaves, and all smothered in a general cataract of untidy foolscap and loose-half sheets.

"My study and workroom," explained Colonel Wragge, with a delightful touch of innocent pride, as though he were a very serious scholar. He placed arm-chairs for us round the fire. "Here," he added significantly, "we shall be safe from interruption and can talk securely."

During dinner the manner of the doctor had been all that was natural and spontaneous, though it was impossible for me, knowing him as I did, not to be aware that he was subconsciously very keenly alert and already receiving upon the ultra-sensitive surface of his mind various and vivid impressions; and there was now something in the gravity of his face, as well as in the significant tone of Colonel Wragge's speech, and something, too, in the fact that we three were shut away in this private chamber about to listen to things probably strange, and certainly mysterious—something in all this that touched my imagination sharply and sent an undeniable thrill along my nerves. Taking the chair indicated by my host, I lit my cigar and waited for the opening of the attack, fully conscious that we were now too far gone in the adventure to admit of withdrawal, and wondering a little anxiously where it was going to lead.

What I expected precisely, it is hard to say. Nothing definite, perhaps. Only the sudden change was dramatic. A few hours before the prosaic atmosphere of Piccadilly was about me, and now I was sitting in a secret chamber of this remote old building waiting to hear an account of things that held possibly the genuine heart of terror. I thought of the dreary moors and hills outside, and the dark pine copses soughing in the wind of night; I remembered my companion's singular words up in my bedroom before dinner; and then I turned and noted carefully the stern countenance of the Colonel as he faced us and lit his big black cigar before speaking.

The threshold of an adventure, I reflected as I waited for the first words, is always the most thrilling moment—until the climax comes.

But Colonel Wragge hesitated—mentally—a long time before he began. He talked briefly of our journey, the weather, the country, and other comparatively trivial topics, while he sought about in his mind for an appropriate entry into the subject that was uppermost in the thoughts of all of us. The fact was he found it a difficult matter to speak of at all, and it was Dr. Silence who finally showed him the way over the hedge.

"Mr. Hubbard will take a few notes when you are ready—you won't object," he suggested; "I can give my undivided attention in this way."

"By all means," turning to reach some of the loose sheets on the writing table, and glancing at me. He still hesitated a little, I thought. "The fact is," he said apologetically, "I wondered if it was quite fair to trouble you so soon. The daylight might suit you better to hear what I have to tell. Your sleep, I mean, might be less disturbed, perhaps."

"I appreciate your thoughtfulness," John Silence replied with his gentle smile, taking command as it were from that moment, "but really we are both quite immune. There is nothing, I think, that could prevent either of us sleeping, except—an outbreak of fire, or some such very physical disturbance."

Colonel Wragge raised his eyes and looked fixedly at him. This reference to an outbreak of fire I felt sure was made with a purpose. It certainly had the desired effect of removing from our host's manner the last signs of hesitancy.

"Forgive me," he said. "Of course, I know nothing of your methods in matters of this kind—so, perhaps, you would like me to begin at once and give you an outline of the situation?"

Dr. Silence bowed his agreement. "I can then take my precautions accordingly," he added calmly.

The soldier looked up for a moment as though he did not quite gather the meaning of these words; but he made no further comment and turned at once to tackle a subject on which he evidently talked with diffidence and unwillingness.

"It's all so utterly out of my line of things," he began, puffing out clouds of cigar smoke between his words, "and there's so little to tell with any real evidence behind it, that it's almost impossible to make a consecutive story for you. It's the total cumulative effect that is so—so disquieting." He chose his words with care, as though determined not to travel one hair's breadth beyond the truth.

"I came into this place twenty years ago when my elder brother died," he continued, "but could not afford to live here then. My sister, whom you met at dinner, kept house for him till the end, and during all these years, while I was seeing service abroad, she had an eye to the place—for we never got a satisfactory tenant—and saw that it was not allowed to go to ruin. I myself took possession, however, only a year ago.

"My brother," he went on, after a perceptible pause, "spent much of his time away, too. He was a great traveller, and filled the house with stuff he brought home from all over the world. The laundry—a small detached building beyond the servants' quarters—he turned into a regular little museum. The curios and things I have cleared away—they collected dust and were always getting broken—but the laundry-house you shall see tomorrow."

Colonel Wragge spoke with such deliberation and with so many pauses that this beginning took him a long time. But at this point he came to a full stop altogether. Evidently there was something he wished to say that cost him considerable effort. At length he looked up steadily into my companion's face.

"May I ask you—that is, if you won't think it strange," he said, and a sort of hush came over his voice and manner, "whether you have noticed anything at all unusual—anything queer, since you came into the house?"

Dr. Silence answered without a moment's hesitation.

"I have," he said. "There is a curious sensation of heat in the place."

"Ah!" exclaimed the other, with a slight start. "You *have* noticed it. This unaccountable heat——"

"But its cause, I gather, is not in the house itself—but outside," I was astonished to hear the doctor add.

Colonel Wragge rose from his chair and turned to unhook a framed map that hung upon the wall. I got the impression that the movement was made with the deliberate purpose of concealing his face.

"Your diagnosis, I believe, is amazingly accurate," he said after a moment, turning round with the map in his hands. "Though, of course, I can have no idea how you should guess——"

John Silence shrugged his shoulders expressively. "Merely my impression," he said. "If you pay attention to impressions, and do not allow them to be confused by deductions of the intellect, you will often find them surprisingly, uncannily, accurate."

Colonel Wragge resumed his seat and laid the map upon his knees. His face was very thoughtful as he plunged abruptly again into his story.

"On coming into possession," he said, looking us alternately in the face, "I found a crop of stories of the most extraordinary and impossible kind I had ever heard—stories which at first I treated with amused indifference, but later was forced to regard seriously, if only to keep my servants. These stories I thought I traced to the fact of my brother's death—and, in a way, I think so still."

He leant forward and handed the map to Dr. Silence.

"It's an old plan of the estate," he explained, "but accurate enough for our purpose, and I wish you would note the position of the plantations marked upon it, especially those near the house. That one," indicating the spot with his finger, "is called the Twelve Acre Plantation. It was just there, on the side nearest the house, that my brother and the head keeper met their deaths."

He spoke as a man forced to recognise facts that he deplored, and would have preferred to leave untouched—things he personally would rather have treated with ridicule if possible. It made his words peculiarly dignified and impressive, and I listened with an increasing uneasiness as to the sort of help the doctor would look to me for later. It seemed as though I were a spectator of some drama of mystery in which any moment I might be summoned to play a part.

"It was twenty years ago," continued the Colonel, "but there was much talk about it at the time, unfortunately, and you may, perhaps, have heard of the affair. Stride, the keeper, was a passionate, hot-tempered man but I regret to say, so was my brother, and quarrels between them seem to have been frequent."

"I do not recall the affair," said the doctor. "May I ask what was the cause of death?" Something in his voice made me prick up my ears for the reply.

"The keeper, it was said, from suffocation. And at the inquest the doctors averred that both men had been dead the same length of time when found."

"And your brother?" asked John Silence, noticing the omission, and listening intently.

"Equally mysterious," said our host, speaking in a low voice with effort. "But there was one distressing feature I think I ought to mention. For those who saw the face—I did not see it myself—and though Stride carried a gun its chambers were undischarged——" He stammered and hesitated with confusion. Again that sense of terror moved between his words. He stuck.

"Yes," said the chief listener sympathetically.

"My brother's face, they said, looked as though it had been scorched. It had been swept, as it were, by something that burned—blasted. It was, I am told, quite dreadful. The bodies were found lying side by side, faces downwards, both pointing away from the wood, as though they had been in the act of running, and not more than a dozen yards from its edge."

Dr. Silence made no comment. He appeared to be studying the map attentively.

"I did not see the face myself," repeated the other, his manner somehow expressing the sense of awe he contrived to keep out of his voice, "but my sister unfortunately did, and her present state I believe to be entirely due to the shock it gave to her nerves. She never can be brought to refer to it, naturally, and I am even inclined to think that the memory has mercifully been permitted to vanish from her mind. But she spoke of it at the time as a face swept by flame—blasted."

John Silence looked up from his contemplation of the map, but with the air of one who wished to listen, not to speak, and presently Colonel Wragge went on with his account. He stood on the mat, his broad shoulders hiding most of the mantelpiece.

"They all centred about this particular plantation, these stories. That was to be expected, for the people here are as superstitious as Irish peasantry, and though I made one or two examples among them to stop the foolish talk, it had no effect, and new versions came to my ears every week. You may imagine how little good dismissals did, when I tell you that the servants dismissed themselves. It was not the house servants, but the men who worked on the estate outside. The keepers gave notice one after another, none of them with any reason I could accept; the foresters refused to enter the wood, and the beaters to beat in it. Word flew all over the countryside that Twelve Acre Plantation was a place to be avoided, day or night.

"There came a point," the Colonel went on, now well in his swing, "when I felt compelled to make investigations on my own account. I could not kill the thing by ignoring it; so I collected and analysed the stories at first hand. For this Twelve Acre Wood, you will see by the map, comes rather near home. Its lower end, if you will look, almost touches the end of the back lawn, as I will show you tomorrow, and its dense growth of pines forms the chief protection the house enjoys from the east winds that blow up from the sea. And in olden days, before my brother interfered with it and frightened all the game away, it was one of the best pheasant coverts on the whole estate."

"And what form, if I may ask, did this interference take?" asked Dr. Silence.

"In detail, I cannot tell you, for I do not know—except that I understand it was the subject of his frequent differences with the head keeper; but during the last two years of his life, when he gave up travelling and settled down here, he took a special interest in this wood, and for some unaccountable reason began to build a low stone wall around it. This wall was never finished, but you shall see the ruins tomorrow in the daylight."

"And the result of your investigations—these stories, I mean?" the doctor broke in, anxious to keep him to the main issues.

"Yes, I'm coming to that," he said slowly, "but the wood first, for this wood out of which they grew like mushrooms has nothing in any way peculiar about it. It is very thickly grown, and rises to a clearer part in the centre, a sort of mound where there is a circle of large boulders— old Druid stones, I'm told. At another place there's a small pond. There's nothing distinctive about it that I could mention—just an ordinary pine-wood, a very ordinary pine-wood—only the trees are a bit twisted in the trunks, some of 'em, and very dense. Nothing more.

"And the stories? Well, none of them had anything to do with my poor brother, or the keeper, as you might have expected; and they were all odd—such odd things, I mean, to invent or imagine. I never could make out how these people got such notions into their heads."

He paused a moment to relight his cigar.

"There's no regular path through it," he resumed, puffing vigorously, "but the fields round it are constantly used, and one of the gardeners whose cottage lies over that way declared he often saw moving lights in it at night, and luminous shapes like globes of fire over the tops of the trees, skimming and floating, and making a soft hissing sound—most of 'em said that, in fact—and another man saw shapes flitting in and out among the trees, things that were neither men nor animals, and all faintly luminous. No one ever pretended to see human forms—always queer, huge things they could not properly describe. Sometimes the whole wood was lit up, and one fellow—he's still here and you shall see him—has a most circumstantial yarn about having seen great stars lying on the ground round the edge of the wood at regular intervals——"

"What kind of stars?" put in John Silence sharply, in a sudden way that made me start.

"Oh, I don't know quite; ordinary stars, I think he said, only very large, and apparently blazing as though the ground was alight. He was too terrified to go close and examine, and he has never seen them since."

He stooped and stirred the fire into a welcome blaze—welcome for its blaze of light rather than for its heat. In the room there was already a strange pervading sensation of warmth that was oppressive in its effect and far from comforting.

"Of course," he went on, straightening up again on the mat, "this was all commonplace enough—this seeing lights and figures at night. Most of these fellows drink, and imagination and terror between them may account for almost anything. But others saw things in broad daylight. One of the woodmen, a sober, respectable man, took the shortcut home to his midday meal, and swore he was followed the whole length of the wood by something that never showed itself, but dodged from tree to tree, always keeping out of sight, yet solid enough to make the branches sway and the twigs snap on the ground. And it made a noise, he declared—but really"—the speaker stopped and gave a short laugh—"it's too absurd——"

"*Please!*" insisted the doctor; "for it is these small details that give me the best clues always."

"——it made a crackling noise, he said, like a bonfire. Those were his very words: like the crackling of a bonfire," finished the soldier, with a repetition of his short laugh.

"Most interesting," Dr. Silence observed gravely. "Please omit nothing."

"Yes," he went on, "and it was soon after that the fires began—the fires in the wood. They started mysteriously burning in the patches of coarse white grass that cover the more open parts of the plantation. No one ever actually saw them start, but many, myself among the number, have seen them burning and smouldering. They are always small and circular in shape, and for all the world like a picnic fire. The head keeper has a dozen explanations, from sparks flying out of the house chimneys to the sunlight focusing through a dewdrop, but none of them, I must admit, convince me as being in the least likely or probable. They are most singular, I consider, most singular, these mysterious fires, and I am glad to say that they come only at rather long intervals and never seem to spread.

"But the keeper had other queer stories as well, and about things that are verifiable. He declared that no life ever willingly entered the plantation; more, that no life existed in it at all. No birds nested in the trees, or flew into their shade. He set countless traps, but never caught so much as a rabbit or a weasel. Animals avoided it, and more than once he had picked up dead creatures round the edges that bore no obvious signs of how they had met their death.

"Moreover, he told me one extraordinary tale about his retriever chasing some invisible creature across the field one day when he was out with his gun. The dog suddenly pointed at something in the field at his feet, and then gave chase, yelping like a mad thing. It followed its imaginary quarry to the borders of the wood, and then went in—a thing he had never known it to do before. The moment it crossed the edge—it is darkish in there even in daylight—it began fighting in the most frenzied and terrific fashion. It made him afraid to interfere, he said. And at last, when the dog came out, hanging its tail down and panting, he found something like white hair stuck to its jaws, and brought it to show me. I tell you these details because——"

"They are important, believe me," the doctor stopped him. "And you have it still, this hair?" he asked.

"It disappeared in the oddest way," the Colonel explained. "It was curious looking stuff, something like asbestos, and I sent it to be analysed by the local chemist. But either the man got wind of its origin, or else he didn't like the look of it for some reason, because he returned it to me and said it was neither animal, vegetable, nor mineral, so far as he could make out, and he didn't wish to have anything to do with it. I put it away in paper, but a week later, on opening the package—it was gone! Oh, the stories are simply endless. I could tell you hundreds all on the same lines."

"And personal experiences of your own, Colonel Wragge?" asked John Silence earnestly, his manner showing the greatest possible interest and sympathy.

The soldier gave an almost imperceptible start. He looked distinctly uncomfortable.

"Nothing, I think," he said slowly, "nothing—er—I should like to rely on. I mean nothing I have the right to speak of, perhaps—yet."

His mouth closed with a snap. Dr. Silence, after waiting a little to see if he would add to his reply, did not seek to press him on the point.

"Well," he resumed presently, and as though he would speak contemptuously, yet dared not, "this sort of thing has gone on at intervals ever since. It spreads like wildfire, of course, mysterious chatter of this kind, and people began trespassing all over the estate, coming to see the wood, and making themselves a general nuisance. Notices of man-traps and spring-guns only seemed to increase their persistence; and—think of it," he snorted, "some local Research Society actually wrote and asked permission for one of their members to spend a night in the wood! Bolder fools, who didn't write for leave, came and took away bits of bark from the trees and gave them to clairvoyants, who invented in their turn a further batch of tales. There was simply no end to it all."

"Most distressing and annoying, I can well believe," interposed the doctor.

"Then suddenly, the phenomena ceased as mysteriously as they had begun, and the interest flagged. The tales stopped. People got interested in something else. It all seemed to die out. This was last July. I can tell you exactly, for I've kept a diary more or less of what happened."

"Ah!"

"But now, quite recently, within the past three weeks, it has all revived again with a rush—with a kind of furious attack, so to speak. It has really become unbearable. You may imagine what it means, and the general state of affairs, when I say that the possibility of leaving has occurred to me."

"Incendiarism?" suggested Dr. Silence, half under his breath, but not so low that Colonel Wragge did not hear him.

"By Jove, sir, you take the very words out of my mouth!" exclaimed the astonished man, glancing from the doctor to me and from me to the doctor, and rattling the money in his pocket as though some explanation of my friend's divining powers were to be found that way.

"It's only that you are thinking very vividly," the doctor said quietly, "and your thoughts form pictures in my mind before you utter them. It's merely a little elementary thought-reading."

His intention, I saw, was not to perplex the good man, but to impress him with his powers so as to ensure obedience later.

"Good Lord! I had no idea——" He did not finish the sentence, and dived again abruptly into his narrative.

"I did not see anything myself, I must admit, but the stories of independent eye-witnesses were to the effect that lines of light, like streams of thin fire, moved through the wood and sometimes were seen to shoot out precisely as flames might shoot out—in the direction of this house. There," he explained, in a louder voice that made me jump, pointing with a thick finger to the map, "where the westerly fringe of the plantation comes up to the end of the lower lawn at the back of the house—where it links on to those dark patches, which are laurel shrubberies, running right up to the back premises—that's where these lights were seen. They passed from the wood to the shrubberies, and in this way reached the house itself. Like silent rockets, one man described them, rapid as lightning and exceedingly bright."

"And this evidence you spoke of?"

"They actually reached the sides of the house. They've left a mark of scorching on the walls—the walls of the laundry building at the other end. You shall see 'em tomorrow." He pointed to the map to indicate the spot, and then straightened himself and glared about the room as though he had said something no one could believe and expected contradiction.

"Scorched—just as the faces were," the doctor murmured, looking significantly at me.

"Scorched—yes," repeated the Colonel, failing to catch the rest of the sentence in his excitement.

There was a prolonged silence in the room, in which I heard the gurgling of the oil in the lamp and the click of the coals and the heavy breathing of our host. The most unwelcome sensations were creeping about my spine, and I wondered whether my companion would scorn me utterly if I asked to sleep on the sofa in his room. It was eleven o'clock, I saw by the clock on the mantelpiece. We had crossed the dividing line and were now well in the movement of the adventure. The fight between my interest and my dread became acute. But, even if turning back had been possible, I think the interest would have easily gained the day.

"I have enemies, of course," I heard the Colonel's rough voice break into the pause presently, "and have discharged a number of servants——"

"It's not that," put in John Silence briefly.

"You think not? In a sense I am glad, and yet—there are some things that can be met and dealt with——"

He left the sentence unfinished, and looked down at the floor with an expression of grim severity that betrayed a momentary glimpse of character. This fighting man loathed and abhorred the thought of an enemy he could not see and come to grips with. Presently he moved over and sat down in the chair between us. Something like a sigh escaped him. Dr. Silence said nothing.

"My sister, of course, is kept in ignorance, as far as possible, of all this," he said disconnectedly, and as if talking to himself. "But even if she knew she would find matter-of-fact explanations. I only wish I could. I'm sure they exist."

There came then an interval in the conversation that was very significant. It did not seem a real pause, or the silence real silence, for both men continued to think so rapidly and strongly that one almost imagined their thoughts clothed themselves in words in the air of the room. I was more than a little keyed up with the strange excitement of all I had heard, but what stimulated my nerves more than anything else was the obvious fact that the doctor was clearly upon the trail of discovery. In his mind at that moment, I believe, he had already solved the nature of this perplexing psychical problem. His face was like a mask, and he employed the absolute minimum of gesture and words. All his energies were directed inwards, and by those incalculable methods and processes he had mastered with such infinite patience and study, I felt sure he was already in touch with the forces behind these singular phenomena and laying his deep plans for bringing them into the open, and then effectively dealing with them.

Colonel Wragge meanwhile grew more and more fidgety. From time to time he turned towards my companion, as though about to speak, yet always changing his mind at the last moment. Once he went over and opened the door suddenly, apparently to see if any one were listening at the keyhole, for he disappeared a moment between the two doors, and I then heard him open the outer one. He stood there for some seconds and made a noise as though he were sniffing the air like a dog. Then he closed both doors cautiously and came back to the fireplace. A strange excitement seemed growing upon him. Evidently he was trying to make up his mind to say something that he found it difficult to say. And John Silence, as I rightly judged, was waiting patiently for him to choose his own opportunity and his own way of saying it. At last he turned and faced us, squaring his great shoulders, and stiffening perceptibly.

Dr. Silence looked up sympathetically.

"Your own experiences help me most," he observed quietly.

"The fact is," the Colonel said, speaking very low, "this past week there have been outbreaks of fire in the house itself. Three separate outbreaks—and all—in my sister's room."

"Yes," the doctor said, as if this was just what he had expected to hear.

"Utterly unaccountable—all of them," added the other, and then sat down. I began to understand something of the reason of his excitement. He was realising at last that the "natural" explanation he had held to all along was becoming impossible, and he hated it. It made him angry.

"Fortunately," he went on, "she was out each time and does not know. But I have made her sleep now in a room on the ground floor."

"A wise precaution," the doctor said simply. He asked one or two questions. The fires had started in the curtains—once by the window and once by the bed. The third time smoke had been discovered by the maid coming from the cupboard, and it was found that Miss Wragge's clothes hanging on the hooks were smouldering. The doctor listened attentively, but made no comment.

"And now can you tell me," he said presently, "what your own feeling about it is—your general impression?"

"It sounds foolish to say so," replied the soldier, after a moment's hesitation, "but I feel exactly as I have often felt on active service in my Indian campaigns: just as if the house and all in it were in a state of siege; as though a concealed enemy were encamped about us—in ambush somewhere." He uttered a soft nervous laugh. "As if the next sign of smoke would precipitate a panic—a dreadful panic."

The picture came before me of the night shadowing the house, and the twisted pine trees he had described crowding about it, concealing some powerful enemy; and, glancing at the resolute face and figure of the old soldier, forced at length to his confession, I understood something of all he had been through before he sought the assistance of John Silence.

"And tomorrow, unless I am mistaken, is full moon," said the doctor suddenly, watching the other's face for the effect of his apparently careless words.

Colonel Wragge gave an uncontrollable start, and his face for the first time showed unmistakable pallor.

"What in the world——?" he began, his lip quivering.

"Only that I am beginning to see light in this extraordinary affair," returned the other calmly, "and, if my theory is correct, each month when the moon is at the full should witness an increase in the activity of the phenomena."

"I don't see the connection," Colonel Wragge answered almost savagely, "but I am bound to say my diary bears you out." He wore the most puzzled expression I have ever seen upon an honest face, but he abhorred this additional corroboration of an explanation that perplexed him.

"I confess," he repeated, "I cannot see the connection."

"Why should you?" said the doctor, with his first laugh that evening. He got up and hung the map upon the wall again. "But I do—because these things are my special study—and let me add that I have yet to come across a problem that is not natural, and has not a natural explanation. It's merely a question of how much one knows—and admits."

Colonel Wragge eyed him with a new and curious respect in his face. But his feelings were soothed. Moreover, the doctor's laugh and change of manner came as a relief to all, and broke the spell of grave suspense that had held us so long. We all rose and stretched our limbs, and took little walks about the room.

"I am glad, Dr. Silence, if you will allow me to say so, that you are here," he said simply, "very glad indeed. And now I fear I have kept you both up very late," with a glance to include me, "for you must be tired, and ready for your beds. I have told you all there is to tell," he added, "and tomorrow you must feel perfectly free to take any steps you think necessary."

The end was abrupt, yet natural, for there was nothing more to say, and neither of these men talked for mere talking's sake.

Out in the cold and chilly hall he lit our candles and took us upstairs. The house was at rest and still, every one asleep. We moved softly. Through the windows on the stairs we saw the moonlight falling across the lawn, throwing deep shadows. The nearer pine trees were just visible in the distance, a wall of impenetrable blackness.

Our host came for a moment to our rooms to see that we had everything. He pointed to a coil of strong rope lying beside the window, fastened to the wall by means of an iron ring. Evidently it had been recently put in.

"I don't think we shall need it," Dr. Silence said, with a smile.

"I trust not," replied our host gravely. "I sleep quite close to you across the landing," he whispered, pointing to his door, "and if you—if you want anything in the night you will know where to find me."

He wished us pleasant dreams and disappeared down the passage into his room, shading the candle with his big muscular hand from the draughts.

John Silence stopped me a moment before I went.

"You know what it is?" I asked, with an excitement that even overcame my weariness.

"Yes," he said, "I'm almost sure. And you?"

"Not the smallest notion."

He looked disappointed, but not half as disappointed as I felt.

"Egypt," he whispered, "Egypt!"

II

Nothing happened to disturb me in the night—nothing, that is, except a nightmare in which Colonel Wragge chased me amid thin streaks of fire, and his sister always prevented my escape by suddenly rising up out of the ground in her chair—dead. The deep baying of dogs woke me once, just before the dawn, it must have been, for I saw the window frame against the sky; there was a flash of lightning, too, I thought, as I turned over in bed. And it was warm, for October oppressively warm.

It was after eleven o'clock when our host suggested going out with the guns, these, we understood, being a somewhat thin disguise for our true purpose. Personally, I was glad to be in the open air, for the atmosphere of the house was heavy with presentiment. The sense of impending disaster hung over all. Fear stalked the passages, and lurked in the corners of every room. It was a house haunted, but really haunted; not by some vague shadow of the dead, but by a definite though incalculable influence that was actively alive, and dangerous. At the least smell of smoke the entire household quivered. An odour of burning, I was convinced, would paralyse all the inmates. For the servants, though professedly ignorant by the master's unspoken orders, yet shared the common dread; and the hideous uncertainty, joined with this display of so spiteful and calculated a spirit of malignity, provided a kind of black doom that draped not only the walls, but also the minds of the people living within them.

Only the bright and cheerful vision of old Miss Wragge being pushed about the house in her noiseless chair, chatting and nodding briskly to every one she met, prevented us from giving way entirely to the depression which governed the majority. The sight of her was like a gleam of sunshine through the depths of some ill-omened wood, and just as we went out I saw her being wheeled along by her attendant into the sunshine of the back lawn, and caught her cheery smile as she turned her head and wished us good sport.

The morning was October at its best. Sunshine glistened on the dew-drenched grass and on leaves turned golden-red. The dainty messengers of coming hoar-frost were already in the air, a search for permanent winter quarters. From the wide moors that everywhere swept up against the sky, like a purple sea splashed by the occasional grey of rocky clefts, there stole down the cool and perfumed wind of the west. And the keen taste of the sea ran through all like a master-flavour, borne over the spaces perhaps by the seagulls that cried and circled high in the air.

But our host took little interest in this sparkling beauty, and had no thought of showing off the scenery of his property. His mind was otherwise intent, and, for that matter, so were our own.

"Those bleak moors and hills stretch unbroken for hours," he said, with a sweep of the hand; "and over there, some four miles," pointing in another direction, "lies S—— Bay, a long, swampy inlet of the sea, haunted by myriads of seabirds. On the other side of the house are the plantations and pine-woods. I thought we would get the dogs and go first to the Twelve Acre Wood I told you about last night. It's quite near."

We found the dogs in the stable, and I recalled the deep baying of the night when a fine bloodhound and two great Danes leaped out to greet us. Singular companions for guns, I thought to myself, as we struck out across the fields and the great creatures bounded and ran beside us, nose to ground.

The conversation was scanty. John Silence's grave face did not encourage talk. He wore the expression I knew well—that look of earnest solicitude which meant that his whole being was deeply absorbed and preoccupied. Frightened, I had never seen him, but anxious often—it always moved me to witness it—and he was anxious now.

"On the way back you shall see the laundry building," Colonel Wragge observed shortly, for he, too, found little to say. "We shall attract less attention then."

Yet not all the crisp beauty of the morning seemed able to dispel the feelings of uneasy dread that gathered increasingly about our minds as we went.

In a very few minutes a clump of pine trees concealed the house from view, and we found ourselves on the outskirts of a densely grown plantation of conifers. Colonel Wragge stopped abruptly, and, producing a map from his pocket, explained once more very briefly its position with regard to the house. He showed how it ran up almost to the

walls of the laundry building—though at the moment beyond our actual view—and pointed to the windows of his sister's bedroom where
the fires had been. The room, now empty, looked straight on to the
wood. Then, glancing nervously about him, and calling the dogs to
heel, he proposed that we should enter the plantation and make as
thorough examination of it as we thought worth while. The dogs, he
added, might perhaps be persuaded to accompany us a little way—and
he pointed to where they cowered at his feet—but he doubted it.
"Neither voice nor whip will get them very far, I'm afraid," he said. "I
know by experience."

"If you have no objection," replied Dr. Silence, with decision, and
speaking almost for the first time, "we will make our examination
alone—Mr. Hubbard and myself. It will be best so."

His tone was absolutely final, and the Colonel acquiesced so politely
that even a less intuitive man than myself must have seen that he was
genuinely relieved.

"You doubtless have good reasons," he said.

"Merely that I wish to obtain my impressions uncoloured. This delicate clue I am working on might be so easily blurred by the thought-
currents of another mind with strongly preconceived ideas."

"Perfectly. I understand," rejoined the soldier, though with an expression of countenance that plainly contradicted his words. "Then I
will wait here with the dogs; and we'll have a look at the laundry on our
way home."

I turned once to look back as we clambered over the low stone wall
built by the late owner, and saw his straight, soldierly figure standing in
the sunlit field watching us with a curiously intent look on his face.
There was something to me incongruous, yet distinctly pathetic, in the
man's efforts to meet all far-fetched explanations of the mystery with
contempt, and at the same time in his stolid, unswerving investigation
of it all. He nodded at me and made a gesture of farewell with his hand.
That picture of him, standing in the sunshine with his big dogs, steadily
watching us, remains with me to this day.

Dr. Silence led the way in among the twisted trunks, planted closely
together in serried ranks, and I followed sharp at his heels. The moment we were out of sight he turned and put down his gun against the
roots of a big tree, and I did likewise.

"We shall hardly want these cumbersome weapons of murder," he
observed, with a passing smile.

"You are sure of your clue, then?" I asked at once, bursting with curiosity, yet fearing to betray it lest he should think me unworthy. His
own methods were so absolutely simple and untheatrical.

"I am sure of my clue," he answered gravely. "And I think we have come just in time. You shall know in due course. For the present—be content to follow and observe. And think, steadily. The support of your mind will help me."

His voice had that quiet mastery in it which leads men to face death with a sort of happiness and pride. I would have followed him anywhere at that moment. At the same time his words conveyed a sense of dread seriousness. I caught the thrill of his confidence; but also, in this broad light of day, I felt the measure of alarm that lay behind.

"You still have no strong impressions?" he asked. "Nothing happened in the night, for instance? No vivid dreamings?"

He looked closely for my answer, I was aware.

"I slept almost an unbroken sleep. I was tremendously tired, you know, and, but for the oppressive heat——"

"Good! You still notice the heat, then," he said to himself, rather than expecting an answer. "And the lightning?" he added, "that lightning out of a clear sky—that flashing—did you notice *that?*"

I answered truly that I thought I had seen a flash during a moment of wakefulness, and he then drew my attention to certain facts before moving on.

"You remember the sensation of warmth when you put the letter to your forehead in the train; the heat generally in the house last evening, and, as you now mention, in the night. You heard, too, the Colonel's stories about the appearances of fire in this wood and in the house itself, and the way his brother and the gamekeeper came to their deaths twenty years ago."

I nodded, wondering what in the world it all meant.

"And you get no clue from these facts?" he asked, a trifle surprised.

I searched every corner of my mind and imagination for some inkling of his meaning, but was obliged to admit that I understood nothing so far.

"Never mind, you will later. And now," he added, "we will go over the wood and see what we can find."

His words explained to me something of his method. We were to keep our minds alert and report to each other the least fancy that crossed the picture-gallery of our thoughts. Then, just as we started, he turned again to me with a final warning.

"And, for your safety," he said earnestly, "imagine *now*—and for that matter, imagine always until we leave this place—imagine with the utmost keenness, that you are surrounded by a shell that protects you. Picture yourself inside a protective envelope, and build it up with the most intense imagination you can evoke. Pour the whole force of your thought and will into it. Believe vividly all through this adventure that such a shell, constructed of your thought, will and imagination, surrounds you completely, and that nothing can pierce it to attack."

He spoke with dramatic conviction, gazing hard at me as though to enforce his meaning, and then moved forward and began to pick his way over the rough, tussocky ground into the wood. And meanwhile, knowing the efficacy of his prescription, I adopted it to the best of my ability.

The trees at once closed about us like the night. Their branches met overhead in a continuous tangle, their stems crept closer and closer, the brambly undergrowth thickened and multiplied. We tore our trousers, scratched our hands, and our eyes filled with fine dust that made it most difficult to avoid the clinging, prickly network of branches and creepers. Coarse white grass that caught our feet like string grew here and there in patches. It crowned the lumps of peaty growth that stuck up like human heads, fantastically dressed, thrusting up at us out of the ground with crests of dead hair. We stumbled and floundered among them. It was hard going, and I could well conceive it impossible to find a way at all in the night-time. We jumped, when possible, from tussock to tussock, and it seemed as though we were springing among heads on a battlefield, and that this dead white grass concealed eyes that turned to stare as we passed.

Here and there the sunlight shot in with vivid spots of white light, dazzling the sight, but only making the surrounding gloom deeper by contrast. And on two occasions we passed dark circular places in the grass where fires had eaten their mark and left a ring of ashes. Dr. Silence pointed to them, but without comment and without pausing, and the sight of them woke in me a singular realisation of the dread that lay so far only just out of sight in this adventure.

It was exhausting work, and heavy going. We kept close together. The warmth, too, was extraordinary. Yet it did not seem the warmth of the body due to violent exertion, but rather an inner heat of the mind that laid glowing hands of fire upon the heart and set the brain in a kind of steady blaze. When my companion found himself too far in advance, he waited for me to come up. The place had evidently been untouched by hand of man, keeper, forester or sportsman, for many a year; and my thoughts, as we advanced painfully, were not unlike the state of the wood itself—dark, confused, full of a haunting wonder and the shadow of fear.

By this time all signs of the open field behind us were hid. No single gleam penetrated. We might have been groping in the heart of some primeval forest. Then, suddenly, the brambles and tussocks and stringlike grass came to an end; the trees opened out; and the ground began to slope upwards towards a large central mound. We had reached the middle of the plantation, and before us stood the broken Druid stones our host had mentioned. We walked easily up the little hill, between the sparser stems, and, resting upon one of the ivy-covered boulders, looked round upon a comparatively open space, as large, perhaps, as a small London Square.

Thinking of the ceremonies and sacrifices this rough circle of prehistoric monoliths might have witnessed, I looked up into my companion's face with an unspoken question. But he read my thought and shook his head.

"Our mystery has nothing to do with these dead symbols," he said, "but with something perhaps even more ancient, and of another country altogether."

"Egypt?" I said half under my breath, hopelessly puzzled, but recalling his words in my bedroom.

He nodded. Mentally I still floundered, but he seemed intensely preoccupied and it was no time for asking questions; so while his words circled unintelligibly in my mind I looked round at the scene before me, glad of the opportunity to recover breath and some measure of composure. But hardly had I time to notice the twisted and contorted shapes of many of the pine trees close at hand when Dr. Silence leaned over and touched me on the shoulder. He pointed down the slope. And the look I saw in his eyes keyed up every nerve in my body to its utmost pitch.

A thin, almost imperceptible column of blue smoke was rising among the trees some twenty yards away at the foot of the mound. It curled up and up, and disappeared from sight among the tangled branches overhead. It was scarcely thicker than the smoke from a small brand of burning wood.

"Protect yourself! Imagine your shell strongly," whispered the doctor sharply, "and follow me closely."

He rose at once and moved swiftly down the slope towards the smoke, and I followed, afraid to remain alone. I heard the soft crunching of our steps on the pine needles. Over his shoulder I watched the thin blue spiral, without once taking my eyes off it. I hardly know how to describe the peculiar sense of vague horror inspired in me by the sight of that streak of smoke pencilling its way upwards among the dark trees. And the sensation of increasing heat as we approached was phenomenal. It was like walking towards a glowing yet invisible fire.

As we drew nearer his pace slackened. Then he stopped and pointed, and I saw a small circle of burnt grass upon the ground. The tussocks were blackened and smouldering, and from the centre rose this line of smoke, pale, blue, steady. Then I noticed a movement of the atmosphere beside us, as if the warm air were rising and the cooler air rushing in to take its place: a little centre of wind in the stillness. Overhead the boughs stirred and trembled where the smoke disappeared. Otherwise, not a tree sighed, not a sound made itself heard. The wood was still as a graveyard. A horrible idea came to me that the course of nature was about to change without warning, *had* changed a little already, that the sky would drop, or the surface of the earth crash inwards like a broken bubble. Something, certainly, reached up to the citadel of my reason, causing its throne to shake.

John Silence moved forward again. I could not see his face, but his attitude was plainly one of resolution, of muscles and mind ready for vigorous action. We were within ten feet of the blackened circle when the smoke of a sudden ceased to rise, and vanished. The tail of the column disappeared in the air above, and at the same instant it seemed to me that the sensation of heat passed from my face, and the motion of the wind was gone. The calm spirit of the fresh October day resumed command.

Side by side we advanced and examined the place. The grass was smouldering, the ground still hot. The circle of burned earth was a foot to a foot and a half in diameter. It looked like an ordinary picnic fireplace. I bent down cautiously to look, but in a second I sprang back with an involuntary cry of alarm, for, as the doctor stamped on the ashes to prevent them spreading, a sound of hissing rose from the spot as though he had kicked a living creature. This hissing was faintly audible in the air. It moved past us, away towards the thicker portion of the wood in the direction of our field, and in a second Dr. Silence had left the fire and started in pursuit.

And then began the most extraordinary hunt of invisibility I can ever conceive.

He went fast even at the beginning, and, of course, it was perfectly obvious that he was following something. To judge by the poise of his head he kept his eyes steadily at a certain level—just above the height of a man—and the consequence was he stumbled a good deal over the roughness of the ground. The hissing sound had stopped. There was no sound of any kind, and what he saw to follow was utterly beyond me. I only know, that in mortal dread of being left behind, and with a biting curiosity to see whatever there was to be seen, I followed as quickly as I could, and even then barely succeeded in keeping up with him.

And, as we went, the whole mad jumble of the Colonel's stories ran through my brain, touching a sense of frightened laughter that was only held in check by the sight of this earnest, hurrying figure before me. For John Silence at work inspired me with a kind of awe. He looked so diminutive among these giant twisted trees, while yet I knew that his purpose and his knowledge were so great, and even in hurry he was dignified. The fancy that we were playing some queer, exaggerated game together met the fact that we were two men dancing upon the brink of some possible tragedy, and the mingling of the two emotions in my mind was both grotesque and terrifying.

He never turned in his mad chase, but pushed rapidly on, while I panted after him like a figure in some unreasoning nightmare. And, as I ran, it came upon me that he had been aware all the time, in his quiet, internal way, of many things that he had kept for his own secret consideration; he had been watching, waiting, planning from the very moment we entered the shade of the wood. By some inner, concentrated process of mind, dynamic if not actually magical, he had been in direct contact with the source of the whole adventure, the very essence of the real mystery. And now the forces were moving to a climax. Something was about to happen, something important, something possibly dreadful. Every nerve, every sense, every significant gesture of the plunging figure before me proclaimed the fact just as surely as the skies, the winds, and the face of the earth tell the birds the time to migrate and warn the animals that danger lurks and they must move.

In a few moments we reached the foot of the mound and entered the tangled undergrowth that lay between us and the sunlight of the field. Here the difficulties of fast travelling increased a hundredfold. There were brambles to dodge, low boughs to dive under, and countless tree trunks closing up to make a direct path impossible. Yet Dr. Silence never seemed to falter or hesitate. He went, diving, jumping, dodging, ducking, but ever in the same main direction, following a clean trail. Twice I tripped and fell, and both times, when I picked myself up again, I saw him ahead of me, still forcing a way like a dog after its quarry. And sometimes, like a dog, he stopped and pointed—human pointing it was, psychic pointing,—and each time he stopped to point I heard that faint high hissing in the air beyond us. The instinct of an infallible dowser possessed him, and he made no mistakes.

At length, abruptly, I caught up with him, and found that we stood at the edge of the shallow pond Colonel Wragge had mentioned in his account the night before. It was long and narrow, filled with dark brown water, in which the trees were dimly reflected. Not a ripple stirred its surface.

"Watch!" he cried out, as I came up. "It's going to cross. It's bound to betray itself. The water is its natural enemy, and we shall see the direction."

And, even as he spoke, a thin line like the track of a water-spider, shot swiftly across the shiny surface; there was a ghost of steam in the air above; and immediately I became aware of an odour of burning.

Dr. Silence turned and shot a glance at me that made me think of lightning. I began to shake all over.

"Quick!" he cried with excitement, "to the trail again! We must run around. It's going to the house!"

The alarm in his voice quite terrified me. Without a false step I dashed round the slippery banks and dived again at his heels into the sea of bushes and tree trunks. We were now in the thick of the very dense belt that ran around the outer edge of the plantation, and the field was near; yet so dark was the tangle that it was some time before the first shafts of white sunlight became visible. The doctor now ran in zigzags. He was following something that dodged and doubled quite wonderfully, yet had begun, I fancied, to move more slowly than before.

"Quick!" he cried. "In the light we shall lose it!"

I still saw nothing, heard nothing, caught no suggestion of a trail; yet this man, guided by some interior divining that seemed infallible, made no false turns, though how he failed to crash headlong into the trees has remained a mystery to me ever since. And then, with a sudden rush, we found ourselves on the skirts of the wood with the open field lying in bright sunshine before our eyes.

"Too late!" I heard him cry, a note of anguish in his voice. "It's out— and, by God, it's making for the house!"

I saw the Colonel standing in the field with his dogs where we had left him. He was bending double, peering into the wood where he heard us running, and he straightened up like a bent whip released. John Silence dashed passed, calling him to follow.

"We shall lose the trail in the light," I heard him cry as he ran. "But quick! We may yet get there in time!"

That wild rush across the open field, with the dogs at our heels, leaping and barking, and the elderly Colonel behind us running as though for his life, shall I ever forget it? Though I had only vague ideas of the meaning of it all, I put my best foot forward, and, being the youngest of the three, I reached the house an easy first. I drew up, panting, and turned to wait for the others. But, as I turned, something moving a little distance away caught my eye, and in that moment I swear I experienced the most overwhelming and singular shock of surprise and terror I have ever known, or can conceive as possible.

For the front door was open, and the waist of the house being narrow, I could see through the hall into the dining-room beyond, and so out on to the back lawn, and there I saw no less a sight than the figure of Miss Wragge—running. Even at that distance it was plain that she had seen me, and was coming fast towards me, running with the frantic gait of a terror-stricken woman. She had recovered the use of her legs.

Her face was a livid grey, as of death itself, but the general expression was one of laughter, for her mouth was gaping, and her eyes, always bright, shone with the light of a wild merriment that seemed the merriment of a child, yet was singularly ghastly. And that very second, as she fled past me into her brother's arms behind, I smelt again most unmistakably the odour of burning, and to this day the smell of smoke and fire can come very near to turning me sick with the memory of what I had seen.

Fast on her heels, too, came the terrified attendant, more mistress of herself, and able to speak—which the old lady could not do—but with a face almost, if not quite, as fearful.

"We were down by the bushes in the sun,"—she gasped and screamed in reply to Colonel Wragge's distracted questionings,— "I was wheeling the chair as usual when she shrieked and leaped—I don't know exactly—I was too frightened to see—Oh, my God! she jumped clean out of the chair—*and ran!* There was a blast of hot air from the wood, and she hid her face and jumped. She didn't make a sound— she didn't cry out, or make a sound. She just ran."

But the nightmare horror of it all reached the breaking point a few minutes later, and while I was still standing in the hall temporarily bereft of speech and movement; for while the doctor, the Colonel and the attendant were half-way up the staircase, helping the fainting woman to the privacy of her room, and all in a confused group of dark figures, there sounded a voice behind me, and I turned to see the butler, his face dripping with perspiration, his eyes starting out of his head.

"The laundry's on fire!" he cried; "the laundry building's a-caught!"

I remember his odd expression "a-caught," and wanting to laugh, but finding my face rigid and inflexible.

"The devil's about again, s'help me Gawd!" he cried, in a voice thin with terror, running about in circles.

And then the group on the stairs scattered as at the sound of a shot, and the Colonel and Dr. Silence came down three steps at a time, leaving the afflicted Miss Wragge to the care of her single attendant.

We were out across the front lawn in a moment and round the corner of the house, the Colonel leading, Silence and I at his heels, and the portly butler puffing some distance in the rear, getting more and more mixed in his addresses to God and the devil; and the moment we passed the stables and came into view of the laundry building, we saw a wicked-looking volume of smoke pouring out of the narrow windows, and the frightened women-servants and grooms running hither and thither, calling aloud as they ran.

The arrival of the master restored order instantly, and this retired soldier, poor thinker perhaps, but capable man of action, had the matter in hand from the start. He issued orders like a martinet, and, almost before I could realise it, there were streaming buckets on the scene and a line of men and women formed between the building and the stable pump.

"Inside," I heard John Silence cry, and the Colonel followed him through the door, while I was just quick enough at their heels to hear him add, "the smoke's the worst part of it. There's no fire yet, I think."

And, true enough, there was no fire. The interior was thick with smoke, but it speedily cleared and not a single bucket was used upon the floor or walls. The air was stifling, the heat fearful.

"There's precious little to burn in here; it's all stone," the Colonel exclaimed, coughing. But the doctor was pointing to the wooden covers of the great cauldron in which the clothes were washed, and we saw that these were smouldering and charred. And when we sprinkled half a bucket of water on them the surrounding bricks hissed and fizzed and sent up clouds of steam. Through the open door and windows this passed out with the rest of the smoke, and we three stood there on the brick floor staring at the spot and wondering, each in our own fashion, how in the name of natural law the place could have caught fire or smoked at all. And each was silent—myself from sheer incapacity and befuddlement, the Colonel from the quiet pluck that faces all things yet speaks little, and John Silence from the intense mental grappling with this latest manifestation of a profound problem that called for concentration of thought rather than for any words.

There was really nothing to say. The facts were indisputable.

Colonel Wragge was the first to utter.

"My sister," he said briefly, and moved off. In the yard I heard him sending the frightened servants about their business in an excellently matter-of-fact voice, scolding some one roundly for making such a big fire and letting the flues get over-heated, and paying no heed to the stammering reply that no fire had been lit there for several days. Then he dispatched a groom on horseback for the local doctor.

Then Dr. Silence turned and looked at me. The absolute control he possessed, not only over the outward expression of emotion by gesture, change of colour, light in the eyes, and so forth, but also, as I well knew, over its very birth in his heart, the masklike face of the dead he could assume at will, made it extremely difficult to know at any given moment what was at work in his inner consciousness. But now, when he turned and looked at me, there was no sphinx-expression there, but rather the keen triumphant face of a man who had solved a dangerous and complicated problem, and saw his way to a clean victory.

"*Now* do you guess?" he asked quietly, as though it were the simplest matter in the world, and ignorance were impossible.

I could only stare stupidly and remain silent. He glanced down at the charred cauldron-lids, and traced a figure in the air with his finger. But I was too excited, or too mortified, or still too dazed, perhaps, to see what it was he outlined, or what it was he meant to convey. I could only go on staring and shaking my puzzled head.

"A fire-elemental," he cried, "a fire-elemental of the most powerful and malignant kind——"

"A what?" thundered the voice of Colonel Wragge behind us, having returned suddenly and overheard.

"It's a fire-elemental," repeated Dr. Silence more calmly, but with a note of triumph in his voice he could not keep out, "and a fire-elemental enraged."

The light began to dawn in my mind at last. But the Colonel—who had never heard the term before, and was besides feeling considerably worked up for a plain man with all this mystery he knew not how to grapple with—the Colonel stood, with the most dumfoundered look ever seen on a human countenance, and continued to roar, and stammer, and stare.

"And why," he began, savage with the desire to find something visible he could fight—"why, in the name of all the blazes——?" and then stopped as John Silence moved up and took his arm.

"There, my dear Colonel Wragge," he said gently, "you touch the heart of the whole thing. You ask 'Why.' That is precisely our problem." He held the soldier's eyes firmly with his own. "And that, too, I think, we shall soon know. Come and let us talk over a plan of action—that room with the double doors, perhaps."

The word "action" calmed him a little, and he led the way, without further speech, back into the house, and down the long stone passage to the room where we had heard his stories on the night of our arrival. I understood from the doctor's glance that my presence would not make the interview easier for our host, and I went upstairs to my own room—shaking.

But in the solitude of my room the vivid memories of the last hour revived so mercilessly that I began to feel I should never in my whole life lose the dreadful picture of Miss Wragge running—that dreadful human climax after all the non-human mystery in the wood—and I was not sorry when a servant knocked at my door and said that Colonel Wragge would be glad if I would join them in the little smoking-room.

"I think it is better you should be present," was all Colonel Wragge said as I entered the room. I took the chair with my back to the window. There was still an hour before lunch, though I imagine that the usual divisions of the day hardly found a place in the thoughts of any one of us.

The atmosphere of the room was what I might call electric. The Colonel was positively bristling; he stood with his back to the fire, fingering an unlit black cigar, his face flushed, his being obviously roused and ready for action. He hated this mystery. It was poisonous to his nature, and he longed to meet something face to face—something he could gauge and fight. Dr. Silence, I noticed at once, was sitting before the map of the estate which was spread upon a table. I knew by his expression the state of his mind. He was in the thick of it all, knew it, delighted in it, and was working at high pressure. He recognised my presence with a lifted eyelid, and the flash of the eye, contrasted with his stillness and composure, told me volumes.

"I was about to explain to our host briefly what seems to me afoot in all this business," he said without looking up, "when he asked that you should join us so that we can all work together." And, while signifying my assent, I caught myself wondering what quality it was in the calm speech of this undemonstrative man that was so full of power, so charged with the strange, virile personality behind it and that seemed to inspire us with his own confidence as by a process of radiation.

"Mr. Hubbard," he went on gravely, turning to the soldier, "knows something of my methods, and in more than one—er—interesting situation has proved of assistance. What we want now"—and here he suddenly got up and took his place on the mat beside the Colonel, and looked hard at him—"is men who have self-control, who are sure of themselves, whose minds at the critical moment will emit positive forces, instead of the wavering and uncertain currents due to negative feelings—due, for instance, to fear."

He looked at us each in turn. Colonel Wragge moved his feet farther apart, and squared his shoulders; and I felt guilty but said nothing, conscious that my latent store of courage was being deliberately hauled to the front. He was winding me up like a clock.

"So that, in what is yet to come," continued our leader, "each of us will contribute his share of power, and ensure success for my plan."

"I'm not afraid of anything I can *see*," said the Colonel bluntly.

"I'm ready," I heard myself say, as it were automatically, "for anything," and then added, feeling the declaration was lamely insufficient, "and everything."

Dr. Silence left the mat and began walking to and fro about the room, both hands plunged deep into the pockets of his shooting-jacket. Tremendous vitality streamed from him. I never took my eyes off the small, moving figure; small yes,—and yet somehow making me think of a giant plotting the destruction of worlds. And his manner was gentle, as always, soothing almost, and his words uttered quietly without emphasis or emotion. Most of what he said was addressed, though not too obviously, to the Colonel.

"The violence of this sudden attack," he said softly, pacing to and fro beneath the bookcase at the end of the room, "is due, of course, partly to the fact that tonight the moon is at the full"—here he glanced at me for a moment—"and partly to the fact that we have all been so deliberately concentrating upon the matter. Our thinking, our investigation, has stirred it into unusual activity. I mean that the intelligent force behind these manifestations has realised that some one is busied about its destruction. And it is now on the defensive: more, it is aggressive."

"But 'it'—what is 'it'?" began the soldier, fuming. "What, in the name of all that's dreadful, *is* a fire-elemental?"

"I cannot give you at this moment," replied Dr. Silence, turning to him, but undisturbed by the interruption, "a lecture on the nature and history of magic, but can only say that an Elemental is the active force behind the elements,—whether earth, air, water, *or fire*,—it is impersonal in its essential nature, but can be focused, personified, ensouled, so to say, by those who know how—by magicians, if you will—for certain purposes of their own, much in the same way that steam and electricity can be harnessed by the practical man of this century.

"Alone, these blind elemental energies can accomplish little, but governed and directed by the trained will of a powerful manipulator they may become potent activities for good or evil. They are the basis of all magic, and it is the motive behind them that constitutes the magic 'black' or 'white'; they can be the vehicles of curses or of blessings, for a curse is nothing more than the thought of a violent will perpetuated. And in such cases—cases like this—the conscious, directing will of the mind that is using the elemental stands always behind the phenomena——"

"You think that my brother——!" broke in the Colonel, aghast.

"Has nothing whatever to do with it—directly. The fire-elemental that has here been tormenting you and your household was sent upon its mission long before you, or your family, or your ancestors, or even the nation you belong to—unless I am much mistaken—was even in existence. We will come to that a little later; after the experiment I propose to make we shall be more positive. At present I can only say we have to deal now, not only with the phenomenon of Attacking Fire merely, but with the vindictive and enraged intelligence that is directing it from behind the scenes—vindictive and enraged,"—he repeated the words.

"That explains——" began Colonel Wragge, seeking furiously for words he could not find quickly enough.

"Much," said John Silence, with a gesture to restrain him.

He stopped a moment in the middle of his walk, and a deep silence came down over the little room. Through the windows the sunlight seemed less bright, the long line of dark hills less friendly, making me think of a vast wave towering to heaven and about to break and overwhelm us. Something formidable had crept into the world about us. For, undoubtedly, there was a disquieting thought, holding terror as well as awe, in the picture his words conjured up: the conception of a human will reaching its deathless hand, spiteful and destructive, down through the ages, to strike the living and afflict the innocent.

"But what *is* its object?" burst out the soldier, unable to restrain himself longer in the silence. "Why does it come from that plantation? And why should it attack us, or any one in particular?" Questions began to pour from him in a stream.

"All in good time," the doctor answered quietly, having let him run on for several minutes. "But I must first discover positively what, or who, it is that directs this particular fire-elemental. And, to do that, we must first"—he spoke with slow deliberation—"seek to capture—to confine by visibility—to limit its sphere in a concrete form."

"Good heavens almighty!" exclaimed the soldier, mixing his words in his unfeigned surprise.

"Quite so," pursued the other calmly; "for in so doing I think we can release it from the purpose that binds it, restore it to its normal condition of latent fire, and also"—he lowered his voice perceptibly—"also discover the face and form of the Being that ensouls it."

"The man behind the gun!" cried the Colonel, beginning to understand something, and leaning forward so as not to miss a single syllable.

"I mean that in the last resort, before it returns to the womb of potential fire, it will probably assume the face and figure of its Director, of the man of magical knowledge who originally bound it with his incantations and sent it forth upon its mission of centuries."

The soldier sat down and gasped openly in his face, breathing hard; but it was a very subdued voice that framed the question.

"And how do you propose to make it visible? How capture and confine it? What d'ye mean, Dr. John Silence?"

"By furnishing it with the materials for a form. By the process of materialisation simply. Once limited by dimensions, it will become slow, heavy, visible. We can then dissipate it. Invisible fire, you see, is dangerous and incalculable; locked up in a form we can perhaps manage it. We must betray it—to its death."

"And this material?" we asked in the same breath, although I think I had already guessed.

"Not pleasant, but effective," came the quiet reply; "the exhalations of freshly spilled blood."

"Not human blood!" cried Colonel Wragge, starting up from his chair with a voice like an explosion. I thought his eyes would start from their sockets.

The face of Dr. Silence relaxed in spite of himself, and his spontaneous little laugh brought a welcome though momentary relief.

"The days of human sacrifice, I hope, will never come again," he explained. "Animal blood will answer the purpose, and we can make the experiment as pleasant as possible. Only, the blood must be freshly spilled and strong with the vital emanations that attract this peculiar class of elemental creature. Perhaps—perhaps if some pig on the estate is ready for the market——"

He turned to hide a smile; but the passing touch of comedy found no echo in the mind of our host, who did not understand how to change quickly from one emotion to another. Clearly he was debating many things laboriously in his honest brain. But, in the end, the earnestness and scientific disinterestedness of the doctor, whose influence over him was already very great, won the day, and he presently looked up more calmly, and observed shortly that he thought perhaps the matter could be arranged.

"There are other and pleasanter methods," Dr. Silence went on to explain, "but they require time and preparation, and things have gone much too far, in my opinion, to admit of delay. And the process need cause you no distress: we sit round the bowl and await results. Nothing more. The emanations of blood—which, as Levi says, is the first incarnation of the universal fluid—furnish the materials out of which the creatures of discarnate life, spirits if you prefer, can fashion themselves a temporary appearance. The process is old, and lies at the root of all blood sacrifice. It was known to the priests of Baal, and it is known to the modern ecstasy dancers who cut themselves to produce objective phantoms who dance with them. And the least gifted clairvoyant could tell you that the forms to be seen in the vicinity of slaughter-houses, or hovering above the deserted battlefields, are—well, simply beyond all description. I do not mean," he added, noticing the uneasy fidgeting of his host, "that anything in our laundry-experiment need appear to terrify us, for this case seems a comparatively simple one, and it is only the vindictive character of the intelligence directing this fire-elemental that causes anxiety and makes for personal danger."

"It is curious," said the Colonel, with a sudden rush of words, drawing a deep breath, and as though speaking of things distasteful to him, "that during my years among the Hill Tribes of Northern India I came across—personally came across—instances of the sacrifices of blood to certain deities being stopped suddenly, and all manner of disasters happening until they were resumed. Fires broke out in the huts, and even on the clothes, of the natives—and—and I admit I have read, in the course of my studies,"—he made a gesture toward his books and heavily laden table,—"of the Yezidis of Syria evoking phantoms by means of cutting their bodies with knives during their whirling dances—enormous globes of fire which turned into monstrous and terrible forms—and I remember an account somewhere, too, how the emaciated forms and pallid countenances of the spectres, that appeared to the Emperor Julian, claimed to be the true Immortals, and told him to renew the sacrifices of blood 'for the fumes of which, since the establishment of Christianity, they had been pining'—that these were in reality the phantoms evoked by the rites of blood."

Both Dr. Silence and myself listened in amazement, for this sudden speech was so unexpected, and betrayed so much more knowledge than we had either of us suspected in the old soldier.

"Then perhaps you have read, too," said the doctor, "how the Cosmic Deities of savage races, elemental in their nature, have been kept alive through many ages by these blood rites?"

"No," he answered; "that is new to me."

"In any case," Dr. Silence added, "I am glad you are not wholly unfamiliar with the subject, for you will now bring more sympathy, and therefore more help, to our experiment. For, of course, in this case, we only want the blood to tempt the creature from its lair and enclose it in a form——"

"I quite understand. And I only hesitated just now," he went on, his words coming much more slowly, as though he felt he had already said too much, "because I wished to be quite sure it was no mere curiosity, but an actual sense of necessity that dictated this horrible experiment."

"It is your safety, and that of your household, and of your sister, that is at stake," replied the doctor. "Once I have *seen*, I hope to discover whence this elemental comes, and what its real purpose is."

Colonel Wragge signified his assent with a bow.

"And the moon will help us," the other said, "for it will be full in the early hours of the morning, and this kind of elemental-being is always most active at the period of full moon. Hence, you see, the clue furnished by your diary."

So it was finally settled. Colonel Wragge would provide the materials for the experiment, and we were to meet at midnight. How he would contrive at that hour—but that was his business. I only know we both realised that he would keep his word, and whether a pig died at midnight, or at noon, was after all perhaps only a question of the sleep and personal comfort of the executioner.

"Tonight, then, in the laundry," said Dr. Silence finally, to clinch the plan; "we three alone—and at midnight, when the household is asleep and we shall be free from disturbance."

He exchanged significant glances with our host, who, at that moment, was called away by the announcement that the family doctor had arrived, and was ready to see him in his sister's room.

For the remainder of the afternoon John Silence disappeared. I had my suspicions that he made a secret visit to the plantation and also to the laundry building; but, in any case, we saw nothing of him, and he kept strictly to himself. He was preparing for the night, I felt sure, but the nature of his preparations I could only guess. There was movement in his room, I heard, and an odour like incense hung about the door, and knowing that he regarded rites as the vehicles of energies, my guesses were probably not far wrong.

Colonel Wragge, too, remained absent the greater part of the afternoon, and, deeply afflicted, had scarcely left his sister's bedside, but in response to my inquiry when we met for a moment at tea-time, he told me that although she had moments of attempted speech, her talk was quite incoherent and hysterical, and she was still quite unable to explain the nature of what she had seen. The doctor, he said, feared she had recovered the use of her limbs, only to lose that of her memory, and perhaps even of her mind.

"Then the recovery of her legs, I trust, may be permanent, at any rate," I ventured, finding it difficult to know what sympathy to offer. And he replied with a curious short laugh, "Oh yes; about that there can be no doubt whatever."

And it was due merely to the chance of my overhearing a fragment of conversation—unwillingly, of course—that a little further light was thrown upon the state in which the old lady actually lay. For, as I came out of my room, it happened that Colonel Wragge and the doctor were going downstairs together, and their words floated up to my ears before I could make my presence known by so much as a cough.

"Then you must find a way," the doctor was saying with decision; "for I cannot insist too strongly upon that—and at all costs she must be kept quiet. These attempts to go out must be prevented—if necessary, by force. This desire to visit some wood or other she keeps talking about is, of course, hysterical in nature. It cannot be permitted for a moment."

"It shall not be permitted," I heard the soldier reply, as they reached the hall below.

"It has impressed her mind for some reason——" the doctor went on, by way evidently of soothing explanation, and then the distance made it impossible for me to hear more.

At dinner Dr. Silence was still absent, on the public plea of a headache, and though food was sent to his room, I am inclined to believe he did not touch it, but spent the entire time fasting.

We retired early, desiring that the household should do likewise, and I must confess that at ten o'clock when I bid my host a temporary goodnight, and sought my room to make what mental preparation I could, I realised in no very pleasant fashion that it was a singular and formidable assignation, this midnight meeting in the laundry building, and that there were moments in every adventure of life when a wise man, and one who knew his own limitations, owed it to his dignity to withdraw discreetly. And, but for the character of our leader, I probably should have then and there offered the best excuse I could think of, and have allowed myself quietly to fall asleep and wait for an exciting story in the morning of what had happened. But with a man like John Silence, such a lapse was out of the question, and I sat before my fire counting the minutes and doing everything I could think of to fortify my resolution and fasten my will at the point where I could be reasonably sure that my self-control would hold against all attacks of men, devils, or elementals.

III

At a quarter before midnight, clad in a heavy ulster, and with slippered feet, I crept cautiously from my room and stole down the passage to the top of the stairs. Outside the doctor's door I waited a moment to listen. All was still; the house in utter darkness; no gleam of light beneath any door; only, down the length of the corridor, from the direction of the sick-room, came faint sounds of laughter and incoherent talk that were not things to reassure a mind already half a-tremble, and I made haste to reach the hall and let myself out through the front door into the night.

The air was keen and frosty, perfumed with night smells, and exquisitely fresh; all the million candles of the sky were alight, and a faint breeze rose and fell with far-away sighings in the tops of the pine trees. My blood leaped for a moment in the spaciousness of the night, for the splendid stars brought courage; but the next instant, as I turned the corner of the house, moving stealthily down the gravel drive, my spirits sank again ominously. For, yonder, over the funereal plumes of the Twelve Acre Plantation, I saw the broken, yellow disc of the half-moon just rising in the east, staring down like some vast Being come to watch upon the progress of our doom. Seen through the distorting vapours of the earth's atmosphere, her face looked weirdly unfamiliar, her usual expression of benignant vacancy somehow a-twist. I slipped along by the shadows of the wall, keeping my eyes upon the ground.

The laundry-house, as already described, stood detached from the other offices, with laurel shrubberies crowding thickly behind it, and the kitchen-garden so close on the other side that the strong smells of soil and growing things came across almost heavily. The shadows of the haunted plantation, hugely lengthened by the rising moon behind them, reached to the very walls and covered the stone tiles of the roof with a dark pall. So keenly were my senses alert at this moment that I believe I could fill a chapter with the endless small details of the impression I received—shadows, odour, shapes, sounds—in the space of the few seconds I stood and waited before the closed wooden door.

Then I became aware of some one moving towards me through the moonlight, and the figure of John Silence, without overcoat and bareheaded, came quickly and without noise to join me. His eyes, I saw at once, were wonderfully bright, and so marked was the shining pallor of his face that I could hardly tell when he passed from the moonlight into the shade.

He passed without a word, beckoning me to follow, and then pushed the door open, and went in.

The chill air of the place met us like that of an underground vault; and the brick floor and whitewashed walls, streaked with damp and smoke, threw back the cold in our faces. Directly opposite gaped the black throat of the huge open fireplace, the ashes of wood fires still piled and scattered about the hearth, and on either side of the projecting chimney-column were the deep recesses holding the big twin cauldrons for boiling clothes. Upon the lids of these cauldrons stood the two little oil lamps, shaded red, which gave all the light there was, and immediately in front of the fireplace there was a small circular table with three chairs set about it. Overhead, the narrow slit windows, high up the walls, pointed to a dim network of wooden rafters half lost among the shadows, and then came the dark vault of the roof. Cheerless and unalluring, for all the red light, it certainly was, reminding me of some unused conventicle, bare of pews or pulpit, ugly and severe, and I was forcibly struck by the contrast between the normal uses to which the place was ordinarily put, and the strange and mediæval purpose which had brought us under its roof tonight.

Possibly an involuntary shudder ran over me, for my companion turned with a confident look to reassure me, and he was so completely master of himself that I at once absorbed from his abundance, and felt the chinks of my failing courage beginning to close up. To meet his eye in the presence of danger was like finding a mental railing that guided and supported thought along the giddy edges of alarm.

"I am quite ready," I whispered, turning to listen for approaching footsteps.

He nodded, still keeping his eyes on mine. Our whispers sounded hollow as they echoed overhead among the rafters.

"I'm glad you are here," he said. "Not all would have the courage. Keep your thoughts controlled, and imagine the protective shell round you—round your *inner* being."

"I'm all right," I repeated, cursing my chattering teeth.

He took my hand and shook it, and the contact seemed to shake into me something of his supreme confidence. The eyes and hands of a strong man can touch the soul. I think he guessed my thought, for a passing smile flashed about the corners of his mouth.

"You will feel more comfortable," he said, in a low tone, "when the chain is complete. The Colonel we can count on, of course. Remember, though," he added warningly, "he may perhaps become controlled—possessed—when the thing comes, because he won't know how to resist. And to explain the business to such a man——!" He shrugged his shoulders expressively. "But it will only be temporary, and I will see that no harm comes to him."

He glanced round at the arrangements with approval.

"Red light," he said, indicating the shaded lamps, "has the lowest rate of vibration. Materialisations are dissipated by strong light—won't form, or hold together—in rapid vibrations."

I was not sure that I approved altogether of this dim light, for in complete darkness there is something protective—the knowledge that one cannot be seen, probably—which a half-light destroys, but I remembered the warning to keep my thoughts steady, and forbore to give them expression.

There was a step outside, and the figure of Colonel Wragge stood in the doorway. Though entering on tiptoe, he made considerable noise and clatter, for his free movements were impeded by the burden he carried, and we saw a large yellowish bowl held out at arms' length from his body, the mouth covered with a white cloth. His face, I noted, was rigidly composed. He, too, was master of himself. And, as I thought of this old soldier moving through the long series of alarms, worn with watching and wearied with assault, unenlightened yet undismayed, even down to the dreadful shock of his sister's terror, and still showing the dogged pluck that persists in the face of defeat, I understood what Dr. Silence meant when he described him as a man "to be counted on."

I think there was nothing beyond this rigidity of his stern features, and a certain greyness of the complexion, to betray the turmoil of the emotions that were doubtless going on within; and the quality of these two men, each in his own way, so keyed me up that, by the time the door was shut and we had exchanged silent greetings, all the latent courage I possessed was well to the fore, and I felt as sure of myself as I knew I ever could feel.

Colonel Wragge set the bowl carefully in the centre of the table.

"Midnight," he said shortly, glancing at his watch, and we all three moved to our chairs.

There, in the middle of that cold and silent place, we sat, with the vile bowl before us, and a thin, hardly perceptible steam rising through the damp air from the surface of the white cloth and disappearing upwards the moment it passed beyond the zone of red light and entered the deep shadows thrown forward by the projecting wall of chimney.

The doctor had indicated our respective places, and I found myself seated with my back to the door and opposite the black hearth. The Colonel was on my left, and Dr. Silence on my right, both half facing me, the latter more in shadow than the former. We thus divided the little table into even sections, and sitting back in our chairs we awaited events in silence.

For something like an hour I do not think there was even the faintest sound within those four walls and under the canopy of that vaulted roof. Our slippers made no scratching on the gritty floor, and our breathing was suppressed almost to nothing; even the rustle of our clothes as we shifted from time to time upon our seats was inaudible. Silence smothered us absolutely—the silence of night, of listening, the silence of a haunted expectancy. The very gurgling of the lamps was too soft to be heard, and if light itself had sound, I do not think we should have noticed the silvery tread of the moonlight as it entered the high narrow windows and threw upon the floor the slender traces of its pallid footsteps.

Colonel Wragge and the doctor, and myself too for that matter, sat thus like figures of stone, without speech and without gesture. My eyes passed in ceaseless journeys from the bowl to their faces, and from their faces to the bowl. They might have been masks, however, for all the signs of life they gave; and the light steaming from the horrid contents beneath the white cloth had long ceased to be visible.

Then presently, as the moon rose higher, the wind rose with it. It sighed, like the lightest of passing wings, over the roof; it crept most softly round the walls; it made the brick floor like ice beneath our feet. With it I saw mentally the desolate moorland flowing like a sea about the old house, the treeless expanse of lonely hills, the nearer copses, sombre and mysterious in the night. The plantation, too, in particular I saw, and imagined I heard the mournful whisperings that must now be a-stirring among its tree-tops as the breeze played down between the twisted stems. In the depth of the room behind us the shafts of moonlight met and crossed in a growing network.

It was after an hour of this wearing and unbroken attention, and I should judge about one o'clock in the morning, when the baying of the dogs in the stableyard first began, and I saw John Silence move suddenly in his chair and sit up in an attitude of attention. Every force in my being instantly leaped into the keenest vigilance. Colonel Wragge moved too, though slowly, and without raising his eyes from the table before him.

The doctor stretched his arm out and took the white cloth from the bowl.

It was perhaps imagination that persuaded me the red glare of the lamps grew fainter and the air over the table before us thickened. I had been expecting something for so long that the movement of my companions, and the lifting of the cloth, may easily have caused the momentary delusion that something hovered in the air before my face, touching the skin of my cheeks with a silken run. But it was certainly not a delusion that the Colonel looked up at the same moment and glanced over his shoulder, as though his eyes followed the movements of something to and fro about the room, and that he then buttoned his overcoat more tightly about him and his eyes sought my own face first, and then the doctor's. And it was no delusion that his face seemed somehow to have turned dark, become spread as it were with a shadowy blackness. I saw his lips tighten and his expression grow hard and stern, and it came to me then with a rush that, of course, this man had told us but a part of the experiences he had been through in the house, and that there was much more he had never been able to bring himself to reveal at all. I felt sure of it. The way he turned and stared about him betrayed a familiarity with other things than those he had described to us. It was not merely a sight of fire he looked for; it was a sight of something alive, intelligent, something able to evade his searching; it was *a person*. It was the watch for the ancient Being who sought to obsess him.

And the way in which Dr. Silence answered his look—though it was only by a glance of subtlest sympathy—confirmed my impression.

"We may be ready now," I heard him say in a whisper, and I understood that his words were intended as a steadying warning, and braced myself mentally to the utmost of my power.

Yet long before Colonel Wragge had turned to stare about the room, and long before the doctor had confirmed my impression that things were at last beginning to stir, I had become aware in most singular fashion that the place held more than our three selves. With the rising of the wind this increase to our numbers had first taken place. The baying of the hounds almost seemed to have signalled it. I cannot say how it may be possible to realise that an empty place has suddenly become—not empty, when the new arrival is nothing that appeals to any one of the senses; for this recognition of an "invisible," as of the change in the balance of personal forces in a human group, is indefinable and beyond proof. Yet it is unmistakable. And I knew perfectly well at what given moment the atmosphere within these four walls became charged with the presence of other living beings besides ourselves. And, on reflection, I am convinced that both my companions knew it too.

"Watch the light," said the doctor under his breath, and then I knew too that it was no fancy of my own that had turned the air darker, and the way he turned to examine the face of our host sent an electric thrill of wonder and expectancy shivering along every nerve in my body.

Yet it was no kind of terror that I experienced, but rather a sort of mental dizziness, and a sensation as of being suspended in some remote and dreadful altitude where things might happen, indeed were about to happen, that had never before happened within the ken of man. Horror may have formed an ingredient, but it was not chiefly horror, and in no sense ghostly horror.

Uncommon thoughts kept beating on my brain like tiny hammers, soft yet persistent, seeking admission; their unbidden tide began to wash along the far fringes of my mind, the currents of unwonted sensations to rise over the remote frontiers of my consciousness. I was

aware of thoughts, and the fantasies of thoughts, that I never knew before existed. Portions of my being stirred that had never stirred before,
and things ancient and inexplicable rose to the surface and beckoned
me to follow. I felt as though I were about to fly off, at some immense
tangent, into an outer space hitherto unknown even in dreams. And so
singular was the result produced upon me that I was uncommonly glad
to anchor my mind, as well as my eyes, upon the masterful personality
of the doctor at my side, for there, I realised, I could draw always upon
the forces of sanity and safety.

With a vigorous effort of will I returned to the scene before me, and
tried to focus my attention, with steadier thoughts, upon the table, and
upon the silent figures seated round it. And then I saw that certain
changes had come about in the place where we sat.

The patches of moonlight on the floor, I noted, had become curiously shaded; the faces of my companions opposite were not so clearly
visible as before; and the forehead and cheeks of Colonel Wragge were
glistening with perspiration. I realised further, that an extraordinary
change had come about in the temperature of the atmosphere. The increased warmth had a painful effect, not alone on Colonel Wragge, but
upon all of us. It was oppressive and unnatural. We gasped figuratively
as well as actually.

"You are the first to feel it," said Dr. Silence in low tones, looking
across at him. "You are in more intimate touch, of course——"

The Colonel was trembling, and appeared to be in considerable distress. His knees shook, so that the shuffling of his slippered feet became
audible. He inclined his head to show that he had heard, but made no
other reply. I think, even then, he was sore put to it to keep himself in
hand. I knew what he was struggling against. As Dr. Silence had
warned me, he was about to be obsessed, and was savagely, though
vainly, resisting.

But, meanwhile, a curious and whirling sense of exhilaration began
to come over me. The increasing heat was delightful, bringing a sensation of intense activity, of thoughts pouring through the mind at high
speed, of vivid pictures in the brain, of fierce desires and lightning energies alive in every part of the body. I was conscious of no physical distress, such as the Colonel felt, but only of a vague feeling that it might
all grow suddenly too intense—that I might be consumed—that my
personality as well as my body, might become resolved into the flame
of pure spirit. I began to live at a speed too intense to last. It was as if a
thousand ecstasies besieged me——

"Steady!" whispered the voice of John Silence in my ear, and I
looked up with a start to see that the Colonel had risen from his chair.

The doctor rose too. I followed suit, and for the first time saw down into the bowl. To my amazement and horror I saw that the contents were troubled. The blood was astir with movement.

The rest of the experiment was witnessed by us standing. It came, too, with a curious suddenness. There was no more dreaming, for me at any rate.

I shall never forget the figure of Colonel Wragge standing there beside me, upright and unshaken, squarely planted on his feet, looking about him, puzzled beyond belief, yet full of a fighting anger. Framed by the white walls, the red glow of the lamps upon his streaming cheeks, his eyes glowing against the deathly pallor of his skin, breathing hard and making convulsive efforts of hands and body to keep himself under control, his whole being roused to the point of savage fighting, yet with nothing visible to get at anywhere—he stood there, immovable against odds. And the strange contrast of the pale skin and the burning face I had never seen before, or wish to see again.

But what has left an even sharper impression on my memory was the blackness that then began crawling over his face, obliterating the features, concealing their human outline, and hiding him inch by inch from view. This was my first realisation that the process of materialisation was at work. His visage became shrouded. I moved from one side to the other to keep him in view, and it was only then I understood that, properly speaking, the blackness was not upon the countenance of Colonel Wragge, but that something had inserted itself between me and him, thus screening his face with the effect of a dark veil. Something that apparently rose through the floor was passing slowly into the air above the table and above the bowl. The blood in the bowl, moreover, was considerably less than before.

And, with this change in the air before us, there came at the same time a further change, I thought, in the face of the soldier. One-half was turned towards the red lamps, while the other caught the pale illumination of the moonlight falling aslant from the high windows, so that it was difficult to estimate this change with accuracy of detail. But it seemed to me that, while the features—eyes, nose, mouth—remained the same, the life informing them had undergone some profound transformation. The signature of a new power had crept into the face and left its traces there—an expression dark, and in some unexplained way, terrible.

Then suddenly he opened his mouth and spoke, and the sound of this changed voice, deep and musical though it was, made me cold and set my heart beating with uncomfortable rapidity. The Being, as he had dreaded, was already in control of his brain, using his mouth.

"I see a blackness like the blackness of Egypt before my face," said the tones of this unknown voice that seemed half his own and half another's. "And out of this darkness they come, they come."

I gave a dreadful start. The doctor turned to look at me for an instant, and then turned to centre his attention upon the figure of our host, and I understood in some intuitive fashion that he was there to watch over the strangest contest man ever saw—to watch over and, if necessary, to protect.

"He is being controlled—possessed," he whispered to me through the shadows. His face wore a wonderful expression, half triumph, half admiration.

Even as Colonel Wragge spoke, it seemed to me that this visible darkness began to increase, pouring up thickly out of the ground by the hearth, rising up in sheets and veils, shrouding our eyes and faces. It stole up from below—an awful blackness that seemed to drink in all the radiations of light in the building, leaving nothing but the ghost of a radiance in their place. Then, out of this rising sea of shadows, issued a pale and spectral light that gradually spread itself about us, and from the heart of this light I saw the shapes of fire crowd and gather. And these were not human shapes, or the shapes of anything I recognised as alive in the world, but outlines of fire that traced globes, triangles, crosses, and the luminous bodies of various geometrical figures. They grew bright, faded, and then grew bright again with an effect almost of pulsation. They passed swiftly to and fro through the air, rising and falling, and particularly in the immediate neighbourhood of the Colonel, often gathering about his head and shoulders, and even appearing to settle upon him like giant insects of flame. They were accompanied, moreover, by a faint sound of hissing—the same sound we had heard that afternoon in the plantation.

"The fire-elementals that precede their master," the doctor said in an undertone. "Be ready."

And while this weird display of the shapes of fire alternately flashed and faded, and the hissing echoed faintly among the dim rafters overhead, we heard the awful voice issue at intervals from the lips of the afflicted soldier. It was a voice of power, splendid in some way I cannot describe, and with a certain sense of majesty in its cadences, and, as I listened to it with quickly beating heart, I could fancy it was some ancient voice of Time itself, echoing down immense corridors of stone, from the depths of vast temples, from the very heart of mountain tombs.

"I have seen my divine Father, Osiris," thundered the great tones. "I have scattered the gloom of the night. I have burst through the earth, and am one with the starry Deities!"

Something grand came into the soldier's face. He was staring fixedly before him, as though seeing nothing.

"Watch," whispered Dr. Silence in my ear, and his whisper seemed to come from very far away.

Again the mouth opened and the awesome voice issued forth.

"Thoth," it boomed, "has loosened the bandages of Set which fettered my mouth. I have taken my place in the great winds of heaven."

I heard the little wind of night, with its mournful voice of ages, sighing round the walls and over the roof.

"Listen!" came from the doctor at my side, and the thunder of the voice continued —

"I have hidden myself with you, O ye stars that never diminish. I remember my name — in — the — House — of — Fire!"

The voice ceased and the sound died away. Something about the face and figure of Colonel Wragge relaxed, I thought. The terrible look passed from his face. The Being that obsessed him was gone.

"The great Ritual," said Dr. Silence aside to me, very low, "the Book of the Dead. Now it's leaving him. Soon the blood will fashion it a body."

Colonel Wragge, who had stood absolutely motionless all this time, suddenly swayed, so that I thought he was going to fall, — and, but for the quick support of the doctor's arm, he probably would have fallen, for he staggered as in the beginning of collapse.

"I am drunk with the wine of Osiris," he cried, — and it was half with his own voice this time — "but Horus, the Eternal Watcher, is about my path — for — safety." The voice dwindled and failed, dying away into something almost like a cry of distress.

"Now, watch closely," said Dr. Silence, speaking loud, "for after the cry will come the Fire!"

I began to tremble involuntarily; an awful change had come without warning into the air; my legs grew weak as paper beneath my weight and I had to support myself by leaning on the table. Colonel Wragge, I saw, was also leaning forward with a kind of droop. The shapes of fire had vanished all, but his face was lit by the red lamps and the pale, shifting moonlight rose behind him like mist.

We were both gazing at the bowl, now almost empty; the Colonel stooped so low I feared every minute he would lose his balance and drop into it; and the shadow, that had so long been in process of forming, now at length began to assume material outline in the air before us.

Then John Silence moved forward quickly. He took his place between us and the shadow. Erect, formidable, absolute master of the situation, I saw him stand there, his face calm and almost smiling, and fire in his eyes. His protective influence was astounding and incalculable. Even the abhorrent dread I felt at the sight of the creature growing into life and substance before us, lessened in some way so that I was able to keep my eyes fixed on the air above the bowl without too vivid a terror.

But as it took shape, rising out of nothing as it were, and growing momentarily more defined in outline, a period of utter and wonderful silence settled down upon the building and all it contained. A hush of ages, like the sudden centre of peace at the heart of the travelling cyclone, descended through the night, and out of this hush, as out of the emanations of the steaming blood, issued the form of the ancient being who had first sent the elemental of fire upon its mission. It grew and darkened and solidified before our eyes. It rose from just beyond the table so that the lower portions remained invisible, but I saw the outline limn itself upon the air, as though slowly revealed by the rising of a curtain. It apparently had not then quite concentrated to the normal proportions, but was spread out on all sides into space, huge, though rapidly condensing, for I saw the colossal shoulders, the neck, the lower portion of the dark jaws, the terrible mouth, and then the teeth and lips—and, as the veil seemed to lift further upon the tremendous face—I saw the nose and cheek bones. In another moment I should have looked straight into the eyes——

But what Dr. Silence did at that moment was so unexpected, and took me so by surprise, that I have never yet properly understood its nature, and he has never yet seen fit to explain in detail to me. He uttered some sound that had a note of command in it—and, in so doing, stepped forward and intervened between me and the face. The figure, just nearing completeness, he therefore hid from my sight—and I have always thought purposely hid from my sight.

"The fire!" he cried out. "The fire! Beware!"

There was a sudden roar as of flame from the very mouth of the pit, and for the space of a single second all grew light as day. A blinding flash passed across my face, and there was heat for an instant that seemed to shrivel skin, and flesh, and bone. Then came steps, and I heard Colonel Wragge utter a great cry, wilder than any human cry I have ever known. The heat sucked all the breath out of my lungs with a rush, and the blaze of light, as it vanished, swept my vision with it into enveloping darkness.

When I recovered the use of my senses a few moments later I saw that Colonel Wragge with a face of death, its whiteness strangely stained, had moved closer to me. Dr. Silence stood beside him, an expression of triumph and success in his eyes. The next minute the soldier tried to clutch me with his hand. Then he reeled, staggered, and, unable to save himself, fell with a great crash upon the brick floor.

After the sheet of flame, a wind raged round the building as though it would lift the roof off, but then passed as suddenly as it came. And in the intense calm that followed I saw that the form had vanished, and the doctor was stooping over Colonel Wragge upon the floor, trying to lift him to a sitting position.

"Light," he said quietly, "more light. Take the shades off."

Colonel Wragge sat up and the glare of the unshaded lamps fell upon his face. It was grey and drawn, still running heat, and there was a look in the eyes and about the corners of the mouth that seemed in this short space of time to have added years to its age. At the same time, the expression of effort and anxiety had left it. It showed relief.

"Gone!" he said, looking up at the doctor in a dazed fashion, and struggling to his feet. "Thank God! it's gone at last." He stared round the laundry as though to find out where he was. "Did it control me — take possession of me? Did I talk nonsense?" he asked bluntly. "After the heat came, I remember nothing——"

"You'll feel yourself again in a few minutes," the doctor said. To my infinite horror I saw that he was surreptitiously wiping sundry dark stains from the face. "Our experiment has been a success and——"

He gave me a swift glance to hide the bowl, standing between me and our host while I hurriedly stuffed it down under the lid of the nearest cauldron.

"—— and none of us the worse for it," he finished.

"And fires?" he asked, still dazed, "there'll be no more fires?"

"It is dissipated — partly, at any rate," replied Dr. Silence cautiously.

"And the man behind the gun," he went on, only half realising what he was saying, I think; "have you discovered *that?*"

"A form materialised," said the doctor briefly. "I know for certain now what the directing intelligence was behind it all."

Colonel Wragge pulled himself together and got upon his feet. The words conveyed no clear meaning to him yet. But his memory was returning gradually, and he was trying to piece together the fragments into a connected whole. He shivered a little, for the place had grown suddenly chilly. The air was empty again, lifeless.

"You feel all right again now," Dr. Silence said, in the tone of a man stating a fact rather than asking a question.

"Thanks to you — both, yes." He drew a deep breath, and mopped his face, and even attempted a smile. He made me think of a man coming from the battlefield with the stains of fighting still upon him, but scornful of his wounds. Then he turned gravely towards the doctor with a question in his eyes. Memory had returned and he was himself again.

"Precisely what I expected," the doctor said calmly; "a fire-elemental sent upon its mission in the days of Thebes, centuries before Christ, and tonight, for the first time all these thousands of years, released from the spell that originally bound it."

We stared at him in amazement, Colonel Wragge opening his lips for words that refused to shape themselves.

"And, if we dig," he continued significantly, pointing to the floor where the blackness had poured up, "we shall find some underground connection—a tunnel most likely—leading to the Twelve Acre Wood. It was made by—your predecessor."

"A tunnel made by my brother!" gasped the soldier. "Then my sister should know—she lived here with him——" He stopped suddenly.

John Silence inclined his head slowly. "I think so," he said quietly. "Your brother, no doubt, was as much tormented as you have been," he continued after a pause in which Colonel Wragge seemed deeply preoccupied with his thoughts, "and tried to find peace by burying it in the wood, and surrounding the wood then, like a large magic circle, with the enchantments of the old formulæ. So the stars the man saw blazing——"

"But burying *what?*" asked the soldier faintly, stepping backwards towards the support of the wall.

Dr. Silence regarded us both intently for a moment before he replied. I think he weighed in his mind whether to tell us now, or when the investigation was absolutely complete.

"The mummy," he said softly, after a moment; "the mummy that your brother took from its resting place of centuries, and brought home—here."

Colonel Wragge dropped down upon the nearest chair, hanging breathlessly on every word. He was far too amazed for speech.

"The mummy of some important person—a priest most likely—protected from disturbance and desecration by the ceremonial magic of the time. For they understood how to attach to the mummy, to lock up with it in the tomb, an elemental force that would direct itself even after ages upon any one who dared to molest it. In this case it was an elemental of fire."

Dr. Silence crossed the floor and turned out the lamps one by one. He had nothing more to say for the moment. Following his example, I folded the table together and took up the chairs, and our host, still dazed and silent, mechanically obeyed him and moved to the door.

We removed all traces of the experiment, taking the empty bowl back to the house concealed beneath an ulster.

The air was cool and fragrant as we walked to the house, the stars beginning to fade overhead and a fresh wind of early morning blowing up out of the east where the sky was already hinting of the coming day. It was after five o'clock.

Stealthily we entered the front hall and locked the door, and as we went on tiptoe upstairs to our rooms, the Colonel, peering at us over his candle as he nodded good-night, whispered that if we were ready the digging should be begun that very day.

Then I saw him steal along to his sister's room and disappear.

IV

But not even the mysterious references to the mummy, or the prospect of a revelation by digging, were able to hinder the reaction that followed the intense excitement of the past twelve hours, and I slept the sleep of the dead, dreamless and undisturbed. A touch on the shoulder woke me, and I saw Dr. Silence standing beside the bed, dressed to go out.

"Come," he said, "it's tea-time. You've slept the best part of a dozen hours."

I sprang up and made a hurried toilet, while my companion sat and talked. He looked fresh and rested, and his manner was even quieter than usual.

"Colonel Wragge has provided spades and pickaxes. We're going out to unearth this mummy at once," he said; "and there's no reason we should not get away by the morning train."

"I'm ready to go tonight, if you are," I said honestly.

But Dr. Silence shook his head.

"I must see this through to the end," he said gravely, and in a tone that made me think he still anticipated serious things, perhaps. He went on talking while I dressed.

"This case is really typical of all stories of mummy-haunting, and none of them are cases to trifle with," he explained, "for the mummies of important people—kings, priests, magicians—were laid away with profoundly significant ceremonial, and were very effectively protected, as you have seen, against desecration, and especially against destruction.

"The general belief," he went on, anticipating my questions, "held, of course, that the perpetuity of the mummy guaranteed that of its Ka,—the owner's spirit,—but it is not improbable that the magical embalming was also used to retard reincarnation, the preservation of the body preventing the return of the spirit to the toil and discipline of earth-life; and, in any case, they knew how to attach powerful guardian-forces to keep off trespassers. And any one who dared to remove the mummy, or especially to unwind it—well," he added, with meaning, "you have seen—and you *will* see."

I caught his face in the mirror while I struggled with my collar. It was deeply serious. There could be no question that he spoke of what he believed and knew.

"The traveller-brother who brought it here must have been haunted too," he continued, "for he tried to banish it by burial in the wood, making a magic circle to enclose it. Something of genuine ceremonial he must have known, for the stars the man saw were of course the remains of the still flaming pentagrams he traced at intervals in the circle. Only he did not know enough, or possibly was ignorant that the mummy's guardian was a fire-force. Fire cannot be enclosed by fire, though, as you saw, it can be released by it."

"Then that awful figure in the laundry?" I asked, thrilled to find him so communicative.

"Undoubtedly the actual Ka of the mummy operating always behind its agent, the elemental, and most likely thousands of years old."

"And Miss Wragge——?" I ventured once more.

"Ah, Miss Wragge," he repeated with increased gravity, "Miss Wragge——"

A knock at the door brought a servant with word that tea was ready, and the Colonel had sent to ask if we were coming down. The thread was broken. Dr. Silence moved to the door and signed to me to follow. But his manner told me that in any case no real answer would have been forthcoming to my question.

"And the place to dig in," I asked, unable to restrain my curiosity, "will you find it by some process of divination or——?"

He paused at the door and looked back at me, and with that he left me to finish my dressing.

It was growing dark when the three of us silently made our way to the Twelve Acre Plantation; the sky was overcast, and a black wind came out of the east. Gloom hung about the old house and the air seemed full of sighings. We found the tools ready laid at the edge of the wood, and each shouldering his piece, we followed our leader at once in among the trees. He went straight forward for some twenty yards and then stopped. At his feet lay the blackened circle of one of the burned places. It was just discernible against the surrounding white grass.

"There are three of these," he said, "and they all lie in a line with one another. Any one of them will tap the tunnel that connects the laundry—the former Museum—with the chamber where the mummy now lies buried."

He at once cleared away the burnt grass and began to dig; we all began to dig. While I used the pick, the others shovelled vigorously. No one spoke. Colonel Wragge worked the hardest of the three. The soil was light and sandy, and there were only a few snake-like roots and occasional loose stones to delay us. The pick made short work of these. And meanwhile the darkness settled about us and the biting wind swept roaring through the trees overhead.

Then, quite suddenly, without a cry, Colonel Wragge disappeared up to his neck.

"The tunnel!" cried the doctor, helping to drag him out, red, breathless, and covered with sand and perspiration. "Now, let me lead the way." And he slipped down nimbly into the hole, so that a moment later we heard his voice, muffled by sand and distance, rising up to us.

"Hubbard, you come next, and then Colonel Wragge—if he wishes," we heard.

"I'll follow you, of course," he said, looking at me as I scrambled in.

The hole was bigger now, and I got down on all-fours in a channel not much bigger than a large sewer-pipe and found myself in total darkness. A minute later a heavy thud, followed by a cataract of loose sand, announced the arrival of the Colonel.

"Catch hold of my heel," called Dr. Silence, "and Colonel Wragge can take yours."

In this slow, laborious fashion we wormed our way along a tunnel that had been roughly dug out of the shifting sand, and was shored up clumsily by means of wooden pillars and posts. Any moment, it seemed to me, we might be buried alive. We could not see an inch before our eyes, but had to grope our way feeling the pillars and the walls. It was difficult to breathe, and the Colonel behind me made but slow progress, for the cramped position of our bodies was very severe.

We had travelled in this way for ten minutes, and gone perhaps as much as ten yards, when I lost my grasp of the doctor's heel.

"Ah!" I heard his voice, sounding above me somewhere. He was standing up in a clear space, and the next moment I was standing beside him. Colonel Wragge came heavily after, and he too rose up and stood. Then Dr. Silence produced his candles and we heard preparations for striking matches.

Yet even before there was light, an indefinable sensation of awe came over us all. In this hole in the sand, some three feet under ground, we stood side by side, cramped and huddled, struck suddenly with an overwhelming apprehension of something ancient, something formidable, something incalculably wonderful, that touched in each one of us a sense of the sublime and the terrible even before we could see an inch before our faces. I know not how to express in language this singular emotion that caught us here in utter darkness, touching no sense directly, it seemed, yet with the recognition that before us in the blackness of this underground night there lay something that was mighty with the mightiness of long past ages.

I felt Colonel Wragge press in closely to my side, and I understood the pressure and welcomed it. No human touch, to me at least, has ever been more eloquent.

Then the match flared, a thousand shadows fled on black wings, and I saw John Silence fumbling with the candle, his face lit up grotesquely by the flickering light below it.

I had dreaded this light, yet when it came there was apparently nothing to explain the profound sensations of dread that preceded it. We stood in a small vaulted chamber in the sand, the sides and roof shored with bars of wood, and the ground laid roughly with what seemed to be tiles. It was six feet high, so that we could all stand comfortably, and may have been ten feet long by eight feet wide. Upon the wooden pillars at the side I saw that Egyptian hieroglyphics had been rudely traced by burning.

Dr. Silence lit three candles and handed one to each of us. He placed a fourth in the sand against the wall on his right, and another to mark the entrance to the tunnel. We stood and stared about us, instinctively holding our breath.

"Empty, by God!" exclaimed Colonel Wragge. His voice trembled with excitement. And then, as his eyes rested on the ground, he added, "And footsteps—look—footsteps in the sand!"

Dr. Silence said nothing. He stooped down and began to make a search of the chamber, and as he moved, my eyes followed his crouching figure and noted the queer distorted shadows that poured over the walls and ceiling after him. Here and there thin trickles of loose sand ran fizzing down the sides. The atmosphere, heavily charged with faint yet pungent odours, lay utterly still, and the flames of the candles might have been painted on the air for all the movement they betrayed.

And, as I watched, it was almost necessary to persuade myself forcibly that I was only standing upright with difficulty in this little sand-hole of a modern garden in the south of England, for it seemed to me that I stood, as in vision, at the entrance of some vast rock-hewn Temple far, far down the river of Time. The illusion was powerful, and persisted. Granite columns, that rose to heaven, piled themselves about me, majestically uprearing, and a roof like the sky itself spread above a line of colossal figures that moved in shadowy procession along endless and stupendous aisles. This huge and splendid fantasy, borne I knew not whence, possessed me so vividly that I was actually obliged to concentrate my attention upon the small stooping figure of the doctor, as he groped about the walls, in order to keep the eye of imagination on the scene before me.

But the limited space rendered a long search out of the question, and his footsteps, instead of shuffling through loose sand, presently struck something of a different quality that gave forth a hollow and resounding echo. He stooped to examine more closely.

He was standing exactly in the centre of the little chamber when this happened, and he at once began scraping away the sand with his feet. In less than a minute a smooth surface became visible—the surface of a wooden covering. The next thing I saw was that he had raised it and was peering down into a space below. Instantly, a strong odour of nitre and bitumen, mingled with the strange perfume of unknown and powdered aromatics, rose up from the uncovered space and filled the vault, stinging the throat and making the eyes water and smart.

"The mummy!" whispered Dr. Silence, looking up into our faces over his candle; and as he said the word I felt the soldier lurch against me, and heard his breathing in my very ear.

"The mummy!" he repeated under his breath, as we pressed forward to look.

It is difficult to say exactly why the sight should have stirred in me so prodigious an emotion of wonder and veneration, for I have had not a little to do with mummies, have unwound scores of them, and even experimented magically with not a few. But there was something in the sight of that grey and silent figure, lying in its modern box of lead and wood at the bottom of this sandy grave, swathed in the bandages of centuries and wrapped in the perfumed linen that the priests of Egypt had prayed over with their mighty enchantments thousands of years before—something in the sight of it lying there and breathing its own spice-laden atmosphere even in the darkness of its exile in this remote land, something that pierced to the very core of my being and touched that root of awe which slumbers in every man near the birth of tears and the passion of true worship.

I remember turning quickly from the Colonel, lest he should see my emotion, yet fail to understand its cause, turn and clutch John Silence by the arm, and then fall trembling to see that he, too, had lowered his head and was hiding his face in his hands.

A kind of whirling storm came over me, rising out of I know not what utter deeps of memory, and in a whiteness of vision I heard the magical old chauntings from the Book of the Dead, and saw the Gods pass by in dim procession, the mighty, immemorial Beings who were yet themselves only the personified attributes of the true Gods, the God with the Eyes of Fire, the God with the Face of Smoke. I saw again Anubis, the dog-faced deity, and the children of Horus, eternal watcher of the ages, as they swathed Osiris, the first mummy of the world, in the scented and mystic bands, and I tasted again something of the ecstasy of the justified soul as it embarked in the golden Boat of Ra, and journeyed onwards to rest in the fields of the blessed.

And then, as Dr. Silence, with infinite reverence, stooped and touched the still face, so dreadfully staring with its painted eyes, there rose again to our nostrils wave upon wave of this perfume of thousands of years, and time fled backwards like a thing of naught, showing me in haunted panorama the most wonderful dream of the whole world.

A gentle hissing became audible in the air, and the doctor moved quickly backwards. It came close to our faces and then seemed to play about the walls and ceiling.

"The last of the Fire—still waiting for its full accomplishment," he muttered; but I heard both words and hissing as things far away, for I was still busy with the journey of the soul through the Seven Halls of Death, listening for echoes of the grandest ritual ever known to men.

The earthen plates covered with hieroglyphics still lay beside the mummy, and round it, carefully arranged at the points of the compass, stood the four jars with the heads of the hawk, the jackal, the cynocephalus, and man, the jars in which were placed the hair, the nail parings, the heart, and other special portions of the body. Even the amulets, the mirror, the blue clay statues of the Ka, and the lamp with seven wicks were there. Only the sacred scarabæus was missing.

"Not only has it been torn from its ancient resting-place," I heard Dr. Silence saying in a solemn voice as he looked at Colonel Wragge with fixed gaze, "but it has been partially unwound,"—he pointed to the wrappings of the breast,—"and—the scarabæus has been removed from the throat."

The hissing, that was like the hissing of an invisible flame, had ceased; only from time to time we heard it as though it passed backwards and forwards in the tunnel; and we stood looking into each other's faces without speaking.

Presently Colonel Wragge made a great effort and braced himself. I heard the sound catch in his throat before the words actually became audible.

"My sister," he said, very low. And then there followed a long pause, broken at length by John Silence.

"It must be replaced," he said significantly.

"I knew nothing," the soldier said, forcing himself to speak the words he hated saying. "Absolutely nothing."

"It must be returned," repeated the other, "if it is not now too late. For I fear—I fear——"

Colonel Wragge made a movement of assent with his head.

"It shall be," he said.

The place was still as the grave.

I do not know what it was then that made us all three turn round with so sudden a start, for there was no sound audible to my ears, at least.

The doctor was on the point of replacing the lid over the mummy, when he straightened up as if he had been shot.

"There's something coming," said Colonel Wragge under his breath, and the doctor's eyes, peering down the small opening of the tunnel, showed me the true direction.

A distant shuffling noise became distinctly audible coming from a point about half-way down the tunnel we had so laboriously penetrated.

"It's the sand falling in," I said, though I knew it was foolish.

"No," said the Colonel calmly, in a voice that seemed to have the ring of iron, "I've heard it for some time past. It is something alive—and it is coming nearer."

He stared about him with a look of resolution that made his face almost noble. The horror in his heart was overmastering, yet he stood there prepared for anything that might come.

"There's no other way out," John Silence said.

He leaned the lid against the sand, and waited. I knew by the mask-like expression of his face, the pallor, and the steadiness of the eyes, that he anticipated something that might be very terrible—appalling.

The Colonel and myself stood on either side of the opening. I still held my candle and was ashamed of the way it shook, dripping the grease all over me; but the soldier had set his into the sand just behind his feet.

Thoughts of being buried alive, of being smothered like rats in a trap, of being caught and done to death by some invisible and merciless force we could not grapple with, rushed into my mind. Then I thought of fire—of suffocation—of being roasted alive. The perspiration began to pour from my face.

"Steady!" came the voice of Dr. Silence to me through the vault.

For five minutes, that seemed fifty, we stood waiting, looking from each other's faces to the mummy, and from the mummy to the hole, and all the time the shuffling sound, soft and stealthy, came gradually nearer. The tension, for me at least, was very near the breaking point when at last the cause of the disturbance reached the edge. It was hidden for a moment just behind the broken rim of soil. A jet of sand, shaken by the close vibration, trickled down on to the ground; I have never in my life seen anything fall with such laborious leisure. The next second, uttering a cry of curious quality, it came into view.

And it was far more distressingly horrible than anything I had anticipated.

For the sight of some Egyptian monster, some god of the tombs, or even of some demon of fire, I think I was already half prepared; but when, instead, I saw the white visage of Miss Wragge framed in that round opening of sand, followed by her body crawling on all-fours, her eyes bulging and reflecting the yellow glare of the candles, my first instinct was to turn and run like a frantic animal seeking a way of escape.

But Dr. Silence, who seemed no whit surprised, caught my arm and steadied me, and we both saw the Colonel then drop upon his knees and come thus to a level with his sister. For more than a whole minute, as though struck in stone, the two faces gazed silently at each other: hers, for all the dreadful emotion in it, more like a gargoyle than anything human; and his, white and blank with an expression that was beyond either astonishment or alarm. She looked up; he looked down. It was a picture in a nightmare, and the candle, stuck in the sand close to the hole, threw upon it the glare of impromptu footlights.

Then John Silence moved forward and spoke in a voice that was very low, yet perfectly calm and natural.

"I am glad you have come," he said. "You are the one person whose presence at this moment is most required. And I hope that you may yet be in time to appease the anger of the Fire, and to bring peace again to your household, and," he added lower still so that no one heard it but myself, "*safety to yourself.*"

And while her brother stumbled backwards, crushing a candle into the sand in his awkwardness, the old lady crawled farther into the vaulted chamber and slowly rose upon her feet.

At the sight of the wrapped figure of the mummy I was fully prepared to see her scream and faint, but on the contrary, to my complete amazement, she merely bowed her head and dropped quietly upon her knees. Then, after a pause of more than a minute, she raised her eyes to the roof and her lips began to mutter as in prayer. Her right hand, meanwhile, which had been fumbling for some time at her throat suddenly came away, and before the gaze of all of us she held it out, palm upwards, over the grey and ancient figure outstretched below. And in it we beheld glistening the green jasper of the stolen scarabæus.

Her brother, leaning heavily against the wall behind, uttered a sound that was half cry, half exclamation, but John Silence, standing directly in front of her, merely fixed his eyes on her and pointed downwards to the staring face below.

"Replace it," he said sternly, "where it belongs."

Miss Wragge was kneeling at the feet of the mummy when this happened. We three men all had our eyes riveted on what followed. Only the reader who by some remote chance may have witnessed a line of mummies, freshly laid from their tombs upon the sand, slowly stir and bend as the heat of the Egyptian sun warms their ancient bodies into the semblance of life, can form any conception of the ultimate horror we experienced when the silent figure before us moved in its grave of lead and sand. Slowly, before our eyes, it writhed, and, with a faint rustling of the immemorial cerements, rose up, and. through sightless and bandaged eyes, stared across the yellow candle-light at the woman who had violated it.

I tried to move—her brother tried to move—but the sand seemed to hold our feet. I tried to cry—her brother tried to cry—but the sand seemed to fill our lungs and throat. We could only stare—and, even so, the sand seemed to rise like a desert storm and cloud our vision. . . .

And when I managed at length to open my eyes again, the mummy was lying once more upon its back, motionless, the shrunken and painted face upturned towards the ceiling, and the old lady had tumbled forward and was lying in the semblance of death with her head and arms upon its crumbling body.

But upon the wrappings of the throat I saw the green jasper of the sacred scarabæus shining again like a living eye.

Colonel Wragge and the doctor recovered themselves long before I did, and I found myself helping them clumsily and unintelligently to raise the frail body of the old lady, while John Silence carefully replaced the covering over the grave and scraped back the sand with his foot, while he issued brief directions.

I heard his voice as in a dream; but the journey back along that cramped tunnel, weighted by a dead woman, blinded with sand, suffocated with heat, was in no sense a dream. It took us the best part of half an hour to reach the open air. And, even then, we had to wait a considerable time for the appearance of Dr. Silence. We carried her undiscovered into the house and up to her own room.

"The mummy will cause no further disturbance," I heard Dr.

Silence say to our host later that evening as we prepared to drive for the night train, "provided always," he added significantly, "that you, and yours, cause *it* no disturbance."

It was in a dream, too, that we left.

"You did not see her face, I know," he said to me as we wrapped our rugs about us in the empty compartment. And when I shook my head, quite unable to explain the instinct that had come to me not to look, he turned toward me, his face pale, and genuinely sad.

"Scorched and blasted," he whispered.

SECRET WORSHIP

Harris, the silk merchant, was in South Germany on his way home from a business trip when the idea came to him suddenly that he would take the mountain railway from Strassbourg and run down to revisit his old school after an interval of something more than thirty years. And it was to this chance impulse of the junior partner in Harris Brothers of St. Paul's Churchyard that John Silence owed one of the most curious cases of his whole experience, for at that very moment he happened to be tramping these same mountains with a holiday knapsack, and from different points of the compass the two men were actually converging towards the same inn.

Now, deep down in the heart that for thirty years had been concerned chiefly with the profitable buying and selling of silk, this school had left the imprint of its peculiar influence, and, though perhaps unknown to Harris, had strongly coloured the whole of his subsequent existence. It belonged to the deeply religious life of a small Protestant community (which it is unnecessary to specify), and his father had sent him there at the age of fifteen, partly because he would learn the German requisite for the conduct of the silk business, and partly because the discipline was strict, and discipline was what his soul and body needed just then more than anything else.

The life, indeed, had proved exceedingly severe, and young Harris benefited accordingly; for though corporal punishment was unknown, there was a system of mental and spiritual correction which somehow made the soul stand proudly erect to receive it, while it struck at the very root of the fault and taught the boy that his character was being cleaned and strengthened, and that he was not merely being tortured in a kind of personal revenge.

That was over thirty years ago, when he was a dreamy and impressionable youth of fifteen; and now, as the train climbed slowly up the winding mountain gorges, his mind travelled back somewhat lovingly over the intervening period, and forgotten details rose vividly again before him out of the shadows. The life there had been very wonderful, it seemed to him, in that remote mountain village, protected from the tumults of the world by the love and worship of the devout Brotherhood that ministered to the needs of some hundred boys from every country in Europe. Sharply the scenes came back to him. He smelt again the

144

long stone corridors, the hot pinewood rooms, where the sultry hours of summer study were passed with bees droning through open windows in the sunshine, and German characters struggling in the mind with dreams of English lawns—and then the sudden awful cry of the master in German—

"Harris, stand up! You sleep!"

And he recalled the dreadful standing motionless for an hour, book in hand, while the knees felt like wax and the head grew heavier than a cannon-ball.

The very smell of the cooking came back to him—the daily *Sauerkraut*, the watery chocolate on Sundays, the flavour of the stringy meat served twice a week at *Mittagessen*; and he smiled to think again of the half-rations that was the punishment for speaking English. The very odour of the milk-bowls,—the hot sweet aroma that rose from the soaking peasant-bread at the six-o'clock breakfast,—came back to him pungently, and he saw the huge *Speisesaal* with the hundred boys in their school uniform, all eating sleepily in silence, gulping down the coarse bread and scalding milk in terror of the bell that would presently cut them short—and, at the far end where the masters sat, he saw the narrow slit windows with the vistas of enticing field and forest beyond.

And this, in turn, made him think of the great barnlike room on the top floor where all slept together in wooden cots, and he heard in memory the clamour of the cruel bell that woke them on winter mornings at five o'clock and summoned them to the stone-flagged *Waschkammer*, where boys and masters alike, after scanty and icy washing, dressed in complete silence.

From this his mind passed swiftly, with vivid picture-thoughts, to other things, and with a passing shiver he remembered how the loneliness of never being alone had eaten into him, and how everything—work, meals, sleep, walks, leisure—was done with his "division" of twenty other boys and under the eyes of at least two masters. The only solitude possible was by asking for half an hour's practice in the cell-like music rooms, and Harris smiled to himself as he recalled the zeal of his violin studies.

Then, as the train puffed laboriously through the great pine forests that cover these mountains with a giant carpet of velvet, he found the pleasanter layers of memory giving up their dead, and he recalled with admiration the kindness of the masters, whom all addressed as Brother, and marvelled afresh at their devotion in burying themselves for years in such a place, only to leave it, in most cases, for the still rougher life of missionaries in the wild places of the world.

He thought once more of the still, religious atmosphere that hung over the little forest community like a veil, barring the distressful world; of the picturesque ceremonies at Easter, Christmas, and New Year; of the numerous feast-days and charming little festivals. The *Beschehr-Fest*, in particular, came back to him, — the feast of gifts at Christmas, — when the entire community paired off and gave presents, many of which had taken weeks to make or the savings of many days to purchase. And then he saw the midnight ceremony in the church at New Year, with the shining face of the *Prediger* in the pulpit, — the village preacher who, on the last night of the old year, saw in the empty gallery beyond the organ loft the faces of all who were to die in the ensuing twelve months, and who at last recognised himself among them, and, in the very middle of his sermon, passed into a state of rapt ecstasy and burst into a torrent of praise.

Thickly the memories crowded upon him. The picture of the small village dreaming its unselfish life on the mountain-tops, clean, wholesome, simple, searching vigorously for its God, and training hundreds of boys in the grand way, rose up in his mind with all the power of an obsession. He felt once more the old mystical enthusiasm, deeper than the sea and more wonderful than the stars; he heard again the winds sighing from leagues of forest over the red roofs in the moonlight; he heard the Brothers' voices talking of the things beyond this life as though they had actually experienced them in the body; and, as he sat in the jolting train, a spirit of unutterable longing passed over his seared and tired soul, stirring in the depths of him a sea of emotions that he thought had long since frozen into immobility.

And the contrast pained him, — the idealistic dreamer then, the man of business now, — so that a spirit of unworldly peace and beauty known only to the soul in meditation laid its feathered finger upon his heart, moving strangely the surface of the waters.

Harris shivered a little and looked out of the window of his empty carriage. The train had long passed Hornberg, and far below the streams tumbled in white foam down the limestone rocks. In front of him, dome upon dome of wooded mountain stood against the sky. It was October, and the air was cool and sharp, woodsmoke and damp moss exquisitely mingled in it with the subtle odours of the pines. Overhead, between the tips of the highest firs, he saw the first stars peeping, and the sky was a clean, pale amethyst that seemed exactly the colour all these memories clothed themselves with in his mind.

He leaned back in his corner and sighed. He was a heavy man, and he had not known sentiment for years; he was a big man, and it took much to move him, literally and figuratively; he was a man in whom the dreams of God that haunt the soul in youth, though overlaid by the scum that gathers in the fight for money, had not, as with the majority, utterly died the death.

He came back into this little neglected pocket of the years, where so much fine gold had collected and lain undisturbed, with all his semi-spiritual emotions aquiver; and, as he watched the mountain-tops come nearer, and smelt the forgotten odours of his boyhood, something melted on the surface of his soul and left him sensitive to a degree he had not known since, thirty years before, he had lived here with his dreams, his conflicts, and his youthful suffering.

A thrill ran through him as the train stopped with a jolt at a tiny station and he saw the name in large black lettering on the grey stone building, and below it, the number of metres it stood above the level of the sea.

"The highest point on the line!" he exclaimed. "How well I remember it—Sommerau—Summer Meadow. The very next station is mine!"

And, as the train ran downhill with brakes on and steam shut off, he put his head out of the window and one by one saw the old familiar landmarks in the dusk. They stared at him like dead faces in a dream. Queer, sharp feelings, half poignant, half sweet, stirred in his heart.

"There's the hot, white road we walked along so often with the two Brüder always at our heels," he thought; "and there, by Jove, is the turn through the forest to 'Die Galgen,' the stone gallows where they hanged the witches in olden days!"

He smiled a little as the train slid past.

"And there's the copse where the Lilies of the Valley powdered the ground in spring; and, I swear,"—he put his head out with a sudden impulse—"if that's not the very clearing where Calame, the French boy, chased the swallow-tail with me, and Bruder Pagel gave us half-rations for leaving the road without permission, and for shouting in our mother tongues!" And he laughed again as the memories came back with a rush, flooding his mind with vivid detail.

The train stopped, and he stood on the grey gravel platform like a man in a dream. It seemed half a century since he last waited there with corded wooden boxes, and got into the train for Strassbourg and home after the two years' exile. Time dropped from him like an old garment and he felt a boy again. Only, things looked so much smaller than his memory of them; shrunk and dwindled they looked, and the distances seemed on a curiously smaller scale.

He made his way across the road to the little Gasthaus, and, as he went, faces and figures of former schoolfellows,—German, Swiss, Italian, French, Russian,—slipped out of the shadowy woods and silently accompanied him. They flitted by his side, raising their eyes questioningly, sadly, to his. But their names he had forgotten. Some of the Brothers, too, came with them, and most of these he remembered by name—Bruder Röst, Bruder Pagel, Bruder Schliemann, and the bearded face of the old preacher who had seen himself in the haunted gallery of those about to die—Bruder Gysin. The dark forest lay all about him like a sea that any moment might rush with velvet waves upon the scene and sweep all the faces away. The air was cool and wonderfully fragrant, but with every perfumed breath came also a pallid memory. . . .

Yet, in spite of the underlying sadness inseparable from such an experience, it was all very interesting, and held a pleasure peculiarly its own, so that Harris engaged his room and ordered supper feeling well pleased with himself, and intending to walk up to the old school that very evening. It stood in the centre of the community's village, some four miles distant through the forest, and he now recollected for the first time that this little Protestant settlement dwelt isolated in a section of the country that was otherwise Catholic. Crucifixes and shrines surrounded the clearing like the sentries of a beleaguering army. Once beyond the square of the village, with its few acres of field and orchard, the forest crowded up in solid phalanxes, and beyond the rim of trees began the country that was ruled by the priests of another faith. He vaguely remembered, too, that the Catholics had showed sometimes a certain hostility towards the little Protestant oasis that flourished so quietly and benignly in their midst. He had quite forgotten this. How trumpery it all seemed now with his wide experience of life and his knowledge of other countries and the great outside world. It was like stepping back, not thirty years, but three hundred.

There were only two others besides himself at supper. One of them, a bearded, middle-aged man in tweeds, sat by himself at the far end, and Harris kept out of his way because he was English. He feared he might be in business, possibly even in the silk business, and that he would perhaps talk on the subject. The other traveller, however, was a Catholic priest. He was a little man who ate his salad with a knife, yet so gently that it was almost inoffensive, and it was the sight of "the cloth" that recalled his memory of the old antagonism. Harris mentioned by way of conversation the object of his sentimental journey, and the priest looked up sharply at him with raised eyebrows and an expression of surprise and suspicion that somehow piqued him. He ascribed it to his difference of belief.

"Yes," went on the silk merchant, pleased to talk of what his mind was so full, "and it was a curious experience for an English boy to be dropped down into a school of a hundred foreigners. I well remember

the loneliness and intolerable Heimweh of it at first." His German was
very fluent.

The priest opposite looked up from his cold veal and potato salad and
smiled. It was a nice face. He explained quietly that he did not belong
here, but was making a tour of the parishes of Württemberg and Baden.

"It was a strict life," added Harris. "We English, I remember, used to
call it Gefängnisleben—prison life!"

The face of the other, for some unaccountable reason, darkened.
After a slight pause, and more by way of politeness than because he
wished to continue the subject, he said quietly—

"It was a flourishing school in those days, of course. Afterwards, I
have heard——" He shrugged his shoulders slightly, and the odd
look—it almost seemed a look of alarm—came back into his eyes. The
sentence remained unfinished.

Something in the tone of the man seemed to his listener uncalled
for—in a sense reproachful, singular. Harris bridled in spite of himself.

"It has changed?" he asked. "I can hardly believe——"

"You have not heard, then?" observed the priest gently, making a gesture as though to cross himself, yet not actually completing it. "You
have not heard what happened there before it was abandoned——?"

It was very childish, of course, and perhaps he was overtired and
overwrought in some way, but the words and manner of the little priest
seemed to him so offensive—so disproportionately offensive—that he
hardly noticed the concluding sentence. He recalled the old bitterness
and the old antagonism, and for a moment he almost lost his temper.

"Nonsense," he interrupted with a forced laugh, "Unsinn! You
must forgive me, sir, for contradicting you. But I was a pupil there myself. I was at school there. There was no place like it. I cannot believe
that anything serious could have happened to—to take away its
character. The devotion of the Brothers would be difficult to equal anywhere——"

He broke off suddenly, realising that his voice had been raised un-
duly and that the man at the far end of the table might understand
German; and at the same moment he looked up and saw that this individual's eyes were fixed upon his face intently. They were peculiarly
bright. Also they were rather wonderful eyes, and the way they met his
own served in some way he could not understand to convey both a reproach and a warning. The whole face of the stranger, indeed, made a
vivid impression upon him, for it was a face, he now noticed for the first
time, in whose presence one would not willingly have said or done anything unworthy. Harris could not explain to himself how it was he had
not become conscious sooner of its presence.

But he could have bitten off his tongue for having so far forgotten himself. The little priest lapsed into silence. Only once he said, looking up and speaking in a low voice that was not intended to be overheard, but that evidently *was* overheard, "You will find it different." Presently he rose and left the table with a polite bow that included both the others.

And, after him, from the far end rose also the figure in the tweed suit, leaving Harris by himself.

He sat on for a bit in the darkening room, sipping his coffee and smoking his fifteen-pfennig cigar, till the girl came in to light the oil lamps. He felt vexed with himself for his lapse from good manners, yet hardly able to account for it. Most likely, he reflected, he had been annoyed because the priest had unintentionally changed the pleasant character of his dream by introducing a jarring note. Later he must seek an opportunity to make amends. At present, however, he was too impatient for his walk to the school, and he took his stick and hat and passed out into the open air.

And, as he crossed before the Gasthaus, he noticed that the priest and the man in the tweed suit were engaged already in such deep conversation that they hardly noticed him as he passed and raised his hat.

He started off briskly, well remembering the way, and hoping to reach the village in time to have a word with one of the Brüder. They might even ask him in for a cup of coffee. He felt sure of his welcome, and the old memories were in full possession once more. The hour of return was a matter of no consequence whatever.

It was then just after seven o'clock, and the October evening was drawing in with chill airs from the recesses of the forest. The road plunged straight from the railway clearing into its depths, and in a very few minutes the trees engulfed him and the clack of his boots fell dead and echoless against the serried stems of a million firs. It was very black; one trunk was hardly distinguishable from another. He walked smartly, swinging his holly stick. Once or twice he passed a peasant on his way to bed, and the guttural "Gruss Got," unheard for so long, emphasised the passage of time, while yet making it seem as nothing. A fresh group of pictures crowded his mind. Again the figures of former schoolfellows flitted out of the forest and kept pace by his side, whispering of the doings of long ago. One reverie stepped hard upon the heels of another. Every turn in the road, every clearing of the forest, he knew, and each in turn brought forgotten associations to life. He enjoyed himself thoroughly.

He marched on and on. There was powdered gold in the sky till the moon rose, and then a wind of faint silver spread silently between the earth and stars. He saw the tips of the fir trees shimmer, and heard them whisper as the breeze turned their needles towards the light. The mountain air was indescribably sweet. The road shone like the foam of a river through the gloom. White moths flitted here and there like silent thoughts across his path, and a hundred smells greeted him from the forest caverns across the years.

Then, when he least expected it, the trees fell away abruptly on both sides, and he stood on the edge of the village clearing.

He walked faster. There lay the familiar outlines of the houses, sheeted with silver; there stood the trees in the little central square with the fountain and small green lawns; there loomed the shape of the church next to the Gasthof der Brüdergemeinde; and just beyond, dimly rising into the sky, he saw with a sudden thrill the mass of the huge school building, blocked castlelike with deep shadows in the moonlight, standing square and formidable to face him after the silences of more than a quarter of a century.

He passed quickly down the deserted village street and stopped close beneath its shadow, staring up at the walls that had once held him prisoner for two years—two unbroken years of discipline and homesickness. Memories and emotions surged through his mind; for the most vivid sensations of his youth had focused about this spot, and it was here he had first begun to live and learn values. Not a single footstep broke the silence, though lights glimmered here and there through cottage windows; but when he looked up at the high walls of the school, draped now in shadow, he easily imagined that well-known faces crowded to the windows to greet him—closed windows that really reflected only moonlight and the gleam of stars.

This, then, was the old school building, standing foursquare to the world, with its shuttered windows, its lofty, tiled roof, and the spiked lightning-conductors pointing like black and taloned fingers from the corners. For a long time he stood and stared. Then, presently, he came to himself again, and realised to his joy that a light still shone in the windows of the *Bruderstube*.

He turned from the road and passed through the iron railings; then climbed the twelve stone steps and stood facing the black wooden door with the heavy bars of iron, a door he had once loathed and dreaded with the hatred and passion of an imprisoned soul, but now looked upon tenderly with a sort of boyish delight.

Almost timorously he pulled the rope and listened with a tremor of excitement to the clanging of the bell deep within the building. And the long-forgotten sound brought the past before him with such a vivid sense of reality that he positively shivered. It was like the magic bell in

the fairy-tale that rolls back the curtain of Time and summons the figures from the shadows of the dead. He had never felt so sentimental in
his life. It was like being young again. And, at the same time, he began
to bulk rather large in his own eyes with a certain spurious importance.
He was a big man from the world of strife and action. In this little place
of peaceful dreams would he, perhaps, not cut something of a figure?

"I'll try once more," he thought after a long pause, seizing the iron
bell-rope, and was just about to pull it when a step sounded on the
stone passage within, and the huge door slowly swung open.

A tall man with a rather severe cast of countenance stood facing him
in silence.

"I must apologise — it is somewhat late," he began a trifle pompously,
"but the fact is I am an old pupil. I have only just arrived and really
could not restrain myself." His German seemed not quite so fluent as
usual. "My interest is so great. I was here in '70."

The other opened the door wider and at once bowed him in with a
smile of genuine welcome.

"I am Bruder Kalkmann," he said quietly in a deep voice. "I myself was a master here about that time. It is a great pleasure always to
welcome a former pupil." He looked at him very keenly for a few seconds, and then added, "I think, too, it is splendid of you to come — very
splendid."

"It is a very great pleasure," Harris replied, delighted with his
reception.

The dimly lighted corridor with its flooring of grey stone, and the familiar sound of a German voice echoing through it, — with the peculiar
intonation the Brothers always used in speaking, — all combined to lift
him bodily, as it were, into the dream-atmosphere of long-forgotten
days. He stepped gladly into the building and the door shut with the familiar thunder that completed the reconstruction of the past. He almost felt the old sense of imprisonment, of aching nostalgia, of having
lost his liberty.

Harris sighed involuntarily and turned towards his host, who returned his smile faintly and then led the way down the corridor.

"The boys have retired," he explained, "and, as you remember, we
keep early hours here. But, at least, you will join us for a little while in
the *Bruderstube* and enjoy a cup of coffee." This was precisely what the
silk merchant had hoped, and he accepted with an alacrity that he intended to be tempered by graciousness. "And tomorrow," continued
the Bruder, "you must come and spend a whole day with us. You may
even find acquaintances, for several pupils of your day have come back
here as masters."

For one brief second there passed into the man's eyes a look that made the visitor start. But it vanished as quickly as it came. It was impossible to define. Harris convinced himself it was the effect of a shadow cast by the lamp they had just passed on the wall. He dismissed it from his mind.

"You are very kind, I'm sure," he said politely. "It is perhaps a greater pleasure to me than you can imagine to see the place again. Ah,"—he stopped short opposite a door with the upper half of glass and peered in—"surely there is one of the music rooms where I used to practise the violin. How it comes back to me after all these years!"

Bruder Kalkmann stopped indulgently, smiling, to allow his guest a moment's inspection.

"You still have the boys' orchestra? I remember I used to play 'zweite Geige' in it. Bruder Schliemann conducted at the piano. Dear me, I can see him now with his long black hair and—and——" He stopped abruptly. Again the odd, dark look passed over the stern face of his companion. For an instant it seemed curiously familiar.

"We still keep up the pupils' orchestra," he said, "but Bruder Schliemann, I am sorry to say——" he hesitated an instant, and then added, "Bruder Schliemann is dead."

"Indeed, indeed," said Harris quickly. "I am sorry to hear it." He was conscious of a faint feeling of distress, but whether it arose from the news of his old music teacher's death, or—from something else—he could not quite determine. He gazed down the corridor that lost itself among shadows. In the street and village everything had seemed so much smaller than he remembered, but here, inside the school building, everything seemed so much bigger. The corridor was loftier and longer, more spacious and vast, than the mental picture he had preserved. His thoughts wandered dreamily for an instant.

He glanced up and saw the face of the Bruder watching him with a smile of patient indulgence.

"Your memories possess you," he observed gently, and the stern look passed into something almost pitying.

"You are right," returned the man of silk, "they do. This was the most wonderful period of my whole life in a sense. At the time I hated it——" He hesitated, not wishing to hurt the Brother's feelings.

"According to English ideas it seemed strict, of course," the other said persuasively, so that he went on.

"——Yes, partly that; and partly the ceaseless nostalgia, and the solitude which came from never being really alone. In English schools the boys enjoy peculiar freedom, you know."

Bruder Kalkmann, he saw, was listening intently.

"But it produced one result that I have never wholly lost," he continued self-consciously, "and am grateful for."

"*Ach! Wie so, denn?*"

"The constant inner pain threw me headlong into your religious life, so that the whole force of my being seemed to project itself towards the search for a deeper satisfaction—a real resting-place for the soul. During my two years here I yearned for God in my boyish way as perhaps I have never yearned for anything since. Moreover, I have never quite lost that sense of peace and inward joy which accompanied the search. I can never quite forget this school and the deep things it taught me."

He paused at the end of his long speech, and a brief silence fell between them. He feared he had said too much, or expressed himself clumsily in the foreign language, and when Bruder Kalkmann laid a hand upon his shoulder, he gave a little involuntary start.

"So that my memories perhaps do possess me rather strongly," he added apologetically; "and this long corridor, these rooms, that barred and gloomy front door, all touch chords that—that——" His German failed him and he glanced at his companion with an explanatory smile and gesture. But the Brother had removed the hand from his shoulder and was standing with his back to him, looking down the passage.

"Naturally, naturally so," he said hastily without turning round. "*Es ist doch selbstverständlich.* We shall all understand."

Then he turned suddenly, and Harris saw that his face had turned most oddly and disagreeably sinister. It may only have been the shadows again playing their tricks with the wretched oil lamps on the wall, for the dark expression passed instantly as they retraced their steps down the corridor, but the Englishman somehow got the impression that he had said something to give offence, something that was not quite to the other's taste. Opposite the door of the *Bruderstube* they stopped. Harris realised that it was late and he had possibly stayed talking too long. He made a tentative effort to leave, but his companion would not hear of it.

"You must have a cup of coffee with us," he said firmly as though he meant it, "and my colleagues will be delighted to see you. Some of them will remember you, perhaps."

The sound of voices came pleasantly through the door, men's voices talking together. Bruder Kalkmann turned the handle and they entered a room ablaze with light and full of people.

"Ah,—but your name?" he whispered, bending down to catch the reply; "you have not told me your name yet."

"Harris," said the Englishman quickly as they went in. He felt nervous as he crossed the threshold, but ascribed the momentary trepidation to the fact that he was breaking the strictest rule of the whole establishment, which forbade a boy under severest penalties to come near this holy of holies where the masters took their brief leisure.

"Ah, yes, of course—Harris," repeated the other as though he remembered it. "Come in, Herr Harris, come in, please. Your visit will be immensely appreciated. It is really very fine, very wonderful of you to have come in this way."

The door closed behind them and, in the sudden light which made his sight swim for a moment, the exaggeration of the language escaped his attention. He heard the voice of Bruder Kalkmann introducing him. He spoke very loud, indeed, unnecessarily,—absurdly loud, Harris thought.

"Brothers," he announced, "it is my pleasure and privilege to introduce to you Herr Harris from England. He has just arrived to make us a little visit, and I have already expressed to him on behalf of us all the satisfaction we feel that he is here. He was, as you remember, a pupil in the year '70."

It was a very formal, a very German introduction, but Harris rather liked it. It made him feel important and he appreciated the tact that made it almost seem as though he had been expected.

The black forms rose and bowed; Harris bowed; Kalkmann bowed. Every one was very polite and very courtly. The room swam with moving figures; the light dazzled him after the gloom of the corridor, there was thick cigar smoke in the atmosphere. He took the chair that was offered to him between two of the Brothers, and sat down, feeling vaguely that his perceptions were not quite as keen and accurate as usual. He felt a trifle dazed perhaps, and the spell of the past came strongly over him, confusing the immediate present and making everything dwindle oddly to the dimensions of long ago. He seemed to pass under the mastery of a great mood that was a composite reproduction of all the moods of his forgotten boyhood.

Then he pulled himself together with a sharp effort and entered into the conversation that had begun again to buzz round him. Moreover, he entered into it with keen pleasure, for the Brothers—there were perhaps a dozen of them in the little room—treated him with a charm of manner that speedily made him feel one of themselves. This, again, was a very subtle delight to him. He felt that he had stepped out of the greedy, vulgar, self-seeking world, the world of silk and markets and profit-making—stepped into the cleaner atmosphere where spiritual ideals were paramount and life was simple and devoted. It all charmed him inexpressibly, so that he realised—yes, in a sense—the degradation of his twenty years' absorption in business. This keen atmosphere under the stars where men thought only of their souls, and of the souls of others, was too rarefied for the world he was now associated with. He found himself making comparisons to his own disadvantage, — comparisons with the mystical little dreamer that had stepped thirty years before from the stern peace of this devout community, and the man of the world that he had since become, — and the contrast made him shiver with a keen regret and something like self-contempt.

He glanced round at the other faces floating towards him through tobacco smoke — this acrid cigar smoke he remembered so well: how keen they were, how strong, placid, touched with the nobility of great aims and unselfish purposes. At one or two he looked particularly. He hardly knew why. They rather fascinated him. There was something so very stern and uncompromising about them, and something, too, oddly, subtly, familiar, that yet just eluded him. But whenever their eyes met his own they held undeniable welcome in them; and some held more — a kind of perplexed admiration, he thought, something that was between esteem and deference. This note of respect in all the faces was very flattering to his vanity.

Coffee was served presently, made by a black-haired Brother who sat in the corner by the piano and bore a marked resemblance to Bruder Schliemann, the musical director of thirty years ago. Harris exchanged bows with him when he took the cup from his white hands, which he noticed were like the hands of a woman. He lit a cigar, offered to him by his neighbour, with whom he was chatting delightfully, and who, in the glare of the lighted match, reminded him sharply for a moment of Bruder Pagel, his former room-master.

"*Es ist wirklich merkwürdig,*" he said, "how many resemblances I see, or imagine. It is really *very* curious!"

"Yes," replied the other, peering at him over his coffee cup, "the spell of the place is wonderfully strong. I can well understand that the old faces rise before your mind's eye — almost to the exclusion of ourselves perhaps."

They both laughed presently. It was soothing to find his mood understood and appreciated. And they passed on to talk of the mountain village, its isolation, its remoteness from worldly life, its peculiar fitness for meditation and worship, and for spiritual development — of a certain kind.

"And your coming back in this way, Herr Harris, has pleased us all so much," joined in the Bruder on his left. "We esteem you for it most highly. We honour you for it."

Harris made a deprecating gesture. "I fear, for my part, it is only a very selfish pleasure," he said a trifle unctuously.

"Not all would have had the courage," added the one who resembled Bruder Pagel.

"You mean," said Harris, a little puzzled, "the disturbing memories——?"

Bruder Pagel looked at him steadily, with unmistakable admiration and respect. "I mean that most men hold so strongly to life, and can give up so little for their beliefs," he said gravely.

The Englishman felt slightly uncomfortable. These worthy men really made too much of his sentimental journey. Besides, the talk was getting a little out of his depth. He hardly followed it.

"The worldly life still has *some* charms for me," he replied smilingly, as though to indicate that sainthood was not yet quite within his grasp.

"All the more, then, must we honour you for so freely coming," said the Brother on his left; "so unconditionally!"

A pause followed, and the silk merchant felt relieved when the conversation took a more general turn, although he noted that it never travelled very far from the subject of his visit and the wonderful situation of the lonely village for men who wished to develop their spiritual powers and practise the rites of a high worship. Others joined in, complimenting him on his knowledge of the language, making him feel utterly at his ease, yet at the same time a little uncomfortable by the excess of their admiration. After all, it was such a very small thing to do, this sentimental journey.

The time passed along quickly; the coffee was excellent, the cigars soft and of the nutty flavour he loved. At length, fearing to outstay his welcome, he rose reluctantly to take his leave. But the others would not hear of it. It was not often a former pupil returned to visit them in this simple, unaffected way. The night was young. If necessary they could even find him a corner in the great *Schlafzimmer* upstairs. He was easily persuaded to stay a little longer. Somehow he had become the centre of the little party. He felt pleased, flattered, honoured.

"And perhaps Bruder Schliemann will play something for us—now."

It was Kalkmann speaking, and Harris started visibly as he heard the name, and saw the black-haired man by the piano turn with a smile. For Schliemann was the name of his old music director, who was dead. Could this be his son? They were so exactly alike.

"If Bruder Meyer has not put his Amati to bed, I will accompany him," said the musician suggestively, looking across at a man whom Harris had not yet noticed, and who, he now saw, was the very image of a former master of that name.

Meyer rose and excused himself with a little bow, and the

Englishman quickly observed that he had a peculiar gesture as though his neck had a false join on to the body just below the collar and feared it might break. Meyer of old had this trick of movement. He remembered how the boys used to copy it.

He glanced sharply from face to face, feeling as though some silent, unseen process were changing everything about him. All the faces seemed oddly familiar. Pagel, the Brother he had been talking with, was of course the image of Pagel, his former room-master, and Kalkmann, he now realised for the first time, was the very twin of another master whose name he had quite forgotten, but whom he used to dislike intensely in the old days. And, through the smoke, peering at him from the corners of the room, he saw that all the Brothers about him had the faces he had known and lived with long ago—Röst, Fluheim, Meinert, Rigel, Gysin.

He stared hard, suddenly grown more alert, and everywhere saw, or fancied he saw, strange likenesses, ghostly resemblances,—more, the identical faces of years ago. There was something queer about it all, something not quite right, something that made him feel uneasy. He shook himself, mentally and actually, blowing the smoke from before his eyes with a long breath, and as he did so he noticed to his dismay that every one was fixedly staring. They were watching him.

This brought him to his senses. As an Englishman, and a foreigner, he did not wish to be rude, or to do anything to make himself foolishly conspicuous and spoil the harmony of the evening. He was a guest, and a privileged guest at that. Besides, the music had already begun. Bruder Schliemann's long white fingers were caressing the keys to some purpose.

He subsided into his chair and smoked with half-closed eyes that yet saw everything.

But the shudder had established itself in his being, and, whether he would or not, it kept repeating itself. As a town, far up some inland river, feels the pressure of the distant sea, so he became aware that mighty forces from somewhere beyond his ken were urging themselves up against his soul in this smoky little room. He began to feel exceedingly ill at ease.

And as the music filled the air his mind began to clear. Like a lifted veil there rose up something that had hitherto obscured his vision. The words of the priest at the railway inn flashed across his brain unbidden: "You will find it different." And also, though why he could not tell, he saw mentally the strong, rather wonderful eyes of that other guest at the supper-table, the man who had overheard his conversation, and had later got into earnest talk with the priest. He took out his watch

and stole a glance at it. Two hours had slipped by. It was already eleven
o'clock.

Schliemann, meanwhile, utterly absorbed in his music, was playing
a solemn measure. The piano sang marvellously. The power of a great
conviction, the simplicity of great art, the vital spiritual message of a
soul that had found itself—all this, and more, were in the chords, and
yet somehow the music was what can only be described as impure—
atrociously and diabolically impure. And the piece itself, although
Harris did not recognise it as anything familiar, was surely the music of
a Mass—huge, majestic, sombre? It stalked through the smoky room
with slow power, like the passage of something that was mighty, yet profoundly intimate, and as it went there stirred into each and every face
about him the signature of the enormous forces of which it was the audible symbol. The countenances round him turned sinister, but not
idly, negatively sinister: they grew dark with purpose. He suddenly recalled the face of Bruder Kalkmann in the corridor earlier in the
evening. The motives of their secret souls rose to the eyes, and mouths,
and foreheads, and hung there for all to see like the black banners of
an assembly of ill-starred and fallen creatures. Demons—was the horrible word that flashed through his brain like a sheet of fire.

When this sudden discovery leaped out upon him, for a moment he
lost his self-control. Without waiting to think and weigh his extraordinary impression, he did a very foolish but a very natural thing. Feeling
himself irresistibly driven by the sudden stress to some kind of action,
he sprang to his feet—and screamed! To his own utter amazement he
stood up and shrieked aloud!

But no one stirred. No one, apparently, took the slightest notice of
his absurdly wild behaviour. It was almost as if no one but himself had
heard the scream at all—as though the music had drowned it and swallowed it up—as though after all perhaps he had not really screamed as
loudly as he imagined, or had not screamed at all.

Then, as he glanced at the motionless, dark faces before him, something of utter cold passed into his being, touching his very soul. . . . All
emotion cooled suddenly, leaving him like a receding tide. He sat
down again, ashamed, mortified, angry with himself for behaving like
a fool and a boy. And the music, meanwhile, continued to issue from
the white and snakelike fingers of Bruder Schliemann, as poisoned
wine might issue from the weirdly fashioned necks of antique phials.

And, with the rest of them, Harris drank it in.

Forcing himself to believe that he had been the victim of some kind
of illusory perception, he vigorously restrained his feelings. Then the
music presently ceased, and every one applauded and began to talk at

once, laughing, changing seats, complimenting the player, and behaving naturally and easily as though nothing out of the way had happened. The faces appeared normal once more. The Brothers crowded round their visitor, and he joined in their talk and even heard himself thanking the gifted musician.

But, at the same time, he found himself edging towards the door, nearer and nearer, changing his chair when possible, and joining the groups that stood closest to the way of escape.

"I must thank you all *tausendmal* for my little reception and the great pleasure—the very great honour you have done me," he began in decided tones at length, "but I fear I have trespassed far too long already on your hospitality. Moreover, I have some distance to walk to my inn."

A chorus of voices greeted his words. They would not hear of his going,—at least not without first partaking of refreshment. They produced pumpernickel from one cupboard, and rye-bread and sausage from another, and all began to talk again and eat. More coffee was made, fresh cigars lighted, and Bruder Meyer took out his violin and began to tune it softly.

"There is always a bed upstairs if Herr Harris will accept it," said one.

"And it is difficult to find the way out now, for all the doors are locked," laughed another loudly.

"Let us take our simple pleasures as they come," cried a third. "Bruder Harris will understand how we appreciate the honour of this last visit of his."

They made a dozen excuses. They all laughed, as though the politeness of their words was but formal, and veiled thinly—more and more thinly—a very different meaning.

"And the hour of midnight draws near," added Bruder Kalkmann with a charming smile, but in a voice that sounded to the Englishman like the grating of iron hinges.

Their German seemed to him more and more difficult to understand. He noted that they called him "Bruder" too, classing him as one of themselves.

And then suddenly he had a flash of keener perception, and realised with a creeping of his flesh that he had all along misinterpreted— grossly misinterpreted all they had been saying. They had talked about the beauty of the place, its isolation and remoteness from the world, its peculiar fitness for certain kinds of spiritual development and worship—yet hardly, he now grasped, in the sense in which he had taken the words. They had meant something different. Their spiritual powers, their desire for loneliness, their passion for worship, were not the powers, the solitude, or the worship that *he* meant and understood. He was playing a part in some horrible masquerade; he was among men who cloaked their lives with religion in order to follow their real purposes unseen of men.

What did it all mean? How had he blundered into so equivocal a situation? Had he blundered into it at all? Had he not rather been led into it, deliberately led? His thoughts grew dreadfully confused, and his confidence in himself began to fade. And why, he suddenly thought again, were they so impressed by the mere fact of his coming to revisit his old school? What was it they so admired and wondered at in his simple act? Why did they set such store upon his having the courage to come, to "give himself so freely," "unconditionally" as one of them had expressed it with such a mockery of exaggeration?

Fear stirred in his heart most horribly, and he found no answer to any of his questionings. Only one thing he now understood quite clearly: it was their purpose to keep him here. They did not intend that he should go. And from this moment he realised that they were sinister, formidable and, in some way he had yet to discover, inimical to himself, inimical to his life. And the phrase one of them had used a moment ago— "this *last* visit of his"—rose before his eyes in letters of flame.

Harris was not a man of action, and had never known in all the course of his career what it meant to be in a situation of real danger. He was not necessarily a coward, though, perhaps, a man of untried nerve. He realised at last plainly that he was in a very awkward predicament indeed, and that he had to deal with men who were utterly in earnest. What their intentions were he only vaguely guessed. His mind, indeed, was too confused for definite ratiocination, and he was only able to follow blindly the strongest instincts that moved in him. It never occurred to him that the Brothers might all be mad, or that he himself might have temporarily lost his senses and be suffering under some terrible delusion. In fact, nothing occurred to him—he realised nothing—except that he meant to escape—and the quicker the better. A tremendous revulsion of feeling set in and overpowered him.

Accordingly, without further protest for the moment, he ate his pumpernickel and drank his coffee, talking meanwhile as naturally and pleasantly as he could, and when a suitable interval had passed, he rose to his feet and announced once more that he must now take his leave. He spoke very quietly, but very decidedly. No one hearing him could doubt that he meant what he said. He had got very close to the door by this time.

"I regret," he said, using his best German, and speaking to a hushed room, "that our pleasant evening must come to an end, but it is now time for me to wish you all good-night." And then, as no one said anything, he added, though with a trifle less assurance, "And I thank you all most sincerely for your hospitality."

"On the contrary," replied Kalkmann instantly, rising from his chair and ignoring the hand the Englishman had stretched out to him, "it is we who have to thank you; and we do so most gratefully and sincerely."

And at the same moment at least half a dozen of the Brothers took up their position between himself and the door.

"You are very good to say so," Harris replied as firmly as he could manage, noticing this movement out of the corner of his eye, "but really I had no conception that—my little chance visit could have afforded you so much pleasure." He moved another step nearer the door, but Bruder Schliemann came across the room quickly and stood in front of him. His attitude was uncompromising. A dark and terrible expression had come into his face.

"But it was *not* by chance that you came, Bruder Harris," he said so that all the room could hear; "surely we have not misunderstood your presence here?" He raised his black eyebrows.

"No, no," the Englishman hastened to reply, "I was—I am delighted to be here. I told you what pleasure it gave me to find myself among you. Do not misunderstand me, I beg." His voice faltered a little, and he had difficulty in finding the words. More and more, too, he had difficulty in understanding *their* words.

"Of course," interposed Bruder Kalkmann in his iron bass, "*we* have not misunderstood. You have come back in the spirit of true and unselfish devotion. You offer yourself freely, and we all appreciate it. It is your willingness and nobility that have so completely won our veneration and respect." A faint murmur of applause ran round the room. "What we all delight in—what our great Master will especially delight in—is the value of your spontaneous and voluntary——"

He used a word Harris did not understand. He said "*Opfer.*" The bewildered Englishman searched his brain for the translation, and searched in vain. For the life of him he could not remember what it meant. But the word, for all his inability to translate it, touched his soul with ice. It was worse, far worse, than anything he had imagined. He felt like a lost, helpless creature, and all power to fight sank out of him from that moment.

"It is magnificent to be such a willing——" added Schliemann, sidling up to him with a dreadful leer on his face. He made use of the same word—"*Opfer.*"

"God! What could it all mean?" "Offer himself!" "True spirit of devotion!" "Willing," "unselfish," "magnificent!" *Opfer, Opfer, Opfer!*

What in the name of heaven did it mean, that strange, mysterious word that struck such terror into his heart?

He made a valiant effort to keep his presence of mind and hold his nerves steady. Turning, he saw that Kalkmann's face was a dead white. Kalkmann! He understood that well enough. *Kalkmann* meant "Man of Chalk": he knew that. But what did *"Opfer"* mean? That was the real key to the situation. Words poured through his disordered mind in an endless stream—unusual, rare words he had perhaps heard but once in his life—while *"Opfer,"* a word in common use, entirely escaped him. What an extraordinary mockery it all was!

Then Kalkmann, pale as death, but his face hard as iron, spoke a few low words that he did not catch, and the Brothers standing by the walls at once turned the lamps down so that the room became dim. In the half light he could only just discern their faces and movements.

"It is time," he heard Kalkmann's remorseless voice continue just behind him. "The hour of midnight is at hand. Let us prepare. He comes! He comes; Bruder Asmodelius comes!" His voice rose to a chant.

And the sound of that name, for some extraordinary reason, was terrible—utterly terrible; so that Harris shook from head to foot as he heard it. Its utterance filled the air like soft thunder, and a hush came over the whole room. Forces rose all about him, transforming the normal into the horrible, and the spirit of craven fear ran through all his being, bringing him to the verge of collapse.

Asmodelius! Asmodelius! The name was appalling. For he understood at last to whom it referred and the meaning that lay between its great syllables. At the same instant, too, he suddenly understood the meaning of that unremembered word. The import of the word *"Opfer"* flashed upon his soul like a message of death.

He thought of making a wild effort to reach the door, but the weakness of his trembling knees, and the row of black figures that stood between, dissuaded him at once. He would have screamed for help, but remembering the emptiness of the vast building, and the loneliness of the situation, he understood that no help could come that way, and he kept his lips closed. He stood still and did nothing. But he knew now what was coming.

Two of the Brothers approached and took him gently by the arm.

"Bruder Asmodelius accepts you," they whispered; "are you ready?"

Then he found his tongue and tried to speak. "But what have I to do with this Bruder Asm—Asmo——?" he stammered, a desperate rush of words crowding vainly behind the halting tongue.

The name refused to pass his lips. He could not pronounce it as they did. He could not pronounce it at all. His sense of helplessness then en-

tered the acute stage, for this inability to speak the name produced a
fresh sense of quite horrible confusion in his mind, and he became extraordinarily agitated.

"I came here for a friendly visit," he tried to say with a great effort,
but, to his intense dismay, he heard his voice saying something quite
different, and actually making use of that very word they had all used:
"I came here as a willing *Opfer*," he heard his own voice say, "and *I am
quite ready.*"

He was lost beyond all recall now! Not alone his mind, but the very
muscles of his body had passed out of control. He felt that he was hovering on the confines of a phantom or demon-world,—a world in
which the name they had spoken constituted the Master-name, the
word of ultimate power.

What followed he heard and saw as in a nightmare.

"In the half light that veils all truth, let us prepare to worship
and adore," chanted Schliemann, who had preceded him to the end of
the room.

"In the mists that protect our faces before the Black Throne, let us
make ready the willing victim," echoed Kalkmann in his great bass.

They raised their faces, listening expectantly, as a roaring sound, like
the passing of mighty projectiles, filled the air, far, far away, very wonderful, very forbidding. The walls of the room trembled.

"He comes! He comes! He comes!" chanted the Brothers in chorus.

The sound of roaring died away, and an atmosphere of still and utter
cold established itself over all. Then Kalkmann, dark and unutterably
stern, turned in the dim light and faced the rest.

"Asmodelius, our *Hauptbruder*, is about us," he cried in a voice that
even while it shook was yet a voice of iron; "Asmodelius is about us.
Make ready."

There followed a pause in which no one stirred or spoke. A tall
Brother approached the Englishman; but Kalkmann held up his hand.

"Let the eyes remain uncovered," he said, "in honour of so freely giving himself." And to his horror Harris then realised for the first time
that his hands were already fastened to his sides.

The Brother retreated again silently, and in the pause that followed
all the figures about him dropped to their knees, leaving him standing
alone, and as they dropped, in voices hushed with mingled reverence
and awe, they cried, softly, odiously, appallingly, the name of the Being
whom they momentarily expected to appear.

Then, at the end of the room, where the windows seemed to have
disappeared so that he saw the stars, there rose into view far up
against the night sky, grand and terrible, the outline of a man. A

kind of grey glory enveloped it so that it resembled a steel-cased statue, immense, imposing, horrific in its distant splendour; while, at the same time, the face was so spiritually mighty, yet so proudly, so austerely sad, that Harris felt as he stared, that the sight was more than his eyes could meet, and that in another moment the power of vision would fail him altogether, and he must sink into utter nothingness.

So remote and inaccessible hung this figure that it was impossible to gauge anything as to its size, yet at the same time so strangely close, that when the grey radiance from its mightily broken visage, august and mournful, beat down upon his soul, pulsing like some dark star with the powers of spiritual evil, he felt almost as though he were looking into a face no farther removed from him in space than the face of any one of the Brothers who stood by his side.

And then the room filled and trembled with sounds that Harris understood full well were the failing voices of others who had preceded him in a long series down the years. There came first a plain, sharp cry, as of a man in the last anguish, choking for his breath, and yet, with the very final expiration of it, breathing the name of the Worship—of the dark Being who rejoiced to hear it. The cries of the strangled; the short, running gasp of the suffocated; and the smothered gurgling of the tightened throat, all these, and more, echoed back and forth between the walls, the very walls in which he now stood a prisoner, a sacrificial victim. The cries, too, not alone of the broken bodies, but—far worse—of beaten, broken souls. And as the ghastly chorus rose and fell, there came also the faces of the lost and unhappy creatures to whom they belonged, and, against that curtain of pale grey light, he saw float past him in the air, an array of white and piteous human countenances that seemed to beckon and gibber at him as though he were already one of themselves.

Slowly, too, as the voices rose, and the pallid crew sailed past, that giant form of grey descended from the sky and approached the room that contained the worshippers and their prisoner. Hands rose and sank about him in the darkness, and he felt that he was being draped in other garments than his own; a circlet of ice seemed to run about his head, while round the waist, enclosing the fastened arms, he felt a girdle tightly drawn. At last, about his very throat, there ran a soft and silken touch which, better than if there had been full light, and a mirror held to his face, he understood to be the cord of sacrifice—and of death.

At this moment the Brothers, still prostrate upon the floor, began again their mournful, yet impassioned chanting, and as they did so a strange thing happened. For, apparently without moving or altering its position, the huge Figure seemed, at once and suddenly, to be inside the room, almost beside him, and to fill the space around him to the exclusion of all else.

He was now beyond all ordinary sensations of fear, only a drab feeling as of death—the death of the soul—stirred in his heart. His thoughts no longer even beat vainly for escape. The end was near, and he knew it.

The dreadfully chanting voices rose about him in a wave: "We worship! We adore! We offer!" The sounds filled his ears and hammered, almost meaningless, upon his brain.

Then the majestic grey face turned slowly downwards upon him, and his very soul passed outwards and seemed to become absorbed in the sea of those anguished eyes. At the same moment a dozen hands forced him to his knees, and in the air before him he saw the arm of Kalkmann upraised, and felt the pressure about his throat grow strong.

It was in this awful moment, when he had given up all hope, and the help of gods or men seemed beyond question, that a strange thing happened. For before his fading and terrified vision there slid, as in a dream of light,—yet without apparent rhyme or reason—wholly unbidden and unexplained,—the face of that other man at the supper table of the railway inn. And the sight, even mentally, of that strong, wholesome, vigorous English face, inspired him suddenly with a new courage.

It was but a flash of fading vision before he sank into a dark and terrible death, yet, in some inexplicable way, the sight of that face stirred in him unconquerable hope and the certainty of deliverance. It was a face of power, a face, he now realised, of simple goodness such as might have been seen by men of old on the shores of Galilee; a face, by heaven, that could conquer even the devils of outer space.

And, in his despair and abandonment, he called upon it, and called with no uncertain accents. He found his voice in this overwhelming moment to some purpose; though the words he actually used, and whether they were in German or English, he could never remember. Their effect, nevertheless, was instantaneous. The Brothers understood, and that grey Figure of evil understood.

For a second the confusion was terrific. There came a great shattering sound. It seemed that the very earth trembled. But all Harris remembered afterwards was that voices rose about him in the clamour of terrified alarm—

"A man of power is among us! A man of God!"

The vast sound was repeated—the rushing through space as of huge projectiles—and he sank to the floor of the room, unconscious. The entire scene had vanished, vanished like smoke over the roof of a cottage when the wind blows.

And, by his side, sat down a slight un-German figure,—the figure of the stranger at the inn,—the man who had the "rather wonderful eyes."

When Harris came to himself he felt cold. He was lying under the open sky, and the cool air of field and forest was blowing upon his face. He sat up and looked about him. The memory of the late scene was still horribly in his mind, but no vestige of it remained. No walls or ceiling enclosed him; he was no longer in a room at all. There were no lamps turned low, no cigar smoke, no black forms of sinister worshippers, no tremendous grey Figure hovering beyond the windows.

Open space was about him, and he was lying on a pile of bricks and mortar, his clothes soaked with dew, and the kind stars shining brightly overhead. He was lying, bruised and shaken, among the heaped-up débris of a ruined building.

He stood up and stared about him. There, in the shadowy distance, lay the surrounding forest, and here, close at hand, stood the outline of the village buildings. But, underfoot, beyond question, lay nothing but the broken heaps of stones that betokened a building long since crumbled to dust. Then he saw that the stones were blackened, and that great wooden beams, half burnt, half rotten, made lines through the general débris. He stood, then, among the ruins of a burnt and shattered building, the weeds and nettles proving conclusively that it had lain thus for many years.

The moon had already set behind the encircling forest, but the stars that spangled the heavens threw enough light to enable him to make quite sure of what he saw. Harris, the silk merchant, stood among these broken and burnt stones and shivered.

Then he suddenly became aware that out of the gloom a figure had risen and stood beside him. Peering at him, he thought he recognised the face of the stranger at the railway inn.

"Are *you* real?" he asked in a voice he hardly recognised as his own.

"More than real—I'm friendly," replied the stranger; "I followed you up here from the inn."

Harris stood and stared for several minutes without adding anything. His teeth chattered. The least sound made him start; but the simple words in his own language, and the tone in which they were uttered, comforted him inconceivably.

"You're English too, thank God," he said inconsequently. "These German devils——" He broke off and put a hand to his eyes. "But what's become of them all—and the room—and—and——" The hand travelled down to his throat and moved nervously round his neck. He drew a long, long breath of relief. "Did I dream everything—everything?" he said distractedly.

He stared wildly about him, and the stranger moved forward and took his arm. "Come," he said soothingly, yet with a trace of command in the voice, "we will move away from here. The high-road, or even the woods will be more to your taste, for we are standing now on one of the most haunted—and most terribly haunted—spots of the whole world."

He guided his companion's stumbling footsteps over the broken masonry until they reached the path, the nettles stinging their hands, and Harris feeling his way like a man in a dream. Passing through the twisted iron railing they reached the path, and thence made their way to the road, shining white in the night. Once safely out of the ruins, Harris collected himself and turned to look back.

"But, how is it possible?" he exclaimed, his voice still shaking. "How can it be possible? When I came in here I saw the building in the moonlight. They opened the door. I saw the figures and heard the voices and touched, yes touched their very hands, and saw their damned black faces, saw them far more plainly than I see you now." He was deeply bewildered. The glamour was still upon his eyes with a degree of reality stronger than the reality even of normal life. "Was I so utterly deluded?"

Then suddenly the words of the stranger, which he had only half heard or understood, returned to him.

"Haunted?" he asked, looking hard at him; "haunted, did you say?" He paused in the roadway and stared into the darkness where the building of the old school had first appeared to him. But the stranger hurried him forward.

"We shall talk more safely farther on," he said. "I followed you from the inn the moment I realised where you had gone. When I found you it was eleven o'clock——"

"Eleven o'clock," said Harris, remembering with a shudder.

"——I saw you drop. I watched over you till you recovered consciousness of your own accord, and now—now I am here to guide you safely back to the inn. I have broken the spell—the glamour——"

"I owe you a great deal, sir," interrupted Harris again, beginning to understand something of the stranger's kindness, "but I don't understand it all. I feel dazed and shaken." His teeth still chattered, and spells of violent shivering passed over him from head to foot. He found that he was clinging to the other's arm. In this way they passed beyond the deserted and crumbling village and gained the highroad that led homewards through the forest.

"That school building has long been in ruins," said the man at his side presently; "it was burnt down by order of the Elders of the community at least ten years ago. The village has been uninhabited ever since. But the simulacra of certain ghastly events that took place under that roof in past days still continue. And the 'shells' of the chief participants still enact there the dreadful deeds that led to its final destruction, and to the desertion of the whole settlement. They were devil-worshippers!"

Harris listened with beads of perspiration on his forehead that did not come alone from their leisurely pace through the cool night. Although he had seen this man but once before in his life, and had never before exchanged so much as a word with him, he felt a degree of confidence and a subtle sense of safety and well-being in his presence that were the most healing influences he could possibly have wished after the experience he had been through. For all that, he still felt as if he were walking in a dream, and though he heard every word that fell from his companion's lips, it was only the next day that the full import of all he said became fully clear to him. The presence of this quiet stranger, the man with the wonderful eyes which he felt now, rather than saw, applied a soothing anodyne to his shattered spirit that healed him through and through. And this healing influence, distilled from the dark figure at his side, satisfied his first imperative need, so that he almost forgot to realise how strange and opportune it was that the man should be there at all.

It somehow never occurred to him to ask his name, or to feel any undue wonder that one passing tourist should take so much trouble on behalf of another. He just walked by his side, listening to his quiet words, and allowing himself to enjoy the very wonderful experience after his recent ordeal, of being helped, strengthened, blessed. Only once, remembering vaguely something of his reading of years ago, he turned to the man beside him, after some more than usually remarkable words, and heard himself, almost involuntarily it seemed, putting the question: "Then are you a Rosicrucian, sir, perhaps?" But the stranger had ignored the words, or possibly not heard them, for he continued with his talk as though unconscious of any interruption, and Harris became aware that another somewhat unusual picture had taken possession of his mind, as they walked there side by side through the cool reaches of the forest, and that he had found his imagination suddenly charged with the childhood memory of Jacob wrestling with an angel,—wrestling all night with a being of superior quality whose strength eventually became his own.

"It was your abrupt conversation with the priest at supper that first put me upon the track of this remarkable occurrence," he heard the man's quiet voice beside him in the darkness, "and it was from him I learned after you left the story of the devil-worship that became secretly established in the heart of this simple and devout little community."

"Devil-worship! Here——!" Harris stammered, aghast.

"Yes—here;—conducted secretly for years by a group of Brothers before unexplained disappearances in the neighbourhood led to its discovery. For where could they have found a safer place in the whole wide world for their ghastly traffic and perverted powers than here, in the very precincts—under cover of the very shadow of saintliness and holy living?"

"Awful, awful!" whispered the silk merchant, "and when I tell you the words they used to me——"

"I know it all," the stranger said quietly. "I saw and heard everything. My plan first was to wait till the end and then to take steps for their destruction, but in the interest of your personal safety,"—he spoke with the utmost gravity and conviction,—"in the interest of the safety of your soul, I made my presence known when I did, and before the conclusion had been reached——"

"My safety! The danger, then, was real. They were alive and——" Words failed him. He stopped in the road and turned towards his companion, the shining of whose eyes he could just make out in the gloom.

"It was a concourse of the shells of violent men, spiritually developed but evil men, seeking after death—the death of the body—to prolong their vile and unnatural existence. And had they accomplished their object you, in turn, at the death of your body, would have passed into their power and helped to swell their dreadful purposes."

Harris made no reply. He was trying hard to concentrate his mind upon the sweet and common things of life. He even thought of silk and St. Paul's Churchyard and the faces of his partners in business.

"For you came all prepared to be caught," he heard the other's voice like some one talking to him from a distance; "your deeply introspective mood had already reconstructed the past so vividly, so intensely, that you were *en rapport* at once with any forces of those days that chanced still to be lingering. And they swept you up all unresistingly."

Harris tightened his hold upon the stranger's arm as he heard. At the moment he had room for one emotion only. It did not seem to him odd that this stranger should have such intimate knowledge of his mind.

"It is, alas, chiefly the evil emotions that are able to leave their photographs upon surrounding scenes and objects," the other added, "and who ever heard of a place haunted by a noble deed, or of beautiful and lovely ghosts revisiting the glimpses of the moon? It is unfortunate. But the wicked passions of men's hearts alone seem strong enough to leave pictures that persist; the good are ever too lukewarm."

The stranger sighed as he spoke. But Harris, exhausted and shaken as he was to the very core, paced by his side, only half listening. He moved as in a dream still. It was very wonderful to him, this walk home under the stars in the early hours of the October morning, the peaceful forest all about them, mist rising here and there over the small clearings, and the sound of water from a hundred little invisible streams filling in the pauses of the talk. In after life he always looked back to it as something magical and impossible, something that had seemed too beautiful, too curiously beautiful, to have been quite true. And, though at the time he heard and understood but a quarter of what the stranger said, it came back to him afterwards, staying with him till the end of his days, and always with a curious, haunting sense of unreality, as though he had enjoyed a wonderful dream of which he could recall only faint and exquisite portions.

But the horror of the earlier experience was effectually dispelled; and when they reached the railway inn, somewhere about three o'clock in the morning, Harris shook the stranger's hand gratefully, effusively, meeting the look of those rather wonderful eyes with a full heart, and went up to his room, thinking in a hazy, dream-like way of the words with which the stranger had brought their conversation to an end as they left the confines of the forest—

"And if thought and emotion can persist in this way so long after the brain that sent them forth has crumbled into dust, how vitally important it must be to control their very birth in the heart, and guard them with the keenest possible restraint."

But Harris, the silk merchant, slept better than might have been expected, and with a soundness that carried him half-way through the day. And when he came downstairs and learned that the stranger had already taken his departure, he realised with keen regret that he had never once thought of asking his name.

"Yes, he signed the visitors' book," said the girl in reply to his question.

And he turned over the blotted pages and found there, the last entry, in a very delicate and individual handwriting—

"*John Silence*, London."

THE CAMP OF THE DOG

I

Islands of all shapes and sizes troop northward from Stockholm by the hundred, and the little steamer that threads their intricate mazes in summer leaves the traveller in a somewhat bewildered state as regards the points of the compass when it reaches the end of its journey at Waxholm. But it is only after Waxholm that the true islands begin, so to speak, to run wild, and start up the coast on their tangled course of a hundred miles of deserted loveliness, and it was in the very heart of this delightful confusion that we pitched our tents for a summer holiday. A veritable wilderness of islands lay about us: from the mere round button of a rock that bore a single fir, to the mountainous stretch of a square mile, densely wooded, and bounded by precipitous cliffs; so close together often that a strip of water ran between no wider than a country lane, or, again, so far that an expanse stretched like the open sea for miles.

Although the larger islands boasted farms and fishing stations, the majority were uninhabited. Carpeted with moss and heather, their coast-lines showed a series of ravines and clefts and little sandy bays, with a growth of splendid pine-woods that came down to the water's edge and led the eye through unknown depths of shadow and mystery into the very heart of primitive forest.

The particular islands to which we had camping rights by virtue of paying a nominal sum to a Stockholm merchant lay together in a picturesque group far beyond the reach of the steamer, one being a mere reef with a fringe of fairy-like birches, and two others, cliff-bound monsters rising with wooded heads out of the sea. The fourth, which we selected because it enclosed a little lagoon suitable for anchorage, bathing, night-lines, and what-not, shall have what description is necessary as the story proceeds; but, so far as paying rent was concerned, we might equally well have pitched our tents on any one of a hundred others that clustered about us as thickly as a swarm of bees.

It was in the blaze of an evening in July, the air clear as crystal, the sea a cobalt blue, when we left the steamer on the borders of civilisation and sailed away with maps, compasses, and provisions for the little group of dots in the Skägård that were to be our home for the next two months. The dinghy and my Canadian canoe trailed behind us, with tents and dunnage carefully piled aboard, and when the point of cliff intervened to hide the steamer and the Waxholm hotel we realised for the first time that the horror of trains and houses was far behind us, the fever of men and cities, the weariness of streets and confined spaces. The wilderness opened up on all sides into endless blue reaches, and the map and compasses were so frequently called into requisition that we went astray more often than not and progress was enchantingly slow. It took us, for instance, two whole days to find our crescent-shaped home, and the camps we made on the way were so fascinating that we left them with difficulty and regret, for each island seemed more desirable than the one before it, and over all lay the spell of haunting peace, remoteness from the turmoil of the world, and the freedom of open and desolate spaces.

And so many of these spots of world-beauty have I sought out and dwelt in, that in my mind remains only a composite memory of their faces, a true map of heaven, as it were, from which this particular one stands forth with unusual sharpness because of the strange things that happened there, and also, I think, because anything in which John Silence played a part has a habit of fixing itself in the mind with a living and lasting quality of vividness.

For the moment, however, Dr. Silence was not of the party. Some private case in the interior of Hungary claimed his attention, and it was not till later—the 15th of August, to be exact—that I had arranged to meet him in Berlin and then return to London together for our harvest of winter work. All the members of our party, however, were known to him more or less well, and on this third day as we sailed through the narrow opening into the lagoon and saw the circular ridge of trees in a gold and crimson sunset before us, his last words to me when we parted in London for some unaccountable reason came back very sharply to my memory, and recalled the curious impression of prophecy with which I had first heard them:

"Enjoy your holiday and store up all the force you can," he had said as the train slipped out of Victoria; "and we will meet in Berlin on the 15th—unless you should send for me sooner."

And now suddenly the words returned to me so clearly that it seemed I almost heard his voice in my ear: "Unless you should send for me sooner"; and returned, moreover, with a significance I was wholly at a loss to understand that touched somewhere in the depths of my mind a vague sense of apprehension that they had all along been intended in the nature of a prophecy.

In the lagoon, then, the wind failed us this July evening, as was only natural behind the shelter of the belt of woods, and we took to the oars, all breathless with the beauty of this first sight of our island home, yet all talking in somewhat hushed voices of the best place to land, the depth of water, the safest place to anchor, to put up the tents in, the most sheltered spot for the camp-fires, and a dozen things of importance that crop up when a home in the wilderness has actually to be made.

And during this busy sunset hour of unloading before the dark, the souls of my companions adopted the trick of presenting themselves very vividly anew before my mind, and introducing themselves afresh.

In reality, I suppose, our party was in no sense singular. In the conventional life at home they certainly seemed ordinary enough, but suddenly, as we passed through these gates of the wilderness, I saw them more sharply than before, with characters stripped of the atmosphere of men and cities. A complete change of setting often furnishes a startlingly new view of people hitherto held for well-known; they present another facet of their personalities. I seemed to see my own party almost as new people—people I had not known properly hitherto, people who would drop all disguises and henceforth reveal themselves as they really were. And each one seemed to say: "Now you will see me as I am. You will see me here in this primitive life of the wilderness without clothes. All my masks and veils I have left behind in the abodes of men. So, look out for surprises!"

The Reverend Timothy Maloney helped me to put up the tents, long practice making the process easy, and while he drove in pegs and tightened ropes, his coat off, his flannel collar flying open without a tie, it was impossible to avoid the conclusion that he was cut out for the life of a pioneer rather than the church. He was fifty years of age, muscular, blue-eyed and hearty, and he took his share of the work, and more, without shirking. The way he handled the axe in cutting down saplings for the tent-poles was a delight to see, and his eye in judging the level was unfailing.

Bullied as a young man into a lucrative family living, he had in turn bullied his mind into some semblance of orthodox beliefs, doing the honours of the little country church with an energy that made one think of a coal-heaver tending china; and it was only in the past few years that he had resigned the living and taken instead to cramming young men for their examinations. This suited him better. It enabled him, too, to indulge his passion for spells of "wild life," and to spend the summer months of most years under canvas in one part of the world or another where he could take his young men with him and combine "reading" with open air.

His wife usually accompanied him, and there was no doubt she enjoyed the trips, for she possessed, though in less degree, the same joy of the wilderness that was his own distinguishing characteristic. The only difference was that while he regarded it as the real life, she regarded it as an interlude. While he camped out with his heart and mind, she played at camping out with her clothes and body. None the less, she made a splendid companion, and to watch her busy cooking dinner over the fire we had built among the stones was to understand that her heart was in the business for the moment and that she was happy even with the detail.

Mrs. Maloney at home, knitting in the sun and believing that the world was made in six days, was one woman; but Mrs. Maloney, standing with bare arms over the smoke of a wood fire under the pine trees, was another; and Peter Sangree, the Canadian pupil, with his pale skin, and his loose, though not ungainly figure, stood beside her in very unfavourable contrast as he scraped potatoes and sliced bacon with slender white fingers that seemed better suited to hold a pen than a knife. She ordered him about like a slave, and he obeyed, too, with willing pleasure, for in spite of his general appearance of debility he was as happy to be in camp as any of them.

But more than any other member of the party, Joan Maloney, the daughter, was the one who seemed a natural and genuine part of the landscape, who belonged to it all just in the same way that the trees and the moss and the grey rocks running out into the water belonged to it. For she was obviously in her right and natural setting, a creature of the wilds, a gipsy in her own home.

To any one with a discerning eye this would have been more or less apparent, but to me, who had known her during all the twenty-two years of her life and was familiar with the ins and outs of her primitive, utterly un-modern type, it was strikingly clear. To see her there made it impossible to imagine her again in civilisation. I lost all recollection of how she looked in a town. The memory somehow evaporated. This slim creature before me, flitting to and fro with the grace of the woodland life, swift, supple, adroit, on her knees blowing the fire, or stirring the frying-pan through a veil of smoke, suddenly seemed the only way I had ever really seen her. Here she was at home; in London she became some one concealed by clothes, an artificial doll overdressed and moving by clockwork, only a portion of her alive. Here she was alive all over.

I forget altogether how she was dressed, just as I forget how any particular tree was dressed, or how the markings ran on any one of the boulders that lay about the Camp. She looked just as wild and natural and untamed as everything else that went to make up the scene, and more than that I cannot say.

Pretty, she was decidedly not. She was thin, skinny, dark-haired, and possessed of great physical strength in the form of endurance. She had, too, something of the force and vigorous purpose of a man, tempestuous sometimes and wild to passionate, frightening her mother, and puzzling her easy-going father with her storms of waywardness, while at the same time she stirred his admiration by her violence. A pagan of the pagans she was besides, and with some haunting suggestion of old-world pagan beauty about her dark face and eyes. Altogether an odd and difficult character, but with a generosity and high courage that made her very lovable.

In town life she always seemed to me to feel cramped, bored, a devil in a cage, in her eyes a hunted expression as though any moment she dreaded to be caught. But up in these spacious solitudes all this disappeared. Away from the limitations that plagued and stung her, she would show at her best, and as I watched her moving about the Camp I repeatedly found myself thinking of a wild creature that had just obtained its freedom and was trying its muscles.

Peter Sangree, of course, at once went down before her. But she was so obviously beyond his reach, and besides so well able to take care of herself, that I think her parents gave the matter but little thought, and he himself worshipped at a respectful distance, keeping admirable control of his passion in all respects save one; for at his age the eyes are difficult to master, and the yearning, almost the devouring, expression often visible in them was probably there unknown even to himself. He, better than any one else, understood that he had fallen in love with something most hard of attainment, something that drew him to the very edge of life, and almost beyond it. It, no doubt, was a secret and terrible joy to him, this passionate worship from afar; only I think he suffered more than any one guessed, and that his want of vitality was due in large measure to the constant stream of unsatisfied yearning that poured for ever from his soul and body. Moreover, it seemed to me, who now saw them for the first time together, that there was an unnamable something—an elusive quality of some kind—that marked them as belonging to the same world, and that although the girl ignored him she was secretly, and perhaps unknown to herself, drawn by some attribute very deep in her own nature to some quality equally deep in his.

This, then, was the party when we first settled down into our two months' camp on the island in the Baltic Sea. Other figures flitted from time to time across the scene, and sometimes one reading man, sometimes another, came to join us and spend his four hours a day in the clergyman's tent, but they came for short periods only, and they went without leaving much trace in my memory, and certainly they played no important part in what subsequently happened.

The weather favoured us that night, so that by sunset the tents were up, the boats unloaded, a store of wood collected and chopped into lengths, and the candle-lanterns hung round ready for lighting on the trees. Sangree, too, had picked deep mattresses of balsam boughs for the women's beds, and had cleared little paths of brushwood from their tents to the central fireplace. All was prepared for bad weather. It was a cosy supper and a well-cooked one that we sat down to and ate under the stars, and, according to the clergyman, the only meal fit to eat we had seen since we left London a week before.

The deep stillness, after that roar of steamers, trains, and tourists, held something that thrilled, for as we lay round the fire there was no sound but the faint sighing of the pines and the soft lapping of the waves along the shore and against the sides of the boat in the lagoon. The ghostly outline of her white sails was just visible through the trees, idly rocking to and fro in her calm anchorage, her sheets flapping gently against the mast. Beyond lay the dim blue shapes of other islands floating in the night, and from all the great spaces about us came the murmur of the sea and the soft breathing of great woods. The odours of the wilderness—smells of wind and earth, of trees and water, clean, vigorous, and mighty—were the true odours of a virgin world unspoilt by men, more penetrating and more subtly intoxicating than any other perfume in the whole world. Oh!—and dangerously strong, too, no doubt, for some natures!

"Ahhh!" breathed out the clergyman after supper, with an indescribable gesture of satisfaction and relief. "Here there is freedom, and room for body and mind to turn in. Here one can work and rest and play. Here one can be alive and absorb something of the earth-forces that never get within touching distance in the cities. By George, I shall make a permanent camp here and come when it is time to die!"

The good man was merely giving vent to his delight at being under canvas. He said the same thing every year, and he said it often. But it more or less expressed the superficial feelings of us all. And when, a little later, he turned to compliment his wife on the fried potatoes, and discovered that she was snoring, with her back against a tree, he grunted with content at the sight and put a ground-sheet over her feet, as if it were the most natural thing in the world for her to fall asleep after dinner, and then moved back to his own corner, smoking his pipe with great satisfaction.

And I, smoking mine too, lay and fought against the most delicious sleep imaginable, while my eyes wandered from the fire to the stars peeping through the branches, and then back again to the group about me. The Rev. Timothy soon let his pipe go out, and succumbed as his wife had done, for he had worked hard and eaten well. Sangree, also smoking, leaned against a tree with his gaze fixed on the girl, a depth of yearning in his face that he could not hide, and that really distressed me for him. And Joan herself, with wide staring eyes, alert, full of the new forces of the place, evidently keyed up by the magic of finding herself among all the things her soul recognised as "home," sat rigid by the fire, her thoughts roaming through the spaces, the blood stirring about her heart. She was as unconscious of the Canadian's gaze as she was that her parents both slept. She looked to me more like a tree, or something that had grown out of the island, than a living girl of the century; and when I spoke across to her in a whisper and suggested a tour of investigation, she started and looked up at me as though she heard a voice in her dreams.

Sangree leaped up and joined us, and without waking the others we three went over the ridge of the island and made our way down to the shore behind. The water lay like a lake before us still coloured by the sunset. The air was keen and scented, wafting the smell of the wooded islands that hung about us in the darkening air. Very small waves tumbled softly on the sand. The sea was sown with stars, and everywhere breathed and pulsed the beauty of the northern summer night. I confess I speedily lost consciousness of the human presences beside me, and I have little doubt Joan did too. Only Sangree felt otherwise, I suppose, for presently we heard him sighing; and I can well imagine that he absorbed the whole wonder and passion of the scene into his aching heart, to swell the pain there that was more searching even than the pain at the sight of such matchless and incomprehensible beauty.

The splash of a fish jumping broke the spell.

"I wish we had the canoe now," remarked Joan; "we could paddle out to the other islands."

"Of course," I said; "wait here and I'll go across for it," and was turning to feel my way back through the darkness when she stopped me in a voice that meant what it said.

"No; Mr. Sangree will get it. We will wait here and cooee to guide him."

The Canadian was off in a moment, for she had only to hint of her wishes and he obeyed.

"Keep out from shore in case of rocks," I cried out as he went, "and turn to the right out of the lagoon. That's the shortest way round by the map."

My voice travelled across the still waters and woke echoes in the distant islands that came back to us like people calling out of space. It was only thirty or forty yards over the ridge and down the other side to the lagoon where the boats lay, but it was a good mile to coast round the shore in the dark to where we stood and waited. We heard him stumbling away among the boulders, and then the sounds suddenly ceased as he topped the ridge and went down past the fire on the other side.

"I didn't want to be left alone with him," the girl said presently in a low voice. "I'm always afraid he's going to say or do something——" She hesitated a moment, looking quickly over her shoulder towards the ridge where he had just disappeared—"something that might lead to unpleasantness."

She stopped abruptly.

"*You* frightened, Joan!" I exclaimed, with genuine surprise. "This is a new light on your wicked character. I thought the human being who could frighten you did not exist." Then I suddenly realised she was talking seriously—looking to me for help of some kind—and at once I dropped the teasing attitude.

"He's very far gone, I think, Joan," I added gravely. "You must be kind to him, whatever else you may feel. He's exceedingly fond of you."

"I know, but I can't help it," she whispered, lest her voice should carry in the stillness; "there's something about him that—that makes me feel creepy and half afraid."

"But, poor man, it's not his fault if he is delicate and sometimes looks like death," I laughed gently, by way of defending what I felt to be a very innocent member of my sex.

"Oh, but it's not that I mean," she answered quickly; "it's something I feel about him, something in his soul, something he hardly knows himself, but that may come out if we are much together. It draws me, I feel, tremendously. It stirs what is wild in me—deep down—oh, very deep down,—yet at the same time makes me feel afraid."

"I suppose his thoughts are always playing about you," I said, "but he's nice-minded and——"

"Yes, yes," she interrupted impatiently, "I can trust myself absolutely with him. He's gentle and singularly pure-minded. But there's something else that——" She stopped again sharply to listen. Then she came up close beside me in the darkness, whispering—

"You know, Mr. Hubbard, sometimes my intuitions warn me a little too strongly to be ignored. Oh, yes, you needn't tell me again that it's difficult to distinguish between fancy and intuition. I know all that. But I also know that there's something deep down in that man's soul that calls to something deep down in mine. And at present it frightens me. Because I cannot make out what it is; and I know, I *know*, he'll do something some day that—that will shake my life to the very bottom." She laughed a little at the strangeness of her own description.

I turned to look at her more closely, but the darkness was too great to show her face. There was an intensity, almost of suppressed passion, in her voice that took me completely by surprise.

"Nonsense, Joan," I said, a little severely; "you know him well. He's been with your father for months now."

"But that was in London; and up here it's different—I mean, I feel that it may be different. Life in a place like this blows away the restraints of the artificial life at home. I know, oh, I know what I'm saying. I feel all untied in a place like this; the rigidity of one's nature begins to melt and flow. Surely *you* must understand what I mean!"

"Of course I understand," I replied, yet not wishing to encourage her in her present line of thought, "and it's a grand experience—for a short time. But you're overtired to-night, Joan, like the rest of us. A few days in this air will set you above all fears of the kind you mention."

Then, after a moment's silence, I added, feeling I should estrange her confidence altogether if I blundered any more and treated her like a child—

"I think, perhaps, the true explanation is that you pity him for loving you, and at the same time you feel the repulsion of the healthy, vigorous animal for what is weak and timid. If he came up boldly and took you by the throat and shouted that he would force you to love him— well, then you would feel no fear at all. You would know exactly how to deal with him. Isn't it, perhaps, something of that kind?"

The girl made no reply, and when I took her hand I felt that it trembled a little and was cold.

"It's not his love that I'm afraid of," she said hurriedly, for at this moment we heard the dip of a paddle in the water, "it's something in his very soul that terrifies me in a way I have never been terrified before,— yet fascinates me. In town I was hardly conscious of his presence. But the moment we got away from civilisation, it began to come. He seems so—so *real* up here. I dread being alone with him. It makes me feel that something must burst and tear its way out—that he would do something—or I should do something—I don't know exactly what I mean, probably,—but that I should let myself go and scream——"

"Joan!"

"Don't be alarmed," she laughed shortly; "I shan't do anything silly, but I wanted to tell you my feelings in case I needed your help. When I have intuitions as strong as this they are never wrong, only I don't know yet what it means exactly."

"You must hold out for the month, at any rate," I said in as matter-of-fact a voice as I could manage, for her manner had somehow changed my surprise to a subtle sense of alarm. "Sangree only stays the month, you know. And, anyhow, you are such an odd creature yourself that you should feel generously towards other odd creatures," I ended lamely, with a forced laugh.

She gave my hand a sudden pressure. "I'm glad I've told you at any rate," she said quickly under her breath, for the canoe was now gliding up silently like a ghost to our feet, "and I'm glad you're here, too," she added as we moved down towards the water to meet it.

I made Sangree change into the bows and got into the steering seat myself, putting the girl between us so that I could watch them both by keeping their outlines against the sea and stars. For the intuitions of certain folk—women and children usually, I confess—I have always felt a great respect that has more often than not been justified by experience; and now the curious emotion stirred in me by the girl's words remained somewhat vividly in my consciousness. I explained it in some measure by the fact that the girl, tired out by the fatigue of many days' travel, had suffered a vigorous reaction of some kind from the strong, desolate scenery, and further, perhaps, that she had been treated to my own experience of seeing the members of the party in a new light—the Canadian, being partly a stranger, more vividly than the rest of us. But, at the same time, I felt it was quite possible that she had sensed some subtle link between his personality and her own, some quality that she had hitherto ignored and that the routine of town life had kept buried out of sight. The only thing that seemed difficult to explain was the fear she had spoken of, and this I hoped the wholesome effects of camp-life and exercise would sweep away naturally in the course of time.

We made the tour of the island without speaking. It was all too beautiful for speech. The trees crowded down to the shore to hear us pass. We saw their fine dark heads, bowed low with splendid dignity to watch us, forgetting for a moment that the stars were caught in the needled network of their hair. Against the sky in the west, where still lingered the sunset gold, we saw the wild toss of the horizon, shaggy with forest and cliff, gripping the heart like the motive in a symphony, and sending the sense of beauty all a-shiver through the mind—all these surrounding islands standing above the water like low clouds, and like them seeming to post along silently into the engulfing night. We heard the musical drip-drip of the paddle, and the little wash of our waves on the shore, and then suddenly we found ourselves at the opening of the lagoon again, having made the complete circuit of our home.

The Reverend Timothy had awakened from sleep and was singing to himself; and the sound of his voice as we glided down the fifty yards of enclosed water was pleasant to hear and undeniably wholesome. We saw the glow of the fire up among the trees on the ridge, and his shadow moving about as he threw on more wood.

"There you are!" he called aloud. "Good again! Been setting the night-lines, eh? Capital! And your mother's still fast asleep, Joan."

His cheery laugh floated across the water; he had not been in the least disturbed by our absence, for old campers are not easily alarmed.

"Now, remember," he went on, after we had told our little tale of travel by the fire, and Mrs. Maloney had asked for the fourth time exactly where her tent was and whether the door faced east or south, "every one takes their turn at cooking breakfast, and one of the men is always out at sunrise to catch it first. Hubbard, I'll toss you which you do in the morning and which I do!" He lost the toss. "Then I'll catch it," I said, laughing at his discomfiture, for I knew he loathed stirring porridge. "And mind you don't burn it as you did every blessed time last year on the Volga," I added by way of reminder.

Mrs. Maloney's fifth interruption about the door of her tent, and her further pointed observation that it was past nine o'clock, set us lighting lanterns and putting the fire out for safety.

But before we separated for the night the clergyman had a time-honoured little ritual of his own to go through that no one had the heart to deny him. He always did this. It was a relic of his pulpit habits. He glanced briefly from one to the other of us, his face grave and earnest, his hands lifted to the stars and his eyes all closed and puckered up beneath a momentary frown. Then he offered up a short, almost inaudible prayer, thanking Heaven for our safe arrival, begging for good weather, no illness or accidents, plenty of fish, and strong sailing winds.

And then, unexpectedly—no one knew why exactly—he ended up with an abrupt request that nothing from the kingdom of darkness should be allowed to afflict our peace, and no evil thing come near to disturb us in the night-time.

And while he uttered these last surprising words, so strangely unlike his usual ending, it chanced that I looked up and let my eyes wander round the group assembled about the dying fire. And it certainly seemed to me that Sangree's face underwent a sudden and visible alteration. He was staring at Joan, and as he stared the change ran over it like a shadow and was gone. I started in spite of myself, for something oddly concentrated, potent, collected, had come into the expression usually so scattered and feeble. But it was all swift as a passing meteor, and when I looked a second time his face was normal and he was looking among the trees.

And Joan, luckily, had not observed him, her head being bowed and her eyes tightly closed while her father prayed.

"The girl has a vivid imagination indeed," I thought, half laughing, as I lit the lanterns, "if her thoughts can put a glamour upon mine in this way"; and yet somehow, when we said good-night, I took occasion to give her a few vigorous words of encouragement, and went to her tent to make sure I could find it quickly in the night in case anything happened. In her quick way the girl understood and thanked me, and the last thing I heard as I moved off to the men's quarters was Mrs. Maloney crying that there were beetles in her tent, and Joan's laughter as she went to help her turn them out.

Half an hour later the island was silent as the grave, but for the mournful voices of the wind as it sighed up from the sea. Like white sentries stood the three tents of the men on one side of the ridge, and on the other side, half hidden by some birches, whose leaves just shivered as the breeze caught them, the women's tents, patches of ghostly grey, gathered more closely together for mutual shelter and protection. Something like fifty yards of broken ground, grey rock, moss and lichen, lay between, and over all lay the curtain of the night and the great whispering winds from the forests of Scandinavia.

And the very last thing, just before floating away on that mighty wave that carries one so softly off into the deeps of forgetfulness, I again heard the voice of John Silence as the train moved out of Victoria Station; and by some subtle connection that met me on the very threshold of consciousness there rose in my mind simultaneously the memory of the girl's half-given confidence, and of her distress. As by some wizardry of approaching dreams they seemed in that instant to be related; but before I could analyse the why and the wherefore, both sank away out of sight again, and I was off beyond recall.

"Unless you should send for me sooner."

II

Whether Mrs. Maloney's tent door opened south or east I think she never discovered, for it is quite certain she always slept with the flap tightly fastened; I only know that my own little "five by seven, all silk" faced due east, because next morning the sun, pouring in as only the wilderness sun knows how to pour, woke me early, and a moment later, with a short run over soft moss and a flying dive from the granite ledge, I was swimming in the most sparkling water imaginable.

It was barely four o'clock, and the sun came down a long vista of blue islands that led out to the open sea and Finland. Nearer by rose the wooded domes of our own property, still capped and wreathed with smoky trails of fast-melting mist, and looking as fresh as though it was the morning of Mrs. Maloney's Sixth Day and they had just issued, clean and brilliant, from the hands of the great Architect.

In the open spaces the ground was drenched with dew, and from the sea a cool salt wind stole in among the trees and set the branches trembling in an atmosphere of shimmering silver. The tents shone white where the sun caught them in patches. Below lay the lagoon, still dreaming of the summer night; in the open the fish were jumping busily, sending musical ripples towards the shore; and in the air hung the magic of dawn—silent, incommunicable.

I lit the fire, so that an hour later the clergyman should find good ashes to stir his porridge over, and then set forth upon an examination of the island, but hardly had I gone a dozen yards when I saw a figure standing a little in front of me where the sunlight fell in a pool among the trees.

It was Joan. She had already been up an hour, she told me, and had bathed before the last stars had left the sky. I saw at once that the new spirit of this solitary region had entered into her, banishing the fears of the night, for her face was like the face of a happy denizen of the wilderness, and her eyes stainless and shining. Her feet were bare, and drops of dew she had shaken from the branches hung in her loose-flying hair. Obviously she had come into her own.

"I've been all over the island," she announced laughingly, "and there are two things wanting."

"You're a good judge, Joan. What are they?"

"There's no animal life, and there's no—water."

"They go together," I said. "Animals don't bother with a rock like this unless there's a spring on it."

And as she led me from place to place, happy and excited, leaping adroitly from rock to rock, I was glad to note that my first impressions were correct. She made no reference to our conversation of the night before. The new spirit had driven out the old. There was no room in her heart for fear or anxiety, and Nature had everything her own way.

The island, we found, was some three-quarters of a mile from point to point, built in a circle, or wide horseshoe, with an opening of twenty feet at the mouth of the lagoon. Pine-trees grew thickly all over, but here and there were patches of silver birch, scrub oak, and considerable colonies of wild raspberry and gooseberry bushes. The two ends of the horseshoe formed bare slabs of smooth granite running into the sea and forming dangerous reefs just below the surface, but the rest of the island rose in a forty-foot ridge and sloped down steeply to the sea on either side, being nowhere more than a hundred yards wide.

The outer shore-line was much indented with numberless coves and bays and sandy beaches, with here and there caves and precipitous little cliffs against which the sea broke in spray and thunder. But the inner shore, the shore of the lagoon, was low and regular, and so well protected by the wall of trees along the ridge that no storm could ever send more than a passing ripple along its sandy marges. Eternal shelter reigned there.

On one of the other islands, a few hundred yards away—for the rest of the party slept late this first morning, and we took to the canoe—we discovered a spring of fresh water untainted by the brackish flavour of the Baltic, and having thus solved the most important problem of the Camp, we next proceeded to deal with the second—fish. And in half an hour we reeled in and turned homewards, for we had no means of storage, and to clean more fish than may be stored or eaten in a day is no wise occupation for experienced campers.

And as we landed towards six o'clock we heard the clergyman singing as usual and saw his wife and Sangree shaking out their blankets in the sun, and dressed in a fashion that finally dispelled all memories of streets and civilisation.

"The Little People lit the fire for me," cried Maloney, looking natural and at home in his ancient flannel suit and breaking off in the middle of his singing, "so I've got the porridge going—and this time it's *not* burnt."

We reported the discovery of water and held up the fish.

"Good! Good again!" he cried. "We'll have the first decent breakfast we've had this year. Sangree'll clean 'em in no time, and the Bo'sun's Mate——"

"Will fry them to a turn," laughed the voice of Mrs. Maloney, appearing on the scene in a tight blue jersey and sandals, and catching up the frying-pan. Her husband always called her the Bo'sun's Mate in Camp, because it was her duty, among others, to pipe all hands to meals.

"And as for you, Joan," went on the happy man, "you look like the spirit of the island, with moss in your hair and wind in your eyes, and sun and stars mixed in your face." He looked at her with delighted admiration. "Here, Sangree, take these twelve, there's a good fellow, they're the biggest; and we'll have 'em in butter in less time than you can say Baltic island!"

I watched the Canadian as he slowly moved off to the cleaning pail. His eyes were drinking in the girl's beauty, and a wave of passionate, almost feverish, joy passed over his face, expressive of the ecstasy of true worship more than anything else. Perhaps he was thinking that he still had three weeks to come with that vision always before his eyes; perhaps he was thinking of his dreams in the night. I cannot say. But I noticed the curious mingling of yearning and happiness in his eyes, and the strength of the impression touched my curiosity. Something in his face held my gaze for a second, something to do with its intensity. That so timid, so gentle a personality should conceal so virile a passion almost seemed to require explanation.

But the impression was momentary, for that first breakfast in Camp permitted no divided attentions, and I dare swear that the porridge, the tea, the Swedish "flatbread," and the fried fish flavoured with points of frizzled bacon, were better than any meal eaten elsewhere that day in the whole world.

The first clear day in a new camp is always a furiously busy one, and we soon dropped into the routine upon which in large measure the real comfort of every one depends. About the cooking-fire, greatly improved with stones from the shore, we built a high stockade consisting of upright poles thickly twined with branches, the roof lined with moss and lichen and weighted with rocks, and round the interior we made low wooden seats so that we could lie round the fire even in rain and eat our meals in peace. Paths, too, outlined themselves from tent to tent, from the bathing places and the landing stage, and a fair division of the island was decided upon between the quarters of the men and the women. Wood was stacked, awkward trees and boulders removed, hammocks slung, and tents strengthened. In a word, Camp was established, and duties were assigned and accepted as though we expected to live on this Baltic island for years to come and the smallest detail of the Community life was important.

Moreover, as the Camp came into being, this sense of a community developed, proving that we were a definite whole, and not merely separate human beings living for a while in tents upon a desert island. Each fell willingly into the routine. Sangree, as by natural selection, took upon himself the cleaning of the fish and the cutting of the wood into lengths sufficient for a day's use. And he did it well. The pan of water was never without a fish, cleaned and scaled, ready to fry for whoever was hungry; the nightly fire never died down for lack of material to throw on without going farther afield to search.

And Timothy, once reverend, caught the fish and chopped down the trees. He also assumed responsibility for the condition of the boat, and did it so thoroughly that nothing in the little cutter was ever found wanting. And when, for any reason, his presence was in demand, the first place to look for him was—in the boat, and there, too, he was usually found, tinkering away with sheets, sails, or rudder and singing as he tinkered.

"Nor was the "reading" neglected; for most mornings there came a sound of droning voices form the white tent by the raspberry bushes, which signified that Sangree, the tutor, and whatever other man chanced to be in the party at the time, were hard at it with history or the classics.

And while Mrs. Maloney, also by natural selection, took charge of the larder and the kitchen, the mending and general supervision of the rough comforts, she also made herself peculiarly mistress of the megaphone which summoned to meals and carried her voice easily from one end of the island to the other; and in her hours of leisure she daubed the surrounding scenery on to a sketching block with all the honesty and devotion of her determined but unreceptive soul.

Joan, meanwhile, Joan, elusive creature of the wilds, became I know not exactly what. She did plenty of work in the Camp, yet seemed to have no very precise duties. She was everywhere and anywhere. Sometimes she slept in her tent, sometimes under the stars with a blanket. She knew every inch of the island and kept turning up in places where she was least expected—for ever wandering about, reading her books in sheltered corners, making little fires on sunless days to "worship by to the gods," as she put it, ever finding new pools to dive and bathe in, and swimming day and night in the warm and waveless lagoon like a fish in a huge tank. She went bare-legged and bare-footed, with her hair down and her skirts caught up to the knees, and if ever a human being turned into a jolly savage within the compass of a single week, Joan Maloney was certainly that human being. She ran wild.

So completely, too, was she possessed by the strong spirit of the place that the little human fear she had yielded to so strangely on our arrival seemed to have been utterly dispossessed. As I hoped and expected, she made no reference to our conversation of the first evening. Sangree bothered her with no special attentions, and after all they were very little together. His behaviour was perfect in that respect, and I, for my part, hardly gave the matter another thought. Joan was ever a prey to vivid fancies of one kind or another, and this was one of them. Mercifully for the happiness of all concerned, it had melted away before the spirit of busy, active life and deep content that reigned over the island. Every one was intensely alive, and peace was upon all.

Meanwhile the effect of the camp-life began to tell. Always a searching test of character, its results, sooner or later, are infallible, for it acts upon the soul as swiftly and surely as the hypo bath upon the negative of a photograph. A readjustment of the personal forces takes place quickly; some parts of the personality go to sleep, others wake up: but the first sweeping change that the primitive life brings about is that the artificial portions of the character shed themselves one after another like dead skins. Attitudes and poses that seemed genuine in the city drop away. The mind, like the body, grows quickly hard, simple, uncomplex. And in a camp as primitive and close to nature as ours was, these effects became speedily visible.

Some folk, of course, who talk glibly about the simple life when it is safely out of reach, betray themselves in camp by for ever peering about for the artificial excitements of civilisation which they miss. Some get bored at once; some grow slovenly; some reveal the animal in most unexpected fashion; and some, the select few, find themselves in very short order and are happy.

And, in our little party, we could flatter ourselves that we all belonged to the last category, so far as the general effect was concerned. Only there were certain other changes as well, varying with each individual, and all interesting to note.

It was only after the first week or two that these changes became marked, although this is the proper place, I think, to speak of them. For, having myself no other duty than to enjoy a well-earned holiday, I used to load my canoe with blankets and provisions and journey forth on exploration trips among the islands of several days together; and it was on my return from the first of these—when I rediscovered the party, so to speak—that these changes first presented themselves vividly to me, and in one particular instance produced a rather curious impression.

In a word, then, while every one had grown wilder, naturally wilder, Sangree, it seemed to me, had grown much wilder, and what I can only call unnaturally wilder. He made me think of a savage.

To begin with, he had changed immensely in mere physical appearance, and the full brown cheeks, the brighter eyes of absolute health, and the general air of vigour and robustness that had come to replace his customary lassitude and timidity, had worked such an improvement that I hardly knew him for the same man. His voice, too, was deeper and his manner bespoke for the first time a greater measure of confidence in himself. He now had some claims to be called nice-looking, or at least to a certain air of virility that would not lessen his value in the eyes of the opposite sex.

All this, of course, was natural enough, and most welcome. But, altogether apart from this physical change, which no doubt had also been going forward in the rest of us, there was a subtle note in his personality that came to me with a degree of surprise that almost amounted to shock.

And two things—as he came down to welcome me and pull up the canoe—leaped up in my mind unbidden, as though connected in some way I could not at the moment divine—first, the curious judgment formed of him by Joan; and secondly, that fugitive expression I had caught in his face while Maloney was offering up his strange prayer for special protection from Heaven.

The delicacy of manner and feature—to call it by no milder term—which had always been a distinguishing characteristic of the man, had been replaced by something far more vigorous and decided, that yet utterly eluded analysis. The change which impressed me so oddly was not easy to name. The others—singing Maloney, the bustling Bo'sun's Mate, and Joan, that fascinating half-breed of undine and salamander—all showed the effects of a life so close to nature; but in their case the change was perfectly natural and what was to be expected, whereas with Peter Sangree, the Canadian, it was something unusual and unexpected.

It is impossible to explain how he managed gradually to convey to my mind the impression that something in him had turned savage, yet this, more or less, is the impression that he did convey. It was not that he seemed really less civilised, or that his character had undergone any definite alteration, but rather that something in him, hitherto dormant, had awakened to life. Some quality, latent till now—so far, at least, as we were concerned, who, after all, knew him but slightly—had stirred into activity and risen to the surface of his being.

And while, for the moment, this seemed as far as I could get, it was but natural that my mind should continue the intuitive process and acknowledge that John Silence, owing to his peculiar faculties, and the girl, owing to her singularly receptive temperament, might each in a different way have divined this latent quality in his soul, and feared its manifestation later.

On looking back to this painful adventure, too, it now seems equally natural that the same process, carried to its logical conclusion, should have wakened some deep instinct in me that, wholly without direction from my will, set itself sharply and persistently upon the watch from that very moment. Thenceforward the personality of Sangree was never far from my thoughts, and I was for ever analysing and searching for the explanation that took so long in coming.

"I declare, Hubbard, you're tanned like an aboriginal, and you look like one, too," laughed Maloney.

"And I can return the compliment," was my reply, as we all gathered round a brew of tea to exchange news and compare notes.

And later, at supper, it amused me to observe that the distinguished tutor, once clergyman, did not eat his food quite as "nicely" as he did at home—he devoured it; that Mrs. Maloney ate more, and, to say the least, with less delay, than was her custom in the select atmosphere of her English dining-room; and that while Joan attacked her tin plateful with genuine avidity, Sangree, the Canadian, bit and gnawed at his, laughing and talking and complimenting the cook all the while, and making me think with secret amusement of a starved animal at its first meal. While, from their remarks about myself, I judged that I had changed and grown wild as much as the rest of them.

In this and in a hundred other little ways the change showed, ways difficult to define in detail, but all proving—not the coarsening effect of leading the primitive life, but, let us say, the more direct and unvarnished methods that became prevalent. For all day long we were in the bath of the elements—wind, water, sun—and just as the body became insensible to cold and shed unnecessary clothing, the mind grew straightforward and shed many of the disguises required by the conventions of civilisation.

And in each, according to temperament and character, there stirred the life-instincts that were natural, untamed, and, in a sense—savage.

III

So it came about that I stayed with our island party, putting off my second exploring trip from day to day, and I think that this far-fetched instinct to watch Sangree was really the cause of my postponement.

For another ten days the life of the Camp pursued its even and delightful way, blessed by perfect summer weather, a good harvest of fish, fine winds for sailing, and calm, starry nights. Maloney's selfish prayer had been favourably received. Nothing came to disturb or perplex. There was not even the prowling of night animals to vex the rest of Mrs. Maloney; for in previous camps it had often been her peculiar affliction that she heard the porcupines scratching against the canvas, or the squirrels dropping fir-cones in the early morning with a sound of miniature thunder upon the roof of her tent. But on this island there was not even a squirrel or a mouse. I think two toads and a small and harmless snake were the only living creatures that had been discovered during the whole of the first fortnight. And these two toads in all probability were not two toads, but one toad.

Then, suddenly, came the terror that changed the whole aspect of the place—the devastating terror.

It came, at first, gently, but from the very start it made me realise the unpleasant loneliness of our situation, our remote isolation in this wilderness of sea and rock, and how the islands in this tideless Baltic ocean lay about us like the advance guard of a vast besieging army. Its entry, as I say, was gentle, hardly noticeable, in fact, to most of us: singularly undramatic it certainly was. But, then, in actual life this is often the way the dreadful climaxes move upon us, leaving the heart undisturbed almost to the last minute, and then overwhelming it with a sudden rush of horror. For it was the custom at breakfast to listen patiently while each in turn related the trivial adventures of the night—how they slept, whether the wind shook their tent, whether the spider on the ridge pole had moved, whether they had heard the toad, and so forth—and on this particular morning Joan, in the middle of a little pause, made a truly novel announcement:

"In the night I heard the howling of a dog," she said, and then flushed up to the roots of her hair when we burst out laughing. For the idea of there being a dog on this forsaken island that was only able to support a snake and two toads was distinctly ludicrous, and I remember Maloney, half-way through his burnt porridge, capping the announcement by declaring that he had heard a "Baltic turtle" in the lagoon, and his wife's expression of frantic alarm before the laughter undeceived her.

But the next morning Joan repeated the story with additional and convincing detail.

"Sounds of whining and growling woke me," she said, "and I distinctly heard sniffing under my tent, and the scratching of paws."

"Oh, Timothy! Can it be a porcupine?" exclaimed the Bo'sun's Mate with distress, forgetting that Sweden was not Canada.

But the girl's voice had sounded to me in quite another key, and looking up I saw that her father and Sangree were staring at her hard. They, too, understood that she was in earnest, and had been struck by the serious note in her voice.

"Rubbish, Joan! You are always dreaming something or other wild," her father said a little impatiently.

"There's not an animal of any size on the whole island," added Sangree with a puzzled expression. He never took his eyes from her face.

"But there's nothing to prevent one swimming over," I put in briskly, for somehow a sense of uneasiness that was not pleasant had woven itself into the talk and pauses. "A deer, for instance, might easily land in the night and take a look round——"

"Or a bear!" gasped the Bo'sun's Mate, with a look so portentous that we all welcomed the laugh.

But Joan did not laugh. Instead, she sprang up and called to us to follow.

"There," she said, pointing to the ground by her tent on the side farthest from her mother's; "there are the marks close to my head. You can see for yourselves."

We saw plainly. The moss and lichen—for earth there was hardly any—had been scratched up by paws. An animal about the size of a large dog it must have been, to judge by the marks. We stood and stared in a row.

"Close to my head," repeated the girl, looking round at us. Her face, I noticed, was very pale, and her lip seemed to quiver for an instant. Then she gave a sudden gulp—and burst into a flood of tears.

The whole thing had come about in the brief space of a few minutes, and with a curious sense of inevitableness, moreover, as though it had all been carefully planned from all time and nothing could have stopped it. It had all been rehearsed before—had actually happened before, as the strange feeling sometimes has it; it seemed like the opening movement in some ominous drama, and that I knew exactly what would happen next. Something of great moment was impending.

For this sinister sensation of coming disaster made itself felt from the very beginning, and an atmosphere of gloom and dismay pervaded the entire Camp from that moment forward.

I drew Sangree to one side and moved away, while Maloney took the distressed girl into her tent, and his wife followed them, energetic and greatly flustered.

For thus, in undramatic fashion, it was that the terror I have spoken of first attempted the invasion of our Camp, and, trivial and unimportant though it seemed, every little detail of this opening scene is photographed upon my mind with merciless accuracy and precision. It happened exactly as described. This was exactly the language used. I see it written before me in black and white. I see, too, the faces of all concerned with the sudden ugly signature of alarm where before had been peace. The terror had stretched out, so to speak, a first tentative feeler toward us and had touched the hearts of each with a horrid directness. And from this moment the Camp changed.

Sangree in particular was visibly upset. He could not bear to see the girl distressed, and to hear her actually cry was almost more than he could stand. The feeling that he had no right to protect her hurt him keenly, and I could see that he was itching to do something to help, and liked him for it. His expression said plainly that he would tear in a thousand pieces anything that dared to injure a hair of her head.

We lit our pipes and strolled over in silence to the men's quarters, and it was his odd Canadian expression "Gee whiz!" that drew my attention to a further discovery.

"The brute's been scratching round my tent too," he cried, as he pointed to similar marks by the door and I stooped down to examine them. We both stared in amazement for several minutes without speaking.

"Only I sleep like the dead," he added, straightening up again, "and so heard nothing, I suppose."

We traced the paw-marks from the mouth of his tent in a direct line across to the girl's, but nowhere else about the Camp was there a sign of the strange visitor. The deer, dog, or whatever it was that had twice favoured us with a visit in the night, had confined its attentions to these two tents. And, after all, there was really nothing out of the way about these visits of an unknown animal, for although our own island was destitute of life, we were in the heart of a wilderness, and the mainland and larger islands must be swarming with all kinds of four-footed creatures, and no very prolonged swimming was necessary to reach us. In any other country it would not have caused a moment's interest—interest of the kind we felt, that is. In our Canadian camps the bears were for ever grunting about among the provision bags at night, porcupines scratching unceasingly, and chipmunks scuttling over everything.

"My daughter is overtired, and that's the truth of it," explained Maloney presently when he rejoined us and had examined in turn the other paw-marks. "She's been overdoing it lately, and camp-life, you know, always means a great excitement to her. It's natural enough. If we take no notice she'll be all right." He paused to borrow my tobacco pouch and fill his pipe, and the blundering way he filled it and spilled the precious weed on the ground visibly belied the calm of his easy language. "You might take her out for a bit of fishing, Hubbard, like a good chap; she's hardly up to the long day in the cutter. Show her some of the other islands in your canoe, perhaps. Eh?"

And by lunch-time the cloud had passed away as suddenly, and as suspiciously, as it had come.

But in the canoe, on our way home, having till then purposely ignored the subject uppermost in our minds, she suddenly spoke to me in a way that again touched the note of sinister alarm—the note that kept on sounding and sounding until finally John Silence came with his great vibrating presence and relieved it; yes, and even after he came, too, for a while.

"I'm ashamed to ask it," she said abruptly, as she steered me home, her sleeves rolled up, her hair blowing in the wind, "and ashamed of my silly tears too, because I really can't make out what caused them; but, Mr. Hubbard, I want you to promise me not to go off for your long expeditions—just yet. I beg it of you." She was so in earnest that she forgot the canoe, and the wind caught it sideways and made us roll dangerously. "I have tried hard not to ask this," she added, bringing the canoe round again, "but I simply can't help myself."

It was a good deal to ask, and I suppose my hesitation was plain; for she went on before I could reply, and her beseeching expression and intensity of manner impressed me very forcibly.

"For another two weeks only——"

"Mr. Sangree leaves in a fortnight," I said, seeing at once what she was driving at, but wondering if it was best to encourage her or not.

"If I knew you were to be on the island till then," she said, her face alternately pale and blushing, and her voice trembling a little, "I should feel so much happier."

I looked at her steadily, waiting for her to finish.

"And safer," she added almost in a whisper; "especially—at night, I mean."

"Safer, Joan?" I repeated, thinking I had never seen her eyes so soft and tender. She nodded her head, keeping her gaze fixed on my face.

It was really difficult to refuse, whatever my thoughts and judgment may have been, and somehow I understood that she spoke with good reason, though for the life of me I could not have put it into words.

"Happier—and safer," she said gravely, the canoe giving a dangerous lurch as she leaned forward in her seat to catch my answer. Perhaps, after all, the wisest way was to grant her request and make light of it, easing her anxiety without too much encouraging its cause.

"All right, Joan, you queer creature; I promise," and the instant look of relief in her face, and the smile that came back like sunlight to her eyes, made me feel that, unknown to myself and the world, I was capable of considerable sacrifice after all.

"But, you know, there's nothing to be afraid of," I added sharply; and she looked up in my face with the smile women use when they know we are talking idly, yet do not wish to tell us so.

"*You* don't feel afraid, I know," she observed quietly.

"Of course not; why should I?"

"So, if you will just humour me this once I—I will never ask any-thing foolish of you again as long as I live," she said gratefully.

"You have my promise," was all I could find to say.

She headed the nose of the canoe for the lagoon lying a quarter of a mile ahead, and paddled swiftly; but a minute or two later she paused again and stared hard at me with the dripping paddle across the thwarts.

"You've not heard anything at night yourself, have you?" she asked.

"I never hear anything at night," I replied shortly, "from the moment I lie down till the moment I get up."

"That dismal howling, for instance," she went on, determined to get it out, "far away at first and then getting closer, and stopping just out-side the Camp?"

"Certainly not."

"Because, sometimes I think I almost dreamed it."

"Most likely you did," was my unsympathetic response.

"And you don't think father has heard it either, then?"

"No. He would have told me if he had."

This seemed to relieve her mind a little. "I know mother hasn't," she added, as if speaking to herself, "for she hears nothing—ever."

It was two nights after this conversation that I woke out of deep sleep and heard sounds of screaming. The voice was really horrible, breaking the peace and silence with its shrill clamour. In less than ten seconds I was half dressed and out of my tent. The screaming had stopped abruptly, but I knew the general direction, and ran as fast as the dark-ness would allow over to the women's quarters, and on getting close I heard sounds of suppressed weeping. It was Joan's voice. And just as I came up I saw Mrs. Maloney, marvellously attired, fumbling with a lantern. Other voices became audible in the same moment behind me, and Timothy Maloney arrived, breathless, less than half dressed, and carrying another lantern that had gone out on the way from being banged against a tree. Dawn was just breaking, and a chill wind blew in from the sea. Heavy black clouds drove low overhead.

The scene of confusion may be better imagined than described. Questions in frightened voices filled the air against this background of suppressed weeping. Briefly—Joan's silk tent had been torn, and the girl was in a state bordering upon hysterics. Somewhat reassured by our noisy presence, however,—for she was plucky at heart,—she pulled herself together and tried to explain what had happened; and her bro-ken words, told there on the edge of night and morning upon this wild island ridge, were oddly thrilling and distressingly convincing.

"Something touched me and I woke," she said simply, but in a voice still hushed and broken with the terror of it, "something pushing against the tent; I felt it through the canvas. There was the same sniffing and scratching as before, and I felt the tent give a little as when wind shakes it. I heard breathing—very loud, very heavy breathing— and then came a sudden great tearing blow, and the canvas ripped open close to my face."

She had instantly dashed out through the open flap and screamed at the top of her voice, thinking the creature had actually got into the tent. But nothing was visible, she declared, and she heard not the faintest sound of an animal making off under cover of the darkness. The brief account seemed to exercise a paralysing effect upon us all as we listened to it. I can see the dishevelled group to this day, the wind blowing the women's hair, and Maloney craning his head forward to listen, and his wife, open-mouthed and gasping, leaning against a pine tree.

"Come over to the stockade and we'll get the fire going," I said; "that's the first thing," for we were all shaking with the cold in our scanty garments. And at that moment Sangree arrived wrapped in a blanket and carrying his gun; he was still drunken with sleep.

"The dog again," Maloney explained briefly, forestalling his questions; "been at Joan's tent. Torn it, by Gad! this time. It's time we did something." He went on mumbling confusedly to himself.

Sangree gripped his gun and looked about swiftly in the darkness. I saw his eyes aflame in the glare of the flickering lanterns. He made a movement as though to start out and hunt—and kill. Then his glance fell on the girl crouching on the ground, her face hidden in her hands, and there leaped into his features an expression of savage anger that transformed them. He could have faced a dozen lions with a walking-stick at that moment, and again I liked him for the strength of his anger, his self-control, and his hopeless devotion.

But I stopped him going off on a blind and useless chase.

"Come and help me start the fire, Sangree," I said, anxious also to relieve the girl of our presence; and a few minutes later the ashes, still growing from the night's fire, had kindled the fresh wood, and there was a blaze that warmed us well while it also lit up the surrounding trees within a radius of twenty yards.

"I heard nothing," he whispered; "what in the world do you think it is? It surely can't be only a dog!"

"We'll find that out later," I said, as the others came up to the grateful warmth; "the first thing is to make as big a fire as we can."

Joan was calmer now, and her mother had put on some warmer, and less miraculous, garments. And while they stood talking in low voices

Maloney and I slipped off to examine the tent. There was little enough to see, but that little was unmistakable. Some animal had scratched up the ground at the head of the tent, and with a great blow of a powerful paw — a paw clearly provided with good claws — had struck the silk and torn it open. There was a hole large enough to pass a fist and arm through.

"It can't be far away," Maloney said excitedly. "We'll organise a hunt at once; this very minute."

We hurried back to the fire, Maloney talking boisterously about his proposed hunt. "There's nothing like prompt action to dispel alarm," he whispered in my ear; and then turned to the rest of us.

"We'll hunt the island from end to end at once," he said, with excitement; "that's what we'll do. The beast can't be far away. And the Bo'sun's Mate and Joan must come too, because they can't be left alone. Hubbard, you take the right shore, and you, Sangree, the left, and I'll go in the middle with the women. In this way we can stretch clean across the ridge, and nothing bigger than a rabbit can possibly escape us." He was extraordinarily excited, I thought. Anything affecting Joan, of course, stirred him prodigiously. "Get your guns and we'll start the drive at once," he cried. He lit another lantern and handed one each to his wife and Joan, and while I ran to fetch my gun I heard him singing to himself with the excitement of it all.

Meanwhile the dawn had come on quickly. It made the flickering lanterns look pale. The wind, too, was rising, and I heard the trees moaning overhead and the waves breaking with increasing clamour on the shore. In the lagoon the boat dipped and splashed, and the sparks from the fire were carried aloft in a stream and scattered far and wide.

We made our way to the extreme end of the island, measured our distances carefully, and then began to advance. None of us spoke. Sangree and I, with cocked guns, watched the shore lines, and all within easy touch and speaking distance. It was a slow and blundering drive, and there were many false alarms, but after the best part of half an hour we stood on the farther end, having made the complete tour, and without putting up so much as a squirrel. Certainly there was no living creature on that island but ourselves.

"I know what it is!" cried Maloney, looking out over the dim expanse of grey sea, and speaking with the air of a man making a discovery; "it's a dog from one of the farms on the larger islands" — he pointed seawards where the archipelago thickened — "and it's escaped and turned wild. Our fires and voices attracted it, and it's probably half starved as well as savage, poor brute!"

No one said anything in reply, and he began to sing again very low to himself.

The point where we stood—a huddled, shivering group—faced the wider channels that led to the open sea and Finland. The grey dawn had broken in earnest at last, and we could see the racing waves with their angry crests of white. The surrounding islands showed up as dark masses in the distance, and in the east, almost as Maloney spoke, the sun came up with a rush in a stormy and magnificent sky of red and gold. Against this splashed and gorgeous background black clouds, shaped like fantastic and legendary animals, filed past swiftly in a tearing stream, and to this day I have only to close my eyes to see again that vivid and hurrying procession in the air. All about us the pines made black splashes against the sky. It was an angry sunrise. Rain, indeed, had already begun to fall in big drops.

We turned, as by a common instinct, and, without speech, made our way back slowly to the stockade, Maloney humming snatches of his songs, Sangree in front with his gun, prepared to shoot at a moment's notice, and the women floundering in the rear with myself and the extinguished lanterns.

Yet it was only a dog!

Really, it was most singular when one came to reflect soberly upon it all. Events, say the occultists, have souls, or at least that agglomerate life due to the emotions and thoughts of all concerned in them, so that cities, and even whole countries, have great astral shapes which may become visible to the eye of vision; and certainly here, the soul of this drive—this vain, blundering, futile drive—stood somewhere between ourselves and—laughed.

All of us heard that laugh, and all of us tried hard to smother the sound, or at least to ignore it. Every one talked at once, loudly, and with exaggerated decision, obviously trying to say something plausible against heavy odds, striving to explain naturally that an animal might so easily conceal itself from us, or swim away before we had time to light upon its trail. For we all spoke of that "trail" as though it really existed, and we had more to go upon than the mere marks of paws about the tents of Joan and the Canadian. Indeed, but for these, and the torn tent, I think it would, of course, have been possible to ignore the existence of this beast intruder altogether.

And it was here, under this angry dawn, as we stood in the shelter of the stockade from the pouring rain, weary yet so strangely excited—it was here, out of this confusion of voices and explanations, that—very stealthily—the ghost of something horrible slipped in and stood among us. It made all our explanations seem childish and untrue; the false relation was instantly exposed. Eyes exchanged quick, anxious glances, questioning, expressive of dismay. There was a sense of wonder, of poignant distress, and of trepidation. Alarm stood waiting at our elbows. We shivered.

Then, suddenly, as we looked into each other's faces, came the long, unwelcome pause in which this new arrival established itself in our hearts.

And, without further speech, or attempt at explanation, Maloney moved off abruptly to mix the porridge for an early breakfast; Sangree to clean the fish; myself to chop wood and tend the fire; Joan and her mother to change their wet garments; and, most significant of all, to prepare her mother's tent for its future complement of two.

Each went to his duty, but hurriedly, awkwardly, silently; and this new arrival, this shape of terror and distress stalked, viewless, by the side of each.

"If only I could have traced that dog," I think was the thought in the minds of all.

But in Camp, where every one realises how important the individual contribution is to the comfort and well-being of all, the mind speedily recovers tone and pulls itself together.

During the day, a day of heavy and ceaseless rain, we kept more or less to our tents, and though there were signs of mysterious conferences between the three members of the Maloney family, I think that most of us slept a good deal and stayed alone with his thoughts. Certainly, I did, because when Maloney came to say that his wife invited us all to a special "tea" in her tent, he had to shake me awake before I realised that he was there at all.

And by supper-time we were more or less even-minded again, and almost jolly. I only noticed that there was an undercurrent of what is best described as "jumpiness," and that the merest snapping of a twig, or plop of a fish in the lagoon, was sufficient to make us start and look over our shoulders. Pauses were rare in our talk, and the fire was never for one instant allowed to get low. The wind and rain had ceased, but the dripping of the branches still kept up an excellent imitation of a downpour. In particular, Maloney was vigilant and alert, telling us a series of tales in which the wholesome humorous element was especially strong. He lingered, too, behind with me after Sangree had gone to bed, and while I mixed myself a glass of hot Swedish punch, he did a thing I had never known him do before—he mixed one for himself, and then asked me to light him over to his tent. We said nothing on the way, but I felt that he was glad of my companionship.

I returned alone to the stockade, and for a long time after that kept the fire blazing, and sat up smoking and thinking. I hardly knew why; but sleep was far from me for one thing, and for another, an idea was taking form in my mind that required the comfort of tobacco and a bright fire for its growth. I lay against a corner of the stockade seat, listening to the wind whispering and to the ceaseless drip-drip of the trees. The night, otherwise, was very still, and the sea quiet as a lake. I remember that I was conscious, peculiarly conscious, of this host of desolate islands crowding about us in the darkness, and that we were the one little spot of humanity in a rather wonderful kind of wilderness.

But this, I think, was the only symptom that came to warn me of highly strung nerves, and it certainly was not sufficiently alarming to destroy my peace of mind. One thing, however, did come to disturb my peace, for just as I finally made ready to go, and had kicked the embers of the fire into a last effort, I fancied I saw, peering at me round the farther end of the stockade wall, a dark and shadowy mass that might have been—that strongly resembled, in fact—the body of a large animal. Two glowing eyes shone for an instant in the middle of it. But the next second I saw that it was merely a projecting mass of moss and lichen in the wall of our stockade, and the eyes were a couple of wandering sparks from the dying ashes I had kicked. It was easy enough, too, to imagine I saw an animal moving here and there between the trees, as I picked my way stealthily to my tent. Of course, the shadows tricked me.

And though it was after one o'clock, Maloney's light was still burning, for I saw his tent shining white among the pines.

It was, however, in the short space between consciousness and sleep—that time when the body is low and the voices of the submerged region tell sometimes true—that the idea which had been all this while maturing reached the point of an actual decision, and I suddenly realised that I had resolved to send word to Dr. Silence. For, with a sudden wonder that I had hitherto been so blind, the unwelcome conviction dawned upon me all at once that some dreadful thing was lurking about us on this island, and that the safety of at least one of us was threatened by something monstrous and unclean that was too horrible to contemplate. And, again remembering those last words of his as the train moved out of the platform, I understood that Dr. Silence would hold himself in readiness to come.

"Unless you should send for me sooner," he had said.

I found myself suddenly wide awake. It is impossible to say what woke me, but it was no gradual process, seeing that I jumped from deep sleep to absolute alertness in a single instant. I had evidently slept for an hour and more, for the night had cleared, stars crowded the sky, and a pallid half-moon just sinking into the sea threw a spectral light between the trees.

I went outside to sniff the air, and stood upright. A curious impression that something was astir in the Camp came over me, and when I glanced across at Sangree's tent, some twenty feet away, I saw that it was moving. He too, then, was awake and restless, for I saw the canvas sides bulge this way and that as he moved within.

The the flap pushed forward. He was coming out, like myself, to sniff the air; and I was not surprised, for its sweetness after the rain was intoxicating. And he came on all fours, just as I had done. I saw a head thrust round the edge of the tent.

And then I saw that it was not Sangree at all. It was an animal. And the same instant I realised something else too—it was *the* animal; and its whole presentment for some unaccountable reason was unutterably malefic.

A cry I was quite unable to suppress escaped me, and the creature turned on the instant and stared at me with baleful eyes. I could have dropped on the spot, for the strength all ran out of my body with a rush. Something about it touched in me the living terror that grips and paralyses. If the mind requires but the tenth of a second to form an impression, I must have stood there stockstill for several seconds while I seized the ropes for support and stared. Many and vivid impressions flashed through my mind, but not one of them resulted in action, because I was in instant dread that the beast any moment would leap in my direction and be upon me. Instead, however, after what seemed a vast period, it slowly turned its eyes from my face, uttered a low whining sound, and came out altogether into the open.

Then, for the first time, I saw it in its entirety and noted two things: it was about the size of a large dog, but at the same time it was utterly unlike any animal that I had ever seen. Also, that the quality that had impressed me first as being malefic was really only its singular and original strangeness. Foolish as it may sound, and impossible as it is for me to adduce proof, I can only say that the animal seemed to me then to be—not real.

But all this passed through my mind in a flash, almost subconsciously, and before I had time to check my impressions, or even properly verify them, I made an involuntary movement, catching the tight rope in my hand so that it twanged like a banjo string, and in that instant the creature turned the corner of Sangree's tent and was gone into the darkness.

Then, of course, my senses in some measure returned to me, and I realised only one thing: it had been inside his tent!

I dashed out, reached the door in half a dozen strides, and looked in. The Canadian, thank God! lay upon his bed of branches. His arm was stretched outside, across the blankets, the fist tightly clenched, and the body had an appearance of unusual rigidity that was alarming. On his face there was an expression of effort, almost of painful effort, so far as the uncertain light permitted me to see, and his sleep seemed to be very profound. He looked, I thought, so stiff, so unnaturally stiff, and in some indefinable way, too, he looked smaller—shrunken.

I called to him to wake, but called many times in vain. Then I decided to shake him, and had already moved forward to do so vigorously when there came a sound of footsteps padding softly behind me, and I felt a stream of hot breath burn my neck as I stooped. I turned sharply. The tent door was darkened and something silently swept in. I felt a rough and shaggy body push past me, and knew that the animal had returned. It seemed to leap forward between me and Sangree—in fact, to leap upon Sangree, for its dark body hid him momentarily from view, and in that moment my soul turned sick and coward with a horror that rose from the very dregs and depths of life, and gripped my existence at its central source.

The creature seemed somehow to melt away into him, almost as though it belonged to him and were a part of himself, but in the same instant—that instant of extraordinary confusion and terror in my mind—it seemed to pass over and behind him, and, in some utterly unaccountable fashion, it was gone. And the Canadian woke and sat up with a start.

"Quick! You fool!" I cried, in my excitement, "the beast has been in your tent, here at your very throat while you sleep like the dead. Up, man! Get your gun! Only this second it disappeared over there behind your head. Quick! or Joan——!"

And somehow the fact that he was there, wide-awake now, to corroborate me, brought the additional conviction to my own mind that this was no animal, but some perplexing and dreadful form of life that drew upon my deeper knowledge, that much reading had perhaps assented to, but that had never yet come within actual range of my senses.

He was up in a flash, and out. He was trembling, and very white. We searched hurriedly, feverishly, but found only the traces of paw-marks passing from the door of his own tent across the moss to the women's. And the sight of the tracks about Mrs. Maloney's tent, where Joan now slept, set him in a perfect fury.

"Do you know what it is, Hubbard, this beast?" he hissed under his breath at me; "it's a damned wolf, that's what it is—a wolf lost among the islands, and starving to death—desperate. So help me God, I believe it's that!"

He talked a lot of rubbish in his excitement. He declared he would

sleep by day and sit up every night until he killed it. Again his rage
touched my admiration; but I got him away before he made enough
noise to wake the whole Camp.

"I have a better plan than that," I said, watching his face closely. "I
don't think this is anything we can deal with. I'm going to send for the
only man I know who can help. We'll go to Waxholm this very morning and get a telegram through."

Sangree stared at me with a curious expression as the fury died out
of his face and a new look of alarm took its place.

"John Silence," I said, "will know——"

"You think it's something—of that sort?" he stammered.

"I am sure of it."

There was a moment's pause. "That's worse, far worse than anything
material," he said, turning visibly paler. He looked from my face to the
sky, and then added with sudden resolution, "Come; the wind's rising.
Let's get off at once. From there you can telephone to Stockholm and
get a telegram sent without delay."

I sent him down to get the boat ready, and seized the opportunity myself to run and wake Maloney. He was sleeping very lightly, and sprang
up the moment I put my head inside his tent. I told him briefly what I
had seen, and he showed so little surprise that I caught myself wondering for the first time whether he himself had seen more going on than
he had deemed wise to communicate to the rest of us.

He agreed to my plan without a moment's hesitation, and my last
words to him were to let his wife and daughter think that the great psychic doctor was coming merely as a chance visitor, and not with any
professional interest.

So, with frying-pan, provisions, and blankets aboard, Sangree and I
sailed out of the lagoon fifteen minutes later, and headed with a good
breeze for the direction of Waxholm and the borders of civilisation.

IV

Although nothing John Silence did ever took me, properly speaking, by
surprise, it was certainly unexpected to find a letter from Stockholm
waiting for me. "I have finished my Hungary business," he wrote, "and
am here for ten days. Do not hesitate to send if you need me. If you
telephone any morning from Waxholm I can catch the afternoon
steamer."

My years of intercourse with him were full of "coincidences" of this
description, and although he never sought to explain them by claiming
any magical system of communication with my mind, I have never

doubted that there actually existed some secret telepathic method by which he knew my circumstances and gauged the degree of my need. And that this power was independent of time in the sense that it saw into the future, always seemed to me equally apparent.

Sangree was as much relieved as I was, and within an hour of sunset that very evening we met him on the arrival of the little coasting steamer, and carried him off in the dinghy to the camp we had prepared on a neighbouring island, meaning to start for home early next morning.

"Now," he said, when supper was over and we were smoking round the fire, "let me hear your story." He glanced from one to the other, smiling.

"You tell it, Mr. Hubbard," Sangree interrupted abruptly, and went off a little way to wash the dishes, yet not so far as to be out of earshot. And while he splashed with the hot water, and scraped the tin plates with sand and moss, my voice, unbroken by a single question from Dr. Silence, ran on for the next half-hour with the best account I could give of what had happened.

My listener lay on the other side of the fire, his face half hidden by a big sombrero; sometimes he glanced up questioningly when a point needed elaboration, but he uttered no single word till I had reached the end, and his manner all through the recital was grave and attentive. Overhead, the wash of the wind in the pine branches filled in the pauses; the darkness settled down over the sea, and the stars came out in thousands, and by the time I finished the moon had risen to flood the scene with silver. Yet, by his face and eyes, I knew quite well that the doctor was listening to something he had expected to hear, even if he had not actually anticipated all the details.

"You did well to send for me," he said very low, with a significant glance at me when I finished; "very well,"—and for one swift second his eye took in Sangree,—"for what we have to deal with here is nothing more than a werewolf—rare enough, I am glad to say, but often very sad, and sometimes very terrible."

I jumped as though I had been shot, but the next second was heartily ashamed of my want of control; for this brief remark, confirming as it did my own worst suspicions, did more to convince me of the gravity of the adventure than any number of questions or explanations. It seemed to draw close the circle about us, shutting a door somewhere that locked us in with the animal and the horror, and turning the key. Whatever it was had now to be faced and dealt with.

"No one has been actually injured so far?" he asked aloud, but in a matter-of-fact tone that lent reality to grim possibilities.

"Good heavens, no!" cried the Canadian, throwing down his dish-cloths and coming forward into the circle of firelight. "Surely there can be no question of this poor starved beast injuring anybody, can there?" His hair straggled untidily over his forehead, and there was a gleam in his eyes that was not all reflection from the fire. His words made me turn sharply. We all laughed a little short, forced laugh.

"I trust not, indeed," Dr. Silence said quietly. "But what makes you think the creature is starved?" He asked the question with his eyes straight on the other's face. The prompt question explained to me why I had started, and I waited with just a tremor of excitement for the reply.

Sangree hesitated a moment, as though the question took him by surprise. But he met the doctor's gaze unflinchingly across the fire, and with complete honesty.

"Really," he faltered, with a little shrug of the shoulders, "I can hardly tell you. The phrase seemed to come out of its own accord. I have felt from the beginning that it was in pain and—starved, though why I felt this never occurred to me till you asked."

"You really know very little about it, then?" said the other, with a sudden gentleness in his voice.

"No more than that," Sangree replied, looking at him with a puzzled expression that was unmistakably genuine. "In fact, nothing at all, really," he added, by way of further explanation.

"I am glad of that," I heard the doctor murmur under his breath, but so low that I only just caught the words, and Sangree missed them altogether, as evidently he was meant to do.

"And now," he cried, getting on his feet and shaking himself with a characteristic gesture, as though to shake out the horror and the mystery, "let us leave the problem till to-morrow and enjoy this wind and sea and stars. I've been living lately in the atmosphere of many people, and feel that I want to wash and be clean. I propose a swim and then bed. Who'll second me?" And two minutes later we were all diving from the boat into cool, deep water, that reflected a thousand moons as the waves broke away from us in countless ripples.

We slept in blankets under the open sky, Sangree and I taking the outside places, and were up before sunrise to catch the dawn wind. Helped by this early start we were half-way home by noon, and then the wind shifted to a few points behind us so that we fairly ran. In and out among a thousand islands, down narrow channels where we lost the wind, out into open spaces where we had to take in a reef, racing along under a hot and cloudless sky, we flew through the very heart of the bewildering and lonely scenery.

"A real wilderness," cried Dr. Silence from his seat in the bows where he held the jib sheet. His hat was off, his hair tumbled in the wind, and his lean brown face gave him the touch of an Oriental. Presently he changed places with Sangree, and came down to talk with me by the tiller.

"A wonderful region, all this world of islands," he said, waving his hand to the scenery rushing past us, "but doesn't it strike you there's something lacking?"

"It's—hard," I answered, after a moment's reflection. "It has a superficial, glittering prettiness, without——" I hesitated to find the word I wanted.

John Silence nodded his head with approval.

"Exactly," he said. "The picturesqueness of stage scenery that is not real, not alive. It's like a landscape by a clever painter, yet without true imagination. Soulless—that's the word you wanted."

"Something like that," I answered, watching the gusts of wind on the sails. "Not dead so much, as without soul. That's it."

"Of course," he went on, in a voice calculated, it seemed to me, not to reach our companion in the bows, "to live long in a place like this—long and alone—might bring about a strange result in some men."

I suddenly realised he was talking with a purpose and pricked up my ears.

"There's no life here. These islands are mere dead rocks pushed up from below the sea—not living land; and there's nothing really alive on them. Even the sea, this tideless, brackish sea, neither salt water nor fresh, is dead. It's all a pretty image of life without the real heart and soul of life. To a man with too strong desires who came here and lived close to nature, strange things might happen."

"Let her out a bit," I shouted to Sangree, who was coming aft. "The wind's gusty and we've got hardly any ballast."

He went back to the bows, and Dr. Silence continued—

"Here, I mean, a long sojourn would lead to deterioration, to degeneration. The place is utterly unsoftened by human influences, by any humanising associations of history, good or bad. This landscape has never awakened into life; it's still dreaming in its primitive sleep."

"In time," I put in, "you mean a man living here might become brutal?"

"The passions would run wild, selfishness become supreme, the instincts coarsen and turn savage probably."

"But——"

"In other places just as wild, parts of Italy for instance, where there are other moderating influences, it could not happen. The character might grow wild, savage too in a sense, but with a human wildness one could understand and deal with. But here, in a hard place like this, it might be otherwise." He spoke slowly, weighing his words carefully.

I looked at him with many questions in my eyes, and a precautionary cry to Sangree to stay in the fore part of the boat, out of earshot.

"First of all there would come callousness to pain, and indifference to the rights of others. Then the soul would turn savage, not from passionate human causes, or with enthusiasm, but by deadening down into a kind of cold, primitive, emotionless savagery—by turning, like the landscape, soulless."

"And a man with strong desires, you say, might change?"

"Without being aware of it, yes; he might turn savage, his instincts and desires turn animal. And if"—he lowered his voice and turned for a moment towards the bows, and then continued in his most weighty manner—"owing to delicate health or other predisposing causes, his Double—you know what I mean, of course—his etheric Body of Desire, or astral body, as some term it—that part in which the emotions, passions and desires reside—if this, I say, were for some constitutional reason loosely joined to his physical organism, there might well take place an occasional projection——"

Sangree came aft with a sudden rush, his face aflame, but whether with wind or sun, or with what he had heard, I cannot say. In my surprise I let the tiller slip and the cutter gave a great plunge as she came sharply into the wind and flung us all together in a heap on the bottom. Sangree said nothing, but while he scrambled up and made the jib sheet fast my companion found a moment to add to his unfinished sentence the words, too low for any ear but mine—

"Entirely unknown to himself, however."

We righted the boat and laughed, and then Sangree produced the map and explained exactly where we were. Far away on the horizon, across an open stretch of water, lay a blue cluster of islands with our crescent-shaped home among them and the safe anchorage of the lagoon. An hour with this wind would get us there comfortably, and while Dr. Silence and Sangree fell into conversation, I sat and pondered over the strange suggestions that had just been put into my mind concerning the "Double," and the possible form it might assume when dissociated temporarily from the physical body.

The whole way home these two chatted, and John Silence was as gentle and sympathetic as a woman. I did not hear much of their talk, for the wind grew occasionally to the force of a hurricane and the sails and tiller absorbed my attention; but I could see that Sangree was pleased and happy, and was pouring out intimate revelations to his companion in the way that most people did—when John Silence wished them to do so.

But it was quite suddenly, while I sat all intent upon wind and sails, that the true meaning of Sangree's remark about the animal flared up in me with its full import. For his admission that he knew it was in pain and starved was in reality nothing more or less than a revelation of his deeper self. It was in the nature of a confession. He was speaking of something that he knew positively, something that was beyond question or argument, something that had to do directly with himself. "Poor starved beast" he had called it in words that had "come out of their own accord," and there had not been the slightest evidence of any desire to conceal or explain away. He had spoken instinctively—from his heart, and as though about his own self.

And half an hour before sunset we raced through the narrow opening of the lagoon and saw the smoke of the dinner-fire blowing here and there among the trees, and the figures of Joan and the Bo'sun's Mate running down to meet us at the landing-stage.

V

Everything changed from the moment John Silence set foot on that island; it was like the effect produced by calling in some big doctor, some great arbiter of life and death, for consultation. The sense of gravity increased a hundredfold. Even inanimate objects took upon themselves a subtle alteration, for the setting of the adventure—this deserted bit of sea with its hundreds of uninhabited islands—somehow turned sombre. An element that was mysterious, and in a sense disheartening, crept unbidden into the severity of grey rock and dark pine forest and took the sparkle from the sunshine and the sea.

I, at least, was keenly aware of the change, for my whole being shifted, as it were, a degree higher, becoming keyed up and alert. The figures from the background of the stage moved forward a little into the light—nearer to the inevitable action. In a word this man's arrival intensified the whole affair.

And, looking back down the years to the time when all this happened, it is clear to me that he had a pretty sharp idea of the meaning of it from the very beginning. How much he knew beforehand by his strange divining powers, it is impossible to say, but from the moment he came upon the scene and caught within himself the note of what was going on amongst us, he undoubtedly held the true solution of the puzzle and had no need to ask questions. And this certitude it was that set him in such an atmosphere of power and made us all look to him instinctively; for he took no tentative steps, made no false moves, and while the rest of us floundered he moved straight to the climax. He was indeed a true diviner of souls.

I can now read into his behaviour a good deal that puzzled me at the time, for though I had dimly guessed the solution, I had no idea how he would deal with it. And the conversations I can reproduce almost verbatim, for, according to my invariable habit, I kept full notes of all he said.

To Mrs. Maloney, foolish and dazed; to Joan, alarmed, yet plucky; and to the clergyman, moved by his daughter's distress below his usual shallow emotions, he gave the best possible treatment in the best possible way, yet all so easily and simply as to make it appear naturally spontaneous. For he dominated the Bo'sun's Mate, taking the measure of her ignorance with infinite patience; he keyed up Joan, stirring her courage and interest to the highest point for her own safety; and the Reverend Timothy he soothed and comforted, while obtaining his implicit obedience, by taking him into his confidence, and leading him gradually to a comprehension of the issue that was bound to follow.

And Sangree—here his wisdom was most wisely calculated—he neglected outwardly because inwardly he was the object of his unceasing and most concentrated attention. Under the guise of apparent indifference his mind kept the Canadian under constant observation.

There was a restless feeling in the Camp that evening and none of us lingered round the fire after supper as usual. Sangree and I busied ourselves with patching up the torn tent for our guest and with finding heavy stones to hold the ropes, for Dr. Silence insisted on having it pitched on the highest point of the island ridge, just where it was most rocky and there was no earth for pegs. The place, moreover, was midway between the men's and women's tents, and, of course, commanded the most comprehensive view of the Camp.

"So that if your dog comes," he said simply, "I may be able to catch him as he passes across."

The wind had gone down with the sun and an unusual warmth lay over the island that made sleep heavy, and in the morning we assembled at a late breakfast, rubbing our eyes and yawning. The cool north wind had given way to the warm southern air that sometimes came up with haze and moisture across the Baltic, bringing with it the relaxing sensations that produced enervation and listlessness.

And this may have been the reason why at first I failed to notice that anything unusual was about, and why I was less alert than normally; for it was not till after breakfast that the silence of our little party struck me and I discovered that Joan had not yet put in an appearance. And then, in a flash, the last heaviness of sleep vanished and I saw that Maloney was white and troubled and his wife could not hold a plate without trembling.

A desire to ask questions was stopped in me by a swift glance from Dr. Silence, and I suddenly understood in some vague way that they were waiting till Sangree should have gone. How this idea came to me I cannot determine, but the soundness of the intuition was soon proved, for the moment he moved off to his tent, Maloney looked up at me and began to speak in a low voice.

"You slept through it all," he half whispered.

"Through what?" I asked, suddenly thrilled with the knowledge that something dreadful had happened.

"We didn't wake you for fear of getting the whole Camp up," he went on, meaning, by the Camp, I supposed, Sangree. "It was just before dawn when the screams woke me."

"The dog again?" I asked, with a curious sinking of the heart.

"Got right into the tent," he went on, speaking passionately but very low, "and woke my wife by scrambling all over her. Then she realised that Joan was struggling beside her. And, by God! the beast had torn her arm; scratched all down the arm she was, and bleeding."

"Joan injured?" I gasped.

"Merely scratched—this time," put in John Silence, speaking for the first time; "suffering more from shock and fright than actual wounds."

"Isn't it a mercy the doctor was here?" said Mrs. Maloney, looking as if she would never know calmness again. "I think we should both have been killed."

"It has been a most merciful escape," Maloney said, his pulpit voice struggling with his emotion. "But, of course, we cannot risk another— we must strike Camp and get away at once——"

"Only poor Mr. Sangree must not know what has happened. He is so attached to Joan and would be so terribly upset," added the Bo'sun's Mate distractedly, looking all about in her terror.

"It is perhaps advisable that Mr. Sangree should not know what has occurred," Dr. Silence said with quiet authority, "but I think, for the safety of all concerned, it will be better not to leave the island just now." He spoke with great decision and Maloney looked up and followed his words closely.

"If you will agree to stay here a few days longer, I have no doubt we can put an end to the attentions of your strange visitor, and incidentally have the opportunity of observing a most singular and interesting phenomenon——"

"What!" gasped Mrs. Maloney, "a phenomenon?—you mean that you know what it is?"

"I am quite certain I know what it is," he replied very low, for we heard the footsteps of Sangree approaching, "though I am not so certain yet as to the best means of dealing with it. But in any case it is not wise to leave precipitately——"

"Oh, Timothy, does he think it's a devil——?" cried the Bo'sun's Mate in a voice that even the Canadian must have heard.

"In my opinion," continued John Silence, looking across at me and the clergyman, "it is a case of modern lycanthropy with other complications that may——" He left the sentence unfinished, for Mrs. Maloney got up with a jump and fled to her tent fearful she might hear a worse thing, and at that moment Sangree turned the corner of the stockade and came into view.

"There are footmarks all round the mouth of my tent," he said with excitement. "The animal has been here again in the night. Dr. Silence, you really must come and see them for yourself. They're as plain on the moss as tracks in snow."

But later in the day, while Sangree went off in the canoe to fish the pools near the larger islands, and Joan still lay, bandaged and resting, in her tent, Dr. Silence called me and the tutor and proposed a walk to the granite slabs at the far end. Mrs. Maloney sat on a stump near her daughter, and busied herself energetically with alternate nursing and painting.

"We'll leave you in charge," the doctor said with a smile that was meant to be encouraging, "and when you want us for lunch, or anything, the megaphone will always bring us back in time."

For, though the very air was charged with strange emotions, every one talked quietly and naturally as with a definite desire to counteract unnecessary excitement.

"I'll keep watch," said the plucky Bo'sun's Mate, "and meanwhile I find comfort in my work." She was busy with the sketch she had begun on the day after our arrival. "For even a tree," she added proudly, pointing to her little easel, "is a symbol of the divine, and the thought makes me feel safer." We glanced for a moment at a daub which was more like the symptom of a disease than a symbol of the divine—and then took the path round the lagoon.

At the far end we made a little fire and lay round it in the shadow of a big boulder. Maloney stopped his humming suddenly and turned to his companion.

"And what do you make of it all?" he asked abruptly.

"In the first place," replied John Silence, making himself comfortable against the rock, "it is of human origin, this animal; it is undoubted lycanthropy."

His words had the effect precisely of a bombshell. Maloney listened as though he had been struck.

"You puzzle me utterly," he said, sitting up closer and staring at him.

"Perhaps," replied the other, "but if you'll listen to me for a few moments you may be less puzzled at the end—or more. It depends how much you know. Let me go further and say that you have underestimated, or miscalculated, the effect of this primitive wild life upon all of you."

"In what way?" asked the clergyman, bristling a trifle.

"It is strong medicine for any town-dweller, and for some of you it has been too strong. One of you has gone wild." He uttered these last words with great emphasis.

"Gone savage," he added, looking from one to the other.

Neither of us found anything to reply.

"To say that the brute has awakened in a man is not a mere metaphor always," he went on presently.

"Of course not!"

"But, in the sense I mean, may have a very literal and terrible significance," pursued Dr. Silence. "Ancient instincts that no one dreamed of, least of all their possessor, may leap forth——"

"Atavism can hardly explain a roaming animal with teeth and claws and sanguinary instincts," interrupted Maloney with impatience.

"The term is of your own choice," continued the doctor equably, "not mine, and it is a good example of a word that indicates a result while it conceals the process; but the explanation of this beast that haunts your island and attacks your daughter is of far deeper significance than mere atavistic tendencies, or throwing back to animal origin, which I suppose is the thought in your mind."

"You spoke just now of lycanthropy," said Maloney, looking bewildered and anxious to keep to plain facts evidently; "I think I have come across the word, but really—really—it can have no actual significance today, can it? These superstitions of mediæval times can hardly——"

He looked round at me with his jolly red face, and the expression of astonishment and dismay on it would have made me shout with laughter at any other time. Laughter, however, was never farther from my mind than at this moment when I listened to Dr. Silence as he carefully suggested to the clergyman the very explanation that had gradually been forcing itself upon my own mind.

"However mediæval ideas may have exaggerated the idea is not of much importance to us now," he said quietly, "when we are face to face with a modern example of what, I take it, has always been a profound fact. For the moment let us leave the name of any one in particular out of the matter and consider certain possibilities."

We all agreed with that at any rate. There was no need to speak of Sangree, or of any one else, until we knew a little more.

"The fundamental fact in this most curious case," he went on, "is that the 'Double' of a man——"

"You mean the astral body? I've heard of that, of course," broke in Maloney with a snort of triumph.

"No doubt," said the other, smiling, "no doubt you have;—that this Double, or fluidic body of a man, as I was saying, has the power under certain conditions of projecting itself and becoming visible to others. Certain training will accomplish this, and certain drugs likewise; illnesses, too, that ravage the body may produce temporarily the result that death produces permanently, and let loose this counterpart of a human being and render it visible to the sight of others.

"Every one, of course, knows this more or less today; but it is not so generally known, and probably believed by none who have not witnessed it, that this fluidic body can, under certain conditions, assume other forms than human, and that such other forms may be determined by the dominating thought and wish of the owner. For this Double, or astral body as you call it, is really the seat of the passions, emotions and desires in the psychical economy. It is the Passion Body; and, in projecting itself, it can often assume a form that gives expression to the overmastering desire that moulds it; for it is composed of such tenuous matter that it lends itself readily to the moulding by thought and wish."

"I follow you perfectly," said Maloney, looking as if he would much rather be chopping firewood elsewhere and singing.

"And there are some persons so constituted," the doctor went on with increasing seriousness, "that the fluid body in them is but loosely associated with the physical, persons of poor health as a rule, yet often of strong desires and passions; and in these persons it is easy for the Double to dissociate itself during deep sleep from their system, and, driven forth by some consuming desire, to assume an animal form and seek the fulfilment of that desire."

There, in broad daylight, I saw Maloney deliberately creep closer to the fire and heap the wood on. We gathered in to the heat, and to each other, and listened to Dr. Silence's voice as it mingled with the swish and whirr of the wind about us, and the falling of the little waves.

"For instance, to take a concrete example," he resumed; "suppose some young man, with the delicate constitution I have spoken of, forms an overpowering attachment to a young woman, yet perceives that it is not welcomed, and is man enough to repress its outward manifestations. In such a case, supposing his Double be easily projected, the very repression of his love in the daytime would add to the intense force of his desire when released in deep sleep from the control of his will, and his fluidic body might issue forth in monstrous or animal shape and become actually visible to others. And, if his devotion were dog-like in its fidelity, yet concealing the fires of a fierce passion beneath, it might well assume the form of a creature that seemed to be half dog, half wolf——"

"A werewolf, you mean?" cried Maloney, pale to the lips as he listened.

John Silence held up a restraining hand. "A werewolf," he said, "is a true psychical fact of profound significance, however absurdly it may have been exaggerated by the imaginations of a superstitious peasantry in the days of unenlightenment, for a werewolf is nothing but the savage, and possibly sanguinary, instincts of a passionate man scouring the world in his fluidic body, his passion body, his body of desire. As in the case at hand, he may not know it——"

"It is not necessarily deliberate, then?" Maloney put in quickly, with relief.

"——It is hardly ever deliberate. It is the desires released in sleep from the control of the will finding a vent. In all savage races it has been recognised and dreaded, this phenomenon styled 'Wehr Wolf,' but to-day it is rare. And it is becoming rarer still, for the world grows tame and civilised, emotions have become refined, desires lukewarm, and few men have savagery enough left in them to generate impulses of such intense force, and certainly not to project them in animal form."

"By Gad!" exclaimed the clergyman breathlessly, and with increasing excitement, "then I feel I must tell you—what has been given to me in confidence—that Sangree has in him an admixture of savage blood—of Red Indian ancestry——"

"Let us stick to our supposition of a man as described," the doctor stopped him calmly, "and let us imagine that he has in him this admixture of savage blood; and further, that he is wholly unaware of his dreadful physical and psychical infirmity; and that he suddenly finds himself leading the primitive life together with the object of his desires; with the result that the strain of the untamed wild-man in his blood——"

"Red Indian, for instance," from Maloney.

"Red Indian, perfectly," agreed the doctor; "the result, I say, that this savage strain in him is awakened and leaps into passionate life. What then?"

He looked hard at Timothy Maloney, and the clergyman looked hard at him.

"The wild life such as you lead here on this island, for instance, might quickly awaken his savage instincts—his buried instincts—and with profoundly disquieting results."

"You mean his Subtle Body, as you call it, might issue forth automatically in deep sleep and seek the object of its desire?" I said, coming to Maloney's aid, who was finding it more and more difficult to get words.

"Precisely;—yet the desire of the man remaining utterly unmalefic—pure and wholesome in every sense——"

"Ah!" I heard the clergyman gasp.

"The lover's desire for union run wild, run savage, tearing its way out in primitive, untamed fashion, I mean," continued the doctor, striving to make himself clear to a mind bounded by conventional thought and knowledge; "for the desire to possess, remember, may easily become importunate, and, embodied in this animal form of the Subtle Body which acts as its vehicle, may go forth to tear in pieces all that obstructs, to reach to the very heart of the loved object and seize it. *Au fond*, it is nothing more than the aspiration for union, as I said—the splendid and perfectly clean desire to absorb utterly into itself——"

He paused a moment and looked into Maloney's eyes.

"To bathe in the very heart's blood of the one desired," he added with grave emphasis.

The fire spurted and crackled and made me start, but Maloney found relief in a genuine shudder, and I saw him turn his head and look about him from the sea to the trees. The wind dropped just at that moment and the doctor's words rang sharply through the stillness.

"Then it might even kill?" stammered the clergyman presently in a hushed voice, and with a little forced laugh by way of protest that sounded quite ghastly.

"In the last resort it might kill," repeated Dr. Silence. Then, after another pause, during which he was clearly debating how much or how little it was wise to give to his audience, he continued: "And if the Double does not succeed in getting back to its physical body, that physical body would wake an imbecile—an idiot—or perhaps never wake at all."

Maloney sat up and found his tongue.

"You mean that if this fluid animal thing, or whatever it is, should be prevented getting back, the man might never wake again?" he asked, with shaking voice.

"He might be dead," replied the other calmly. The tremor of a positive sensation shivered in the air about us.

"Then isn't that the best way to cure the fool—the brute——?" thundered the clergyman, half rising to his feet.

"Certainly it would be an easy and undiscoverable form of murder," was the stern reply, spoken as calmly as though it were a remark about the weather.

Maloney collapsed visibly, and I gathered the wood over the fire and coaxed up a blaze.

"The greater part of the man's life—of his vital forces—goes out with this Double," Dr. Silence resumed, after a moment's consideration, "and a considerable portion of the actual material of his physical body. So the physical body that remains behind is depleted, not only of force, but of matter. You would see it small, shrunken, dropped together, just like the body of a materialising medium at a séance. Moreover, any mark or injury inflicted upon this Double will be found exactly reproduced by the phenomenon of repercussion upon the shrunken physical body lying in its trance——"

"An injury inflicted upon the one you say would be reproduced also on the other?" repeated Maloney, his excitement growing again.

"Undoubtedly," replied the other quietly; "for there exists all the time a continuous connection between the physical body and the Double—a connection of matter, though of exceedingly attenuated, possibly of etheric, matter. The wound *travels*, so to speak, from one to the other, and if this connection were broken the result would be death."

"Death," repeated Maloney to himself, "death!" He looked anxiously at our faces, his thoughts evidently beginning to clear.

"And this solidity?" he asked presently, after a general pause; "this tearing of tents and flesh; this howling, and the marks of paws? You mean that the Double——?"

"Has sufficient material drawn from the depleted body to produce physical results? Certainly!" the doctor took him up. "Although to explain at this moment such problems as the passage of matter through matter would be as difficult as to explain how the thought of a mother can actually break the bones of the child unborn."

Dr. Silence pointed out to sea, and Maloney, looking wildly about him, turned with a violent start. I saw a canoe, with Sangree in the stern-seat, slowly coming into view round the farther point. His hat was off, and his tanned face for the first time appeared to me—to us all, I think—as though it were the face of some one else. He looked like a wild man. Then he stood up in the canoe to make a cast with the rod, and he looked for all the world like an Indian. I recalled the expression of his face as I had seen it once or twice, notably on that occasion of the evening prayer, and an involuntary shudder ran down my spine.

At that very instant he turned and saw us where we lay, and his face broke into a smile, so that his teeth showed white in the sun. He looked in his element, and exceedingly attractive. He called out something about his fish, and soon after passed out of sight into the lagoon.

For a time none of us said a word.

"And the cure?" ventured Maloney at length.

"Is not to quench this savage force," replied Dr. Silence, "but to steer it better, and to provide other outlets. This is the solution of all these problems of accumulated force, for this force is the raw material of usefulness, and should be increased and cherished, not by separating it from the body by death, but by raising it to higher channels. The best and quickest cure of all," he went on, speaking very gently and with a hand upon the clergyman's arm, "is to lead it towards its object, provided that object is not unalterably hostile—to let it find rest where——"

He stopped abruptly, and the eyes of the two men met in a single glance of comprehension.

"Joan?" Maloney exclaimed, under his breath.

"Joan!" replied John Silence.

We all went to bed early. The day had been unusually warm, and after sunset a curious hush descended on the island. Nothing was audible but that faint, ghostly singing which is inseparable from a pinewood even on the stillest day—a low, searching sound, as though the wind had hair and trailed it o'er the world.

With the sudden cooling of the atmosphere a sea fog began to form. It appeared in isolated patches over the water, and then these patches slid together and a white wall advanced upon us. Not a breath of air stirred; the firs stood like flat metal outlines; the sea became as oil. The whole scene lay as though held motionless by some huge weight in the air; and the flames from our fire—the largest we had ever made—rose upwards, straight as a church steeple.

As I followed the rest of our party tent-wards, having kicked the embers of the fire into safety, the advance guard of the fog was creeping slowly among the trees, like white arms feeling their way. Mingled with the smoke was the odour of moss and soil and bark, and the peculiar flavour of the Baltic, half salt, half brackish, like the smell of an estuary at low water.

It is difficult to say why it seemed to me that this deep stillness masked an intense activity; perhaps in every mood lies the suggestion of its opposite, so that I became aware of the contrast of furious energy, for it was like moving through the deep pause before a thunderstorm, and I trod gently lest by breaking a twig or moving a stone I might set the whole scene into some sort of tumultuous movement. Actually, no doubt, it was nothing more than a result of overstrung nerves.

There was no more question of undressing and going to bed than there was of undressing and going to bathe. Some sense in me was alert and expectant. I sat in my tent and waited. And at the end of half an hour or so my waiting was justified, for the canvas suddenly shivered, and some one tripped over the ropes that held it to the earth. John Silence came in.

The effect of his quiet entry was singular and prophetic: it was just as though the energy lying behind all this stillness had pressed forward to the edge of action. This, no doubt, was merely the quickening of my own mind, and had no other justification; for the presence of John Silence always suggested the near possibility of vigorous action, and as a matter of fact, he came in with nothing more than a nod and a significant gesture.

He sat down on a corner of my ground-sheet, and I pushed the blanket over so that he could cover his legs. He drew the flap of the tent after him and settled down, but hardly had he done so when the canvas shook a second time, and in blundered Maloney.

"Sitting in the dark?" he said self-consciously, pushing his head inside, and hanging up his lantern on the ridge-pole nail. "I just looked in for a smoke. I suppose——"

He glanced round, caught the eye of Dr. Silence, and stopped. He put his pipe back into his pocket and began to hum softly—that under-breath humming of a nondescript melody I knew so well and had come to hate.

Dr. Silence leaned forward, opened the lantern and blew the light out. "Speak low," he said, "and don't strike matches. Listen for sounds and movements about the Camp, and be ready to follow me at a moment's notice." There was light enough to distinguish our faces easily, and I saw Maloney glance again hurriedly at both of us.

"Is the Camp asleep?" the doctor asked presently, whispering.

"Sangree is," replied the clergyman, in a voice equally low. "I can't answer for the women; I think they're sitting up."

"That's for the best." And then he added: "I wish the fog would thin a bit and let the moon through; later—we may want it."

"It is lifting now, I think," Maloney whispered back. "It's over the tops of the trees already."

I cannot say what it was in this commonplace exchange of remarks that thrilled. Probably Maloney's swift acquiescence in the doctor's mood had something to do with it; for his quick obedience certainly impressed me a good deal. But, even without that slight evidence, it

was clear that each recognised the gravity of the occasion, and understood that sleep was impossible and sentry duty was the order of the
night.

"Report to me," repeated John Silence once again, "the least sound,
and do nothing precipitately."

He shifted across to the mouth of the tent and raised the flap, fas-
tening it against the pole so that he could see out. Maloney stopped
humming and began to force the breath through his teeth with a kind
of faint hissing, treating us to a medley of church hymns and popular
songs of the day.

Then the tent trembled as though some one had touched it.

"That's the wind rising," whispered the clergyman, and pulled the
flap open as far as it would go. A waft of cold damp air entered and
made us shiver, and with it came a sound of the sea as the first wave
washed its way softly along the shores.

"It's got round to the north," he added, and following his voice came
a long-drawn whisper that rose from the whole island as the trees sent
forth a sighing response. "The fog'll move a bit now. I can make out a
lane across the sea already."

"Hush!" said Dr. Silence, for Maloney's voice had risen above a
whisper, and we settled down again to another long period of watching
and waiting, broken only by the occasional rubbing of shoulders
against the canvas as we shifted our positions, and the increasing noise
of waves on the outer coast-line of the island. And over all whirred the
murmur of wind sweeping the tops of the trees like a great harp, and
the faint tapping on the tent as drops fell from the branches with a
sharp pinging sound.

We had sat for something over an hour in this way, and Maloney and
I were finding it increasingly hard to keep awake, when suddenly Dr.
Silence rose to his feet and peered out. The next minute he was gone.

Relieved of the dominating presence, the clergyman thrust his face
close into mine. "I don't much care for this waiting game," he whispered, "but Silence wouldn't hear of my sitting up with the others; he
said it would prevent anything happening if I did."

"He knows," I answered shortly.

"No doubt in the world about that," he whispered back; "it's this
'Double' business, as he calls it, or else it's obsession as the Bible
describes it. But it's bad, whichever it is, and I've got my Winchester
outside ready cocked, and I brought this too." He shoved a pocket
Bible under my nose. At one time in his life it had been his inseparable companion.

"One's useless and the other's dangerous," I replied under my breath, conscious of a keen desire to laugh, and leaving him to choose. "Safety lies in following our leader——"

"I'm not thinking of myself," he interrupted sharply; "only, if anything happens to Joan tonight I'm going to shoot first—and pray afterwards!"

Maloney put the book back into his hip-pocket, and peered out of the doorway. "What is he up to now, in the devil's name, I wonder!" he added; "going round Sangree's tent and making gestures. How weird he looks disappearing in and out of the fog."

"Just trust him and wait," I said quickly, for the doctor was already on his way back. "Remember, he has the knowledge, and knows what he's about. I've been with him through worse cases than this."

Maloney moved back as Dr. Silence darkened the doorway and stooped to enter.

"His sleep is very deep," he whispered, seating himself by the door again. "He's in a cataleptic condition, and the Double may be released any minute now. But I've taken steps to imprison it in the tent, and it can't get out till I permit it. Be on the watch for signs of movement." Then he looked hard at Maloney. "But no violence, or shooting, remember, Mr. Maloney, unless you want a murder on your hands. Anything done to the Double acts by repercussion upon the physical body. You had better take out the cartridges at once."

His voice was stern. The clergyman went out, and I heard him emptying the magazine of his rifle. When he returned he sat nearer the door than before, and from that moment until we left the tent he never once took his eyes from the figure of Dr. Silence, silhouetted there against sky and canvas.

And, meanwhile, the wind came steadily over the sea and opened the mist into lanes and clearings, driving it about like a living thing.

It must have been well after midnight when a low booming sound drew my attention; but at first the sense of hearing was so strained that it was impossible exactly to locate it, and I imagined it was the thunder of big guns far out at sea carried to us by the rising wind. Then Maloney, catching hold of my arm and leaning forward, somehow brought the true relation, and I realised the next second that it was only a few feet away.

"Sangree's tent," he exclaimed in a loud and startled whisper.

I craned my head round the corner, but at first the effect of the fog was so confusing that every patch of white driving about before the wind looked like a moving tent and it was some seconds before I discovered the one patch that held steady. Then I saw that it was shaking all over, and the sides, flapping as much as the tightness of the ropes allowed, were the cause of the booming sound we had heard. Something alive was tearing frantically about inside, banging against the stretched canvas in a way that made me think of a great moth dashing against the walls and ceiling of a room. The tent bulged and rocked.

"It's trying to get out, by Jupiter!" muttered the clergyman, rising to his feet and turning to the side where the unloaded rifle lay. I sprang up too, hardly knowing what purpose was in my mind, but anxious to be prepared for anything. John Silence, however, was before us both, and his figure slipped past and blocked the doorway of the tent. And there was some quality in his voice next minute when he began to speak that brought our minds instantly to a state of calm obedience.

"First—the women's tent," he said low, looking sharply at Maloney, "and if I need your help, I'll call."

The clergyman needed no second bidding. He dived past me and was out in a moment. He was labouring evidently under intense excitement. I watched him picking his way silently over the slippery ground, giving the moving tent a wide berth, and presently disappearing among the floating shapes of fog.

Dr. Silence turned to me. "You heard those footsteps about half an hour ago?" he asked significantly.

"I heard nothing."

"They were extraordinarily soft—almost the soundless tread of a wild creature. But now, follow me closely," he added, "for we must waste no time if I am to save this poor man from his affliction and lead his were-wolf Double to its rest. And, unless I am much mistaken"—he peered at me through the darkness, whispering with the utmost distinctness— "Joan and Sangree are absolutely made for one another. And I think she knows it too—just as well as he does."

My head swam a little as I listened, but at the same time something cleared in my brain and I saw that he was right. Yet it was all so weird and incredible, so remote from the commonplace facts of life as commonplace people know them; and more than once it flashed upon me that the whole scene—people, words, tents, and all the rest of it—were delusions created by the intense excitement of my own mind somehow, and that suddenly the sea-fog would clear off and the world become normal again.

The cold air from the sea stung our cheeks sharply as we left the close atmosphere of the little crowded tent. The sighing of the trees, the waves breaking below on the rocks, and the lines and patches of mist driving about us seemed to create the momentary illusion that the whole island had broken loose and was floating out to sea like a mighty raft.

The doctor moved just ahead of me, quickly and silently; he was making straight for the Canadian's tent where the sides still boomed and shook as the creature of sinister life raced and tore about impatiently within. A little distance from the door he paused and held up a hand to stop me. We were, perhaps, a dozen feet away.

"Before I release it, you shall see for yourself," he said, "that the reality of the werewolf is beyond all question. The matter of which it is composed is, of course, exceedingly attenuated, but you are partially clairvoyant—and even if it is not dense enough for normal sight you will see something."

He added a little more I could not catch. The fact was that the curiously strong vibrating atmosphere surrounding his person somewhat confused my senses. It was the result, of course, of his intense concentration of mind and forces, and pervaded the entire Camp and all the persons in it. And as I watched the canvas shake and heard it boom and flap I heartily welcomed it. For it was also protective.

At the back of Sangree's tent stood a thin group of pine trees, but in front and at the sides the ground was comparatively clear. The flap was wide open and any ordinary animal would have been out and away without the least trouble. Dr. Silence led me up to within a few feet, evidently careful not to advance beyond a certain limit, and then stooped down and signalled to me to do the same. And looking over his shoulder I saw the interior lit faintly by the spectral light reflected from the fog, and the dim blot upon the balsam boughs and blankets signifying Sangree; while over him, and round him, and up and down him, flew the dark mass of "something" on four legs, with pointed muzzle and sharp ears plainly visible against the tent sides, and the occasional gleam of fiery eyes and white fangs.

I held my breath and kept utterly still, inwardly and outwardly, for fear, I suppose, that the creature would become conscious of my presence; but the distress I felt went far deeper than the mere sense of personal safety, or the fact of watching something so incredibly active and real. I became keenly aware of the dreadful psychic calamity it involved. The realisation that Sangree lay confined in that narrow space with this species of monstrous projection of himself—that he was wrapped there in the cataleptic sleep, all unconscious that this thing was masquerading with his own life and energies—added a distressing touch of horror to the scene. In all the cases of John Silence—and they were many and often terrible—no other psychic affliction has ever, before or since, impressed me so convincingly with the pathetic impermanence of the human personality, with its fluid nature, and with the alarming possibilities of its transformations.

"Come," he whispered, after we had watched for some minutes the frantic efforts to escape from the circle of thought and will that held it prisoner, "come a little farther away while I release it."

We moved back a dozen yards or so. It was like a scene in some impossible play, or in some ghastly and oppressive nightmare from which I should presently awake to find the blankets all heaped up upon my chest.

By some method undoubtedly mental, but which, in my confusion and excitement, I failed to understand, the doctor accomplished his purpose, and the next minute I heard him say sharply under his breath, "It's out! Now watch!"

At this very moment a sudden gust from the sea blew aside the mist, so that a lane opened to the sky, and the moon, ghastly and unnatural as the effect of stage limelight, dropped down in a momentary gleam upon the door of Sangree's tent, and I perceived that something had moved forward from the interior darkness and stood clearly defined upon the threshold. And, at the same moment, the tent ceased its shuddering and held still.

There, in the doorway, stood an animal, with neck and muzzle thrust forward, its head poking into the night, its whole body poised in that attitude of intense rigidity that precedes the spring into freedom, the running leap of attack. It seemed to be about the size of a calf, leaner than a mastiff, yet more squat than a wolf, and I can swear that I saw the fur ridged sharply upon its back. Then its upper lip slowly lifted, and I saw the whiteness of its teeth.

Surely no human being ever stared as hard as I did in those next few minutes. Yet, the harder I stared the clearer appeared the amazing and monstrous apparition. For, after all, it was Sangree—and yet it was not Sangree. It was the head and face of an animal, and yet it was the face of Sangree: the face of a wild dog, a wolf, and yet his face. The eyes were sharper, narrower, more fiery, yet they were his eyes—his eyes run wild; the teeth were longer, whiter, more pointed—yet they were his teeth, his teeth grown cruel; the expression was flaming, terrible, exultant—yet it was his expression carried to the border of savagery—his expression as I had already surprised it more than once, only dominant now, fully released from human constraint, with the mad yearning of a hungry and importunate soul. It was the soul of Sangree, the long suppressed, deeply loving Sangree, expressed in its single and intense desire—pure utterly and utterly wonderful.

Yet, at the same time, came the feeling that it was all an illusion. I suddenly remembered the extraordinary changes the human face can undergo in circular insanity, when it changes from melancholia to elation; and I recalled the effect of hascheesh, which shows the human countenance in the form of the bird or animal to which in character it most approximates; and for a moment I attributed this mingling of Sangree's face with a wolf to some kind of similar delusion of the senses. I was mad, deluded, dreaming! The excitement of the day, and this dim light of stars and bewildering mist combined to trick me. I had been amazingly imposed upon by some false wizardry of the senses. It was all absurd and fantastic; it would pass.

And then, sounding across this sea of mental confusion like a bell through a fog, came the voice of John Silence bringing me back to a consciousness of the reality of it all—

"Sangree—in his Double!"

And when I looked again more calmly, I plainly saw that it was indeed the face of the Canadian, but his face turned animal, yet mingled with the brute expression a curiously pathetic look like the soul seen sometimes in the yearning eyes of a dog,—the face of an animal shot with vivid streaks of the human.

The doctor called to him softly under his breath—

"Sangree! Sangree, you poor afflicted creature! Do you know me? Can you understand what it is you're doing in your 'Body of Desire'?"

For the first time since its appearance the creature moved. Its ears twitched and it shifted the weight of its body on to the hind legs. Then, lifting its head and muzzle to the sky, it opened its long jaws and gave vent to a dismal and prolonged howling.

But, when I heard that howling rise to heaven, the breath caught and strangled in my throat and it seemed that my heart missed a beat; for, though the sound was entirely animal, it was at the same time entirely human. But, more than that, it was the cry I had so often heard in the Western States of America where the Indians still fight and hunt and struggle—it was the cry of the Redskin!

"The Indian blood!" whispered John Silence, when I caught his arm for support; "the ancestral cry."

And that poignant, beseeching cry, that broken human voice, mingling with the savage howl of the brute beast, pierced straight to my very heart and touched there something that no music, no voice, passionate or tender, of man, woman or child has ever stirred before or since for one second into life. It echoed away among the fog and the trees and lost itself somewhere out over the hidden sea. And some part of myself—something that was far more than the mere act of intense listening—went out with it, and for several minutes I lost consciousness of my surroundings and felt utterly absorbed in the pain of another stricken fellow-creature.

Again the voice of John Silence recalled me to myself.

"Hark!" he said aloud. "Hark!"

His tone galvanised me afresh. We stood listening side by side. Far across the island, faintly sounding through the trees and brushwood, came a similar, answering cry. Shrill, yet wonderfully musical, shaking the heart with a singular wild sweetness that defies description, we heard it rise and fall upon the night air.

"It's across the lagoon," Dr. Silence cried, but this time in full tones that paid no tribute to caution. "It's Joan! She's answering him!"

Again the wonderful cry rose and fell, and that same instant the animal lowered its head, and, muzzle to earth, set off on a swift easy canter that took it off into the mist and out of our sight like a thing of wind and vision.

The doctor made a quick dash to the door of Sangree's tent, and, following close at his heels, I peered in and caught a momentary glimpse of the small, shrunken body lying upon the branches but half covered by the blankets—the cage from which most of the life, and not a little of the actual corporeal substance, had escaped into that other form of life and energy, the body of passion and desire.

By another of those swift, incalculable processes which at this stage of my apprenticeship I failed often to grasp, Dr. Silence reclosed the circle about the tent and body.

"Now it cannot return till I permit it," he said, and the next second was off at full speed into the woods, with myself close behind him. I had already had some experience of my companion's ability to run swiftly through a dense wood, and I now had the further proof of his power almost to see in the dark. For, once we left the open space about the tents, the trees seemed to absorb all the remaining vestiges of light, and I understood that special sensibility that is said to develop in the blind—the sense of obstacles.

And twice as we ran we heard the sound of that dismal howling drawing nearer and nearer to the answering faint cry from the point of the island whither we were going.

Then, suddenly, the trees fell away, and we emerged, hot and breathless, upon the rocky point where the granite slabs ran bare into the sea. It was like passing into the clearness of open day. And there, sharply defined against sea and sky, stood the figure of a human being. It was Joan.

I at once saw that there was something about her appearance that was singular and unusual, but it was only when we had moved quite close that I recognised what caused it. For while the lips wore a smile that lit the whole face with a happiness I had never seen there before, the eyes themselves were fixed in a steady, sightless stare as though they were lifeless and made of glass.

I made an impulsive forward movement, but Dr. Silence instantly dragged me back.

"No," he cried, "don't wake her!"

"What do you mean?" I replied aloud, struggling in his grasp.

"She's asleep. It's somnambulistic. The shock might injure her permanently."

I turned and peered closely into his face. He was absolutely calm. I began to understand a little more, catching, I suppose, something of his strong thinking.

"Walking in her sleep, you mean?"

He nodded. "She's on her way to meet him. From the very beginning he must have drawn her—irresistibly."

"But the torn tent and the wounded flesh?"

"When she did not sleep deep enough to enter the somnambulistic trance he missed her—he went instinctively and in all innocence to seek her out—with the result, of course, that she woke and was terrified——"

"Then in their heart of hearts they love?" I asked finally.

John Silence smiled his inscrutable smile. "Profoundly," he answered, "and as simply as only primitive souls can love. If only they both come to realise it in their normal waking states his Double will cease these nocturnal excursions. He will be cured, and at rest."

The words had hardly left his lips when there was a sound of rustling branches on our left, and the very next instant the dense brushwood parted where it was darkest and out rushed the swift form of an animal at full gallop. The noise of feet was scarcely audible, but in that utter stillness I heard the heavy panting breath and caught the swish of the low bushes against its sides. It went straight towards Joan—and as it went the girl lifted her head and turned to meet it. And the same instant a canoe that had been creeping silently and unobserved round the inner shore of the lagoon, emerged from the shadows and defined itself upon the water with a figure at the middle thwart. It was Maloney.

It was only afterwards I realised that we were invisible to him where we stood against the dark background of trees; the figures of Joan and the animal he saw plainly, but not Dr. Silence and myself standing just beyond them. He stood up in the canoe and pointed with his right arm. I saw something gleam in his hand.

"Stand aside, Joan girl, or you'll get hit," he shouted, his voice ringing horribly through the deep stillness, and the same instant a pistol-shot cracked out with a burst of flame and smoke, and the figure of the animal, with one tremendous leap into the air, fell back in the shadows and disappeared like a shape of night and fog. Instantly, then, Joan opened her eyes, looked in a dazed fashion about her, and pressing both hands against her heart, fell with a sharp cry into my arms that were just in time to catch her.

And an answering cry sounded across the lagoon—thin, wailing, piteous. It came from Sangree's tent.

"Fool!" cried Dr. Silence, "you've wounded him!" and before we could move or realise quite what it meant, he was in the canoe and half-way across the lagoon.

Some kind of similar abuse came in a torrent from my lips, too—though I cannot remember the actual words—as I cursed the man for his disobedience and tried to make the girl comfortable on the ground. But the clergyman was more practical. He was spreading his coat over her and dashing water on her face.

"It's not Joan I've killed at any rate," I heard him mutter as she turned and opened her eyes and smiled faintly up in his face. "I swear the bullet went straight."

Joan stared at him; she was still dazed and bewildered, and still imagined herself with the companion of her trance. The strange lucidity of the somnambulist still hung over her brain and mind, though outwardly she appeared troubled and confused.

"Where has he gone to? He disappeared so suddenly, crying that he was hurt," she asked, looking at her father as though she did not recognise him. "And if they've done anything to him—they have done it to me too—for he is more to me than——"

Her words grew vaguer and vaguer as she returned slowly to her normal waking state, and now she stopped altogether, as though suddenly aware that she had been surprised into telling secrets. But all the way back, as we carried her carefully through the trees, the girl smiled and murmured Sangree's name and asked if he was injured, until it finally became clear to me that the wild soul of the one had called to the wild soul of the other and in the secret depths of their beings the call had been heard and understood. John Silence was right. In the abyss of her heart, too deep at first for recognition, the girl loved him, and had loved him from the very beginning. Once her normal waking consciousness recognised the fact they would leap together like twin flames, and his affliction would be at an end; his intense desire would be satisfied; he would be cured.

And in Sangree's tent Dr. Silence and I sat up for the remainder of the night—this wonderful and haunted night that had shown us such strange glimpses of a new heaven and a new hell—for the Canadian tossed upon his balsam boughs with high fever in his blood, and upon each cheek a dark and curious contusion showed, throbbing with severe pain although the skin was not broken and there was no outward and visible sign of blood.

"Maloney shot straight, you see," whispered Dr. Silence to me after the clergyman had gone to his tent, and had put Joan to sleep beside her mother, who, by the way, had never once awakened. "The bullet must have passed clean through the face, for both cheeks are stained. He'll wear these marks all his life—smaller, but always there. They're the most curious scars in the world, these scars transferred by repercussion from an injured Double. They'll remain visible until just before his death, and then with the withdrawal of the subtle body they will disappear finally."

His words mingled in my dazed mind with the sighs of the troubled sleeper and the crying of the wind about the tent. Nothing seemed to paralyse my powers of realisation so much as these twin stains of mysterious significance upon the face before me.

It was odd, too, how speedily and easily the Camp resigned itself again to sleep and quietness, as though a stage curtain had suddenly dropped down upon the action and concealed it; and nothing contributed so vividly to the feeling that I had been a spectator of some kind of visionary drama as the dramatic nature of the change in the girl's attitude.

Yet, as a matter of fact, the change had not been so sudden and revolutionary as appeared. Underneath, in those remoter regions of consciousness where the emotions, unknown to their owners, do secretly mature, and owe thence their abrupt revelation to some abrupt psychological climax, there can be no doubt that Joan's love for the Canadian had been growing steadily and irresistibly all the time. It had now rushed to the surface so that she recognised it; that was all.

And it has always seemed to me that the presence of John Silence, so potent, so quietly efficacious, produced an effect, if one may say so, of a psychic forcing-house, and hastened incalculably the bringing together of these two "wild" lovers. In that sudden awakening had occurred the very psychological climax required to reveal the passionate emotion accumulated below. The deeper knowledge had leaped across and transferred itself to her ordinary consciousness, and in that shock the collision of the personalities had shaken them to the depths and shown her the truth beyond all possibility of doubt.

"He's sleeping quietly now," the doctor said, interrupting my reflections. "If you will watch alone for a bit I'll go to Maloney's tent and help him to arrange his thoughts." He smiled in anticipation of that "arrangement." "He'll never quite understand how a wound on the Double can transfer itself to the physical body, but at least I can persuade him that the less he talks and 'explains' tomorrow, the sooner the forces will run their natural course now to peace and quietness."

He went away softly, and with the removal of his presence Sangree, sleeping heavily, turned over and groaned with the pain of his broken head.

And it was in the still hour just before the dawn, when all the islands were hushed, the wind and sea still dreaming, and the stars visible through clearing mists, that a figure crept silently over the ridge and reached the door of the tent where I dozed beside the sufferer, before I was aware of its presence. The flap was cautiously lifted a few inches and in looked — Joan.

That same instant Sangree woke and sat up on his bed of branches. He recognised her before I could say a word, and uttered a low cry. It was pain and joy mingled, and this time all human. And the girl too was no longer walking in her sleep, but fully aware of what she was doing. I was only just able to prevent him springing from his blankets.

"Joan, Joan!" he cried, and in a flash she answered him, "I'm here — I'm with you always now," and had pushed past me into the tent and flung herself upon his breast.

"I knew you would come to me in the end," I heard him whisper.

"It was all too big for me to understand at first," she murmured, "and for a long time I was frightened ——"

"But not now!" he cried louder; "you don't feel afraid now of — of anything that's in me ——"

"I fear nothing," she cried, "nothing, nothing!"

I led her outside again. She looked steadily into my face with eyes shining and her whole being transformed. In some intuitive way, surviving probably from the somnambulism, she knew or guessed as much as I knew.

"You must talk tomorrow with John Silence," I said gently, leading her towards her own tent. "He understands everything."

I left her at the door, and as I went back softly to take up my place of sentry again with the Canadian, I saw the first streaks of dawn lighting up the far rim of the sea behind the distant islands.

And, as though to emphasise the eternal closeness of comedy to tragedy, two small details rose out of the scene and impressed me so vividly that I remember them to this very day. For in the tent where I had just left Joan, all aquiver with her new happiness, there rose plainly to my ears the grotesque sounds of the Bo'sun's Mate heavily snoring, oblivious of all things in heaven or hell; and from Maloney's tent, so still was the night, where I looked across and saw the lantern's glow, there came to me, through the trees, the monotonous rising and falling of a human voice that was beyond question the sound of a man praying to his God.

A VICTIM OF HIGHER SPACE

"There's a hextraordinary gentleman to see you, sir," said the new man.

"Why 'extraordinary'?" asked Dr. Silence, drawing the tips of his thin fingers through his brown beard. His eyes twinkled pleasantly. "Why 'extraordinary,' Barker?" he repeated encouragingly, noticing the perplexed expression in the man's eyes.

"He's so—so thin, sir. I could hardly see 'im at all—at first. He was inside the house before I could ask the name," he added, remembering strict orders.

"And who brought him here?"

"He come alone, sir, in a closed cab. He pushed by me before I could say a word—making no noise not what I could hear. He seemed to move so soft like——"

The man stopped short with obvious embarrassment, as though he had already said enough to jeopardise his new situation, but trying hard to show that he remembered the instructions and warnings he had received with regard to the admission of strangers not properly accredited.

"And where is the gentleman now?" asked Dr. Silence, turning away to conceal his amusement.

"I really couldn't exactly say, sir. I left him standing in the 'all——"

The doctor looked up sharply. "But why in the hall, Barker? Why not in the waiting-room?" He fixed his piercing though kindly eyes on the man's face. "Did he frighten you?" he asked quickly.

"I think he did, sir, if I may say so. I seemed to lose sight of him, as it were——" The man stammered, evidently convinced by now that he had earned his dismissal. "He come in so funny, just like a cold wind," he added boldly, setting his heels at attention and looking his master full in the face.

The doctor made an internal note of the man's halting description; he was pleased that the slight signs of psychic intuition which had induced him to engage Barker had not entirely failed at the first trial. Dr. Silence sought for this qualification in all his assistants, from secretary to serving man, and if it surrounded him with a somewhat singular crew, the drawbacks were more than compensated for on the whole by their occasional flashes of insight.

"So the gentleman made you feel queer, did he?"

"That was it, I think, sir," repeated the man stolidly.

"And he brings no kind of introduction to me—no letter or any-thing?" asked the doctor, with feigned surprise, as though he knew what was coming.

The man fumbled, both in mind and pockets, and finally produced an envelope.

"I beg pardon, sir," he said, greatly flustered; "the gentleman handed me this for you."

It was a note from a discerning friend, who had never yet sent him a case that was not vitally interesting from one point or another.

"Please see the bearer of this note," the brief message ran, "though I doubt if even you can do much to help him."

John Silence paused a moment, so as to gather from the mind of the writer all that lay behind the brief words of the letter. Then he looked up at his servant with a graver expression than he had yet worn.

"Go back and find this gentleman," he said, "and show him into the green study. Do not reply to his question, or speak more than actually necessary; but think kind, helpful, sympathetic thoughts as strongly as you can, Barker. You remember what I told you about the importance of *thinking*, when I engaged you. Put curiosity out of your mind, and think gently, sympathetically, affectionately, if you can."

He smiled, and Barker, who had recovered his composure in the doctor's presence, bowed silently and went out.

There were two different reception-rooms in Dr. Silence's house. One (intended for persons who imagined they needed spiritual assistance when really they were only candidates for the asylum) had padded walls, and was well supplied with various concealed contrivances by means of which sudden violence could be instantly met and overcome. It was, however, rarely used. The other, intended for the reception of genuine cases of spiritual distress and out-of-the-way afflictions of a psychic nature, was entirely draped and furnished in a soothing deep green, calculated to induce calmness and repose of mind. And this room was the one in which Dr. Silence interviewed the majority of his "queer" cases, and the one into which he had directed Barker to show his present caller.

To begin with, the arm-chair in which the patient was always directed to sit, was nailed to the floor, since its immovability tended to impart this same excellent characteristic to the occupant. Patients invariably grew excited when talking about themselves, and their excitement tended to confuse their thoughts and to exaggerate their language. The inflexibility of the chair helped to counteract this. After repeated endeavours to drag it forward, or push it back, they ended by resigning themselves to sitting quietly. And with the futility of fidgeting there followed a calmer state of mind.

Upon the floor, and at intervals in the wall immediately behind, were certain tiny green buttons, practically unnoticeable, which on being pressed permitted a soothing and persuasive narcotic to rise invisibly about the occupant of the chair. The effect upon the excitable patient was rapid, admirable, and harmless. The green study was further provided with a secret spy-hole; for John Silence liked when possible to observe his patient's face before it had assumed that mask the features of the human countenance invariably wear in the presence of another person. A man sitting alone wears a psychic expression; and this expression is the man himself. It disappears the moment another person joins him. And Dr. Silence often learned more from a few moments' secret observation of a face than from hours of conversation with its owner afterwards.

A very light, almost a dancing, step followed Barker's heavy tread towards the green room, and a moment afterwards the man came in and announced that the gentleman was waiting. He was still pale and his manner nervous.

"Never mind, Barker," the doctor said kindly; "if you were not psychic the man would have had no effect upon you at all. You only need training and development. And when you have learned to interpret these feelings and sensations better, you will feel no fear, but only a great sympathy."

"Yes, sir; thank you, sir!" And Barker bowed and made his escape, while Dr. Silence, an amused smile lurking about the corners of his mouth, made his way noiselessly down the passage and put his eye to the spy-hole in the door of the green study.

This spy-hole was so placed that it commanded a view of almost the entire room, and, looking through it, the doctor saw a hat, gloves, and umbrella lying on a chair by the table, but searched at first in vain for their owner.

The windows were both closed and a brisk fire burned in the grate. There were various signs—signs intelligible at least to a keenly intuitive soul—that the room was occupied, yet so far as human beings were concerned, it was empty, utterly empty. No one sat in the chairs; no one stood on the mat before the fire; there was no sign even that a patient was anywhere close against the wall, examining the Böcklin reproductions—as patients so often did when they thought they were alone—and therefore rather difficult to see from the spy-hole. Ordinarily speaking, there was no one in the room. It was undeniable.

Yet Dr. Silence was quite well aware that a human being *was* in the room. His psychic apparatus never failed in letting him know the proximity of an incarnate or discarnate being. Even in the dark he could tell that. And he now knew positively that his patient—the patient who had alarmed Barker, and had then tripped down the corridor with that dancing footstep—was somewhere concealed within the four walls commanded by his spy-hole. He also realised—and this was most unusual—that this individual whom he desired to watch knew that he was being watched. And, further, that the stranger himself was also watching! In fact, that it was he, the doctor, who was being observed—and by an observer as keen and trained as himself.

An inkling of the true state of the case began to dawn upon him, and he was on the verge of entering—indeed, his hand already touched the door-knob—when his eye, still glued to the spy-hole, detected a slight movement. Directly opposite, between him and the fireplace, something stirred. He watched very attentively and made certain that he was not mistaken. An object on the mantelpiece—it was a blue vase—disappeared from view. It passed out of sight together with the portion of the marble mantelpiece on which it rested. Next, that part of the fire and grate and brass fender immediately below it vanished entirely, as though a slice had been taken clean out of them.

Dr. Silence then understood that something between him and these objects was slowly coming into being, something that concealed them and obstructed his vision by inserting itself in the line of sight between them and himself.

He quietly awaited further results before going in.

First he saw a thin perpendicular line tracing itself from just above the height of the clock and continuing downwards till it reached the woolly fire-mat. This line grew wider, broadened, grew solid. It was no shadow; it was something substantial. It defined itself more and more. Then suddenly, at the top of the line, and about on a level with the face of the clock, he saw a round luminous disc gazing steadily at him. It was a human eye, looking straight into his own, pressed there against the spy-hole. And it was bright with intelligence. Dr. Silence held his breath for a moment—and stared back at it.

Then, like some one moving out of deep shadow into light, he saw the figure of a man come sliding sideways into view, a whitish face following the eye, and the perpendicular line he had first observed broadening out and developing into the complete figure of a human being. It was the patient. He had apparently been standing there in front of the fire all the time. A second eye had followed the first, and both of them stared steadily at the spy-hole, sharply concentrated, yet with a sly twinkle of humour and amusement that made it impossible for the doctor to maintain his position any longer.

He opened the door and went in quickly. As he did so he noticed for the first time the sound of a German band coming in gaily through the open ventilators. In some intuitive, unaccountable fashion the music connected itself with the patient he was about to interview. This sort of prevision was not unfamiliar to him. It always explained itself later.

The man, he saw, was of middle age and of very ordinary appearance; so ordinary, in fact, that he was difficult to describe—his only peculiarity being his extreme thinness. Pleasant—that is, good—vibrations issued from his atmosphere and met Dr. Silence as he advanced to greet him, yet vibrations alive with currents and discharges betraying the perturbed and disordered condition of his mind and brain. There was evidently something wholly out of the usual in the state of his thoughts. Yet, though strange, it was not altogether distressing; it was not the impression that the broken and violent atmosphere of the insane produces upon the mind. Dr. Silence realised in a flash that here was a case of absorbing interest that might require all his powers to handle properly.

"I was watching you through my little peep-hole—as you saw," he began, with a pleasant smile, advancing to shake hands. "I find it of the greatest assistance sometimes——"

But the patient interrupted him at once. His voice was hurried and had odd, shrill changes in it, breaking from high to low in unexpected fashion. One moment it thundered, the next it almost squeaked.

"I understand without explanation," he broke in rapidly. "You get the true note of a man in this way—when he thinks himself unobserved. I quite agree. Only, in my case, I fear, you saw very little. My case, as you of course grasp, Dr. Silence, is extremely peculiar, uncomfortably peculiar. Indeed, unless Sir William had positively assured me——"

"My friend has sent you to me," the doctor interrupted gravely, with a gentle note of authority, "and that is quite sufficient. Pray, be seated, Mr. ——"

"Mudge—Racine Mudge," returned the other.

"Take this comfortable one, Mr. Mudge," leading him to the fixed chair, "and tell me your condition in your own way and at your own pace. My whole day is at your service if you require it."

Mr. Mudge moved towards the chair in question and then hesitated.

"You will promise me not to use the narcotic buttons," he said, before sitting down. "I do not need them. Also I ought to mention that anything you think of vividly will reach my mind. That is apparently part of my peculiar case." He sat down with a sigh and arranged his thin

legs and body into a position of comfort. Evidently he was very sensitive to the thoughts of others, for the picture of the green buttons had
only entered the doctor's mind for a second, yet the other had instantly
snapped it up. Dr. Silence noticed, too, that Mr. Mudge held on tightly
with both hands to the arms of the chair.

"I'm rather glad the chair is nailed to the floor," he remarked, as he
settled himself more comfortably. "It suits me admirably. The fact is—
and this is my case in a nutshell—which is all that a doctor of your marvellous development requires—the fact is, Dr. Silence, I am a victim of
Higher Space. That's what's the matter with me—Higher Space!"

The two looked at each other for a space in silence, the little patient
holding tightly to the arms of the chair which "suited him admirably,"
and looking up with staring eyes, his atmosphere positively trembling
with the waves of some unknown activity; while the doctor smiled
kindly and sympathetically, and put his whole person as far as possible
into the mental condition of the other.

"Higher Space," repeated Mr. Mudge, "that's what it is. Now, do you
think you can help me with *that?*"

There was a pause during which the men's eyes steadily searched
down below the surface of their respective personalities. Then Dr.
Silence spoke.

"I am quite sure I can help," he answered quietly; "sympathy must
always help, and suffering always owns my sympathy. I see you have suffered cruelly. You must tell me all about your case, and when I hear the
gradual steps by which you reached this strange condition, I have no
doubt I can be of assistance to you."

He drew a chair up beside his interlocutor and laid a hand on his
shoulder for a moment. His whole being radiated kindness, intelligence, desire to help.

"For instance," he went on, "I feel sure it was the result of no mere
chance that you became familiar with the terrors of what you term
Higher Space; for Higher Space is no mere external measurement. It
is, of course, a spiritual state, a spiritual condition, an inner development, and one that we must recognise as abnormal, since it is beyond
the reach of the world at the present stage of evolution. Higher Space
is a mythical state."

"Oh!" cried the other, rubbing his birdlike hands with pleasure, "the
relief it is to be able to talk to some one who can understand! Of course
what you say is the utter truth. And you are right that no mere chance
led me to my present condition, but, on the other hand, prolonged and
deliberate study. Yet chance in a sense now governs it. I mean, my entering the condition of Higher Space seems to depend upon the

chance of this and that circumstance. For instance, the mere sound of that German band sent me off. Not that all music will do so, but certain sounds, certain vibrations, at once key me up to the requisite pitch, and off I go. Wagner's music always does it, and that band must have been playing a stray bit of Wagner. But I'll come to all that later. Only first, I must ask you to send away your man from the spy-hole."

John Silence looked up with a start, for Mr. Mudge's back was to the door, and there was no mirror. He saw the brown eye of Barker glued to the little circle of glass, and he crossed the room without a word and snapped down the black shutter provided for the purpose, and then heard Barker snuffle away along the passage.

"Now," continued the little man in the chair, "I can begin. You have managed to put me completely at my ease, and I feel I may tell you my whole case without shame or reserve. You will understand. But you must be patient with me if I go into details that are already familiar to you—details of Higher Space, I mean—and if I seem stupid when I have to describe things that transcend the power of language and are really therefore indescribable."

"My dear friend," put in the other calmly, "that goes without saying. To know Higher Space is an experience that defies description, and one is obliged to make use of more or less intelligible symbols. But, pray, proceed. Your vivid thoughts will tell me more than your halting words."

An immense sigh of relief proceeded from the little figure half lost in the depths of the chair. Such intelligent sympathy meeting him halfway was a new experience to him, and it touched his heart at once. He leaned back, relaxing his tight hold of the arms, and began in his thin, scale-like voice.

"My mother was a Frenchwoman, and my father an Essex bargeman," he said abruptly. "Hence my name—Racine and Mudge. My father died before I ever saw him. My mother inherited money from her Bordeaux relations, and when she died soon after, I was left alone with wealth and a strange freedom. I had no guardian, trustees, sisters, brothers, or any connection in the world to look after me. I grew up, therefore, utterly without education. This much was to my advantage; I learned none of that deceitful rubbish taught in schools, and so had nothing to unlearn when I awakened to my true love—mathematics, higher mathematics and higher geometry. These, however, I seemed to know instinctively. It was like the memory of what I had deeply studied before; the principles were in my blood, and I simply raced through the ordinary stages, and beyond, and then did the same with geometry. Afterwards, when I read the books on these subjects, I understood how swift and undeviating the knowledge had come back to me. It was simply memory. It was simply *re-collecting* the memories of what I had known before in a previous existence and required no books to teach me."

In his growing excitement, Mr. Mudge attempted to drag the chair forward a little nearer to his listener, and then smiled faintly as he resigned himself instantly again to its immovability, and plunged anew into the recital of his singular "disease."

"The audacious speculations of Bolyai, the amazing theories of Gauss—that through a point more than one line could be drawn parallel to a given line; the possibility that the angles of a triangle are together *greater* than two right angles, if drawn upon immense curvatures—the breathless intuitions of Beltrami and Lobatchewsky—all these I hurried through, and emerged, panting but unsatisfied, upon the verge of my—my new world, my Higher Space possibilities—in a word, my disease!

"How I got there," he resumed after a brief pause, during which he appeared to be listening intently for an approaching sound, "is more than I can put intelligibly into words. I can only hope to leave your mind with an intuitive comprehension of the possibility of what I say.

"Here, however, came a change. At this point I was no longer absorbing the fruits of studies I had made before; it was the beginning of new efforts to learn for the first time, and I had to go slowly and laboriously through terrible work. Here I sought for the theories and speculations of others. But books were few and far between, and with the exception of one man—a 'dreamer,' the world called him—whose audacity and piercing intuition amazed and delighted me beyond description, I found no one to guide or help.

"You, of course, Dr. Silence, understand something of what I am driving at with these stammering words, though you cannot perhaps yet guess what depths of pain my new knowledge brought me to, nor why an acquaintance with a new development of space should prove a source of misery and terror."

Mr. Racine Mudge, remembering that the chair would not move, did the next best thing he could in his desire to draw nearer to the attentive man facing him, and sat forward upon the very edge of the cushions, crossing his legs and gesticulating with both hands as though he saw into this region of new space he was attempting to describe, and might any moment tumble into it bodily from the edge of the chair and disappear form view. John Silence, separated from him by three paces, sat with his eyes fixed upon the thin white face opposite, noting every word and every gesture with deep attention.

"This room we now sit in, Dr. Silence, has one side open to space—to Higher Space. A closed box only *seems* closed. There is a way in and out of a soap bubble without breaking the skin."

"You tell me no new thing," the doctor interposed gently.

"Hence, if Higher Space exists and our world borders upon it and lies partially in it, it follows necessarily that we see only portions of all objects. We never see their true and complete shape. We see their three measurements, but not their fourth. The new direction is concealed from us, and when I hold this book and move my hand all round it I have not really made a complete circuit. We only perceive those portions of any object which exist in our three dimensions; the rest escapes us. But, once we learn to see in Higher Space, objects will appear as they actually are. Only they will thus be hardly recognisable!

"Now, you may begin to grasp something of what I am coming to."

"I am beginning to understand something of what you must have suffered," observed the doctor soothingly, "for I have made similar experiments myself, and only stopped just in time——"

"You are the one man in all the world who can hear and understand, *and* sympathise," exclaimed Mr. Mudge, grasping his hand and holding it tightly while he spoke. The nailed chair prevented further excitability.

"Well," he resumed, after a moment's pause, "I procured the implements and the coloured blocks for practical experiment, and I followed the instructions carefully till I had arrived at a working conception of four-dimensional space. The tessaract, the figure whose boundaries are cubes, I knew by heart. That is to say, I knew it and saw it mentally, for my eye, of course, could never take in a new measurement, or my hands and feet handle it.

"So, at least, I thought," he added, making a wry face. "I had reached the stage, you see, when I could *imagine* in a new dimension. I was able to conceive the shape of that new figure which is intrinsically different to all we know—the shape of the tessaract. I could perceive in four dimensions. When, therefore, I looked at a cube I could see all its sides at once. Its top was not foreshortened, nor its farther side and base invisible. I saw the whole thing out flat, so to speak. And this tessaract was bounded by cubes! Moreover, I also saw its content—its insides."

"You were not yourself able to enter this new world," interrupted Dr. Silence.

"Not then. I was only able to conceive intuitively what it was like and how exactly it must look. Later, when I slipped in there and saw objects in their entirety, unlimited by the paucity of our poor three measurements, I very nearly lost my life. For, you see, space does not stop at a single new dimension, a fourth. It extends in all possible new ones, and we must conceive it as containing any number of new dimensions. In other words, there is no space at all, but only a spiritual condition. But, meanwhile, I had come to grasp the strange fact that the objects in our normal world appear to us only partially."

Mr. Mudge moved farther forward till he was balanced dangerously on the very edge of the chair. "From this starting point," he resumed, "I began my studies and experiments, and continued them for years. I had money, and I was without friends. I lived in solitude and experimented. My intellect, of course, had little part in the work, for intellectually it was all unthinkable. Never was the limitation of mere reason more plainly demonstrated. It was mystically, intuitively, spiritually that I began to advance. And what I learnt, and knew, and did is all impossible to put into language, since it all describes experiences transcending the experiences of men. It is only some of the results—what you would call the symptoms of my disease—that I can give you, and even these must often appear absurd contradictions and impossible paradoxes.

"I can only tell you, Dr. Silence"—his manner became exceedingly impressive—"that I reached sometimes a point of view whence all the great puzzle of the world became plain to me, and I understood what they call in the Yoga books 'The Great Heresy of Separateness'; why all great teachers have urged the necessity of man loving his neighbour as himself; how men are all really *one*; and why the utter loss of self is necessary to salvation and the discovery of the true life of the soul."

He paused a moment and drew breath.

"Your speculations have been my own long ago," the doctor said quietly. "I fully realise the force of your words. Men are doubtless not separate at all—in the sense they imagine——"

"All this about the very much Higher Space I only dimly, very dimly, conceived, of course," the other went on, raising his voice again by jerks; "but what did happen to me was the humbler accident of—the simpler disaster—oh, dear, how shall I put it——?"

He stammered and showed visible signs of distress.

"It was simply this," he resumed with a sudden rush of words, "that, accidentally, as the result of my years of experiment, I one day slipped bodily into the next world, the world of four dimensions, yet without knowing precisely how I got there, or how I could get back again. I discovered, that is, that my ordinary three-dimensional body was but an expression—a projection—of my higher four-dimensional body!

"Now you understand what I meant much earlier in our talk when I spoke of chance. I cannot control my entrance or exit. Certain people, certain human atmospheres, certain wandering forces, thoughts, desires even—the radiations of certain combinations of colour, and above all, the vibrations of certain kinds of music, will suddenly throw me into a state of what I can only describe as an intense and terrific inner vibration—and behold I am off! Off in the direction at right angles to all our known directions! Off in the direction the cube takes when it begins to trace the outlines of the new figure! Off into my breathless and semi-divine Higher Space! Off, *inside myself*, into the world of four dimensions!"

He gasped and dropped back into the depths of the immovable chair.

"And there," he whispered, his voice issuing from among the cushions, "there I have to stay until these vibrations subside, or until they do something which I cannot find words to describe properly or intelligibly to you—and then, behold, I am back again. First, that is, I disappear. Then I reappear."

"Just so," exclaimed Dr. Silence, "and that is why a few——"

"Why a few moments ago," interrupted Mr. Mudge, taking the words out of his mouth, "you found me gone, and then saw me return. The music of that wretched German band sent me off. Your intense thinking about me brought me back—when the band had stopped its Wagner. I saw you approach the peep-hole and I saw Barker's intention of doing so later. For me no interiors are hidden. I see inside. When in that state the content of your mind, as of your body, is open to me as the day. Oh, dear, oh, dear, oh, dear!"

Mr. Mudge stopped and again mopped his brow. A light trembling ran over the surface of his small body like wind over grass. He still held tightly to the arms of the chair.

"At first," he presently resumed, "my new experiences were so vividly interesting that I felt no alarm. There was no room for it. The alarm came a little later."

"Then you actually penetrated far enough into that state to experience yourself as a normal portion of it?" asked the doctor, leaning forward, deeply interested.

Mr. Mudge nodded a perspiring face in reply.

"I did," he whispered, "undoubtedly I did. I am coming to all that. It began first at night, when I realised that sleep brought no loss of consciousness——"

"The spirit, of course, can never sleep. Only the body becomes unconscious," interposed John Silence.

"Yes, we know that—theoretically. At night, of course, the spirit is active elsewhere, and we have no memory of where and how, simply because the brain stays behind and receives no record. But I found that, while remaining conscious, I also retained memory. I had attained to the state of continuous consciousness, for at night I regularly, with the first approaches of drowsiness, entered *nolens volens* the four-dimensional world.

"For a time this happened regularly, and I could not control it; though later I found a way to regulate it better. Apparently sleep is unnecessary in the higher—the four-dimensional—body. Yes, perhaps. But I should infinitely have preferred dull sleep to the knowledge. For, unable to control my movements, I wandered to and fro, attracted, owing to my partial development and premature arrival, to parts of this new world that alarmed me more and more. It was the awful waste and drift of a monstrous world, so utterly different to all we know and see that I cannot even hint at the nature of the sights and objects and beings in it. More than that, I cannot even remember them. I cannot now picture them to myself even, but can recall only the *memory of the impression* they made upon me, the horror and devastating terror of it all. To be in several places at once, for instance——"

"Perfectly," interrupted John Silence, noticing the increase of the other's excitement, "I understand exactly. But now, please, tell me a little more of this alarm you experienced, and how it affected you."

"It's not the disappearing and reappearing *per se* that I mind," continued Mr. Mudge, "so much as certain other things. It's seeing people and objects in their weird entirety, in their true and complete shapes, that is so distressing. It introduces me to a world of monsters. Horses, dogs, cats, all of which I loved; people, trees, children; all that I have considered beautiful in life—everything, from a human face to a cathedral—appear to me in a different shape and aspect to all I have known before. I cannot perhaps convince you why this should be terrible, but I assure you that it is so. To hear the human voice proceeding from this novel appearance which I scarcely recognise as a human body is ghastly, simply ghastly. To see inside everything and everybody is a form of insight peculiarly distressing. To be so confused in geography as to find myself one moment at the North Pole, and the next at Clapham Junction—or possibly at both places simultaneously—is absurdly terrifying. Your imagination will readily furnish other details without my multiplying my experiences now. But you have no idea what it all means, and how I suffer."

Mr. Mudge paused in his panting account and lay back in his chair. He still held tightly to the arms as though they could keep him in the world of sanity and three measurements, and only now and again released his left hand in order to mop his face. He looked very thin and white and oddly unsubstantial, and he stared about him as though he saw into this other space he had been talking about.

John Silence, too, felt warm. He had listened to every word and had made many notes. The presence of this man had an exhilarating effect upon him. It seemed as if Mr. Racine Mudge still carried about with him something of that breathless Higher-Space condition he had been describing. At any rate, Dr. Silence had himself advanced sufficiently far along the legitimate paths of spiritual and psychic transformations to realise that the visions of this extraordinary little person had a basis of truth for their origin.

After a pause that prolonged itself into minutes, he crossed the room and unlocked a drawer in a bookcase, taking out a small book with a red cover. It had a lock to it, and he produced a key out of his pocket and proceeded to open the covers. The bright eyes of Mr. Mudge never left him for a single second.

"It almost seems a pity," he said at length, "to cure you, Mr. Mudge. You are on the way to discovery of great things. Though you may lose your life in the process—that is, your life here in the world of three dimensions— you would lose thereby nothing of great value—you will pardon my apparent rudeness, I know—and you might gain what is infinitely greater. Your suffering, of course, lies in the fact that you alternate between the two worlds and are never wholly in one or the other. Also, I rather imagine, though I cannot be certain of this from any personal experiments, that you have here and there penetrated even into space of more than four dimensions, and have hence experienced the terror you speak of."

The perspiring son of the Essex bargeman and the woman of Normandy bent his head several times in assent, but uttered no word in reply.

"Some strange psychic predisposition, dating no doubt from one of your former lives, has favoured the development of your 'disease'; and the fact that you had no normal training at school or college, no leading by the poor intellect into the culs-de-sac falsely called knowledge, has further caused your exceedingly rapid movement along the lines of direct inner experience. None of the knowledge you have foreshadowed has come to you through the senses, of course."

Mr. Mudge, sitting in his immovable chair, began to tremble slightly. A wind again seemed to pass over his surface and again to set it curiously in motion like a field of grass.

"You are merely talking to gain time," he said hurriedly, in a shaking voice. "This thinking aloud delays us. I see ahead what you are coming to, only please be quick, for something is going to happen. A band is again coming down the street, and if it plays—if it plays Wagner—I shall be off in a twinkling."

"Precisely. I will be quick. I was leading up to the point of how to effect your cure. The way is this: You must simply learn to *block the entrances.*"

"True, true, utterly true!" exclaimed the little man, dodging about nervously in the depths of the chair. "But how, in the name of space, is that to be done?"

"By concentration. They are all within you, these entrances, although outer cases such as colour, music and other things lead you towards them. These external things you cannot hope to destroy, but once the entrances are blocked, they will lead you only to bricked walls and closed channels. You will no longer be able to find the way."

"Quick, quick!" cried the bobbing figure in the chair. "How is this concentration to be effected?"

"This little book," continued Dr. Silence calmly, "will explain to you the way." He tapped the cover. "Let me now read out to you certain simple instructions, composed, as I see you divine, entirely from my own personal experiences in the same direction. Follow these instructions and you will no longer enter the state of Higher Space. The entrances will be blocked effectively."

Mr. Mudge sat bolt upright in his chair to listen, and John Silence cleared his throat and began to read slowly in a very distinct voice.

But before he had uttered a dozen words, something happened. A sound of street music entered the room through the open ventilators, for a band had begun to play in the stable mews at the back of the house—the March from *Tannhäuser.* Odd as it may seem that a German band should twice within the space of an hour enter the same mews and play Wagner, it was nevertheless the fact.

Mr. Racine Mudge heard it. He uttered a sharp, squeaking cry and twisted his arms with nervous energy round the chair. A piteous look that was not far from tears spread over his white face. Grey shadows followed it—the grey of fear. He began to struggle convulsively.

"Hold me fast! Catch me! For God's sake, keep me here! I'm on the rush already. Oh, it's frightful!" he cried in tones of anguish, his voice as thin as a reed.

Dr. Silence made a plunge forward to seize him, but in a flash, before he could cover the space between them, Mr. Racine Mudge, screaming and struggling, seemed to shoot past him into invisibility. He disappeared like an arrow from a bow propelled at infinite speed, and his voice no longer sounded in the external air, but seemed in some curious way to make itself heard somewhere within the depths of the doctor's own being. It was almost like a faint singing cry in his head, like a voice of dream, a voice of vision and unreality.

"Alcohol, alcohol!" it cried, "give me alcohol! It's the quickest way. Alcohol, before I'm out of reach!"

The doctor, accustomed to rapid decisions and even more rapid action, remembered that a brandy flask stood upon the mantelpiece, and in less than a second he had seized it and was holding it out towards the space above the chair recently occupied by the visible Mudge. Then, before his very eyes, and long ere he could unscrew the metal stopper, he saw the contents of the closed glass phial sink and lessen as though some one were drinking violently and greedily of the liquor within.

"Thanks! Enough! It deadens the vibrations!" cried the faint voice in his interior, as he withdrew the flask and set it back upon the mantelpiece. He understood that in Mudge's present condition one side of the flask was open to space and he could drink without removing the stopper. He could hardly have had a more interesting proof of what he had been hearing described at such length.

But the next moment—the very same moment it almost seemed—the German band stopped midway in its tune—and there was Mr. Mudge back in his chair again, gasping and panting!

"Quick!" he shrieked, "stop that band! Send it away! Catch hold of me! Block the entrances! Block the entrances! Give me the red book! Oh, oh, oh-h-h-h!!!"

The music had begun again. It was merely a temporary interruption. The *Tannhäuser* March started again, this time at a tremendous pace that made it sound like a rapid two-step as though the instruments played against time.

But the brief interruption gave Dr. Silence a moment in which to collect his scattering thoughts, and before the band had got through half a bar, he had flung forward upon the chair and held Mr. Racine Mudge, the struggling little victim of Higher Space, in a grip of iron. His arms went all round his diminutive person, taking in a good part of the chair at the same time. He was not a big man, yet he seemed to smother Mudge completely.

Yet, even as he did so, and felt the wriggling form underneath him, it began to melt and slip away like air or water. The wood of the arm-chair somehow disentangled itself from between his own arms and those of Mudge. The phenomenon known as the passage of matter through matter took place. The little man seemed actually to get mixed up in his own being. Dr. Silence could just see his face beneath him. It puckered and grew dark as though from some great internal effort. He heard the thin, reedy voice cry in his ear to "Block the entrances, block the entrances!" and then—but how in the world describe what is indescribable?

John Silence half rose up to watch. Racine Mudge, his face distorted beyond all recognition, was making a marvellous inward movement, as though doubling back upon himself. He turned funnel-wise like water in a whirling vortex, and then appeared to break up somewhat as a reflection breaks up and divides in a distorting convex mirror. He went neither forward nor backwards, neither to the right nor the left, neither up nor down. But he went. He went utterly. He simply flashed away out of sight like a vanishing projectile.

All but one leg! Dr. Silence just had the time and the presence of mind to seize upon the left ankle and boot as it disappeared, and to this he held on for several seconds like grim death. Yet all the time he knew it was a foolish and useless thing to do.

The foot was in his grasp one moment, and the next it seemed—this was the only way he could describe it—inside his own skin and bones, and at the same time outside his hand and all round it. It seemed mixed up in some amazing way with his own flesh and blood. Then it was gone, and he was tightly grasping a draught of heated air.

"Gone! gone! gone!" cried a thick, whispering voice, somewhere deep within his own consciousness. "Lost! lost! lost!" it repeated, growing fainter and fainter till at length it vanished into nothing and the last signs of Mr. Racine Mudge vanished with it.

John Silence locked his red book and replaced it in the cabinet, which he fastened with a click, and when Barker answered the bell he inquired if Mr. Mudge had left a card upon the table. It appeared that he had, and when the servant returned with it, Dr. Silence read the address and made a note of it. It was in North London.

"Mr. Mudge has gone," he said quietly to Barker, noticing his expression of alarm.

"He's not taken his 'at with him, sir."

"Mr. Mudge requires no hat where he is now," continued the doctor, stooping to poke the fire. "But he may return for it——"

"And the humbrella, sir."

"And the umbrella."

"He didn't go out *my* way, sir, if you please," stuttered the amazed servant, his curiosity overcoming his nervousness.

"Mr. Mudge has his own way of coming and going, and prefers it. If he returns by the door at any time remember to bring him instantly to me, and be kind and gentle with him and ask no questions. Also, remember, Barker, to think pleasantly, sympathetically, affectionately of him while he is away. Mr. Mudge is a very suffering gentleman."

Barker bowed and went out of the room backwards, gasping and feeling round the inside of his collar with three very hot fingers of one hand.

It was two days later when he brought in a telegram to the study. Dr. Silence opened it, and read as follows:

"Bombay. Just slipped out again. All safe. Have blocked entrances. Thousand thanks. Address Cooks, London.—MUDGE."

Dr. Silence looked up and saw Barker staring at him bewilderingly. It occurred to him that somehow he knew the contents of the telegram.

"Make a parcel of Mr. Mudge's things," he said briefly, "and address them Thomas Cook & Sons, Ludgate Circus. And send them there exactly a month from to-day and marked 'To be called for.'"

"Yes, sir," said Barker, leaving the room with a deep sigh and a hurried glance at the waste-paper basket where his master had dropped the pink paper.

A CATALOG OF SELECTED
DOVER BOOKS
IN ALL FIELDS OF INTEREST

A CATALOG OF SELECTED DOVER BOOKS IN ALL FIELDS OF INTEREST

100 BEST-LOVED POEMS, Edited by Philip Smith. "The Passionate Shepherd to His Love," "Shall I compare thee to a summer's day?" "Death, be not proud," "The Raven," "The Road Not Taken," plus works by Blake, Wordsworth, Byron, Shelley, Keats, many others. 96pp. $5\frac{3}{16}$ x $8\frac{1}{4}$. 0-486-28553-7

100 SMALL HOUSES OF THE THIRTIES, Brown-Blodgett Company. Exterior photographs and floor plans for 100 charming structures. Illustrations of models accompanied by descriptions of interiors, color schemes, closet space, and other amenities. 200 illustrations. 112pp. $8\frac{3}{8}$ x 11. 0-486-44131-8

1000 TURN-OF-THE-CENTURY HOUSES: With Illustrations and Floor Plans, Herbert C. Chivers. Reproduced from a rare edition, this showcase of homes ranges from cottages and bungalows to sprawling mansions. Each house is meticulously illustrated and accompanied by complete floor plans. 256pp. $9\frac{3}{8}$ x $12\frac{1}{4}$. 0-486-45596-3

101 GREAT AMERICAN POEMS, Edited by The American Poetry & Literacy Project. Rich treasury of verse from the 19th and 20th centuries includes works by Edgar Allan Poe, Robert Frost, Walt Whitman, Langston Hughes, Emily Dickinson, T. S. Eliot, other notables. 96pp. $5\frac{3}{16}$ x $8\frac{1}{4}$. 0-486-40158-8

101 GREAT SAMURAI PRINTS, Utagawa Kuniyoshi. Kuniyoshi was a master of the warrior woodblock print — and these 18th-century illustrations represent the pinnacle of his craft. Full-color portraits of renowned Japanese samurais pulse with movement, passion, and remarkably fine detail. 112pp. $8\frac{3}{8}$ x 11. 0-486-46523-3

ABC OF BALLET, Janet Grosser. Clearly worded, abundantly illustrated little guide defines basic ballet-related terms: arabesque, battement, pas de chat, relevé, sissonne, many others. Pronunciation guide included. Excellent primer. 48pp. $4\frac{3}{16}$ x $5\frac{3}{4}$. 0-486-40871-X

ACCESSORIES OF DRESS: An Illustrated Encyclopedia, Katherine Lester and Bess Viola Oerke. Illustrations of hats, veils, wigs, cravats, shawls, shoes, gloves, and other accessories enhance an engaging commentary that reveals the humor and charm of the many-sided story of accessorized apparel. 644 figures and 59 plates. 608pp. $6\frac{1}{8}$ x $9\frac{1}{4}$. 0-486-43378-1

ADVENTURES OF HUCKLEBERRY FINN, Mark Twain. Join Huck and Jim as their boyhood adventures along the Mississippi River lead them into a world of excitement, danger, and self-discovery. Humorous narrative, lyrical descriptions of the Mississippi valley, and memorable characters. 224pp. $5\frac{3}{16}$ x $8\frac{1}{4}$. 0-486-28061-6

ALICE STARMORE'S BOOK OF FAIR ISLE KNITTING, Alice Starmore. A noted designer from the region of Scotland's Fair Isle explores the history and techniques of this distinctive, stranded-color knitting style and provides copious illustrated instructions for 14 original knitwear designs. 208pp. $8\frac{3}{8}$ x $10\frac{7}{8}$. 0-486-47218-3

Browse over 9,000 books at www.doverpublications.com

ALICE'S ADVENTURES IN WONDERLAND, Lewis Carroll. Beloved classic about a little girl lost in a topsy-turvy land and her encounters with the White Rabbit, March Hare, Mad Hatter, Cheshire Cat, and other delightfully improbable characters. 42 illustrations by Sir John Tenniel. 96pp. 5³⁄₁₆ x 8¼.   0-486-27543-4

AMERICA'S LIGHTHOUSES: An Illustrated History, Francis Ross Holland. Profusely illustrated fact-filled survey of American lighthouses since 1716. Over 200 stations — East, Gulf, and West coasts, Great Lakes, Hawaii, Alaska, Puerto Rico, the Virgin Islands, and the Mississippi and St. Lawrence Rivers. 240pp. 8 x 10¾.
     0-486-25576-X

AN ENCYCLOPEDIA OF THE VIOLIN, Alberto Bachmann. Translated by Frederick H. Martens. Introduction by Eugene Ysaye. First published in 1925, this renowned reference remains unsurpassed as a source of essential information, from construction and evolution to repertoire and technique. Includes a glossary and 73 illustrations. 496pp. 6½ x 9¼.   0-486-46618-3

ANIMALS: 1,419 Copyright-Free Illustrations of Mammals, Birds, Fish, Insects, etc., Selected by Jim Harter. Selected for its visual impact and ease of use, this outstanding collection of wood engravings presents over 1,000 species of animals in extremely lifelike poses. Includes mammals, birds, reptiles, amphibians, fish, insects, and other invertebrates. 284pp. 9 x 12.   0-486-23766-4

THE ANNALS, Tacitus. Translated by Alfred John Church and William Jackson Brodribb. This vital chronicle of Imperial Rome, written by the era's great historian, spans A.D. 14-68 and paints incisive psychological portraits of major figures, from Tiberius to Nero. 416pp. 5³⁄₁₆ x 8¼.   0-486-45236-0

ANTIGONE, Sophocles. Filled with passionate speeches and sensitive probing of moral and philosophical issues, this powerful and often-performed Greek drama reveals the grim fate that befalls the children of Oedipus. Footnotes. 64pp. 5³⁄₁₆ x 8 ¼.   0-486-27804-2

ART DECO DECORATIVE PATTERNS IN FULL COLOR, Christian Stoll. Reprinted from a rare 1910 portfolio, 160 sensuous and exotic images depict a breathtaking array of florals, geometrics, and abstracts — all elegant in their stark simplicity. 64pp. 8⅜ x 11.   0-486-44862-2

THE ARTHUR RACKHAM TREASURY: 86 Full-Color Illustrations, Arthur Rackham. Selected and Edited by Jeff A. Menges. A stunning treasury of 86 full-page plates span the famed English artist's career, from *Rip Van Winkle* (1905) to masterworks such as *Undine, A Midsummer Night's Dream,* and *Wind in the Willows* (1939). 96pp. 8⅜ x 11.
     0-486-44685-9

THE AUTHENTIC GILBERT & SULLIVAN SONGBOOK, W. S. Gilbert and A. S. Sullivan. The most comprehensive collection available, this songbook includes selections from every one of Gilbert and Sullivan's light operas. Ninety-two numbers are presented uncut and unedited, and in their original keys. 410pp. 9 x 12.
     0-486-23482-7

THE AWAKENING, Kate Chopin. First published in 1899, this controversial novel of a New Orleans wife's search for love outside a stifling marriage shocked readers. Today, it remains a first-rate narrative with superb characterization. New introductory Note. 128pp. 5³⁄₁₆ x 8¼.   0-486-27786-0

BASIC DRAWING, Louis Priscilla. Beginning with perspective, this commonsense manual progresses to the figure in movement, light and shade, anatomy, drapery, composition, trees and landscape, and outdoor sketching. Black-and-white illustrations throughout. 128pp. 8⅜ x 11.   0-486-45815-6

Browse over 9,000 books at www.doverpublications.com

THE BATTLES THAT CHANGED HISTORY, Fletcher Pratt. Historian profiles 16 crucial conflicts, ancient to modern, that changed the course of Western civilization. Gripping accounts of battles led by Alexander the Great, Joan of Arc, Ulysses S. Grant, other commanders. 27 maps. 352pp. 5⅜ x 8½. 0-486-41129-X

BEETHOVEN'S LETTERS, Ludwig van Beethoven. Edited by Dr. A. C. Kalischer. Features 457 letters to fellow musicians, friends, greats, patrons, and literary men. Reveals musical thoughts, quirks of personality, insights, and daily events. Includes 15 plates. 410pp. 5⅜ x 8½. 0-486-22769-3

BERNICE BOBS HER HAIR AND OTHER STORIES, F. Scott Fitzgerald. This brilliant anthology includes 6 of Fitzgerald's most popular stories: "The Diamond as Big as the Ritz," the title tale, "The Offshore Pirate," "The Ice Palace," "The Jelly Bean," and "May Day." 176pp. 5⅜ x 8½. 0-486-47049-0

BESLER'S BOOK OF FLOWERS AND PLANTS: 73 Full-Color Plates from Hortus Eystettensis, 1613, Basilius Besler. Here is a selection of magnificent plates from the *Hortus Eystettensis,* which vividly illustrated and identified the plants, flowers, and trees that thrived in the legendary German garden at Eichstätt. 80pp. 8⅜ x 11. 0-486-46005-3

THE BOOK OF KELLS, Edited by Blanche Cirker. Painstakingly reproduced from a rare facsimile edition, this volume contains full-page decorations, portraits, illustrations, plus a sampling of textual leaves with exquisite calligraphy and ornamentation. 32 full-color illustrations. 32pp. 9⅜ x 12¼. 0-486-24345-1

THE BOOK OF THE CROSSBOW: With an Additional Section on Catapults and Other Siege Engines, Ralph Payne-Gallwey. Fascinating study traces history and use of crossbow as military and sporting weapon, from Middle Ages to modern times. Also covers related weapons: balistas, catapults, Turkish bows, more. Over 240 illustrations. 400pp. 7¼ x 10⅛. 0-486-28720-3

THE BUNGALOW BOOK: Floor Plans and Photos of 112 Houses, 1910, Henry L. Wilson. Here are 112 of the most popular and economic blueprints of the early 20th century — plus an illustration or photograph of each completed house. A wonderful time capsule that still offers a wealth of valuable insights. 160pp. 8⅜ x 11. 0-486-45104-6

THE CALL OF THE WILD, Jack London. A classic novel of adventure, drawn from London's own experiences as a Klondike adventurer, relating the story of a heroic dog caught in the brutal life of the Alaska Gold Rush. Note. 64pp. 5³⁄₁₆ x 8¼. 0-486-26472-6

CANDIDE, Voltaire. Edited by Francois-Marie Arouet. One of the world's great satires since its first publication in 1759. Witty, caustic skewering of romance, science, philosophy, religion, government — nearly all human ideals and institutions. 112pp. 5³⁄₁₆ x 8¼. 0-486-26689-3

CELEBRATED IN THEIR TIME: Photographic Portraits from the George Grantham Bain Collection, Edited by Amy Pastan. With an Introduction by Michael Carlebach. Remarkable portrait gallery features 112 rare images of Albert Einstein, Charlie Chaplin, the Wright Brothers, Henry Ford, and other luminaries from the worlds of politics, art, entertainment, and industry. 128pp. 8⅜ x 11. 0-486-46754-6

CHARIOTS FOR APOLLO: The NASA History of Manned Lunar Spacecraft to 1969, Courtney G. Brooks, James M. Grimwood, and Loyd S. Swenson, Jr. This illustrated history by a trio of experts is the definitive reference on the Apollo spacecraft and lunar modules. It traces the vehicles' design, development, and operation in space. More than 100 photographs and illustrations. 576pp. 6¾ x 9¼. 0-486-46756-2

Browse over 9,000 books at www.doverpublications.com

A CHRISTMAS CAROL, Charles Dickens. This engrossing tale relates Ebenezer Scrooge's ghostly journeys through Christmases past, present, and future and his ultimate transformation from a harsh and grasping old miser to a charitable and compassionate human being. 80pp. 5³⁄₁₆ x 8¼. 0-486-26865-9

COMMON SENSE, Thomas Paine. First published in January of 1776, this highly influential landmark document clearly and persuasively argued for American separation from Great Britain and paved the way for the Declaration of Independence. 64pp. 5³⁄₁₆ x 8¼. 0-486-29602-4

THE COMPLETE SHORT STORIES OF OSCAR WILDE, Oscar Wilde. Complete texts of "The Happy Prince and Other Tales," "A House of Pomegranates," "Lord Arthur Savile's Crime and Other Stories," "Poems in Prose," and "The Portrait of Mr. W. H." 208pp. 5³⁄₁₆ x 8¼. 0-486-45216-6

COMPLETE SONNETS, William Shakespeare. Over 150 exquisite poems deal with love, friendship, the tyranny of time, beauty's evanescence, death, and other themes in language of remarkable power, precision, and beauty. Glossary of archaic terms. 80pp. 5³⁄₁₆ x 8¼. 0-486-26686-9

THE COUNT OF MONTE CRISTO: Abridged Edition, Alexandre Dumas. Falsely accused of treason, Edmond Dantès is imprisoned in the bleak Chateau d'If. After a hair-raising escape, he launches an elaborate plot to extract a bitter revenge against those who betrayed him. 448pp. 5³⁄₁₆ x 8¼. 0-486-45643-9

CRAFTSMAN BUNGALOWS: Designs from the Pacific Northwest, Yoho & Merritt. This reprint of a rare catalog, showcasing the charming simplicity and cozy style of Craftsman bungalows, is filled with photos of completed homes, plus floor plans and estimated costs. An indispensable resource for architects, historians, and illustrators. 112pp. 10 x 7. 0-486-46875-5

CRAFTSMAN BUNGALOWS: 59 Homes from "The Craftsman," Edited by Gustav Stickley. Best and most attractive designs from Arts and Crafts Movement publication — 1903–1916 — includes sketches, photographs of homes, floor plans, descriptive text. 128pp. 8¼ x 11. 0-486-25829-7

CRIME AND PUNISHMENT, Fyodor Dostoyevsky. Translated by Constance Garnett. Supreme masterpiece tells the story of Raskolnikov, a student tormented by his own thoughts after he murders an old woman. Overwhelmed by guilt and terror, he confesses and goes to prison. 480pp. 5³⁄₁₆ x 8¼. 0-486-41587-2

THE DECLARATION OF INDEPENDENCE AND OTHER GREAT DOCUMENTS OF AMERICAN HISTORY: 1775-1865, Edited by John Grafton. Thirteen compelling and influential documents: Henry's "Give Me Liberty or Give Me Death," Declaration of Independence, The Constitution, Washington's First Inaugural Address, The Monroe Doctrine, The Emancipation Proclamation, Gettysburg Address, more. 64pp. 5³⁄₁₆ x 8¼. 0-486-41124-9

THE DESERT AND THE SOWN: Travels in Palestine and Syria, Gertrude Bell. "The female Lawrence of Arabia," Gertrude Bell wrote captivating, perceptive accounts of her travels in the Middle East. This intriguing narrative, accompanied by 160 photos, traces her 1905 sojourn in Lebanon, Syria, and Palestine. 368pp. 5⅜ x 8½. 0-486-46876-3

A DOLL'S HOUSE, Henrik Ibsen. Ibsen's best-known play displays his genius for realistic prose drama. An expression of women's rights, the play climaxes when the central character, Nora, rejects a smothering marriage and life in "a doll's house." 80pp. 5³⁄₁₆ x 8¼. 0-486-27062-9

Browse over 9,000 books at www.doverpublications.com

DOOMED SHIPS: Great Ocean Liner Disasters, William H. Miller, Jr. Nearly 200 photographs, many from private collections, highlight tales of some of the vessels whose pleasure cruises ended in catastrophe: the *Morro Castle, Normandie, Andrea Doria, Europa,* and many others. 128pp. 8⅝ x 11¼. 0-486-45366-9

THE DORÉ BIBLE ILLUSTRATIONS, Gustave Doré. Detailed plates from the Bible: the Creation scenes, Adam and Eve, horrifying visions of the Flood, the battle sequences with their monumental crowds, depictions of the life of Jesus, 241 plates in all. 241pp. 9 x 12. 0-486-23004-X

DRAWING DRAPERY FROM HEAD TO TOE, Cliff Young. Expert guidance on how to draw shirts, pants, skirts, gloves, hats, and coats on the human figure, including folds in relation to the body, pull and crush, action folds, creases, more. Over 200 drawings. 48pp. 8¼ x 11. 0-486-45591-2

DUBLINERS, James Joyce. A fine and accessible introduction to the work of one of the 20th century's most influential writers, this collection features 15 tales, including a masterpiece of the short-story genre, "The Dead." 160pp. 5³⁄₁₆ x 8¼. 0-486-26870-5

EASY-TO-MAKE POP-UPS, Joan Irvine. Illustrated by Barbara Reid. Dozens of wonderful ideas for three-dimensional paper fun — from holiday greeting cards with moving parts to a pop-up menagerie. Easy-to-follow, illustrated instructions for more than 30 projects. 299 black-and-white illustrations. 96pp. 8⅜ x 11. 0-486-44622-0

EASY-TO-MAKE STORYBOOK DOLLS: A "Novel" Approach to Cloth Dollmaking, Sherralyn St. Clair. Favorite fictional characters come alive in this unique beginner's dollmaking guide. Includes patterns for Pollyanna, Dorothy from *The Wonderful Wizard of Oz,* Mary of *The Secret Garden,* plus easy-to-follow instructions, 263 black-and-white illustrations, and an 8-page color insert. 112pp. 8¼ x 11. 0-486-47360-0

EINSTEIN'S ESSAYS IN SCIENCE, Albert Einstein. Speeches and essays in accessible, everyday language profile influential physicists such as Niels Bohr and Isaac Newton. They also explore areas of physics to which the author made major contributions. 128pp. 5 x 8. 0-486-47011-3

EL DORADO: Further Adventures of the Scarlet Pimpernel, Baroness Orczy. A popular sequel to *The Scarlet Pimpernel,* this suspenseful story recounts the Pimpernel's attempts to rescue the Dauphin from imprisonment during the French Revolution. An irresistible blend of intrigue, period detail, and vibrant characterizations. 352pp. 5³⁄₁₆ x 8¼. 0-486-44026-5

ELEGANT SMALL HOMES OF THE TWENTIES: 99 Designs from a Competition, Chicago Tribune. Nearly 100 designs for five- and six-room houses feature New England and Southern colonials, Normandy cottages, stately Italianate dwellings, and other fascinating snapshots of American domestic architecture of the 1920s. 112pp. 9 x 12. 0-486-46910-7

THE ELEMENTS OF STYLE: The Original Edition, William Strunk, Jr. This is the book that generations of writers have relied upon for timeless advice on grammar, diction, syntax, and other essentials. In concise terms, it identifies the principal requirements of proper style and common errors. 64pp. 5⅜ x 8½. 0-486-44798-7

THE ELUSIVE PIMPERNEL, Baroness Orczy. Robespierre's revolutionaries find their wicked schemes thwarted by the heroic Pimpernel — Sir Percival Blakeney. In this thrilling sequel, Chauvelin devises a plot to eliminate the Pimpernel and his wife. 272pp. 5³⁄₁₆ x 8¼. 0-486-45464-9

AN ENCYCLOPEDIA OF BATTLES: Accounts of Over 1,560 Battles from 1479 B.C. to the Present, David Eggenberger. Essential details of every major battle in recorded history from the first battle of Megiddo in 1479 B.C. to Grenada in 1984. List of battle maps. 99 illustrations. 544pp. 6½ x 9¼. 0-486-24913-1

ENCYCLOPEDIA OF EMBROIDERY STITCHES, INCLUDING CREWEL, Marion Nichols. Precise explanations and instructions, clearly illustrated, on how to work chain, back, cross, knotted, woven stitches, and many more — 178 in all, including Cable Outline, Whipped Satin, and Eyelet Buttonhole. Over 1400 illustrations. 219pp. 8⅜ x 11¼. 0-486-22929-7

ENTER JEEVES: 15 Early Stories, P. G. Wodehouse. Splendid collection contains first 8 stories featuring Bertie Wooster, the deliciously dim aristocrat and Jeeves, his brainy, imperturbable manservant. Also, the complete Reggie Pepper (Bertie's prototype) series. 288pp. 5⅜ x 8½. 0-486-29717-9

ERIC SLOANE'S AMERICA: Paintings in Oil, Michael Wigley. With a Foreword by Mimi Sloane. Eric Sloane's evocative oils of America's landscape and material culture shimmer with immense historical and nostalgic appeal. This original hardcover collection gathers nearly a hundred of his finest paintings, with subjects ranging from New England to the American Southwest. 128pp. 10⅝ x 9. 0-486-46525-X

ETHAN FROME, Edith Wharton. Classic story of wasted lives, set against a bleak New England background. Superbly delineated characters in a hauntingly grim tale of thwarted love. Considered by many to be Wharton's masterpiece. 96pp. 5³⁄₁₆ x 8 ¼. 0-486-26690-7

THE EVERLASTING MAN, G. K. Chesterton. Chesterton's view of Christianity — as a blend of philosophy and mythology, satisfying intellect and spirit — applies to his brilliant book, which appeals to readers' heads as well as their hearts. 288pp. 5⅜ x 8½. 0-486-46036-3

THE FIELD AND FOREST HANDY BOOK, Daniel Beard. Written by a co-founder of the Boy Scouts, this appealing guide offers illustrated instructions for building kites, birdhouses, boats, igloos, and other fun projects, plus numerous helpful tips for campers. 448pp. 5³⁄₁₆ x 8¼. 0-486-46191-2

FINDING YOUR WAY WITHOUT MAP OR COMPASS, Harold Gatty. Useful, instructive manual shows would-be explorers, hikers, bikers, scouts, sailors, and survivalists how to find their way outdoors by observing animals, weather patterns, shifting sands, and other elements of nature. 288pp. 5⅜ x 8½. 0-486-40613-X

FIRST FRENCH READER: A Beginner's Dual-Language Book, Edited and Translated by Stanley Appelbaum. This anthology introduces 50 legendary writers — Voltaire, Balzac, Baudelaire, Proust, more — through passages from *The Red and the Black, Les Misérables, Madame Bovary,* and other classics. Original French text plus English translation on facing pages. 240pp. 5⅜ x 8½. 0-486-46178-5

FIRST GERMAN READER: A Beginner's Dual-Language Book, Edited by Harry Steinhauer. Specially chosen for their power to evoke German life and culture, these short, simple readings include poems, stories, essays, and anecdotes by Goethe, Hesse, Heine, Schiller, and others. 224pp. 5⅜ x 8½. 0-486-46179-3

FIRST SPANISH READER: A Beginner's Dual-Language Book, Angel Flores. Delightful stories, other material based on works of Don Juan Manuel, Luis Taboada, Ricardo Palma, other noted writers. Complete faithful English translations on facing pages. Exercises. 176pp. 5⅜ x 8½. 0-486-25810-6

Browse over 9,000 books at www.doverpublications.com

FIVE ACRES AND INDEPENDENCE, Maurice G. Kains. Great back-to-the-land classic explains basics of self-sufficient farming. The one book to get. 95 illustrations. 397pp. 5⅜ x 8½.   0-486-20974-1

FLAGG'S SMALL HOUSES: Their Economic Design and Construction, 1922, Ernest Flagg. Although most famous for his skyscrapers, Flagg was also a proponent of the well-designed single-family dwelling. His classic treatise features innovations that save space, materials, and cost. 526 illustrations. 160pp. 9⅜ x 12¼.
0-486-45197-6

FLATLAND: A Romance of Many Dimensions, Edwin A. Abbott. Classic of science (and mathematical) fiction — charmingly illustrated by the author — describes the adventures of A. Square, a resident of Flatland, in Spaceland (three dimensions), Lineland (one dimension), and Pointland (no dimensions). 96pp. 5³⁄₁₆ x 8¼.
0-486-27263-X

FRANKENSTEIN, Mary Shelley. The story of Victor Frankenstein's monstrous creation and the havoc it caused has enthralled generations of readers and inspired countless writers of horror and suspense. With the author's own 1831 introduction. 176pp. 5³⁄₁₆ x 8¼.   0-486-28211-2

THE GARGOYLE BOOK: 572 Examples from Gothic Architecture, Lester Burbank Bridaham. Dispelling the conventional wisdom that French Gothic architectural flourishes were born of despair or gloom, Bridaham reveals the whimsical nature of these creations and the ingenious artisans who made them. 572 illustrations. 224pp. 8⅜ x 11.   0-486-44754-5

THE GIFT OF THE MAGI AND OTHER SHORT STORIES, O. Henry. Sixteen captivating stories by one of America's most popular storytellers. Included are such classics as "The Gift of the Magi," "The Last Leaf," and "The Ransom of Red Chief." Publisher's Note. 96pp. 5³⁄₁₆ x 8¼.   0-486-27061-0

THE GOETHE TREASURY: Selected Prose and Poetry, Johann Wolfgang von Goethe. Edited, Selected, and with an Introduction by Thomas Mann. In addition to his lyric poetry, Goethe wrote travel sketches, autobiographical studies, essays, letters, and proverbs in rhyme and prose. This collection presents outstanding examples from each genre. 368pp. 5⅜ x 8½.   0-486-44780-4

GREAT EXPECTATIONS, Charles Dickens. Orphaned Pip is apprenticed to the dirty work of the forge but dreams of becoming a gentleman — and one day finds himself in possession of "great expectations." Dickens' finest novel. 400pp. 5³⁄₁₆ x 8¼.
0-486-41586-4

GREAT WRITERS ON THE ART OF FICTION: From Mark Twain to Joyce Carol Oates, Edited by James Daley. An indispensable source of advice and inspiration, this anthology features essays by Henry James, Kate Chopin, Willa Cather, Sinclair Lewis, Jack London, Raymond Chandler, Raymond Carver, Eudora Welty, and Kurt Vonnegut, Jr. 192pp. 5⅜ x 8½.   0-486-45128-3

HAMLET, William Shakespeare. The quintessential Shakespearean tragedy, whose highly charged confrontations and anguished soliloquies probe depths of human feeling rarely sounded in any art. Reprinted from an authoritative British edition complete with illuminating footnotes. 128pp. 5³⁄₁₆ x 8¼.   0-486-27278-8

THE HAUNTED HOUSE, Charles Dickens. A Yuletide gathering in an eerie country retreat provides the backdrop for Dickens and his friends — including Elizabeth Gaskell and Wilkie Collins — who take turns spinning supernatural yarns. 144pp. 5⅜ x 8½.   0-486-46309-5

Browse over 9,000 books at www.doverpublications.com

HEART OF DARKNESS, Joseph Conrad. Dark allegory of a journey up the Congo River and the narrator's encounter with the mysterious Mr. Kurtz. Masterly blend of adventure, character study, psychological penetration. For many, Conrad's finest, most enigmatic story. 80pp. 5³⁄₁₆ x 8¼.   0-486-26464-5

HENSON AT THE NORTH POLE, Matthew A. Henson. This thrilling memoir by the heroic African-American who was Peary's companion through two decades of Arctic exploration recounts a tale of danger, courage, and determination. "Fascinating and exciting." — *Commonweal.* 128pp. 5⅜ x 8½.   0-486-45472-X

HISTORIC COSTUMES AND HOW TO MAKE THEM, Mary Fernald and E. Shenton. Practical, informative guidebook shows how to create everything from short tunics worn by Saxon men in the fifth century to a lady's bustle dress of the late 1800s. 81 illustrations. 176pp. 5⅜ x 8½.   0-486-44906-8

THE HOUND OF THE BASKERVILLES, Arthur Conan Doyle. A deadly curse in the form of a legendary ferocious beast continues to claim its victims from the Baskerville family until Holmes and Watson intervene. Often called the best detective story ever written. 128pp. 5³⁄₁₆ x 8¼.   0-486-28214-7

THE HOUSE BEHIND THE CEDARS, Charles W. Chesnutt. Originally published in 1900, this groundbreaking novel by a distinguished African-American author recounts the drama of a brother and sister who "pass for white" during the dangerous days of Reconstruction. 208pp. 5⅜ x 8½.   0-486-46144-0

THE HUMAN FIGURE IN MOTION, Eadweard Muybridge. The 4,789 photographs in this definitive selection show the human figure — models almost all undraped — engaged in over 160 different types of action: running, climbing stairs, etc. 390pp. 7⅞ x 10⅝.   0-486-20204-6

THE IMPORTANCE OF BEING EARNEST, Oscar Wilde. Wilde's witty and buoyant comedy of manners, filled with some of literature's most famous epigrams, reprinted from an authoritative British edition. Considered Wilde's most perfect work. 64pp. 5³⁄₁₆ x 8¼.   0-486-26478-5

THE INFERNO, Dante Alighieri. Translated and with notes by Henry Wadsworth Longfellow. The first stop on Dante's famous journey from Hell to Purgatory to Paradise, this 14th-century allegorical poem blends vivid and shocking imagery with graceful lyricism. Translated by the beloved 19th-century poet, Henry Wadsworth Longfellow. 256pp. 5³⁄₁₆ x 8¼.   0-486-44288-8

JANE EYRE, Charlotte Brontë. Written in 1847, *Jane Eyre* tells the tale of an orphan girl's progress from the custody of cruel relatives to an oppressive boarding school and its culmination in a troubled career as a governess. 448pp. 5³⁄₁₆ x 8¼.
0-486-42449-9

JAPANESE WOODBLOCK FLOWER PRINTS, Tanigami Kônan. Extraordinary collection of Japanese woodblock prints by a well-known artist features 120 plates in brilliant color. Realistic images from a rare edition include daffodils, tulips, and other familiar and unusual flowers. 128pp. 11 x 8¼.   0-486-46442-3

JEWELRY MAKING AND DESIGN, Augustus F. Rose and Antonio Cirino. Professional secrets of jewelry making are revealed in a thorough, practical guide. Over 200 illustrations. 306pp. 5⅜ x 8½.   0-486-21750-7

JULIUS CAESAR, William Shakespeare. Great tragedy based on Plutarch's account of the lives of Brutus, Julius Caesar and Mark Antony. Evil plotting, ringing oratory, high tragedy with Shakespeare's incomparable insight, dramatic power. Explanatory footnotes. 96pp. 5³⁄₁₆ x 8¼.   0-486-26876-4

THE JUNGLE, Upton Sinclair. 1906 bestseller shockingly reveals intolerable labor practices and working conditions in the Chicago stockyards as it tells the grim story of a Slavic family that emigrates to America full of optimism but soon faces despair. 320pp. 5³⁄₁₆ x 8¼. 0-486-41923-1

THE KINGDOM OF GOD IS WITHIN YOU, Leo Tolstoy. The soul-searching book that inspired Gandhi to embrace the concept of passive resistance, Tolstoy's 1894 polemic clearly outlines a radical, well-reasoned revision of traditional Christian thinking. 352pp. 5³⁄₁₆ x 8¼. 0-486-45138-0

THE LADY OR THE TIGER?: and Other Logic Puzzles, Raymond M. Smullyan. Created by a renowned puzzle master, these whimsically themed challenges involve paradoxes about probability, time, and change; metapuzzles; and self-referentiality. Nineteen chapters advance in difficulty from relatively simple to highly complex. 1982 edition. 240pp. 5⅜ x 8½. 0-486-47027-X

LEAVES OF GRASS: The Original 1855 Edition, Walt Whitman. Whitman's immortal collection includes some of the greatest poems of modern times, including his masterpiece, "Song of Myself." Shattering standard conventions, it stands as an unabashed celebration of body and nature. 128pp. 5³⁄₁₆ x 8¼. 0-486-45676-5

LES MISÉRABLES, Victor Hugo. Translated by Charles E. Wilbour. Abridged by James K. Robinson. A convict's heroic struggle for justice and redemption plays out against a fiery backdrop of the Napoleonic wars. This edition features the excellent original translation and a sensitive abridgment. 304pp. 6⅛ x 9¼. 0-486-45789-3

LILITH: A Romance, George MacDonald. In this novel by the father of fantasy literature, a man travels through time to meet Adam and Eve and to explore humanity's fall from grace and ultimate redemption. 240pp. 5⅜ x 8½. 0-486-46818-6

THE LOST LANGUAGE OF SYMBOLISM, Harold Bayley. This remarkable book reveals the hidden meaning behind familiar images and words, from the origins of Santa Claus to the fleur-de-lys, drawing from mythology, folklore, religious texts, and fairy tales. 1,418 illustrations. 784pp. 5⅜ x 8½. 0-486-44787-1

MACBETH, William Shakespeare. A Scottish nobleman murders the king in order to succeed to the throne. Tortured by his conscience and fearful of discovery, he becomes tangled in a web of treachery and deceit that ultimately spells his doom. 96pp. 5³⁄₁₆ x 8¼. 0-486-27802-6

MAKING AUTHENTIC CRAFTSMAN FURNITURE: Instructions and Plans for 62 Projects, Gustav Stickley. Make authentic reproductions of handsome, functional, durable furniture: tables, chairs, wall cabinets, desks, a hall tree, and more. Construction plans with drawings, schematics, dimensions, and lumber specs reprinted from 1900s *The Craftsman* magazine. 128pp. 8⅛ x 11. 0-486-25000-8

MATHEMATICS FOR THE NONMATHEMATICIAN, Morris Kline. Erudite and entertaining overview follows development of mathematics from ancient Greeks to present. Topics include logic and mathematics, the fundamental concept, differential calculus, probability theory, much more. Exercises and problems. 641pp. 5⅜ x 8½. 0-486-24823-2

MEMOIRS OF AN ARABIAN PRINCESS FROM ZANZIBAR, Emily Ruete. This 19th-century autobiography offers a rare inside look at the society surrounding a sultan's palace. A real-life princess in exile recalls her vanished world of harems, slave trading, and court intrigues. 288pp. 5⅜ x 8½. 0-486-47121-7

THE METAMORPHOSIS AND OTHER STORIES, Franz Kafka. Excellent new English translations of title story (considered by many critics Kafka's most perfect work), plus "The Judgment," "In the Penal Colony," "A Country Doctor," and "A Report to an Academy." Note. 96pp. 5³⁄₁₆ x 8¼. 0-486-29030-1

MICROSCOPIC ART FORMS FROM THE PLANT WORLD, R. Anheisser. From undulating curves to complex geometrics, a world of fascinating images abound in this classic, illustrated survey of microscopic plants. Features 400 detailed illustrations of nature's minute but magnificent handiwork. The accompanying CD-ROM includes all of the images in the book. 128pp. 9 x 9. 0-486-46013-4

A MIDSUMMER NIGHT'S DREAM, William Shakespeare. Among the most popular of Shakespeare's comedies, this enchanting play humorously celebrates the vagaries of love as it focuses upon the intertwined romances of several pairs of lovers. Explanatory footnotes. 80pp. 5³⁄₁₆ x 8¼. 0-486-27067-X

THE MONEY CHANGERS, Upton Sinclair. Originally published in 1908, this cautionary novel from the author of *The Jungle* explores corruption within the American system as a group of power brokers joins forces for personal gain, triggering a crash on Wall Street. 192pp. 5⅜ x 8½. 0-486-46917-4

THE MOST POPULAR HOMES OF THE TWENTIES, William A. Radford. With a New Introduction by Daniel D. Reiff. Based on a rare 1925 catalog, this architectural showcase features floor plans, construction details, and photos of 26 homes, plus articles on entrances, porches, garages, and more. 250 illustrations, 21 color plates. 176pp. 8⅜ x 11. 0-486-47028-8

MY 66 YEARS IN THE BIG LEAGUES, Connie Mack. With a New Introduction by Rich Westcott. A Founding Father of modern baseball, Mack holds the record for most wins — and losses — by a major league manager. Enhanced by 70 photographs, his warmhearted autobiography is populated by many legends of the game. 288pp. 5⅜ x 8½. 0-486-47184-5

NARRATIVE OF THE LIFE OF FREDERICK DOUGLASS, Frederick Douglass. Douglass's graphic depictions of slavery, harrowing escape to freedom, and life as a newspaper editor, eloquent orator, and impassioned abolitionist. 96pp. 5³⁄₁₆ x 8¼. 0-486-28499-9

THE NIGHTLESS CITY: Geisha and Courtesan Life in Old Tokyo, J. E. de Becker. This unsurpassed study from 100 years ago ventured into Tokyo's red-light district to survey geisha and courtesan life and offer meticulous descriptions of training, dress, social hierarchy, and erotic practices. 49 black-and-white illustrations; 2 maps. 496pp. 5⅜ x 8½. 0-486-45563-7

THE ODYSSEY, Homer. Excellent prose translation of ancient epic recounts adventures of the homeward-bound Odysseus. Fantastic cast of gods, giants, cannibals, sirens, other supernatural creatures — true classic of Western literature. 256pp. 5³⁄₁₆ x 8¼. 0-486-40654-7

OEDIPUS REX, Sophocles. Landmark of Western drama concerns the catastrophe that ensues when King Oedipus discovers he has inadvertently killed his father and married his mother. Masterly construction, dramatic irony. Explanatory footnotes. 64pp. 5³⁄₁₆ x 8¼. 0-486-26877-2

ONCE UPON A TIME: The Way America Was, Eric Sloane. Nostalgic text and drawings brim with gentle philosophies and descriptions of how we used to live — self-sufficiently — on the land, in homes, and among the things built by hand. 44 line illustrations. 64pp. 8⅜ x 11. 0-486-44411-2

ONE OF OURS, Willa Cather. The Pulitzer Prize–winning novel about a young Nebraskan looking for something to believe in. Alienated from his parents, rejected by his wife, he finds his destiny on the bloody battlefields of World War I. 352pp. 5³⁄₁₆ x 8¼. 0-486-45599-8

ORIGAMI YOU CAN USE: 27 Practical Projects, Rick Beech. Origami models can be more than decorative, and this unique volume shows how! The 27 practical projects include a CD case, frame, napkin ring, and dish. Easy instructions feature 400 two-color illustrations. 96pp. 8¼ x 11. 0-486-47057-1

OTHELLO, William Shakespeare. Towering tragedy tells the story of a Moorish general who earns the enmity of his ensign Iago when he passes him over for a promotion. Masterly portrait of an archvillain. Explanatory footnotes. 112pp. 5³⁄₁₆ x 8¼.
0-486-29097-2

PARADISE LOST, John Milton. Notes by John A. Himes. First published in 1667, *Paradise Lost* ranks among the greatest of English literature's epic poems. It's a sublime retelling of Adam and Eve's fall from grace and expulsion from Eden. Notes by John A. Himes. 480pp. 5³⁄₁₆ x 8¼. 0-486-44287-X

PASSING, Nella Larsen. Married to a successful physician and prominently ensconced in society, Irene Redfield leads a charmed existence — until a chance encounter with a childhood friend who has been "passing for white." 112pp. 5⅜ x 8½. 0-486-43713-2

PERSPECTIVE DRAWING FOR BEGINNERS, Len A. Doust. Doust carefully explains the roles of lines, boxes, and circles, and shows how visualizing shapes and forms can be used in accurate depictions of perspective. One of the most concise introductions available. 33 illustrations. 64pp. 5⅜ x 8½. 0-486-45149-6

PERSPECTIVE MADE EASY, Ernest R. Norling. Perspective is easy; yet, surprisingly few artists know the simple rules that make it so. Remedy that situation with this simple, step-by-step book, the first devoted entirely to the topic. 256 illustrations. 224pp. 5⅜ x 8½. 0-486-40473-0

THE PICTURE OF DORIAN GRAY, Oscar Wilde. Celebrated novel involves a handsome young Londoner who sinks into a life of depravity. His body retains perfect youth and vigor while his recent portrait reflects the ravages of his crime and sensuality. 176pp. 5³⁄₁₆ x 8¼. 0-486-27807-7

PRIDE AND PREJUDICE, Jane Austen. One of the most universally loved and admired English novels, an effervescent tale of rural romance transformed by Jane Austen's art into a witty, shrewdly observed satire of English country life. 272pp. 5³⁄₁₆ x 8¼.
0-486-28473-5

THE PRINCE, Niccolò Machiavelli. Classic, Renaissance-era guide to acquiring and maintaining political power. Today, nearly 500 years after it was written, this calculating prescription for autocratic rule continues to be much read and studied. 80pp. 5³⁄₁₆ x 8¼. 0-486-27274-5

QUICK SKETCHING, Carl Cheek. A perfect introduction to the technique of "quick sketching." Drawing upon an artist's immediate emotional responses, this is an extremely effective means of capturing the essential form and features of a subject. More than 100 black-and-white illustrations throughout. 48pp. 11 x 8¼.
0-486-46608-6

RANCH LIFE AND THE HUNTING TRAIL, Theodore Roosevelt. Illustrated by Frederic Remington. Beautifully illustrated by Remington, Roosevelt's celebration of the Old West recounts his adventures in the Dakota Badlands of the 1880s, from round-ups to Indian encounters to hunting bighorn sheep. 208pp. 6¼ x 9¼. 0-486-47340-6

THE RED BADGE OF COURAGE, Stephen Crane. Amid the nightmarish chaos of a Civil War battle, a young soldier discovers courage, humility, and, perhaps, wisdom. Uncanny re-creation of actual combat. Enduring landmark of American fiction. 112pp. 5³⁄₁₆ x 8¼. 0-486-26465-3

RELATIVITY SIMPLY EXPLAINED, Martin Gardner. One of the subject's clearest, most entertaining introductions offers lucid explanations of special and general theories of relativity, gravity, and spacetime, models of the universe, and more. 100 illustrations. 224pp. 5⅜ x 8½. 0-486-29315-7

REMBRANDT DRAWINGS: 116 Masterpieces in Original Color, Rembrandt van Rijn. This deluxe hardcover edition features drawings from throughout the Dutch master's prolific career. Informative captions accompany these beautifully reproduced landscapes, biblical vignettes, figure studies, animal sketches, and portraits. 128pp. 8⅜ x 11. 0-486-46149-1

THE ROAD NOT TAKEN AND OTHER POEMS, Robert Frost. A treasury of Frost's most expressive verse. In addition to the title poem: "An Old Man's Winter Night," "In the Home Stretch," "Meeting and Passing," "Putting in the Seed," many more. All complete and unabridged. 64pp. 5³⁄₁₆ x 8¼. 0-486-27550-7

ROMEO AND JULIET, William Shakespeare. Tragic tale of star-crossed lovers, feuding families and timeless passion contains some of Shakespeare's most beautiful and lyrical love poetry. Complete, unabridged text with explanatory footnotes. 96pp. 5³⁄₁₆ x 8¼. 0-486-27557-4

SANDITON AND THE WATSONS: Austen's Unfinished Novels, Jane Austen. Two tantalizing incomplete stories revisit Austen's customary milieu of courtship and venture into new territory, amid guests at a seaside resort. Both are worth reading for pleasure and study. 112pp. 5⅜ x 8½. 0-486-45793-1

THE SCARLET LETTER, Nathaniel Hawthorne. With stark power and emotional depth, Hawthorne's masterpiece explores sin, guilt, and redemption in a story of adultery in the early days of the Massachusetts Colony. 192pp. 5³⁄₁₆ x 8¼.
0-486-28048-9

THE SEASONS OF AMERICA PAST, Eric Sloane. Seventy-five illustrations depict cider mills and presses, sleds, pumps, stump-pulling equipment, plows, and other elements of America's rural heritage. A section of old recipes and household hints adds additional color. 160pp. 8⅜ x 11. 0-486-44220-9

SELECTED CANTERBURY TALES, Geoffrey Chaucer. Delightful collection includes the General Prologue plus three of the most popular tales: "The Knight's Tale," "The Miller's Prologue and Tale," and "The Wife of Bath's Prologue and Tale." In modern English. 144pp. 5³⁄₁₆ x 8¼. 0-486-28241-4

SELECTED POEMS, Emily Dickinson. Over 100 best-known, best-loved poems by one of America's foremost poets, reprinted from authoritative early editions. No comparable edition at this price. Index of first lines. 64pp. 5³⁄₁₆ x 8¼. 0-486-26466-1

SIDDHARTHA, Hermann Hesse. Classic novel that has inspired generations of seekers. Blending Eastern mysticism and psychoanalysis, Hesse presents a strikingly original view of man and culture and the arduous process of self-discovery, reconciliation, harmony, and peace. 112pp. 5³⁄₁₆ x 8¼. 0-486-40653-9

SKETCHING OUTDOORS, Leonard Richmond. This guide offers beginners step-by-step demonstrations of how to depict clouds, trees, buildings, and other outdoor sights. Explanations of a variety of techniques include shading and constructional drawing. 48pp. 11 x 8¼. 0-486-46922-0

Browse over 9,000 books at www.doverpublications.com

SMALL HOUSES OF THE FORTIES: With Illustrations and Floor Plans, Harold E. Group. 56 floor plans and elevations of houses that originally cost less than $15,000 to build. Recommended by financial institutions of the era, they range from Colonials to Cape Cods. 144pp. 8⅜ x 11. 0-486-45598-X

SOME CHINESE GHOSTS, Lafcadio Hearn. Rooted in ancient Chinese legends, these richly atmospheric supernatural tales are recounted by an expert in Oriental lore. Their originality, power, and literary charm will captivate readers of all ages. 96pp. 5⅜ x 8½. 0-486-46306-0

SONGS FOR THE OPEN ROAD: Poems of Travel and Adventure, Edited by The American Poetry & Literacy Project. More than 80 poems by 50 American and British masters celebrate real and metaphorical journeys. Poems by Whitman, Byron, Millay, Sandburg, Langston Hughes, Emily Dickinson, Robert Frost, Shelley, Tennyson, Yeats, many others. Note. 80pp. 5³⁄₁₆ x 8¼. 0-486-40646-6

SPOON RIVER ANTHOLOGY, Edgar Lee Masters. An American poetry classic, in which former citizens of a mythical midwestern town speak touchingly from the grave of the thwarted hopes and dreams of their lives. 144pp. 5³⁄₁₆ x 8¼. 0-486-27275-3

STAR LORE: Myths, Legends, and Facts, William Tyler Olcott. Captivating retellings of the origins and histories of ancient star groups include Pegasus, Ursa Major, Pleiades, signs of the zodiac, and other constellations. "Classic." — *Sky & Telescope*. 58 illustrations. 544pp. 5⅜ x 8½. 0-486-43581-4

THE STRANGE CASE OF DR. JEKYLL AND MR. HYDE, Robert Louis Stevenson. This intriguing novel, both fantasy thriller and moral allegory, depicts the struggle of two opposing personalities — one essentially good, the other evil — for the soul of one man. 64pp. 5³⁄₁₆ x 8¼. 0-486-26688-5

SURVIVAL HANDBOOK: The Official U.S. Army Guide, Department of the Army. This special edition of the Army field manual is geared toward civilians. An essential companion for campers and all lovers of the outdoors, it constitutes the most authoritative wilderness guide. 288pp. 5³⁄₁₆ x 8¼. 0-486-46184-X

A TALE OF TWO CITIES, Charles Dickens. Against the backdrop of the French Revolution, Dickens unfolds his masterpiece of drama, adventure, and romance about a man falsely accused of treason. Excitement and derring-do in the shadow of the guillotine. 304pp. 5³⁄₁₆ x 8¼. 0-486-40651-2

TEN PLAYS, Anton Chekhov. *The Sea Gull, Uncle Vanya, The Three Sisters, The Cherry Orchard,* and *Ivanov,* plus 5 one-act comedies: *The Anniversary, An Unwilling Martyr, The Wedding, The Bear,* and *The Proposal.* 336pp. 5³⁄₁₆ x 8¼. 0-486-46560-8

THE FLYING INN, G. K. Chesterton. Hilarious romp in which pub owner Humphrey Hump and friend take to the road in a donkey cart filled with rum and cheese, inveighing against Prohibition and other "oppressive forms of modernity." 320pp. 5⅜ x 8½. 0-486-41910-X

THIRTY YEARS THAT SHOOK PHYSICS: The Story of Quantum Theory, George Gamow. Lucid, accessible introduction to the influential theory of energy and matter features careful explanations of Dirac's anti-particles, Bohr's model of the atom, and much more. Numerous drawings. 1966 edition. 240pp. 5⅜ x 8½. 0-486-24895-X

TREASURE ISLAND, Robert Louis Stevenson. Classic adventure story of a perilous sea journey, a mutiny led by the infamous Long John Silver, and a lethal scramble for buried treasure — seen through the eyes of cabin boy Jim Hawkins. 160pp. 5³⁄₁₆ x 8¼. 0-486-27559-0

CATALOG OF DOVER BOOKS

THE TRIAL, Franz Kafka. Translated by David Wyllie. From its gripping first sentence onward, this novel exemplifies the term "Kafkaesque." Its darkly humorous narrative recounts a bank clerk's entrapment in a bureaucratic maze, based on an undisclosed charge. 176pp. 5³⁄₁₆ x 8¼. 0-486-47061-X

THE TURN OF THE SCREW, Henry James. Gripping ghost story by great novelist depicts the sinister transformation of 2 innocent children into flagrant liars and hypocrites. An elegantly told tale of unspoken horror and psychological terror. 96pp. 5³⁄₁₆ x 8¼. 0-486-26684-2

UP FROM SLAVERY, Booker T. Washington. Washington (1856-1915) rose to become the most influential spokesman for African-Americans of his day. In this eloquently written book, he describes events in a remarkable life that began in bondage and culminated in worldwide recognition. 160pp. 5³⁄₁₆ x 8¼. 0-486-28738-6

VICTORIAN HOUSE DESIGNS IN AUTHENTIC FULL COLOR: 75 Plates from the "Scientific American – Architects and Builders Edition," 1885-1894, Edited by Blanche Cirker. Exquisitely detailed, exceptionally handsome designs for an enormous variety of attractive city dwellings, spacious suburban and country homes, charming "cottages" and other structures — all accompanied by perspective views and floor plans. 80pp. 9¼ x 12¼. 0-486-29438-2

VILLETTE, Charlotte Brontë. Acclaimed by Virginia Woolf as "Brontë's finest novel," this moving psychological study features a remarkably modern heroine who abandons her native England for a new life as a schoolteacher in Belgium. 480pp. 5³⁄₁₆ x 8¼. 0-486-45557-2

THE VOYAGE OUT, Virginia Woolf. A moving depiction of the thrills and confusion of youth, Woolf's acclaimed first novel traces a shipboard journey to South America for a captivating exploration of a woman's growing self-awareness. 288pp. 5³⁄₁₆ x 8¼. 0-486-45005-8

WALDEN; OR, LIFE IN THE WOODS, Henry David Thoreau. Accounts of Thoreau's daily life on the shores of Walden Pond outside Concord, Massachusetts, are interwoven with musings on the virtues of self-reliance and individual freedom, on society, government, and other topics. 224pp. 5³⁄₁₆ x 8¼. 0-486-28495-6

WILD PILGRIMAGE: A Novel in Woodcuts, Lynd Ward. Through startling engravings shaded in black and red, Ward wordlessly tells the story of a man trapped in an industrial world, struggling between the grim reality around him and the fantasies his imagination creates. 112pp. 6⅛ x 9¼. 0-486-46583-7

WILLY POGÁNY REDISCOVERED, Willy Pogány. Selected and Edited by Jeff A. Menges. More than 100 color and black-and-white Art Nouveau–style illustrations from fairy tales and adventure stories include scenes from Wagner's "Ring" cycle, The Rime of the Ancient Mariner, Gulliver's Travels, and Faust. 144pp. 8⅜ x 11. 0-486-47046-6

WOOLLY THOUGHTS: Unlock Your Creative Genius with Modular Knitting, Pat Ashforth and Steve Plummer. Here's the revolutionary way to knit — easy, fun, and foolproof! Beginners and experienced knitters need only master a single stitch to create their own designs with patchwork squares. More than 100 illustrations. 128pp. 6½ x 9¼. 0-486-46084-3

WUTHERING HEIGHTS, Emily Brontë. Somber tale of consuming passions and vengeance — played out amid the lonely English moors — recounts the turbulent and tempestuous love story of Cathy and Heathcliff. Poignant and compelling. 256pp. 5³⁄₁₆ x 8¼. 0-486-29256-8

Browse over 9,000 books at www.doverpublications.com